A SECRET WARNING

"What he's doing might be dangerous. He might be using mataglap nano."

A cold chill rose along Gabriel's spine at the very sound of the word.

"Still," Cressida said, "whatever he's doing he's tampering with the Seal, and that compromises almost everything in the Logarchy. Almost every tachline communication is routed through the switching system in the Hyperlogos. Even our private sealed communications—the Seal of the Aristoi won't hold once the Hyperlogos Seal is broken. He's got access to *everything*, and he can tamper with all of it. Our entire civilization is based on free and unlimited access to data. Even the Seal of the Aristoi fades after the Aristos who sealed it dies or retires. Saigo can change data, communications . . . history itself. And we don't know if he's doing this alone, or with others."

A cold wind blew through the seagrass outside. The sun subsided below the murky horizon. Back on the *Pyrrho*, Gabriel shivered.

"Why me?" Gabriel demanded. "Why are you telling me this?"

Also by Walter Jon Williams

ARISTOI

WALTER JON WILLIAMS

A TOM DOHERTY ASSOCIATES BOOK
NEW YORK

ARISTOI

Copyright © 1992 by Walter Jon Williams

All rights reserved, including the right to reproduce this book, or portions thereof, in any form.

Cover art by Jim Burns

A Tor Book
Published by Tom Doherty Associates, Inc.
175 Fifth Avenue
New York, N.Y. 10010

Tor® is a registered trademark of Tom Doherty Associates, Inc.

ISBN: 0-812-51409-2
Library of Congress Catalog Card Number: 92-25452

First edition: September 1992
First mass market printing: September 1993

Printed in the United States of America

0 9 8 7 6 5 4 3 2 1

With thanks and gratitude to Sage Walker, Rebecca Meluch, William F. Wu, Melinda Snodgrass, Pati Nagle, Sally Gwylan, Pat McGraw, Salomon Montoya, Karen McCue, Mr. Bill Packer, Laura J. Mixon, Judith Tarr.

Note

Readers are encouraged to pronounce the foreign words any way that appeals to them, but those interested in the little squiggles over the words might consider the following: The accent marks indicate nothing more than the stress over the syllable. *Therápontes* is accented on the second syllable, *skiagénos* in the third. The horizontal bar over the final vowel of some words (*daimōn, therápōn*) indicates a long vowel. Note that in the plural (*daimones, therápontes*) the vowel turns short.

The words taken from Chinese are transcribed in Pinyin, not Wade-Giles, and are therefore pronounced more or less as the English-speaking reader finds them, with only two exceptions: the *Zh* in "Zhenling" is pronounces like the *j* in "justice," and the word *qi* is pronounced "chee."

As a final note, I should point out that *Aristos* and *Aristoi* have their accent on the first syllable.

Chapter 1

ANIMAL TAMER: Walk in, walk in to my menagerie
Full of life and cruelty.

A t Graduation, every five or seven or ten years, the Aristoi celebrated in Persepolis.

For the most part they celebrated themselves.

Persepolis, in the Realized World, was an interesting artifact. It shaded by degrees into "Persepolis," the real place becoming, through its illusory/electronic deeps and towers, an ever-flexible, ever-unfolding megadimensional dream.

Persepolis, the place, had been reconstructed on its original Persian floor plan, and sat on its reconstructed plain at the meeting of the reconstructed Pulvar and Kor, where it took its place as the (largely symbolic) capital of a reconstructed Earth^2. The city was inhabited only a few days a year, when Pan Wengong, the most senior of the Aristoi, convened the Terran Sessions. Behind the City of a Hundred Columns loomed Kuh-e-Rahmat, the Mount of Mercy, its grey flanks a contrast to the bright gold, vermilion, ivory, and turquoise that accentuated the city. To the hewn tombs of Achaemenid kings carved into the side of the mountain were added those of many Aristoi, laid to rest in their capital beside the descendants of Kurush the Great, whose tenuous spirits were presumed to be flattered by the comparison. Atop the mountain itself, surrounded by a grove of cypress, was the gold monument to the lost Captain Yuan, a place of homage and worship.

"Persepolis," the dream, was a far more interesting place. Most of the people who came here did not do so in the flesh but through the oneirochronon, and the two palaces superimposed on one another in ways both intricate and obscure. Earth²'s archons and senators strolled along the corridors, holding conversations with people others could not see. Corridors that dead-ended in reality possessed doors and branches in the oneirochronic world. Some led to palaces, dominions, grottos, and fantasies that did not exist on Earth², or indeed anywhere, but were instead the special habitats of oneirochronic Aristoi, some of whose bodies were long in the grave. In these palaces the inhabitants danced and discussed and feasted and loved—there had long been competition among them to design the most dazzling sensual experiences for one another, delightful unrealities more striking, more "real," than anything experienced in the flesh.

To Persepolis, the dream, came Gabriel. Demons buzzed insistently in his head, but he kept them on a tight rein.

For Persepolis was a place where demons, as well as dreams, were shared.

A few days before his arrival in Persepolis, in a shimmering predawn on Illyricum, Gabriel glided through his gardens like a ghost. Perfume rose at his footsteps, lingered in the still air. Sometimes he wanted simply to be himself: his daimones were asleep or busy with their own projects, and all was peaceful, as perfect as the plans of this garden he had once built in the oneirochronon before consummating it in the Realized World.

Rectangles cut the solemn sky as solar panels in the Residence, the Red Lacquer Gallery, and the Autumn Pavilion slid from concealment and deployed to catch the first rays of dawn on their surfaces, layers of matte-black photoreactive polymer woven with pure gold. The rising sun turned the gold grids to scarlet flame.

An English bullterrier, Manfred, trotted silently at Gabriel's heels, absorbing in its own fashion the dawn, the garden, the perfume. The terrier had implanted as a nurse and in another few moments would be assisting Gabriel with some minor surgery.

Gabriel climbed the cloudy opal steps of the Autumn Pavilion and stepped into the interior. He seated himself, facing the entrance, on a bench of a black soft-crystal ceramic that reacted to his body heat, yielded and conformed to his shape. Manfred curled up at his feet and yawned. An early bird gave a tentative call.

"Open," Gabriel said.

Silent shutters folded themselves away, inviting the mother-of-pearl dawn. Flower perfume crept into the still building. The Autumn Pavilion featured rooms designed by each of Gabriel's primary daimones, and this room was Horus's contribution: logically eight-sided, the walls covered with Illyrian Workshop ceramic tiles in aspen-yellow and maple-crimson, each featuring a hand-painted harvest scene from preindustrial times. Benevolent Demeter gazed down on all this activity from a ceiling fresco set amid a classic rococo plaster frieze. Tables set beneath the windows were unassuming wrought-iron. Antique vases held dried flowers to the nonexistent wind.

There was a self-portrait in oils by Horus on one wall, Gabriel's pointed face unusually grave and balanced beneath the curling mass of copper hair, brows a little knit but on the whole approving of what he saw. The startling blue of the eyes was a little deemphasized, the wise epicanthal folds pronounced.

Gabriel watched, absorbing the sight, as the spinning globe dropped morning into the garden. Photons' touch caused palati plants to fire pollen from their tube-shaped flowers. Floating particles glowed in the light of the rising sun.

Dawn, in her golden sandals, Gabriel thought, after Sappho. Whatever thought came next drifted away with the palati pollen before he could catch it.

He was going to impregnate the Black-Eyed Ghost, his lover. He thought for a moment about that, about gametes floating like pollen, about bits of himself set adrift in the universe.

His various selves seemed at peace with the notion.

The dog yawned again. The light, as the sun rose, turned bluer, more precise. Reality took on a hard, photographic edge, qualities for which thousands of artists came to this system, this planet. Illyricum, the World of Clear Light.

Gabriel's world. He had built it, designed its effects, contributed to its architecture. Issued decrees to its population, at least when he felt like it, which wasn't often. He had, in fact, owned the whole thing, till he'd given most of it away.

Illyricum was one of several worlds that Gabriel had designed.

He liked to think he hadn't made too many mistakes with any of them.

For the opening-night reception in Persepolis Gabriel dressed his skiagénos in a forest-green jacket covered with gold brocade, tight breeches of a lighter green with Hungarian-style laces on the thigh-tops, black reflective Hessian boots with gold tassels. The cravat was pinned with a diamond, gemstones ornamented the fingers, the hair was drawn back with diamond-and-enamel clips. Atop his head Gabriel put a soft bonnet with a diamond pin and dashing feather. He worked some long moments getting his scent precisely the way he wanted it, just the proper combination, a hint of spice and intrigue.

The finery was not purely ornamental. None of it existed in the Realized World—the outfit was purely oneirochronic—but it all served as advertising for Gabriel's programming skills. The stiff *touch* of the brocade had to be plausibly different from the soft feel of the hat, the tickle of the feather, the pliant mass of copper hair, the warm press of Gabriel's flesh. The reflective *look* of the polished boots was different from the hard, depthless glitter of the stones on his fingers, the cheerful liquid highlights in his eyes, the soft weave of the jacket and the complex patterned loops of the glowing gold brocade. The tassels on the boots were reflected in the boots themselves and cast complex shadows as they danced.

It all had to be not simply real, but finer, more real, than reality itself. True reality was often overlooked in its more exact details, and Gabriel did not want to be overlooked. The careful programming put into Gabriel's appearance, the slight exaggeration built into its visual and tactile dimensions, was meant to give it an impact somewhat greater than the real—the Realized—thing.

For the occasion Gabriel flew up to where his yacht, the *Pyrrho*, waited. He restrained himself with tethers in a null-gee room and had his face constantly scanned by microwatt laser so that his real expression could be transmitted to the skiagénos and that its facial expressions would be Gabriel's own. In zero-gee he could move his real body in synch with the skiagénos in order to enhance his illusion and the conviction of his performance.

The most important people in the Logarchy would be watching. He didn't intend to disappoint them.

Gabriel entered the oneirochronon and told his reno to establish a tachline link to Earth². He materialized his skiagénos in the virtual apartment he'd built in the dream Persepolis and looked about him. The furniture, the hangings, all were as he remembered. Shadow-servants in the shapes of fairy-tale bipedal animals moved toward him, triggered by his appearance. An oneirochronic quintet were frozen in one corner, awaiting only the command to play.

Gabriel inspected the servants' livery and made certain it suited their somewhat inhuman shapes. They hadn't been animals at the last Graduation—their shapes (orange tabby, striped Olivian tetrapus, bright-eyed otter) were a more recent whimsy. He made certain the animals' fur possessed the proper warmth, softness, and resilience—there was even a slight crackle of static as he stroked them—then passed on to the quintet. He triggered their action, gauged and adjusted the tone. The interpretation had been borrowed from his own Residence chamber musicians. The musicians were dressed in eighteenth-century Viennese court dress, white wigs and all.

Everything seemed ready. Gabriel froze the action and then left the suite through carven jade doors.

The doors led to an underground corridor in the palace of Darius I that existed both in reality and in the oneiro-chronic Persepolis. The first person Gabriel saw he recognized: Therápōn Protarchōn Akwasibo, who had served under Gabriel decades before, when Gabriel was a very new, very young Aristos.

As of tomorrow, Akwasibo would be made an Ariste herself.

Her lanky body was clothed in a dress of diamond-shaped mirrors. Invisible spotlights seemed to bounce off the reflective surfaces, casting gold reflections on the walls. Her Ethiopian eyes were rimmed with kohl; her long neck was as supple as that of Nefertiti (and scarcely exaggerated at all, as Gabriel remembered). There was another diamond-shaped mirror set flat in her forehead, and two more dangled from her ears.

"Greetings, Gabriel Aristos." Assuming a Posture of Formal Regard.

Gabriel raised a hand. "Hail, newly immortal."

She smiled. Gabriel embraced her and kissed her hello. Her dream-breath smelled of oranges, and her dream-lips seemed to vibrate slightly, a not unpleasant effect.

"Are you on your way to the reception?" Gabriel asked.

"Point of fact, I was on my way to see you. The city's reno told me you'd arrived and I came right over."

Gabriel lifted an eyebrow. "Is your business that urgent?"

"Depends on your definition of urgent. We can walk to the reception if you like."

"Take my arm."

"A pleasure."

They strolled up the corridor. The wall frescoes were a translucent sea blue, and dolphins, gold and white and deep azure, frolicked thereon. The warm Persian wind brought the fresh scent of cypress. It was autumn here, and somehow that sense had been translated into the oneirochronon. Good programmers, here.

Pan Wengong employed only the best.

"I wanted simply to thank you," Akwasibo said. "I think you were the Aristos who taught me the most."

"I was dreadfully inexperienced. Under thirty, for heaven's sake, and I wasn't that much older than you."

"You taught me while you were teaching yourself. Of course it took me over forty years before I could really put it all in practice."

"But you'll make many fewer mistakes than I."

"The only thing I can say with confidence is that they probably won't be the same mistakes."

The sound of wind chimes floated on the wind, and then the unreal sound of a reed flute. Gabriel and Akwasibo turned toward the Apadana, the great hall of Darius I.

Over the dream-city drifted a dream-moon, half full in a mild blue sky. The real Luna after which it was modeled had long been more Realized than most places—its interior had now been transformed, molecule by molecule, into a huge data store, one of many that made up the Hyperlogos, the universal data pool. Save for that under the Seal of the Aristoi, almost every bit and byte of it was accessible, something that contributed more to peace in the Logarchy than all the social engineers in history.

"I'm a bit nervous," Akwasibo confessed. "What sort of thing goes on at these receptions?"

"Pleasure. Display. Rivalry. Intrigue." Gabriel smiled. "Everything that makes life worth living."

The palati pollen floated through Illyricum's breathless dawn air. Gabriel rose from the bench, and Manfred picked himself up, stretched, yawned yet again, and followed Gabriel from the pavilion. Fading motes of dawn danced in Gabriel's path as he returned to the main building of the Residence.

As he walked past the Shadow Cloister he heard a mumbled, weary chant, and remembered that he'd received a report that the Therápōn Dekarchōn Yaritomo, the demiourgós in charge of tax assessment for one of Illyricum's provinces, had announced he would ere long attempt the ritual of Kavandi. Gabriel told Manfred to wait for him and stepped quietly through a turquoise-encrusted archway to watch the ordeal.

Yaritomo was a stocky man not quite seventeen, a recent graduate of Lincoln College at Illyricum University. He had performed well at the duties that Gabriel had set him in order to acquaint him with the basics of civil administration. Reports from the Psychological Department indicated that Yaritomo's personality had shown a tendency to avoid fragmentation by milder techniques, and Kavandi was his own choice.

Yaritomo was naked beneath the metal frame he had strapped to his body. The frame held over fifty stainless-steel spears, all surgically sharp, all pointed inward to his skin.

Above him was the Shadow Mask on its pillar, the giant robot face—gears, pneumatic systems, and hologram projectors—that Gabriel had designed for his play Mask. The Shadow Mask was set in an expression of harlequin satisfaction, white-featured, thinly smiling, black triangles over the eyes, rosy circles on the cheeks.

Gabriel looked from the mask to the dancing boy below, and approved of Yaritomo's choice of place. The Shadow Mask was a symbol resonant with Yaritomo's announced intent.

The young Therápōn chanted the Sutra of Captain Yuan over and over as he danced in a circle beneath the mask. He'd probably been at this since the previous evening, and he had worn a weary circle in the patient grass. The spears rattled in their frame, driving of their own weight into his flesh. Sweat fell from his forehead.

"*Let madness take my mind,*" he chanted. "*Let daimones take my soul.*"

There was remarkably little blood. Gabriel noted approvingly that even under severe physical and psychic stress Yaritomo had managed to retain mastery over his narrowed capillaries.

"*Let the spirit rise through my body. Let the spirit fill me with power.*"

Gabriel, using his Aristos Override, pulsed a query through his reno concerning Yaritomo's pulse rate and blood pressure. His reno connected with the house reno, which queried Yaritomo's own implant. The Therápōn's reno, monitoring his state from its nest at the base of his skull, returned a reassuring answer. Yaritomo was young and in good condition and with the proper focus of concentration could probably keep this up for days. Gabriel inquired again regarding the level of fatigue toxins, but Yaritomo's reno, unlike Gabriel's, didn't have the ability to make that measurement.

Certain mental states were aided, sometimes even initiated, by the extreme alterations in body chemistry caused by stress. Yaritomo had doubtless been on a moderate fast for several days, lowering his body's reserves against stress, rearranging his brain chemistry. The dancing, chanting, and extremes of pain would have raised stress and fatigue toxins to a high level while lowering reserves of strength, all intended not as an assault on the body, but on the conscious mind . . .

Yaritomo, however, wasn't trying to drive himself out of his mind.

He was trying to drive himself into it.

"*Let the daimōn come. Let me wrestle with this daimōn. Let*

*me overcome the daimōn and make him a part of me. Let me take
the daimōn's power!"*

The last words were a hoarse, determined cry, a shout of
triumph over pain, of mental over physical self.

Gabriel quietly withdrew.

The pain, he knew, was far from over.

Vermilion pillars, capped with gold, supported the roof of the
Apadana. The walls and pillars were encrusted with both the
original Persian script and the complex Involved Ideography
of Captain Yuan. Aristoi, plumed and feathered, thronged the
room. Sebastian, whose oneirochronic body was a shimmering, floating sphere, was conspicuous by his presence.

Entering with Akwasibo, Gabriel acknowledged a few
waves and nods. "I wish I could say that I always knew you
would achieve this," he said. "But in those days I didn't have
the experience to predict these things. And I was too busy to
try."

"Well." She smiled. "I'm not certain that I ever knew
myself. Not till the last three or four years or so, when all my
work started coming together."

Akwasibo's route to the rank of Ariste was the more
common: decades of hard work followed by a kind of synthesis in which the years of diligence paid off, when the accumulated knowledge and ability reached a transcendent
fusion. Gabriel's route was more direct, a blazing vertical
ascent that ranked him as an Aristos before the age of thirty.
Some had predicted that he'd burn out, but were of course
wrong—instead, nearing the age of eighty, he was more pro-
ductive than he'd ever been.

"Do you know everyone?" Gabriel asked. He glanced
over the room again and summoned most of his daimones—
dealing with his peers en masse was usually challenging.

"Sebastian's hard to miss," Akwasibo said. "I've apprenticed with Coetzee and Tallchief. And I probably know most
by sight."

"Their real appearances, certainly. But *here*, if you see a

dark, hovering creature, like a bat, it's most likely Dorothy.
And Salvador likes to appear as a bird of prey—that bird over
there, the"—consulting his reno—"Harris's hawk, that's
probably him." (**Cliché,** said Cyrus, voice echoing in Gabriel's head. **Boring,** said the Welcome Rain.)

"I'm glad I recognized *you*, at least."

"I spent a lot of effort on my physical appearance as well
as my oneirochronic one. No sense in altering it now."

"I remember your eyes being a different color. And the
epicanthal folds . . ."

"Give me a sense of wisdom and maturity, I'd like to
think."

Akwasibo craned her long neck to a somewhat unnatural
angle. (Cyrus and Spring Plum argued back and forth about
whether she had slipped up or not.)

"Who else won't I know?" she said.

"Shankar will look like someone historical from old
Earth[1], Abraham Lincoln or Li Po or Charlie Chaplin. Dorothy St.-John, as distinct from Dorothy, likes to surprise people, so she floats around as something small, a moth or mantis
or—"

"A pair of gold cat's eyes," said a pair of gold cat's eyes
that had been gazing from the nearby pillar. Akwasibo
couldn't quite hide her start of surprise. Gabriel, who had far
more practice at this, efficiently disguised his own.

I *hate* **that!** yelped Spring Plum.

"Hail, Dorothy St.-John Ariste," Gabriel said, assuming
a Posture of Formal Regard. "How're you hanging?"

"Cheshirely, thanks. And you?"

"I hang together, not separately," Gabriel said, meaning
himself and his daimones.

"Pleased to hear it, Flame." The eyes detached themselves from the lintel and floated between Gabriel and Akwasibo. Cyrus and Spring Plum commented on the eyes'
lustrous amber glow; Augenblick lamented the lack of kinesic
clues. "Have you heard what Astoreth and her clique are up
to?"

"No."

"They think we're failing in our duty to motivate and educate the Therápontes and the Demos. Or succeeding all too well. They don't seem to be quite certain on that point. But at any rate they want changes made."

"I thought Astoreth's critique was mainly aesthetic."

"She or her colleagues seem to have discovered a political dimension to their ideas."

"Who's involved?"

"Astoreth. Ctesias. Precious Jade. Han Fu."

"Except for Astoreth they're mostly young," Gabriel said.

"No younger than you. I wouldn't dismiss it as a generational thing."

"I have no intention of dismissing it as a generational thing or anything else." Gabriel gazed into the slitted pupils. "What do you think of their ideas?"

The eyes fluttered like butterfly wings. "They possess a certain merit. But they are expressed with too much force to win over any significant fraction of the Aristoi. The means are too confrontational."

"Astoreth has always been that way."

"She'll regret it eventually. If they'd spent a few decades gathering data, then drawing conclusions, their ideas would have a better foundation—as it is, their notions seem more an artistic impulse than a political creed. If they can't prove their premises, no one's likely to respect their conclusions."

"Far be it from me," Gabriel said, "to denigrate artistic impulse."

"I didn't think you would, Flame." The eyes winked. Dorothy St.-John began to flutter away. "I should go adhere to some other surface and see what news I can gather."

"Best of luck."

"Nice meeting you," Akwasibo said, craning her neck after the golden eyes. (**Aha!** said Cyrus. **Told you it was deliberate.**)

Akwasibo turned back to Gabriel. "I hadn't heard of any of these political developments."

"We have a way of keeping them to ourselves," Gabriel said. "If there's one thing people don't need to see, it's Aristoi yelling at each other."

Akwasibo's eyes widened slightly. "You *yell?*"

"Not me personally, no. But if you were debating someone like Virtue's Icon or Sebastian, you'd be tempted to, wouldn't you?"

"I see your point."

"I should offer my respects to Pan Wengong. Shall I introduce you to him?"

"I met him earlier." She looked about her, absorbing the sight of the Apadana. "Quite a place he built, eh?"

Gabriel laughed. "You should see what he did for Alexandreia, Byzantium, and Peking."

Manfred at his heels, Gabriel entered the Residence's Biomedical Wing and walked through its invisible, sterilizing doors.

Therápōn Hextarchōn Marcus was stretched comfortably on the padded couch in the circular operating theater with its geometrical black-and-white tiles. There was no audience in the seats above. The simple surgical equipment, concealed in a dark wood cabinet brightened by parquetry and bright inlayed silver, had wheeled itself into place. A vase of fresh-cut sunflowers perched happily stop the cabinet like a beaming visitation from Arles.

Marcus wore a dark blue dressing gown over which white birds flocked, in darting flight, through a series of hovering Corinthian columns. His skin was pale, his hair, eyes, and lashes black. Sitting next to him on a stool was Clancy, Therápōn Tritarchōn in charge of the Biomedical Wing. She held Marcus's hand. As Gabriel entered, she rose and assumed, from force of habit, the Second Posture of Formal Regard. Her rosy skin flushed with pleasure.

Marcus, on his table, attempted an approximation of the same stance.

Gabriel kissed them each hello. Affection for Marcus floated warmly through his heart.

"I brought you a gift," he said. He removed from his long red hair a pair of ivory-and-silver hair clips and presented them to Marcus. The ivory had been carved into delicate long helixes, resembling DNA, and each DNA curve had been carved with a delicate bas-relief face resembling either Gabriel or Marcus or some blend of the two.

"The genetic code of our child has been microscopically inscribed into the silver," Gabriel said.

Marcus's pale skin flushed with delight. He kissed Gabriel's hands in thanks, then sat up. Gabriel idly combed his fingers through Marcus's hair. Manfred jumped on the couch between Marcus's legs, and Marcus hugged the dog hello. He stroked Manfred's neck and ears.

"Can I read the code?" he said.

"If you like," Gabriel said. He took the hair clips from Marcus and placed the first, frowned, adjusted it more to his liking. "But it will tell you the sex of the child. I thought you didn't want to know."

Marcus frowned. "Perhaps I can just look at the rest."

"I created a more-or-less random mixture of our genetics—a classical zygote, if you like. I added nothing, I subtracted nothing—I only assured myself that the embryo would be free of genetic defect. I don't think you'd necessarily learn anything from the study." Gabriel fixed the last of the hair clips in place and studied the result. "Are you nervous?" he asked.

"Not as much as I thought I'd be, no."

Marcus's vital signs indicated that he *was* nervous, though only mildly so. "Lie back," Gabriel said. "Perhaps the couch could give you a massage."

GABRIEL: Reno, give me Marcus's pulse and pressure, please. < Priority 2 >
RENO: < Priority 2 > < Linking through Biomed reno > < Linking through Marcus's reno > Heartbeat 87, pressure 150 over 88.

"It won't disturb the procedure?"

"Not at all."

Marcus leaned back on the couch. A faint hum announced he had called up the deep-massage function. Marcus closed his eyes and, with a slight visible effort, summoned his daimones. Gabriel called up those of his own who he thought would have an interest in the procedure. He looked up at Clancy. Sunflowers beamed from over her shoulder.

GABRIEL: Reno, keep that data coming. Horus. Bear. Cyrus. Spring Plum. Psyche. <Priority 2>

HORUS: <Priority 2> Servant.

BEAR: <Priority 2> Servant.

CYRUS: <Priority 2> Servant.

SPRING PLUM: <Priority 2> Servant.

PSYCHE: <Priority 2> Servant.

"Thank you for your offer of assistance." Gabriel had never actually qualified as a doctor and wanted, for form's sake, to have one at hand.

"My pleasure." Clancy stroked Marcus's arm through his dressing gown and smiled down at him. "I've performed a number of these myself, back on Darkbloom."

"I hope you will offer advice when it's needed."

"I doubt I'll be necessary at all," she smiled, and gave a little shake of her head. Cyrus, ever the aesthete, called Gabriel's attention to the pleasant surge of motion through the mass of her hair, to the play of light on its dark sheen. Complex pleasures sang through Gabriel. Clancy was new here. Gabriel had met her several times while discussing this procedure, and found her enthusiasm invigorating.

Gabriel turned to Marcus. "You know you'll have to be a little more careful with yourself than you're used to," he said. "Actually carrying a pregnancy to term within the human body is far more hazardous than other methods."

"I want it, Gabriel Vissarionovich. I want to know every day that it's there."

Gabriel smiled, waved his hands. He found it difficult to refuse anyone a harmless folly. "So be it," he said.

Gabriel undid the buttons of Marcus's dressing gown and revealed the smooth, porcelain-skinned body that had caused him to nickname Marcus "The Black-Eyed Ghost." The rain of sensation from Cyrus fell away, replaced by the presence of Spring Plum. Spring Plum was a female Limited Personality, the most complete and self-possessed of his LPs yet revealed to Gabriel, and though she was as complete a connoisseur as Cyrus, she had firmer aesthetic standards for male beauty, standards that shimmered with complex structures of desire. Cyrus, Gabriel found, was forever and in contrast calling his attention to women.

Marcus was in his forties but had stabilized his body at the age of twenty, as soon as he had graduated from the Demos to the status of Therápōn. The catlike musculature was distinct, but had a pleasant late-adolescent softness that Gabriel found entrancing. The pale, translucent skin was Marcus's own; the contrasting black

SPRING PLUM: *"The expression of a well-made man appears not only in his face, / It is in his limbs and joints also, it is curiously in the joints of his hips and wrists . . ."*

GABRIEL: < kisses >

SPRING PLUM: *"To see him pass conveys as much as the best poem, perhaps more."*

CYRUS: < white birds flocking on blue velvet . . . >

RENO: Pulse 92, pressure 139 over 90.

BEAR: The boy is too nervous.

CYRUS: < the silver curl of Corinthian caps . . . >

GABRIEL: Reno, give me command of the surgical array.

RENO: Do you wish full video?

GABRIEL: Yes.

CYRUS: < Clancy's fine-boned hands, brittle light on nails > < fading >

RENO: < linking with surgical array > Done.

GABRIEL: I'm largely blind. Spring Plum, take command of my body. < Priority 1 >

SPRING PLUM: < Priority 1 > At your service, Aristos.

hair and lashes were benign genetic tinkering. Marcus had served his previous apprenticeships under Deborah and Saigo, and failed his exams the one time he had taken them. He had put off taking them a second time, but finally, with Gabriel's urging, had prepared himself to try again within the next three years.

Perhaps Marcus suspected what Gabriel knew: he would never graduate to the ranks of the Aristoi. He was talented, illustrious in his own chosen sphere of industrial design, but he didn't possess the blazing and brittle brilliance, the cold and all-consuming ambition, needed to rise to the highest ranks of humanity.

Still, Gabriel felt, it would help him to know it, one way or another. *Know* that he hadn't missed an opportunity, that he was right to be just where he was.

It wasn't a coincidence, Gabriel thought, that Marcus's most developed daimōn was a child, an unformed and naive personality who approached the world with delight and transcendent joy. Marcus's aspirations were not those of a steel-willed Aristos, turning the universe to his own account, but those of the talented, ingenuous, warm-hearted young man whose body he had frozen at the age of twenty, and with whom Gabriel had fallen instantly in love.

Perhaps the inner knowledge of his upcoming failure was why Marcus suddenly wanted this child—and not any child, but the child of himself and an Aristos he loved. Some palpable memory of Gabriel, some hope that the child would achieve what Marcus would not . . .

Gabriel had good reason to suspect Marcus's hope. The children of Aristoi did not often achieve their parents' status. None of his other children had—all were talented, but only half had become Therápontes—and the odds were against this one being any different.

But Marcus's child—a girl, Gabriel knew—would be loved. Marcus had a stable future as a talented Therápōn and his own child-daimōn would attach the child to him with bonds of affection and shared interest.

Gabriel placed a mental finger into the oneirochronon and triggered the surgical cabinet, which rolled forward and deployed its array. He reached into the pocket of his brocade jacket (Spring Plum contrasting Marcus's pale skin and black hair with the black-and-white tiles of the theater), brought out the mechanical egg in which the blastocyst lay. The textured surface impressed itself on Gabriel's fingertips, white porcelain lace on Wedgewood blue. Through his reno's connection with the oneirochronon he ordered the egg to open (Spring Plum showing him brightness gleaming on sliding silver bars as the egg opened, as the blue ceramic turned inward, as he found himself with an open metal lotus in his hand, all gleaming silver petals with the treasure at their center).

Gabriel (through Spring Plum) glanced down at Marcus's abdomen, and (through the deploying surgical array and its peritoneoscope) marked a spot just below the navel with a bright spot of low-intensity laser light. "There, Manfred," he said. "Two hundred microns, okay?"

The bullterrier leaned forward and began to lick the area, covering it with sterile saliva. Marcus gave a startled laugh.

"It tickles," he said.

The surgical array dipped a two-millimeter peritoneoscope complex into the silver lotus, carefully absorbed the blastocyst, retracted. The egg folded itself inward again, blue and white flashing in Cyrus's appreciative perception, and was extended toward Marcus.

"A souvenir," he said.

Marcus took the egg, admired it, tried to work the mechanism.

Manfred drew his lips back, extended a carbon tooth tipped with nanodiamond, and stabbed Marcus precisely where Gabriel had indicated with the laser spot. Marcus, absorbed in trying to work the egg, failed to notice. Manfred used modified salivary glands to flood the wound with a fast-working local anesthetic, then licked away the tiny crimson droplet that welled up.

Gabriel (entering the oneirochronon of the peritoneoscope) homed the fiber-optic complex in on the puncture. It entered (Spring Plum relaying Marcus's startled look as he realized that the operation had actually commenced), and Gabriel's visual centers filled with a fish-eye view of the bright colors of Marcus's dermis.

The fiber-optic complex descended between columnar epithelial cells and vascular loops already ruptured by Manfred's diamond incisor. Half-formed fibrin clots were dispersed. Leukocytes tried and failed to come to grips with the seamless surface of the invader.

Yellow fat cells swam through Gabriel's perspective. He slipped through the fibrous tissue surrounding lean, cross-woven muscle tissue of the linea alba, descended through tooth-torn myofibril bands.

"This feels strange. I can feel myself being . . . tugged around down there." Marcus's words came distantly to Gabriel's attention.

"Start a relaxation exercise." Bear spoke with Gabriel's voice. "Straighten your

GABRIEL: Reno, connect me with Clancy, please. < Priority 1 >

RENO: < linking with Clancy's reno > Done, Aristos. < Priority 1 >

CLANCY: < via link > Manfred's done your work for you here. Just follow the puncture to its base.

RENO: Pulse 97. Pressure 139 over 94.

BEAR: The boy is far too nervous. May I speak with him?

GABRIEL: Take my voice. < Priority 2 >

BEAR: < Priority 2 > Done, Aristos.

CLANCY: Careful, here . . . Take your time. There's your place.

CYRUS: < appreciation of the classic geometric array of overlapping muscle tissue >

spine and square your shoulders as much as you can. Inhale through the nose to the count of ten. Hold to the count of fifteen. Exhale through the mouth to the count of ten."

SPRING PLUM: < bemused, slightly alarmed look on Marcus's face >
BEAR: I am commencing a relaxation exercise, Aristos.
GABRIEL: < approval >
SPRING PLUM: *"The true words do not fail . . ."*

Bear was a comforting, warm presence, a parental embrace in daimonic form. It seemed not to possess gender as Gabriel understood the notion, only endless, universal melting reserves of tenderness, forgiveness, and compassion.

Gabriel pushed through muscle tissue and a layer of fat, encountered the semitransparent peritoneum. Bulbous viscera loomed, perceived indistinctly. Distantly Gabriel heard the whisper of Marcus drawing breath. He skated easily along a semifluid layer of fat between the peritoneum and the interior muscle wall. The world seemed to beat in harmony with Marcus's slowing heartbeat, hum with Bear's comforting phrases.

There was an audible popping sound as the peritoneum was punctured. ("What was *that?*"—Marcus's voice, soothed away by Bear.) Fluids pulsed. The yellow fat cells of the omentum, bright with blood and oxygen, swam through the oneirochronon. ("I'm being yanked around!" said Marcus.)

For generations there had existed a nanologic package designed to alter, over a period of months, an individual's sex. Many men in Marcus's situation would simply have opted to become female for the amount of time it took to carry the child. Marcus, on the other hand, preferred remaining biologically male, a decision that increased the number of technological challenges involved.

Gabriel had decided to design the pregnancy package himself. There were standard kits available, but they failed, in Gabriel's view, on one ground or another. Either they depended on brute-force nano to do their work—Gabriel preferred to minimize the amount of nanomachines he actually injected into humans—or they didn't take enough design factors into account. They lacked, in his view, sufficient technological elegance.

Gabriel had united the two gametes eight days before; he had wanted the cell package to reach the more vigorous blastocyst stage before implanting. The blastocyst was surrounded by an array of technologies in the form of a flexible biosculpture, a grey corrugated sphere, two millimeters in diameter, that would nestle among the blood-rich cells of the omentum. The outer layer was designed to dissolve over a period of several days, releasing a supply of hormones that would, in the course of the next week, thicken the omentum and build a thick decidual layer between it and the major blood vessels, a stage intended to preempt the usual difficulty with hemorrhages during abdominal pregnancies. Other hormones would increase the blood supply to the omentum and thicken its walls, strengthening it with cross-grained muscle tissue.

Gabriel was pleased with this aspect of the design. Hormones would encourage the omentum to strengthen itself, but without the intrusive effects of nano invading each cell and restructuring it by force. He wouldn't have to plant a separate hormone package in Marcus's body; he'd made it part of the biosculpture itself, and it would vanish when its work was done, unlike some nanos, which were (rarely, he must admit) disinclined to dismantle themselves when their schedule called for it.

Perhaps because he was the only person on the surface of Illyricum licensed to create nano and use it freely, he employed it only when he must.

The interior of the biosculpture was roughly textured to supply an adequate simulation of the maternal endometrium, providing a firm place for the blastocyst to lodge and the placenta to grow. It would thin and disappear as the placenta grew into the strengthened omentum itself.

Gabriel planted the blastocyst, then withdrew the peritoneoscope to view the nesting grey ball. He felt himself soaring, uniting with his daimones in a moment of ringing transcendence.

Gabriel listened in glowing awe to the rare voice of Psyche. Her verse was presented in ideogrammatic form, each character presenting a delicate grey brush-drawn picture resonant with visual as well as verbal consequence. Gabriel waited for a moment, letting the dying vibrations echo for a moment in his spirit, and then repeated the words to Marcus. He wished he had brush and paper so that he could show Marcus the form in which the poem had been created.

PSYCHE:
The lotus hovers in
*   flawless awareness*
Solipsistic, a solemnity of
*   potential.*
In a nutshell: Shakyamuni.
SPRING PLUM: < applause >
CYRUS: Apposite, as always.
BEAR: Brava!
CLANCY: Beautiful.
HORUS: Proper.
GABRIEL: < the scent of a rose bouquet >

Marcus was deep within his breathing regimen and Gabriel suspected that he wouldn't as yet be able to react to Psyche's effort. That didn't matter: one of Marcus's daimones would memorize the verse and recite it when the time was more appropriate.

Gabriel moved about the blastocyst, in theory assuring himself as to its well-being but in actuality wanting to prolong the soaring moment as long as possible, then he ordered the peritoneoscope to withdraw. As it moved it exuded minute amounts of a growth hormone that would assist with the repair of any damage it had made. The peritoneoscope slipped from Marcus's abdomen, returned to its housing, and then the housing withdrew into the surgical cabinet. Gabriel moved his daimones to a lower priority level and regained full use of body and sight. He looked down at Marcus's form and smiled. He raised his arms in the Fourth Posture of Exuberance. Joy welled up in him. Psyche's words sang through his mind.

"Congratulations," he said. "You're pregnant."

Marcus let go a long breath and looked up. "Thank you," he said. Manfred began to lick Marcus's abdomen again with his sterilizing tongue.

"I hope it's what you really wanted," Gabriel said. "You surprised me with how nervous you were. Much more than I would have expected."

"I surprised myself, Gabriel. Perhaps I'm a little more divided about this than I thought."

"Take the day off," Clancy suggested. "Go up the mountains, to Standing Wave. Talk to yourselves about it."

"Yes." Marcus took Clancy's hand, squeezed it. "I will."

Clancy looked at Gabriel. Her face was a little flushed, her eyes bright enough to dim the sunflowers that smiled behind her. "This is almost as fine as a delivery.

Gabriel looked at her, surprise rolling through him at the power of her incandescence. "I trust you'll have the pleasure of being at the delivery as well," he said. The child would, of course, be delivered by a surgeon, and Clancy was certainly qualified.

"I hope so." She stroked Marcus's hair. "Unless Marcus is an Aristos by then, and off in his capital starting his new empire."

Marcus rose from the table. He gave Clancy a kiss, then hugged Manfred. He turned to Gabriel and held out his arms. Gabriel embraced him and kissed him for a long moment.

GABRIEL: Augenblick. Welcome Rain. < Priority 2 >

AUGENBLICK: < Priority 2 > At your service, Aristos. < absorbing Clancy > Pulse elevated, skin flushed, eyes dilated, both nipples erect.

WELCOME RAIN: Yours.

GABRIEL: Thank you. Fini.

AUGENBLICK: Your servant. < Priority 2, end >

WELCOME RAIN: Your servant. < Priority 2, end >

SCREAM: < Priority 1 > *Fagit!*

HORUS: < Priority 3 > < ??? >

SPRING PLUM: < Priority 3 > Who the hell was *that*?

"I hope you will be happy, Black-Eyed Ghost," Gabriel said. There was a peculiar metallic aftertaste on his tongue.

Marcus smiled, touched the ivory surface of one of his hair clips. "I will. Thank you."

CYRUS: < Priority 3> Someone come to spoil the party.

SPRING PLUM: Was that someone new, or . . . ?

HORUS: From the paleolithic, I think.

GABRIEL: Hush, children.

Marcus made his way out. Gabriel ordered the surgical cabinet to roll itself back into storage and turned to contemplate Clancy. He raised Spring Plum and Cyrus to a higher level of awareness, and Cyrus called attention to her fine, unaltered bone structure, her translucent complexion, roses ever in bloom. Gabriel's heart warmed. He realized he was in love.

"Would you like to have breakfast with me in the Autumn Pavilion?" he asked.

"I'd like that very much. But I'm giving a lecture at ten."

"You might give serious thought to canceling it. Perhaps I'll declare a planetary holiday and make it easy for you."

She smiled. Her full upper lip formed a series of pleasant arches. She had, he remembered, a consort, someone he'd never met.

Someone whose life was going to change.

Gabriel told Manfred to take the day off, took Clancy's arm, and walked with her out of the Biomedical Wing. As he neared the Shadow Cloister, he found himself listening for the sound of rattling steel spears, for Yaritomo's chanting. He didn't hear anything.

He and Clancy passed into the cloister and viewed Yaritomo through the cloister's romanesque, turquoise-encrusted arches. The Therápōn stood still under the bright morning sky, his feet wide apart, sagging under the weight of the spears and their rack. Sweat sheened his skin, and his breath rasped in his throat. His eyes were rolled up into their sockets. The Shadow Mask, a little sinister in the bright light, smiled coldly on the scene.

Gabriel kissed Clancy's hand. "Pardon me for a moment."

He turned to Yaritomo, assumed the First Posture of Confidence, shoulders back, chin high, spine erect, weight distributed evenly on feet that were slightly apart.

"Who are you?"

Yaritomo's eyes slid down from beneath trembling lids, focused with difficulty. His face worked its way into a sneer.

"I am the Burning Tiger," he said. The voice was a deep growl, entirely unlike Yaritomo's voice.

"I see."

"Stay clear!" the Burning Tiger warned.

"I will go where I please," Gabriel said. "I am master here."

The Burning Tiger growled, made a threatening move toward Gabriel. Gabriel did not respond, and the Burning Tiger hesitated. Steel spears rattled in their harness.

GABRIEL: Augenblick. Welcome Rain. < Priority 2 >

AUGENBLICK: < Priority 2 > < scanning Yaritomo > It's someone else.

WELCOME RAIN: We need further definition. Make it talk to us.

AUGENBLICK: Willful, suspicious, powerful. Insensitive, I'd imagine. A fantasy projection of Yaritomo's need for power and control in a stressful situation. But the body language is defeatist.

WELCOME RAIN: Burning Paper Tiger! Confront him, and he'll fade.

AUGENBLICK: Easy enough for us, but it's Therápōn Yaritomo who has to do the confronting.

WELCOME RAIN: It should be easy enough. The Tiger's a berserker—someone who sees only straight ahead is easy enough to trip up from behind.

"If you want to intimidate me," Gabriel said, "you must act like a tiger in truth." He glared at the daimōn that inhabited Yaritomo's body. "Is your demeanor that of a tiger or that of a drunkard in a windstorm?"

The Burning Tiger's eyes widened. He straightened, throwing out his chest. "I will not bear your insults. You have trespassed on my honor."

Augenblick and the Welcome Rain hooted derision from the depths of Gabriel's mind, a verbal echo of the Shadow Mask's mirthless smile. "You're tottering like a broken pinwheel," Gabriel said. "Stand straight if you want to convince me of your mastery."

The Burning Tiger growled, but he dragged his body upright. Spears rattled in their harness. Trails of blood coursed down Yaritomo's arms and legs. He inhaled slowly, filling his chest.

Good, Gabriel thought. The breath showed that somewhere beneath the Burning Tiger's surface awareness, Yaritomo's body had remembered its training.

"Breathe!" Gabriel affirmed. "Fill your lungs with power! And when you exhale, throw weariness and pain away from you!"

The Burning Tiger gave a long snarl as he exhaled. Involuntary tremors stormed through the heavy muscles of his thighs. His hands formed fists, held ready near his waist. Gabriel watched from his commanding stance as the Burning Tiger grew in strength, in resolution. "Are you the master, Tiger?" he asked.

"Yes!"

"Show me your confidence. Imitate my posture!" Gabriel used the Principal Inflection of Command. He drew his right foot back, bent his legs, lowered his stance till his thigh muscles strained, until his center of gravity settled into the swadhishatana chakra in the pit of the abdomen. His spine was still straight and his hands curled into Mudras of Attention and Compulsion.

The Burning Tiger sneered, but certain behaviors had been programmed into Yaritomo's psyche early, and the Burning Tiger was more dominated by reflex than he would have admitted. Driven by the Principal Inflection he snapped into the stance, perhaps without quite meaning to. The doubting look in his eyes demonstrated his uncertainty, and the Welcome Rain mocked him from inside Gabriel's head. The clear blue light of Illyricum etched the merciless strain on the Tiger's face, in his trembling muscles. Augenblick took it all in, pinpointed every weakness, every strength. The Burning Tiger was so unformed, so open, that Augenblick's dissection was scarcely a challenge.

"Now you seem more a tiger," Gabriel said. "Ready to spring."

"Beware me."

"We will see who is master."

"Beware me." The words were chanted, almost a mantra.

Gabriel gave the Tiger a mocking smile resonant with that of the Shadow Mask. "Do you esteem yourself, Tiger?"

"Beware me. I am master here."

Gabriel gave a shout, clearing his lungs, and raised himself into the First Posture of Esteem, his body straightened, hands at sides, feet close together, his center of gravity rising to the manipura chakra at the base of the breastbone. The Burning Tiger gave a startled shuffle backward, then blinked, snarled, firmed his threatening stance.

"Do you esteem yourself, Tiger?" Gabriel taunted.

In a rattle of spears the Burning Tiger shambled into an imitation of Gabriel's posture. Pain twitched across his features. The Welcome Rain cackled amusement.

Gabriel led the Burning Tiger through a series of neural programming exercises designed to firm the Limited Personality's uncertain, newborn character, to give him at least a claim to depth and foundation. Certain stances—codified ages before by Captain Yuan in the *Book of Postures*—were known to possess coherent psychic resonance within the human mind. Gabriel sought to firm the Burning Tiger's psyche by connecting it to a physical, metalinguistic memory that would strengthen it.

Captain Yuan had based his *Postures* on a straightforward

appreciation of the way the human brain was wired to the body that supported and shaped it, and was based on careful study of kinesics as used in classical dance, drama, tantric philosophy, and martial arts. A stance with the legs apart, the center of gravity lowered to the swadhishatana chakra in the abdomen, bespoke confidence and readiness, and did so with a surprising universality, in all surviving human cultures, in all known times. The posture could be made more aggressive by balling the fists or drawing one leg back into a boxer's stance or further back into a classical martial arts pose—all subvariations of the original confident posture, all clearly understood throughout an increasingly divergent humanity. The fingers could form mudras for more psychic impact.

The Poses of Esteem were more straight-legged, raised the center of gravity toward the manipura chakra beneath the breastbone. These postures bespoke seriousness, gravity, and self-regard. Raising the arms lifted the center of gravity yet higher, to the anahata chakra, and bespoke Exuberance. Higher still was Glory. On the other end of the scale were the kneeling postures, those of Submission. Precise arm and leg position, the lift and tilt of the head, flexion of the spine, set of the shoulders, all widened the kinesic vocabulary, allowed it greater flexibility of expression. Lowering the head could transfer esteem and respect to others, while raising the chin high cried out *Look at me!* A vocabulary more important than speech, more fundamental to human nature.

Gabriel resumed the First Posture of Confidence. The Burning Tiger, conditioned by now, followed his example.

"Who are you, Burning Tiger?" Gabriel demanded.

"I am He-Who-Scorches-with-Flame. I am Power-of-the-Daytime. I am That-Which-Drives-Forward. I am Unstoppable-in-Fury. I am master of this place and time."

The growling voice was more confident now, more assured. The fragile Limited Personality had firmed through repeatedly inhabiting kinesics of confidence and strength. If Gabriel advanced on him suddenly, Augenblick advised, the Burning Tiger would not flinch. Welcome Rain advised against closing the distance unless a physical confrontation was desired.

"You are not master here," Gabriel said.

"I am master." The Burning Tiger gestured with one arm, a downward-dropping fist, that emphasized his words. Steel spears quivered in their rack.

"Yaritomo is master," Gabriel said.

"Not so."

"It is true. Shall I call him out?"

The Burning Tiger's eyes were dull, inhuman. "Yaritomo will not come," he said. "He is fainthearted. He summoned me to endure that which he could not."

"I can bring him out."

The Burning Tiger raised his chin in a gesture of contempt. "You are a fool."

Gabriel shouted again, a cry from the pit of his stomach that set the air ringing, and followed it with an arm thrust forward, the hand forming the Mudra of Compulsion. His voice took on the Inflection of Command.

"Therápōn Yaritomo, come forth! Stand before me!"

The Burning Tiger sneered, but there was hesitation in his eyes, an onset of confusion . . .

"Yaritomo, stand forth! I want to speak to you."

The Burning Tiger's eyes turned blank. His jaw muscles worked with the strain of the battle being fought in his psyche. Then the face cleared, the contemptuous sneer vanishing, replaced by the surprised expression of a bewildered youth. Yaritomo staggered under the weight of his spears, went down to one knee with a crash. He propped himself up with one arm as he panted for breath, then dragged himself to his feet. His eyes managed to focus on Gabriel.

"At your service, Aristos," he gasped.

"Do you know what happened?"

"Yes. I think." Yaritomo panted for breath. "I remember . . . someone else."

"He called himself the Burning Tiger."

"I . . ." Yaritomo passed a hand over his eyes. "I don't

remember it very clearly. I was in another place. I only had an impression of him."

"You're going to have to call him back."

Yaritomo swallowed. "I know."

"And defeat him."

"Yes."

"Are you prepared to do that?"

Yaritomo shook his head. His voice was barely audible. "I don't know, Aristos. I suppose so."

"Make yourself ready, then."

He led Yaritomo through the same kinesic exercise he'd used to program the daimōn, then set him to dancing and chanting the Sutra of Captain Yuan again, specifically summoning the Burning Tiger. The Shadow Mask, metaphor for all that took place here, smiled ruthlessly down on them all.

When the Burning Tiger manifested, the desperate rite of chöd would begin. Yaritomo and the Burning Tiger would engage in psychic combat for possession of Yaritomo's body and mind, each trying to conquer the other.

Gabriel suppressed Augenblick and the Welcome Rain, then withdrew to the covered walk where Clancy waited for him. "Thank you for waiting," he said, and kissed her. Her lips were moist, their touch delicate. Cyrus voiced quiet approval.

She took his hand. As they left the Shadow Cloister, Clancy looked over her shoulder at the chanting, rattling figure of Yaritomo. Concern ruffled her brow. "Will he be all right?"

"I believe so."

"He seems so vulnerable, compared to the . . . other."

"The Burning Tiger appears powerful, but it's mostly bluster. He's also rather stupid—he's got Yaritomo's intelligence to draw on, but I suspect he doesn't know how. Yaritomo should have little difficulty coping with him. And when Yaritomo finds more useful LPs, he may decide to suppress this one altogether." Gabriel shrugged. "Still, the Tiger'll do for a start."

"I had to go through some fairly intensive hypnotherapy to bring my daimones out—but nothing like *that*." Looking over her shoulder again. "Nothing like Kavandi." She turned to him. "Did you ever have such difficulty?"

Gabriel smiled. "Not at all. The daimones were my friends from an early age."

"You had imaginary playmates."

"Not so imaginary. But yes. And they required scarcely any coaxing at all to cohere into true shadow personalities." The memory of the shouting daimōn rose in his mind. *Fagit!* "I heard a new voice today," he said. "Someone I didn't know was there. It was rather startling, after all this time. One would have thought I'd know them all by now."

"After breakfast I'll look in on Yaritomo. Make certain that his rite of chöd is going well."

Gabriel felt warmed by her concern. "He's supposed to face his daimōn alone."

"Without even a coach?"

"The struggle should be internal. The outward forms are just props."

"But didn't you just coach him yourself?"

"Ah, well." He laughed. "I'm an Aristos. I can break the rules if I want to."

They emerged into sunlight and delicate flower perfume. Gardeners worked along the patient rows of blossoms. Some, the supervisors, were human, and the rest were either machines or implanted mountain gorillas. The gorillas loved plants above all things, and were good and careful gardeners—also, as a practical point, any harmful grubs or beetles provided them with nourishment.

Above, in a sky precise as the oneirochronon, soared two silhouettes, gliders floating on nanological libelulla wings. The acutely organized perceptions of Cyrus and Spring Plum floated through Gabriel's senses. His heart lifted and he recalled:

> "Early summer, grasses and tall plants
> Around my house, trees flourishing,
> Varieties of birds delighted at finding rest."

Clancy's face turned abstract for a moment as she queried the Hyperlogon for the source of the quote, found it in Tao Chien. Her eyes glowed as she returned the end of the poem.

> "I gaze up and down at heaven and earth.
> Happy? How could I be otherwise?"

Gabriel took her in his arms and kissed her. Her body warmed him. The human gardeners, with accustomed professionalism, affected not to notice.

"It's a day for birth," she said, a moment later. "Burning Tiger, and your child with the Black-Eyed Ghost, and—" She finished the thought with another kiss.

He took her to Psyche's room in the Autumn Pavilion. It was comfortably small but with a tall arched ceiling, the architecture soaring, reaching skyward, making an acoustic cap that turned sound wonderfully to the ear. The walls were white plaster accented with gold; the floor gold-brown and scarlet tile. There was a bed and two couches, a writing desk of light wood with pens, brushes, and paper. A self-portrait by Psyche hung above the bed—a few feathery touches only, a swirling copper line for the hair, the darker suggestion of a cheekbone, brows but no eyes, a mouth but no chin. Hardly anything at all, yet somehow there was the intimation of a complete personality. Caught on canvas, a soul in flight.

Gabriel called for music and made love to Clancy. Melody plucked at his nerves. Cyrus whispered in his inner ear, fine appreciations of skin texture, of curve of limb and breast and abdomen. Spring Plum suggested ways in which Clancy might best be pleasured. The lingering aftertaste of Psyche sang like wine in his consciousness.

Once only saints or madmen could speak to the daimones, could hear whispering the personalities that dwelt within their own minds. The condition could be caused by an imbalance in brain chemistry, a history of abuse in early childhood so severe that the personality fragmented, a deliberately induced ordeal, a spiritual agony like Kavandi or the sun dance or sitting for years on a pillar like St. Simeon. The voices were mislabeled: *angels, past lives, dead spirits, demons.*

All self. Personalities with their own thoughts, their own capabilities, their own glories, wrapped in the primary personality like swaddled children, ready to come out and play in the fields of the mind . . . The ancients had consistently underestimated the glories of their own psyches, preferred to consider these aspects of their own psyches as manifestations of invisible forces, forces divine or demonic.

Daimones. The old Sokratic name resurfaced: the others were all too judgmental, too freighted with obsolete superstition. *Daimones,* meaning Divinities—the godlets of the liberated mind. The word now freed from the centuries of ignorance and superstition, freed like all the little souls the word represented.

How many, Gabriel wondered, made love on Psyche's bed? How many, his own daimones and Clancy's, touched the experience with their own enriched perception?

More than he wanted to count right now, anyway.

The voices sang in his mind, floating like grains of pollen in the sky.

Chapter 2

PABST: Stimulus and response, response and stimulus
Get them right, there's little fuss
They'll do most anything if you pull their
strings
Their response to stimulus.

Aristoi floated through the reception to the sound of a reed flute.

Standing near the buffet table Gabriel paid his respects to Pan Wengong, primary architect for the resurrected Earth². The Eldest Brother was a junior, but sole surviving, member of the first bold generation of Aristoi who had, in the turbulent and dangerous centuries after the Earth¹ disaster, coalesced around Captain Yuan and, with their fearless and absolute command of technology, reordered humanity's future.

Pan Wengong's appearance belied his millennia. He was a round-faced, round-bodied, cheerful man, secure in his place among the Aristoi and in history, and quite pleased with having escaped the law of averages for so long. His domaine included Earth² and the inhabited stars around it, and in the centuries since the great reconstruction he'd been taking it easy; his Therápontes did most of the work while the Eldest Brother relaxed in one or another of the pleasure domes he'd built on or about Earth. He was one of the few Aristoi who was actually, physically present in Persepolis, but he was linked with all the others in the oneirochronon and enjoyed the best of both worlds—the company of his peers, and the fact he could eat and drink.

Pan had been speaking to Saigo, a dour, saturnine man who usually avoided these receptions. Saigo was a specialist in evolution, both human and stellar, and had broadcast his black-browed skiagénos a greater distance than anyone here— he was well out of inhabited space, in a part of distant space called the Gaal Sphere, pursuing his lonely researches.

Saigo saw Gabriel with his melancholy eyes, offered a Posture of Formal Regard, and took his leave. Gabriel and Pan exchanged embraces and the latest jokes. Pan offered Gabriel a ghost drink, and though Gabriel knew the experience would be well crafted, he declined. He avoided eating and drinking while in the oneirochronon—he got only hunger pangs without satisfying his cravings.

Others arrived to pay their respects to Pan. Gabriel spoke briefly to Maryandroid, then found himself approached by Cressida.

"Aristos kaí Athánatos," she began, using the formal title, "forgive me for this interruption."

"Forgiven," said Gabriel, a bit surprised.

Cressida was an older Ariste; she had passed her exams over three hundred years ago and had restricted the size of her domaine so as to devote herself more exclusively to research. She was honored, distant, and briskly eccentric, and in their few meetings had treated Gabriel with courtesy but without great patience.

She gazed from her black-skinned face with intent bird-like eyes. "Therápōn Protarchōn Stephen Rubens y Sedillo, who is in my service, will be visiting Labdakos within a few days to tour the Illyrian Workshop," she said. "I am thinking of setting up a similar academy here on Painter, and I hope you will do me the favor of giving instructions to the Workshop staff to allow him access."

"Really?" Cressida had never shown much interest in crafts. "I will be happy to provide any assistance, of course."

She had not adorned herself for this reception, but dressed in the modest sky-blue uniform worn by her household—the uniform might have been a romantic touch, Gabriel thought, but the design was too relentlessly practical, with many pockets and no ornamentation or badges of rank. Her hair was salt-and-pepper, cut short in a businesslike way.

"I would consider it a favor," she continued, "if you will also give Therápōn Rubens a private appointment at a time convenient to you so that he can present my personal greetings and thanks." She inclined her head, lowered her eyes, the First Posture of Esteem. "At your service, Aristos."

"At your service," Gabriel murmured. Cressida passed on.

What the hell was that about? Gabriel inquired.

Neutral but commanding posture, said Augenblick. **Neutral expression. No involuntary muscle movement, no alteration in pupil dilation. Formally courteous expression.**

That's not much.

My apologies, Aristos. Skiagenoi are difficult to read at the best of times, and perhaps she was taking good care not to be read. Most Aristoi do.

Reno, Gabriel commanded, **report on the whereabouts of Stephen Rubens y Sedillo, class Therápōn, rank Protarchōn, employed by Cressida Ariste. < Priority 2 >**

At your service, Aristos. < Priority 2 > < search program initiated > Done. Therápōn Rubens is aboard the yacht *Lorenz*, currently assuming an orbit about Illyricum. He hailed traffic control four hours ago. The *Lorenz* is owned by Ariste Cressida. Rubens has sent a message to your mailbox requesting a personal audience.

The timing on this is very exact, said the Welcome Rain. **There is more here than we see.**

Gabriel thought for a moment. **Reno,** he said, **how many times has Cressida spoken to me?**

Five, Aristos. On four occasions she merely offered polite greetings, and on the other she criticized your behavior at Coetzee's reception following your Graduation—

I remember very well, thank you.

At your service, Aristos.

He returned his attention to the reception.

Something was afoot. He knew not what it was.

He suspected, however, he would enjoy himself while working out the answer.

Music, angel voices and devil bassoons, eddied in Psyche's perfect acoustic chamber. A piece Gabriel had composed long ago, Sandor Korondi's "Love-Wind" set to music.

After a few hours in the Autumn Pavilion with Clancy, Gabriel decided to call her Blushing Rose. She accepted the new name with what seemed a mixture of pleasure and intelligent skepticism.

She called him Disturber.

Clancy lay facedown on the bed in exactly the naive position in which it pleased Louis XV to have his mistresses painted. Gabriel, sitting beside her, found himself completely charmed by the rosy sight of her soles. She was all warm autumn colors, he thought, like this pavilion, like his thoughts, a contrast to the Black-Eyed Ghost, all pallor and midnight. He let his fingertips graze on the rounded knobs of Clancy's spine as the andante movement sang slowly in his heart.

The Carnation Suite, he remembered, was empty.

"I promised you breakfast," he said. "Shall I tell my reno to order? Kem-Kem, my chef, is an improvisatory genius—he'll cook anything you'd like to order."

Clancy propped her chin on one hand and frowned. "Would you mind having a machine deliver the food?"

"No. Why?"

"Because if Rabjoms is going to find out about this, I'd rather it be from me and not a member of the kitchen staff."

"Ah." He took her hand. "Will that be a problem for you?

She looked at him over her shoulder. "The problem is . . . tactical. *How* I should tell him, not . . ."

"If I can be of any assistance?"

"No. It's my little predicament, I suppose." She gave a tight little smile. "He's an understanding man."

GABRIEL: Reno. < Priority 2 > Query: Rabjoms.

RENO: < Priority 2 > *Rabjoms.* Full name: Thundup Rabjoms Sambhota. Informal consort to Therápōn Clancy. Age: Thirty-one. Class: Demos. Occupation: Artisan < Second Class >, Lowland Machine Works, Labdakos, Illyricum. Born: Gomo Selung, Kampa Province, Phongdo—

GABRIEL: Thank you. Fini.

RENO: At your service.

He looked down at the taut ribbon of knotted muscle that had, in the last few seconds, formed between her shoulder blades, and began to massage it away. The andante sobbed on. Clancy sighed.

"You've been together how long?"

"Six years. Since I came here." She sighed. "He's a good man."

A good man, he thought. Artisan (Second Class), and of the Demos, not even one of the Therápontes. Rabjoms was certainly not the choice of a rising Therápōn eager for a position of power.

"Demos," Gabriel said.

"I'm not ambitious that way." She shrugged. "I'm not ambitious at all. I haven't gone for my exams in nine years, and I don't have any plans to. I like it where I am. Being a doctor. Birth, death, trauma, life, well-being . . . everything I really care about, I'm involved with now."

"You left me off the list."

She smiled, looked over her shoulder again. "*Should* I care for you, Aristos?"

"I love you." Psyche soared through his mind at the words.

"And I you, Aristos." Neatly.

He leaned back and considered her. She was not his usual type. Her body was natural—soft, rounded, without the planed, sculpted, perfected look, genetically or surgically augmented, that normally gratified his taste. The attraction was unusual; Gabriel couldn't predict its outcome, or how long it would last. Perhaps (a sliver of doubt entering) it was merely a shared enthusiasm for Marcus's pregnancy. He thought of calling up Augenblick and the Welcome Rain, but decided he didn't want this *handled*. Not their way.

> "I never was attached to that great sect,
> Whose doctrine is that each one should select
> Out of the crowd a mistress or a friend,
> And all the rest, though fair and wise, commend
> To cold oblivion."

She smiled. "And you're easily bored."

"That as well." Might as well concede that one.

She rolled over and regarded him with wide peridot eyes. "Will you make me your *maîtresse en titre?*"

"Do you want that? I'm surprised."

"May I have it?"

"If that's what you desire."

She shook her head, then laughed. "I don't, as it happens. But I needed to know if you'd give it to me."

Surprise rolled through him. "Fayre eyes," he said, "the myrrour of my mazed hart, what woundrous vertue is contaynd in you . . ."

"I had everything planned. I didn't think"—she considered her words—"this lightning would strike. Not this late." Grinning wryly. "Not this lightning."

"It has struck." He kissed her. "Shall it strike again?"

She fluttered against his lips. "Yes, Aristos. Of course."

Propelled by violas and stinging electric guitar, presto followed andante, and so to finale.

Gabriel continued his rounds about the reception, greeted Pristine Way and Prince Stanislaus. He succeeded in avoiding Virtue's Icon. The reed flute wove its way through the throng, accented every conversation.

He heard his name spoken, turned, and saw Zhenling. Pleasure tingled through his fingertips.

"Hail to the conqueror of Mount Mallory," he said.

Zhenling was a slim woman, tall and taut-muscled, with Tatar cheekbones and tilted dark eyes. Her frame was strong with catlike, augmented muscle, her form perfectly sculpted. She wore cherry-red breeches, boots, sky-blue jacket with gold brocade, and a hussar jacket of a darker blue, trimmed with ermine and more brocade and worn over her shoulders. A fur hat was tipped over one ear and was decorated with a spray of silver and pearls. Her dark hair was braided with gemstones and fell over one shoulder, giving her silhouette a pleasant asymmetry.

She had been among the Aristoi only a short while, having been promoted twelve

GABRIEL: Reno, statistics on Gregory Bonham, if you please.

RENO: Bonham, formal consort of Zhenling Ariste for the last thirteen years. Failed examinations in this last round, placing thirty-first among those who failed to pass. This is his second failure. He resides in the residential annex of Violet Jade Nanotechnology Laboratories in low orbit around Tienjin . . .

GABRIEL: And Zhenling currently resides at . . .?

RENO: Primary residence is at Jade Garden, Ring Island, Tienjin.

SPRING PLUM: < appreciation of contrast between gems and shining hair >

CYRUS:

"All that sternness amid charm,

All that sweetness amid strength."

SPRING PLUM: < amuse-

years ago. She was, astrographically speaking, Gabriel's neighbor, as her domain was expanding from an area near Gabriel's.

"Thank you," she said. "I've got my next ascent mapped—Mount Trasker this time."

ment >

AUGENBLICK: We are interested?

WELCOME RAIN: We are interested.

AUGENBLICK: It's difficult to read skiagenoi. This will take a while.

GABRIEL: Keep me informed.

Her name, translated literally into Demotic, meant "True Sound." Figuratively, however, it meant "True Jade," from the satisfying sound quality jade makes when it's given a good rap.

"You're looking dashing," Gabriel said.

"And you're looking well satisfied."

"Am I? I can't think why."

"Impending fatherhood, perhaps?"

Gabriel permitted himself a look of surprise. "I wasn't aware that anyone knew."

"It wasn't hard to work out. Your schedule of the last week implied a number of things, that among them."

"Should I be flattered that you bothered to study my schedule of the last week?"

"Your schedule for the last year. And various other items concerning you."

Gabriel lifted his shadow-eyebrows. "May one ask why?"

"One may."

Dorothy, mantalike, floated overhead, and Gabriel paused (reno searching files for something apt). The reed flute filled the gap. After Dorothy passed out of immediate eavesdropping range, he spoke. "Questioning," he said, "is not the mode of conversation among gentlefolk."

"I believe Johnson also said that classical quotation is the *parole* of literary men."

"Am I literary? I never thought myself so."

"All that is literature," < De Quincey, said Gabriel's

reno, **after Wordsworth >**, "seeks to communicate power; all that is not literature, to communicate knowledge."

"Our renos seem to have a very good eighteenth-century index," said Gabriel. "Take my arm; let's talk."

"As you like. Though we'll look like a couple of footmen at the Congress of Vienna."

"Not footmen. Equerries at least. Or maybe archdukes. I believe there were plenty to spare."

Her arm, nonexistent though it was, was quite warm: Augenblick and the Welcome Rain both commented hopefully.

"I am told," Gabriel said, "that you and Astoreth are planning to upset our happy galactic order."

"Astoreth intends no such thing."

"That begs a question, but I'm afraid I just forswore that mode of discourse."

"Astoreth wants to create a stir so that she can be at the center of attention. And I—?" She looked at him, and Gabriel found himself admiring the program that had created the liquid depths of her eyes. "I'm willing to put some notions forward," she said. "I'm not certain what it would mean yet."

"You've followed her program otherwise. Rekindling a spirit of adventure through your personal exploits and so on."

"I *like* climbing mountains and stunting around in submarines. It doesn't have to be someone's *program*."

"But the problem, as you see it, requires drastic measures."

"It requires, first of all, an acknowledgment that there's a problem."

"If you gathered data . . ."

"How much data do we need?" She was impatient. "Out of the thousands of Therápontes who took the exams this time, how many passed? Nine. How many Aristoi died or announced impending retirement in the time between this batch of exams and the last? Six."

"This has been discussed, you know. For decades."

"Since most of us restrict population in our own dominions, the only way many of the Demos can have the children they want is to pioneer in new domaines. And since there will be a net increase of only three domaines this time, in essence humanity expands by only three Aristoi."

"Of course the Demos can also have children by moving to underpopulated domaines."

"There's a reason those domaines are underpopulated, you know."

"I know perfectly well. I merely felt I should make mention of all the alternatives available."

"Okay. So the alternative is to queue up for a new planet, moon, or habitat, which can take decades if not centuries, or to be subjected to intrusive social programming in the justly underpopulated domaines."

"I wonder where Pan Aristos got this flute music. It's extraordinary." (Setting his reno on an extended search, < priority 3 >, for a score.)

Zhenling permitted herself an annoyed look. Gabriel inclined toward her. "I beg your pardon. One train of thought intruded on another. I *was* listening."

"To me or the music?"

"I can follow both."

"I was hoping to recruit you."

"Hence your inquiry into my last year's schedule." He sighed. "I'm disappointed. I was hoping your interest was more personal."

Gabriel (and Augenblick) noted that Zhenling didn't seem (or didn't allow herself to seem) as annoyed by this remark as she might have been.

"Isn't your life a little busy without another complication?" she asked. "A child on the way, a new friend moving into the"—her reno floated data along the tachline—"Carnation Suite?"

The Welcome Rain gleefully rubbed metaphysical hands together and whispered in Gabriel's antennae.

"We're Aristoi," Gabriel said. "We're capable of handling any number of complications with grace, with joy, with—"

"Without me," said Zhenling. "I have a consort, as you know."

"Who is not your equal."

"He'll pass the exams." Stubbornly. "He came very close this last time."

"It's more Aristoi that your group wants." Gabriel stroked his chin skiagenically. "Could that be a coincidence, I wonder?"

"You seem to want more Aristoi in your life as well."

"Only one."

"What a shame." She paused for a pensive moment, then carefully shrugged. "Think of it as a rare experience. How often do you experience genuine frustration in your life? Cherish it while it lasts."

"While it lasts." He attempted to lift her hand and kiss it. She turned her skiagénos insubstantial and his hand passed through hers. He straightened and looked at her, and she burst into laughter.

"You should see your face!" she said. "This *is* rare for you, isn't it?"

Gabriel calmed both himself and the Welcome Rain, who was hissing like a kettle.

"Perhaps we'll kiss later," Zhenling said, which soothed Welcome Rain rather more than Gabriel did. "But right now, I'd like to read your brain chemistry."

"My what?"

"Levels of vasopressin," numbering on her fingers, "dopamine, serotonin, lecithin, thiamine, norepinephrine, phosphatidylcholine, endorphins . . . lots of things. Dozens. Your reno has the capability to analyze your chemistry that way?"

"Of course," Gabriel said, "but I'm not certain I'm willing to proceed to that level of intimacy without at least kissing first."

Her look was serious. "I'm going to propose tomorrow

to inaugurate a study concerning what makes Aristoi into Aristoi."

"It's been tried. The category was found to be unquantifiable." He gestured with an arm. Pristine Way, looking at the moment as if she were cut from rose-tinted transparent crystal, nodded back. "Look at all these people," Gabriel said. "Each passed exams, each is licensed for certain dangerous technologies, and each controls a domaine—but each is individual, and over the years the domaine conforms to her image . . . Citizens with an interest in music or architecture migrate to my domaine, those interested in political theory show up in the Icon's territory or Coetzee's, those who yearn for the consolations of philosophy turn up in Sebastian's, and I imagine you get your share of mountain climbers. You know how eccentric some of us are. What d'you think we have in common?"

"I don't think the previous studies were done the right way. Or that they asked the right questions."

"You're an Ariste, of course. You can study what you like."

She tilted her head. Light danced in her eyes. "Which brings me to my next point. I really *would* like to get a look at your brain chemistry. In the normal course of things we're surrounded by people who defer to us, who make things easy, who accept our judgments without question. Some of us are even worshiped."

"Oh, please." Gabriel held up protesting hands. "I just needed to give my mother something to do after she retired."

"Unlike most of us here, I quite believe you. But still, some of us are worshiped. What does that do inside our heads? We're natural leaders—that's one thing we've got in common—and we're still all primates, even the most modified of us. We're more absolute than the leader of any baboon troop ever was. More absolute than Louis the Fourteenth."

"I wish you would come up with more cultivated examples. I don't know which of the two I'd prefer as a houseguest—probably the baboon."

"*Moi aussi, monseigneur. Le roi, c'est l'etat et un cochon.* But then, his brain chemistry must have been as abnormal as ours."

"I *am* going to demand a kiss if you're going to discuss my brain chemistry and make odious comparisons."

She stepped up to him and kissed him quite decisively on the mouth. Her breath had a spicy tint. The Welcome Rain went into ecstacies. The rest of Gabriel wasn't much less affected.

Zhenling stepped back, managing to look both teasing and smug. "What I would like to do," she said, "is compare your brain chemistry now with what it is at the end of Graduation, and with what it will be about six months from now. Because what's happening here is that you're interacting with your peers, not what, for lack of a better term, we'll call your inferiors. It's a greater strain, we're not as deferent as the people you're around normally . . . It's going to do things to your head."

"Where do you plan to go with this?"

"With your head?" She narrowed her tilted eyes. "Very far indeed . . ." Welcome Rain commenced a dance of triumph. "But later, I think." She stepped back, gave him a Posture of Respect subverted by a careless wave. "There are other people I need to speak to. I'm sure we'll be able to see each other at one of the receptions."

"I need to know what you want in the way of brain analysis."

"I'll send you a memo of what I'm interested in."

Gabriel watched her leave and listened to the voices in his head. **Her metalinguistics were consistently flirtatious.** Augenblick's contribution. **Rather deliberately so.**

We're in business, boss, said the Welcome Rain.

Gabriel continued to drift among the throng. He observed that Dorothy St.-John had pasted her cat's eyes to the forehead of Han Fu, and wondered whether Han knew it. Asterion, whose body had been altered for a subaquatic existence, swam elegantly overhead, webbed hands and turned-out dolphin feet moving gracefully through invisible waters.

The music now playing, Gabriel's reno finally reported, **is untitled and unpublished, but is by Tunku Iskander. It is unavailable in the Hyperlogos but a recording exists in the archives of Rival Island, where Tunku played it last week for Aristos MacReady.**

Not in the library, but in obscure records half of human space away—no wonder the search had taken so long, almost four minutes. Tunku Iskander, Gabriel knew, would be installed as an Aristos tomorrow, and had apprenticed under MacReady and Dorothy. Gabriel hadn't ever met him, or heard his music. He told his reno to call up as many recordings as were available and store them for later.

The reception drifted onward to its conclusion.

Gabriel, hair tied back with golden ribbon, performed wushu alone on the sward behind the Red Lacquer Gallery. Cool morning air brushed over his limbs. His mind was in the oneirochronon, and Spring Plum guided the two-sword form, controlling his body with grace and imagination. The heavy broadswords sliced air, one-two, and the red flags tied to the hilts made supersonic cracking sounds as they wove dragon-back images through the air. Gabriel could feel, dim in his conscious mind, the strain on muscles, the beat of pulse and harshness of breath in the throat, the whirls and leaps and stances of wushu, martial arts abstracted to dance, an aesthetic distillation attuned to Spring Plum's psyche. He could see, if he wanted to, the spears of green grass, the long expanse of the Red Lacquer Gallery, grey upthrust mountain peaks beyond the golden web of Labdakos, all whirling in the focused dance . . . but his mind stayed firmly in the oneirochronon, and concentrated on the Involved Ideography of Captain Yuan.

Yuan's Ideography was based on the notion that writing had the greater impact the more senses it evoked. Old-style European script was fine for communicating data efficiently, but it had to work hard to achieve the kind of psychic resonance that Yuan desired—not simply to communicate, but to *involve*.

Old Asian scripts were better, insofar as the ideograms not only communicated words but drew (admittedly rather abstract) pictures. They involved more levels of the mind in the translation, and the impact—at least for Yuan's purposes—was greater.

Yuan's Intermediate Ideography, in which Psyche had presented her conception-poem for Marcus, was based on age-old Chinese characters but adapted for modern grammar, vocabulary, and expression.

The Intermediate characters were only a stage on the way to the Involved Ideography. These intricate hieroglyphs, based on the First Aristos's own ideas about the wiring of the human mind and its relationship to information, were another step toward complexity and many levels higher in symbolism. Looking like a peculiarly convoluted incorporation of baroque Mayan glyphs and circuit diagrams, the Involved Ideography's radicals, modalities, and submodalities were designed to involve as much of the reasoning cortex as possible. They required intense mental concentration to use or read, but were unexcelled in packing complex information into small packages. The system was incomplete, as Yuan hadn't finished his work when he set on his long, presumably fatal quest toward galactic center, but the ideography continued to evolve more or less randomly at the hands of thousands of individual scholars and information theorists.

Gabriel was using the Involved Ideography to design an oneirochronic seal for Clancy, one she could use to get into the secure areas of the Residence. He would be having breakfast with her shortly, in Spring Plum's room of the Autumn Pavilion, and wanted it ready.

He used a glyph for *rose*, a radical for *redden*, modalities for *medicine* and *music* and *pleasure* and *caring* . . . He wanted to evoke her precisely, create a poem in glyph form.

He became aware that Spring Plum had finished the wushu form, that his body was poised in salutation position, swords heavy in his arms. Gabriel had his reno analyze his bodily state. He concluded he'd exercised enough, and he summoned Kouros to perform cool-down exercises. The Kouros daimōn was a child, carefree and happy, innocent of consequence—skipping about the sward and gardens during the cool-down period was something Kouros would find interesting.

He buried himself in the creating of the hieroglyph.

By the time he finished the cool-down period he thought he had finished the seal. He bathed and dressed and had breakfast delivered to Spring Plum's room, where there was a graceful rosewood dining table, and in a matching cabinet a porcelain service rimmed with silver and painted with white plum blossoms. Spring Plum possessed an intent fascination with biological detail: the dark silk wall hangings were covered with exactingly rendered flora, petals, stigmata, anthers, and beaded, glowing droplets of dew.

Clancy arrived at the door. Gabriel embraced her and kissed her hello, then led her to the buffet. There was enough food to feed a dozen guests. Clancy took coffee, a scone, and jam, and sat curled in a chair covered in stitched dogwood blossoms. Gabriel took a plate of fruit and sat by her side.

She cocked an ear at the music. *"Tien Jiang Chun."*

"Yes."

"I played it years ago on Darkbloom. In a recital, at university. Accompanying a friend, who sang Li Jingchao's words."

Gabriel's reno sifted gently through Clancy's biography. "You play piano, flute, persephone."

"The first poorly, due to a lack of time for practice. The second with a bit too much restraint. The third too cleverly, because modern instruments encourage that."

"Do you compose?"

"No."

"You should. You're bound to find a daimōn that will help you."

"I would be mediocre." She sipped coffee. "I'm an outstanding physician and surgeon, however, and a damn good geneticist." There was defensiveness in her tone.

"I know," gently. He took her hand and kissed it.

"Marcus," she said.

"Yes?"

"Is it ended between you?"

" 'How am I fallen from myself, for a long time now I have not seen the Prince of Chang in my dreams.' " He smiled. "I'm building him a house."

"A house? An *estate*, you mean."

"An estate, then. And why not? With a stunning view, and a large nursery, and room for all the playthings and gadgets he likes to build."

"Don't build me such a place, when the time comes."

He sensed the tension in her forearm. He kissed her hand again. "Not if you don't want one, Blushing Rose. But architecture is one of my skills—I hate not to indulge it."

She smiled. "Build me a research clinic if you like. On an asteroid, where I can work with nano."

Gabriel was pleased to discover this hidden thread of ambition.

"Tell me where you want it, and what you want in it, and it's yours. Now. It doesn't have to be a parting gift."

Clancy blinked at him. "Sometimes I forget that you can do that. Wave your hand, and it's done. As easily as if you were in the oneirochronon."

"It takes a little more effort than that."

"But still. It doesn't cost you anything. Does it?"

"Why should it?" He smiled, took a knife, began to peel a hothouse peach. "I like pleasing people. I have the power to do it. Why shouldn't I indulge myself in harmless benevolence?"

She thought about it, then shrugged. "Whyever not?" Another chord chimed briefly. Clancy tilted her head. "I've told Rabjoms."

"I hope it went well."

"I think he's a bit . . . overwhelmed." She gave a tight

little smile. "So am I, really. Rabjoms doesn't want to resist—part of it's the conditioning, okay, but—" There was an uncertain flutter in her eyes. "Well, I don't want to resist either."

Gabriel left his chair, sat cross-legged before her, took her feet into his lap. "I'm pleased, Blushing Rose."

Her look turned uncertain. "Should I move into the Residence? Do you want me to?"

"I would be pleased to have you near me. The Carnation Suite is open, and its decor would suit your coloring very well."

"I'll move, then."

"I've already taken the liberty of designing you an oneirochronic seal that will grant you access to the secure areas and the private passages and galleries in the Residence. I've put it in your message box, and instructed the Residence to open its sealed areas to you."

There was a glimmer of interest in her eyes. "There are secret passages in the Residence?"

"Not secret. Just private. If you want to go somewhere and not have to meet people." He smiled at her. "I find it useful."

She gazed at her plate for a moment, then down at him. "Disturber? Can you tell me why I feel sad?"

Gabriel could not. "How can I make you happy?" he said.

She gave a thin smile. "I should return to work."

"If that's what you wish. But I can still declare that planetary holiday."

Her smile broadened. "That won't be necessary."

"Perhaps," he said, "some other time."

Chapter 3

LULU: You bring them in, you bring them in
You pierce their skin, you pierce their skin
They moan and sigh as you suck them dry
And that is how you win.

LOUISE: (refrain) *Bring me a drink!*

Gabriel was weary after the reception. It was early morning in Persepolis, but early evening here: looking down from *Pyrrho* he could see lights winking across the continent below. As he stepped from the *Pyrrho* into his shuttlecraft he sat in the copilot's seat and gestured to his pilot, White Bear.

"Take the gravity drive," he said. "Try not to destroy the planet."

"I'll do my best, Aristos," White Bear laughed. He was a man who justified his nickname—burly, bearded, pale-skinned, pale blond hair—and Gabriel could see he was pleased. Gabriel enjoyed doing his own piloting and White Bear almost never got to perform the task he was hired for.

Gabriel closed his eyes as White Bear's fingers began to

play over the controls for the specially licensed gravity/inertial generator. White Bear spoke to traffic control through his reno, thus sparing Gabriel half of a dull conversation. The shuttle, in complete silence, detached itself from the *Pyrrho* and began to drop toward the atmosphere.

Speculations on Cressida's conspiracy, whatever it was, floated through Gabriel's head. He didn't want to think about it and instead told his reno to let him look through his mailbox.

Floating up first came a high-priority message from his mother. He made note of it and did not reply.

There was Rubens's request for an audience. Gabriel scheduled it for early the next morning, then sent a note about it to Quiller, his lean, beak-nosed secretary.

Other messages passed before his view. Administrators requested clarifications, guidance, or sought to pass responsibility upward. Some fawned, some flattered, some expressed bewilderment. He preferred the last to the first two. But the fawning and flattery was, he'd discovered, part of the job—the Demos never seemed to realize that their flattery meant little to an Aristos. The work itself was all routine: he dealt with it quickly and impressed on his people, yet again, that he didn't want to deal with trivialities.

Next was a request, from an orchestra director on Thanatogenes in Ariste Dorothy's domaine, to perform some of Gabriel's *Music for the Eye*. Gabriel absorbed the request and wondered. *Music for the Eye* had been intended as closet music for score readers—never intended to be performed, just appreciated as a piece of written amusement, full of the sort of theoretical jokes and ideational cleverness that could only be appreciated by those trained to read a score. It was an intellectual exercise, an abstraction of music that bore the same resemblance to "real" music that a chess problem bore to real chess.

The orchestra director, it seemed, thought otherwise—he made a plausible-sounding case to the effect that actually playing the music would be instructive, and he wanted to provide a way of viewing the score through the oneirochronon simultaneous with the playing of the music.

What the hell. Let it be done, whatever good it would do. Gabriel gave his permission, with the proviso that it be made clear to the audience that the music had not been intended to be presented this way.

The craft swayed as the atmosphere tugged at it. Butterflies danced in Gabriel's belly.

He realized he was putting off calling his mother. He might as well get it over with.

Therápōn ex-Hextarchōn Vashti was one of Gabriel's primary parents—legally speaking, he had six, but shared genes with only the two primaries. She had stabilized her age in her early twenties, several years younger than that of her son. At his decantation Gabriel had supposedly looked like Vashti as a young girl, but both had altered their appearance since childhood and any resemblance had long been obscured.

Vashti (skiagénos-image blossoming in Gabriel's mind) possessed sharp, searching eyes, fine clear skin fashionably bronzed by melanin supplements, lofty winged brows intended to create an air of mystery, and white-blond hair braided and piled high atop her crown. Her long hairpins and jeweled clasps bore religious symbols—mandalas, crescents, swastikas, Gabriel's own Eye-of-Thoth. Since her retirement a dozen years ago she had devoted herself to managing Gabriel's official cult.

"Good evening," Gabriel said. "Or should I say, Hail, Vashti Geneteira? I hope this is not a bad time."

"It's never a bad time for the Geneteira to be visited by the Kouros Athánatos, her divine offspring."

Meaning, Gabriel assumed, she was in public. Her body, wherever it was, would be standing in rapt attention to emanations of the divine, in the company (he presumed) of awed worshippers.

He'd bet anything she'd said that last aloud, just so everyone would know she was receiving a visitation.

As if billions didn't communicate through the oneiro-chronon every passing second.

Gabriel shrugged. "Anything I can do to enhance the mystique."

The skiagénos of Vashti's face raised its lofty eyebrows. "Come now. It's my *job* to take this seriously."

"It isn't mine."

"I'm afraid you have little choice, Kouros. Not any-more." She allowed her image to give a cold little oneiro-chronic smile. "Attendance is up, by the way."

Gabriel knew that he had let himself in for a certain amount of ridicule when he decided to allow himself to be worshiped. In the end he decided that the precedent of actu-ally forbidding a religion was more distasteful than being plagued by the devout, and he allowed the original organizer, a Demotic woman named Diamond, to organize his faith, all the while trying to make it clear to everyone that it was all her idea.

The Demos, Gabriel conceded, desired gods to worship. And, he had to admit, he made a more pleasant god than many he could name.

To make certain that his worshippers didn't make him more ridiculous than absolutely necessary, Gabriel had strictly supervised the unimaginatively named Church of the New Thoth. He made certain that any clergy had genuine credentials as therapists and counselors, and that any spare cash was to be donated to worthwhile efforts, chiefly schools of architecture, music, and design.

Though Diamond had not been pleased by these condi-tions—Gabriel guessed she had other plans entirely, in which she would herself be worshiped as Gabriel's prophet—the result had been a magnificent series of temples and cathedrals in which some very good sacred music was played. Gabriel hoped that the music would be remembered long after his cult had faded.

"Attendance is up?" Gabriel said. "Perhaps it's the choir. I think the new director has improved it."

Vashti slowly shook her head. "I'm afraid you're a god, dear one. Better get used to it. You make things happen. You can intervene to make ordinary lives better."

"How often do I do it? I grant—what?—a few petitions a month?"

"Your mystic interventions are rather more frequent, dear. I hear of miracles every week."

Gabriel managed to avoid wincing. "I hope my fellow Aristoi don't hear it."

"They will if they have an interest. Nothing we do is secret."

"Thanks to the restrictions I put on the church."

The skiagénos nodded graciously. "Thanks to you. The divine will of our Kouros is all-important to us."

She'd probably said that last aloud as well, so her followers would hear. She was, he had to admit, very good at this.

Much better than Diamond had been. Vashti's retirement from her administrative duties in Pan Wengong's domaine—despite her ferocious ambition, or perhaps because of it, she'd never risen above Hextarchōn—had provided an opportunity for Gabriel to set the Mother of Godhead over the church's founder in the hierarchy. Diamond had assumed that Vashti would take only a ceremonial role, but Gabriel knew his mother better than that. Within weeks Diamond, thoroughly bested, set off on missionary work and never returned.

Vashti had never, before or since, had any doubts whether or not she wanted to be worshiped.

"I believe you called me?" Gabriel asked. "Was there any particular message?"

"Ah. I forgot. The Rites of Inanna are next week. Will you be attending in person?"

"I don't believe so. Intoxication and random copulation—"

"—compose a necessary and life-enhancing celebration of the fertility principle." She smiled at him. "That's why I invented the rite."

Gabriel sighed. "Have a nice time, Mom."

"Perhaps the rites are more suitable for the Geneteira, after all. Though you *did* just say you'd do anything to enhance the mystique."

"I was not serious. As you know."

"Could you send a daimōn?"

"I will probably be dealing with Graduation."

"There's sure to be at least one interested in attending. We've got a robot puppet body he could inhabit—the best, quite lifelike."

"A nonfertile one, I hope?"

"Whatever you wish, omniscient one."

Any children born as a result of the orgies were considered, for religious if not legal purposes, Gabriel's own offspring. Women organized their fertility around the celebrations, and some lived ever in hope that Gabriel would attend in person and bless them with his divine essence.

He had attended once—Vashti had talked him into it—and since felt disinclined to return. He preferred sex more spontaneous, and his partners either less intimidated, less worshipful, or less drunk.

"Consult your daimones, then. There will also be the usual requiem service conducted at the Pater's tomb in two days."

"I won't be there." Firmly.

Vashti's brows narrowed. "The service is really quite lovely. I don't understand—"

"My private mourning for my father will not become a public spectacle," Gabriel said, "no matter how tasteful."

Vashti sighed. "Very well. Whatever you desire, Athánatos Kouros."

"Do you really think you should play it up as much as you do? You'd been separated for almost sixty years when he died."

"We are forever united," serenely smiling, "by the glory and divinity of our offspring."

Gabriel gave a hard look at Vashti's skiagénos. The virtual façade was impenetrable. "Sometimes," he said, "I can't tell quite when you're being serious."

The smile widened minutely. "And how is pretty Marcus these days?"

"Pregnant."

"Congratulations. I'm sure he will be a fine father to your child—"

"*Our* child."

"*Your* little godlet. But couldn't you have waited till the Rites of Inanna?"

"No."

Vashti's visage showed mild disappointment. "You *might* try to make my job easier now and again, you know. Now I'll have to have a revelation to the effect that there will be an increase in the divine family." The skiagénos assumed a hopeful cast. "You'll bring the child for baptism?"

"Not if I have anything to say about it."

"Ah." Vashti smiled. "I'll speak to Marcus about it, then."

"Not in the next few days, if you please. He's still adjusting to his condition."

Vashti assumed a searching look. "He's lasted a while, your Marcus. Longer than most, at any rate."

"He has a kind heart."

An eloquently raised eyebrow dismissed the whole notion of kindheartedness. "It's you who are kindhearted," she said. "Too kindhearted, if you ask me. That palace you're building him . . ."

"Standing Wave's not a *palace*."

"It's a *mansion* on an *estate*."

"It's a house your grandchild will live in."

That stopped her. "Well," grudgingly, "you're the Aristos."

"On the contrary." Gabriel smiled. "I'm the god."

Gabriel ended his conversation with Vashti and opened his eyes. The precise flat grid of the Residence landing field, glowing under spotlights, spread out on the other side of the viewscreen. White Bear had landed, noiselessly and without a jounce, while Gabriel was concentrating on the oneirochronon.

"Thank you," Gabriel told him, a bit surprised, and walked toward the Residence while querying its reno for Clancy's location.

Clancy, Gabriel was told, was at the hospital in Labdakos, keeping watch over an emergency case—a six-year-old child with a brain infection.

Gabriel queried further, then arranged for ground transport. Traffic-control renos shifted other traffic out of the way, Gabriel's car raced past, and he was by Clancy's side in ten minutes.

The hospital had been built as a consciously lighthearted place. The rooms and corridors were airy and, in the daytime, full of sun; there were trees and flowers and patios and galleries; the walls were decorated with artwork from the Red Lacquer Gallery—all copies, but copies exact to the last molecule. The routine work of most hospitals concerned cosmetic, alternative, and implant surgery, all elective, all sending home patients cheered by the decor.

Nothing much could be done to make the intensive-care unit cheerful. In it were three cases of Breakdown, all (of course) terminal, and one small child with acute pseudomonas meningitis.

Gabriel found Clancy pacing alone in the doctors' lounge. She wore moccasins, soft trousers, an informal dark-green surgical jacket with pockets. The lounge was a small quiet room with music—a Schubert sonata—a full-wall video tuned to soothing vistas, plush furniture, a molecular restoration of *The Anatomy of Dr. Tulp*, and the scent of flowers.

None of that helped either.

Gabriel entered and kissed her, and then they embraced for a moment. A phantom memory of Zhenling's phantom lips floated through Gabriel's memory, and he reluctantly banished it.

"It's times like these," she said, "when I wish I'd gone in for cosmetic surgery, where all the money and clients are."

"What's happened?"

"People being stupid," Clancy said. "When are we going to work on a cure for that?"

"I'll see what I can do."

Clancy wasn't amused. "I implanted the boy's reno six days ago," she said. "I told the parents there was a tiny chance of infection, and described the symptoms, and three of them *would* go off on vacation to Merrick Peak to celebrate the kid's Implant Day, and once there, they didn't want to spoil their vacation just because he started coming down this morning with what they insisted was an ear infection and a case of contrary behavior. Then he got aphasia, but they thought he was just being cute. Playing with words. It wasn't until he started convulsing that they realized their vacation was over."

Cold anger snarled through Gabriel's nerves at the appalling tale of neglect. Children were rare: therefore precious, therefore adored.

Clancy seemed to sense his mood. "They didn't know what illness *looks* like. None of the parents—not these three, anyway—has ever been sick with anything, and neither had their first child. Neither had this one till now. That's why," waving arms in frustration, "I'm always so careful to describe any likely symptoms."

"What's being done?" he asked.

"We're trying to detonate the bacteria from the inside with hunter-killer virals. The pseudomonas was resistant to the first lot so I gave him another, but it's too early to tell if they're going to work. Spinal fluid and blood cultures have been done, and I linked to Asteroid Semmelweis and put together a nano package that *should* work—well, it works against this bacteria in the simulation. If the hunter-killers don't start working soon I'll ship the package down, but I don't want to put *more* damn mechanisms in his brain than he's got already."

She gnawed her lip, then glanced up at him. "I'll need

your permission to bring the nano package down, of course."

"You'll have it." He called up Horus, then told him to enter the oneirochronon and arrange for the necessary clearances. He also used his Aristos Override to bring the records of the simulation into his reno's memory, where he could look at them and make certain he wasn't importing a deadly mataglap nano by mistake.

He knew Clancy was good. But she was in a hurry, and he wanted to be positive.

"While I was driving here I checked the data on pseudomonas," Gabriel said, "and discovered that it can enter the patient from water in flowerpots. Do we need to rip all the flowers out of this place?"

"Not once we get something that'll kill it, no. And we don't know if the flowers were the vector of transmission or not. No, it's most likely just some bacterium that's mutated to a new form, and . . . Well, we'll check everything thoroughly. The flowers can stay till we know more." She glanced up.

"Do you know how rare this actually is? I looked it up. One in every eleven billion people. I've never *done* a spinal culture outside of training. The hunter-killers I used were all generic—pseudomonas is so rare these days that no one's developed a more specific treatment." Her lips tightened in a thin line. "That's why I want a nano lab, Disturber," she said. "I want to work with these cases that are so rare that nobody's really devised special treatments."

He took her hand. "Blushing Rose. You have the lab whenever you want it."

"It won't make money, Disturber. One in eleven billion people—that's not a very large client base."

"You should see the submissions I get on Nano Day. All the most baroque proposals in the world, building hotels and planets and space habitats from base matter. Hardly any of it has the worth of what you propose. I'll make the investment and—" He smiled. "If I start running out of money, I'll build another planet and sell it."

"Thank you." She embraced him.

" 'Remember the Green-Skirt Girl,' " he said, after Niu Shiji, " 'and everywhere be tender with the grass.' "

He sensed a shift in her body, her attention moving elsewhere as daimones spoke to her. She stepped back, looked at him. "There's movement for the better, Disturber. It looks as if the hunter-killers are doing their work. Would you like to see our patient?"

"Yes. Of course."

The tiny figure lay on his side and looked sick unto death. He was on a respirator, as the brain stem swelling out of the skull had strangled his breathing centers. His muscles had been paralyzed with drugs in order to forestall the convulsions that wracked him. The scar from the reno implant had not yet been removed after the operation. There was a paper-thin monitor on his jugular vein to keep track of the bacterial population in his blood; there was another 'thin on his spine to monitor spinal fluid.

Clancy reached down and brushed the boy's temple lightly with the backs of her knuckles.

Implant Day was one of the two great childhood rites of passage, the moment when the wider universe of the Hyperlogos opened to a young mind. The second, Sterilization Day, occurred in early adolescence and signified the young adult's intention to take responsibility for his own reproduction.

"There'll be scarring of the brain, of course," she said. "We'll have to do a lot of rebuilding with nano, with shunts going into the jugular and carotid to carry away the excess heat. And physical therapy to relearn what he's probably lost." She shook her head. "Normally a patient could inhabit the oneirochronon while something like this was going on, but this boy hasn't had his reno long enough and won't have the practice. I wonder if he'll even *want* his reno after this. It's the one tool he'll most need to survive, and if he develops an aversion to it . . . well, I'll have to recommend a very good therapist." She looked up. "Does your reno have a name, Disturber? Have you programmed it with a personality?"

"I call mine Reno, and it acts like a machine. I find that refreshing—I've got quite enough personalities in my head as it is."

"Mine is named Caroline. I even gave her an appearance. She looks like my sister, if I had a sister—and we're great friends." She looked down at the boy. "I wonder what he will name his. Death?"

He took her hand again. "If he has any sense at all, he'll name it after his deliverer. Reno Blushing Rose."

Her hand tightened in his. He held it until the boy's vital signs strengthened, until it was obvious that the virus was in retreat.

Clancy called off the alert on the nano package, and Gabriel, as long as he was here, visited the other patients in the ward. Breakdown, known as Dorian Gray's disease, was an ugly death and, barring accident or suicide or something very rare like the pseudomonas infection, about the only one available. Every cell in the body revolted against the reprogramming that had kept it young. Cancers erupted overnight, organs suffered massive failure, muscle and neural networks failed . . . incurable, unstoppable, Breakdown had at least the mercy of being quick, usually over in a matter of days. The only treatment was to make the patient as comfortable as possible while it was going on. Breakdown happened to everyone sooner or later—it seemed the result of a kind of chaotic process in the body, in which everything swung out of equilibrium at once, toward a strange attractor of sudden decay—but most people saw at least their third century before Breakdown caught up with them, and a few lucky individuals like Pan Wengong lived into their second millennium.

It was better, all in all, than the alternative.

Gabriel steeled himself to deal with the patients, none of whom were pleasant to look at. One was in a coma, close to death, but the others were awake and aware: Gabriel felt his heart wring as, recognizing him, they tried to struggle into Attitudes of Respect. Images of his father's death fluttered darkly through his mind as he kissed them in greeting.

He spoke quietly and asked the dying if they were comfortable enough. They did not complain—medication had eased their pain and for the most part their minds were journeying in the oneirochronon, where they could meet with their loved ones without either party having to see what was happening to their bodies. Gabriel wished them peace and made his way out to speak to the boy's family, who had just been told by Clancy that the crisis had passed.

There were seven of them. With the average human life span currently set (according to the Hyperlogos) at 355.8 years, and with human space expanding only with an increase in Aristoi, population growth was necessarily restricted. Part of the reason Gabriel had got so many volunteers to help him pioneer his domaine was his promise that each would be entitled to one child whenever they wished. Now Gabriel still allowed his populations to grow, but at a slower rate, and certain social arrangements had been imported from other domaines. Collective families were common: adults agreed to divide the burdens and expenses of child rearing in exchange for a share of the joys. Some even went so far as to assure that the child herself was a collective, with some genetics contributed by each of the legal parents. As a result of this arrangement the children got all the attention a growing psyche could wish, and often more than was really good for them.

As Gabriel arrived he watched relief battle with astonishment on the parents' several faces.

"I came to see your"—Reno supplied the name—"Krishna. Dr. Clancy tells me he will recover and should be up for the Kite-Flying Festival. We've both been very concerned."

The Welcome Rain kept sincerity radiating from his face. His concern for Krishna was perfectly genuine; but because he was an Aristos this visit had, at least a little, become politics; and the Welcome Rain, completely insincere and ruthlessly uncaring as he was, was the best politician Gabriel knew.

Caught by surprise, the family babbled. The guilty three were still dressed for their vacation. Gabriel turned stern for a moment, told them they shouldn't have ignored the early symptoms, then made some general remarks about the life of a child being precious and said his farewells.

Beginning with concern, Gabriel thought, composing a poem to himself, *it ends with politics. Thus does care become governance.*

Clancy would be staying by Krishna's bed. Gabriel kissed her and took his car to the Residence.

Gabriel slept for three hours, so he must have been tired. Clancy, the house reno informed him, was asleep in the Carnation Suite: she'd left a message that Krishna was doing well. Gabriel dressed, went to his office, and ate breakfast there, off his Louis Quinze desk. He conducted business till dawn silvered the windowpane and Quiller, his gangling, knob-wristed secretary, floated him a message that Rubens had arrived.

Gabriel ended his business and thought for a moment about Rubens's purpose in coming here, the intrigue or conspiracy or whatever it was. Thoughts of assassination tingled briefly through his nerves, were dismissed. Cressida had sent Rubens, and sent him obviously, on her own yacht. She would never leave a trail like that if her intentions were violent.

Still, Gabriel had his visitor discreetly scanned for weapons before he summoned (first) some of his daimones, then (second) Rubens.

Cressida's messenger was an olive-skinned man who had stabilized his age at about thirty. There were gill slits on his neck and nictating membranes that, like a cat's, folded over his eyes at each blink—aquatic modifications, but not as drastic as Asterion's. He wore the practical blue uniform of those in Cressida's service, and his manner and kinesics were polite without being overly refined.

Gabriel kissed him hello.

"Would you walk with me?" Gabriel said. "The morning light is very fine."

Rubens nodded carefully. "As you wish, Aristos."

Gabriel's right hand, hidden from Rubens, formed the mudra that opened the private passage to the gallery that connected the rooms of his apartments. Brocade rustled as he took Rubens's arm. Gabriel led him into the passage and down the gallery. Manfred waited there—if this was some hideous plot, Gabriel wanted a dog with diamond teeth and anesthetic saliva on hand. The terrier followed as Gabriel took Rubens out the glass atrium into the gardens. Rubens's nictating membranes partly deployed to protect his eyes from the bright morning light. Augenblick and the Welcome Rain buzzed in Gabriel's head, and Mataglap hovered suspiciously in the background, just in case violence was, after all, the issue.

"I like to conduct business at a brisk walk," Gabriel said. "My reno brings me communication and data, and the rhythm of the walk helps focus my mind."

"I often do my business underwater. I have an office on a coral outcrop ten fathoms down."

"I'm afraid those with little wind or short legs aren't happy with me, though."

Rubens gave a careful smile. "I imagine my clients find my habits inconvenient as well."

Despite the months he'd spent in confinement on the yacht, Rubens had no difficulty keeping up as Gabriel set a fast pace down the gravel walks of the Residence gardens. The gill slits on his neck bloomed slightly at each exhalation. His long shoes—no doubt his toes were extended and webbed—showed no sign of cramping him even at a brisk pace.

Imperial chrysanthemums blossomed warmly on either hand. Manfred's trotting feet ground on gravel. Above, on the horizon, a score of kites lifted to the mild breeze. People practicing for the Kite-Flying Festival, one of Gabriel's holidays.

Holidays in other domains celebrated the birthdays of prominent men or the anniversary of important occasions. Other than Captain Yuan's birthday, which was more or less required, Gabriel's holidays were devoted to nothing other than pleasure outings, kite-flying, picnicking, family banquets, gift-giving.

"I hope your months on the yacht were not burdensome," Gabriel said.

"It's a spacious vessel, fully equipped for long voyages. And there was the crew to keep me company and my work to keep me busy."

"Your work?"

Rubens smiled wryly. "I discovered a new carbon-carbon-silicon ceramic with a radically high thermal diffusivity. It was"—he shrugged—"one of those lucky accidents; I wasn't *looking* for it. The product would be ideal for use in heat shieldings, but we've already got shields almost as good, so there's no real demand, and unfortunately the product has a low tensile strength."

"Too brittle."

"Precisely. But it's ideal for industrial smelters, as well as pottery and so forth, because the high diffusivity means less firing time."

"So you're here to look at the Workshop."

"With intent to set up something like it, though on a modest scale at first. And I've not given up hope that there's

GABRIEL: Can you make him out at all?

AUGENBLICK: I'm trying to get a reading.

WELCOME RAIN: Keep him talking. Turn the conversation to his own business. We'll get a better idea of his natural manner. And keep holding his arm—we get a superior reading on his body that way.

AUGENBLICK: Walking and the outdoors has relaxed him somewhat. There is less tension in his arm and gait. His voice is less strained. He's not thinking about—whatever-it-is.

GABRIEL: Can you read him at all?

AUGENBLICK: He's a Protarchōn Therápōn. The best Cressida could send us without coming herself. If he doesn't want us to read him, it's going to be difficult without the use of extreme measures. Cressida won't like it if we start rummaging in her boy's head.

WELCOME RAIN: Keep

a way of making the product stronger." His gill slits rippled. "So my time on the voyage was spent working on that."

"Any solution in sight?"

"Unfortunately not. But I've learned other things that will prove useful in time. And of course Cressida Ariste assigned me certain duties relating to her Chaos Form studies of interior stellar processes. So I've kept quite busy."

Gabriel paused while Mataglap's dire warning echoed through his skull. He didn't think Rubens was an assassin, but there were always weapons too subtle for a nonintrusive scan, the human body itself was of course a weapon, and the situation was unusual enough that precautions seemed justified.

"Do you have the data on this ceramic?" Gabriel said.

"Yes, Gabriel Aristos."

"Send it to me. Perhaps I'd be interested in licensing it for use at the Workshop." Mataglap's homicidal thunderings sent a river of tension up Gabriel's spine.

him talking. We may yet be able to trip him up.

MATAGLAP: What was that thing with his gills? A preparation for attack?

AUGENBLICK: Tensed neck muscles. Increased tension in the arm.

MATAGLAP: An attack! Ready your free arm. < Visualization of midknuckle strike. >

GABRIEL: Don't be paranoid. < Readying arm anyway >

MATAGLAP: *All* people have *me* in their hearts. Don't forget it.

WELCOME RAIN: I don't think it's violence he's after. Something more personal, I think.

MATAGLAP: What's more personal than violence? After the strike, dazzle him with the Mudra of Domination and get the fuck away from him while Manfred fills him with anesthetic.

AUGENBLICK: Neck tension! Arm tension! Spine rigid! Increased respiration!

MATAGLAP: *KILL HIM NOW!*

WELCOME RAIN: Shut

Rubens smiled. "I'd be delighted, Aristos." His expression turned briefly abstract as he made some internal communication. "I've transmitted the data from my ship to your Hyperlogos address. You may absorb it at leisure, Aristos."

"You'll be on Illyricum for a few days, yes? I'll try to communicate with you by the end of your stay."

"Thank you, Aristos."

Gabriel slowly exhaled, sending the tension from his body. The Welcome Rain's inevitable cynicism was like a chill, refreshing downpour after a humid summer day. The daimōn was a sociopathic manipulator, utterly without conscience, who usually worked in tandem with the intuitive Augenblick—the two were cognates, mirror images of the same personality, the same way that Horus was cognate with Cyrus, who was (in a somewhat more complex fashion) also cognate with Spring Plum.

up and let me think! That's not what's happening here.
AUGENBLICK: Relief! Relaxation of tension! Capillary dilation! Low threat potential!
WELCOME RAIN: Hah. He just wanted you to make his fortune by buying his ceramic. I thought I smelled self-interest.
GABRIEL: You   always smell self-interest.
WELCOME RAIN: There always is self-interest. Let me negotiate the contract. He'll end up with vacuum where his trust fund should be. The least we can do after he scared us like this.
MATAGLAP: < sulk >
AUGENBLICK: Increasing relaxation. Lowered and deeper respiration. Pupil dilation.   Nictating   membranes withdrawn.
WELCOME RAIN: His guard is down—and he's vulnerable now. Ask him why he's here. He or Cressida could have told you about the ceramic by tachline, so he's here for some other reason.

Mataglap, the paranoid, homicidal berserker, was cōgnate with no one. Gabriel had never needed him, and was happy to keep it that way.

"Still," Gabriel said. "You're here on a mission from Ariste Cressida, aren't you?"

Gabriel could feel the tension return to Rubens's body. "Yes," he said. "I was to deliver this, in person, to your hand alone."

Rubens's pace slowed as his free hand reached into one of his uniform pockets. Gabriel mentally shook off another renewed bellow of anxiety from Mataglap.

Rubens produced a data wafer. Gabriel stopped, took it with his free hand, and examined it. The wafer was in a transparent polymer coat to keep it from harm, and had Cressida's seal stamped on both sides. Gabriel gave Rubens a sidelong glance.

"Do you know what's on it?"

"No, Aristos. I was told it was under her seal and will not open to anyone but you." Rubens's face plainly showed a nervous uncertainty. "Cressida's instructions came entirely without warning—she gave me only two days' notice. I'm unaware of Cressida's giving a similar assignment to anyone during the time I've been with her. Usually she's quite thought-

AUGENBLICK: Nictating membranes pulsing. Narrowed pupils. Overall increase in tension.

WELCOME RAIN: Got him.

MATAGLAP: Careful! He'll kill you!

WELCOME RAIN: Oh, shut up.

AUGENBLICK: Stance uncertain. High focus of attention. Low threat potential, but he's thinking about something.

WELCOME RAIN: Keep him talking.

AUGENBLICK: Nictating membranes partially deployed, possibly indicative of deception, but deception is contraindicated by open stance, eye focus, eyelid steadiness, status of capillary dilation. See that? A slight hunch there, a shrug aborted by training. Indication of genuine puzzlement.

GABRIEL: Could his reactions be feigned?

AUGENBLICK: He is highly trained. It is possible.

WELCOME RAIN: We could do it.

GABRIEL: How can we be certain?

ful concerning the people to whom she assigns special duty."

Gabriel put the wafer in an interior pocket. "So whatever this is about, you have good cause to think it important."

"More important than anything since I've been in her service."

"Were you cautioned on what to say to me?"

"Not at all. Her orders were brief and direct—well, they always are." Rubens's brows furrowed. "I was simply to take the *Lorenz* to Illyricum, or wherever you were, after which I would inspect the Illyricum Workshop in order to get an idea of what I would need in my own ceramics workshop."

"Which of course you could have done through the oneirochronon."

"Naturally. And had every intention of doing. Cressida's message was via skiagénos, by the way—I checked."

"Very thorough of you." Which meant he wouldn't gain anything by persuading Rubens to let him look at his original message.

WELCOME RAIN: Keep him talking. But we'll never know for certain unless we use the Mudra of Compulsion or go to extremes.

AUGENBLICK: You could seduce him. Try to woo him from his former allegiance.

GABRIEL: Is it plausible?

AUGENBLICK: His metalinguistics suggest the possibility. His weight is very slightly adjusted in your direction, opening himself to your influence, and his near leg is just slightly turned out toward you, displaying his genitals. The indications are so slight that they are probably unconscious, but they could of course be feigned, or indicative merely of his willingness to be of assistance to you. I'd get a better idea if you look directly into his eyes for a few seconds.

WELCOME RAIN: Take the fellow. He's well trained. A Protarchōn spy would be diverting after this recent dull mingling of sexuality and sincerity.

GABRIEL: I'll view the message first, then think about it.

Gabriel paused and glanced about him. They had left the Red Lacquer Gallery and the Autumn Pavilion far behind, and the border of the formal gardens was just ahead. On a flat sward nearby, the sons and daughters of Residence workers who attended the Residence School were going through a Postures class, everyone from five-year-olds to early adolescents wiring their body and mind with the metalinguistic culture of the Logarchy, the common ground on which all humanity communicated. Behind them were forests, canals, and carefully calculated prospects.

"Would you like to see the deer park or zoo?" Gabriel asked. "The warrens? Little Venice or the Palazzo?"

Rubens glanced back at Manfred. "I imagine your terrier would be happier in the warrens," he said.

Gabriel found himself warming to a man who deferred to a dog, even if in the end he turned out to be some kind of spy. "The warrens, then," he said, and set off again.

Later, back in his office, Gabriel sat at his Louis Quinze desk and tapped the scrolled Illyrian Workshop mother-of-pearl inlay on its surface. A square of mahogany rose from the polished desktop. Gabriel took Cressida's data wafer from his pocket, pressed his thumb to the seal on the plastic envelope, broke the seal, and slipped the wafer into the waiting slit on the desk. The mahogany block seamlessly resumed its place.

The desk informed him that the data was under the Seal of the Aristoi and that Gabriel's positive identification would be needed to release it. Gabriel tapped mother-of-pearl, pressed his fingers to the desktop, and leaned over it so that embedded microwatts could scan his retinas. The mahogany surface deepened, grew bright. Cressida's skiagénos gazed from its depths with bright brown eyes.

"Enclosed are plans for setting up a direct tachline transmitter between your current location and Painter. I presume you will be able to oblige me by preparing this as soon as possible.

"I hope," eyes boring in, "that you will assist me in this

matter. I cannot compel you, but I can say that my reasons are of the utmost urgency, and although our present sealed tachline communications through the Hyperlogos may not be compromised, this alternative is the safest. My apologies if this places you at any inconvenience."

She's mad, suggested Welcome Rain. **One of her daimones is in charge.**

Cressida? Gabriel wondered. **She's been among the Aristoi for centuries—if anyone were firmly in command of her daimones, it should be she.**

She got soft. Couldn't take it anymore. *Science, science, science; discipline, discipline, discipline.* **Had to be in control even over interior stellar processes.**

I don't think that's what Chaos Form theory is about.

You want proof? She used a skiagénos to communicate with you. She didn't dare use a live vidcam—you'd be able to tell it was a daimōn speaking.

Perhaps there's some genuine danger.

From whom? Or what? No . . . she's just lost her grip. She's trying to involve you in her delusions.

Perhaps. But in that case, why *me?*

The Welcome Rain didn't have an answer for that. Gabriel called on his other daimones, none of whom contributed any useful analysis. Through his reno he accessed the Hyperlogos via tachline; he went through public and nonpublic biographical data both of Cressida and Rubens. Cressida's data told him nothing he didn't already know. Rubens's showed a steady ascent under Sebastian and Cressida—two Aristoi notoriously difficult to please—and he had failed his exams eight years ago by only a narrow margin. He might well become an Aristos during the next exam cycle.

So much for biography.

Through his reno he called Therápōn Tritarchōn Fleta, who looked after his communications net, and ordered her to set up the tachline rig.

"This is confidential, Therápōn," he said. "I don't want

anyone to know about this except the people doing the work."

"I will arrange for emplacement by robot, Aristos," Fleta purred. "The programming and telemetry, both of the robots and the tachline, I will do myself." She had altered her appearance to that of a fey elflike creature, all smooth curves, wide dark eyes, skin tinted a shiny, rather acrylic blue. She lowered her lashes suggestively. "No one will know but the two of us, Aristos," she said.

"I thank you," Gabriel said. "Fini."

Something, he was reminded, had always suggested to him that he save Fleta for later. The body shape, with its wide-eyed innocence mixed with catlike sensuality, was just a little *too* manipulative, and sent little warning twinges climbing his spine.

Gabriel's reno reminded him of appointments waiting, postponed, waiting still. A message from Marcus winked at him.

He ran the recording of Cressida again. No answers.

BELIEVE HER! The voice rolled through his mind. His nerves crackled. Daimones chattered in bewilderment.

He told them to be silent and probed gently for the source of the unknown voice. No luck.

The tachline would be set up within a few hours.

Soon he'd know.

Chapter 4

PABST: The human will, a plastic thing . . .
Doubt afflicts the mighty king.

The new Aristoi, moments short of investiture, stood in flickering torchlight beneath pillars of gold and ivory. Asterion loomed over them, propped with ease on fluke-like feet. *All of this compromised?* Gabriel wondered. *By whom?*

"You have demonstrated," Asterion said, "your ability to take your place among the few who can be trusted with the most powerful technology the universe has to offer. You have earned the trust of humanity."

It was Asterion's turn to address the new graduates. His opening was the most conventional possible, but the words had a certain additional impact, coming as they were from the glabrous-skinned modified human.

Akwasibo, Tunku Iskander, and the seven others were all in Postures of Esteem. Standing ranked in torchlight in the center of the Apadana of Darius, the great audience hall, and surrounded by other, older Aristoi, they were no doubt conscious that they were the center of all eyes. Not just of this group, but of the Logarchic millions, perhaps billions, watching via tachline and waiting for a hint as to the direction the future might take.

This, and this alone, was public. Everything else going on in the oneirochronic Persepolis was under the Seal of the Aristoi.

And much of the Aristois' communication with one another was also under privacy seal.

All of it compromised? That was supposed to have been made impossible when the system was created hundreds of years before.

Within an hour or so Gabriel would have his tachline set up. The new communications net wouldn't go through the Hyperlogos, and he and Cressida would talk.

Perhaps, he thought hopefully, she was mad.

For the ceremony Gabriel had dressed Cyrus-style in Phrygian cap and a brilliantly woven Median robe that flashed and flickered in the torchlight. He held by a diamond-studded leash a skiagénos of Manfred, which watched the performance with rapt, solemn attention.

Asterion spoke on, his style conventional, his words uninspired. Gabriel set his skiagénos in the same attentive, respectful attitude as his dog and allowed his thoughts to wander.

An idea came to him.

He sent a message, < Priority 1 >, to Zhenling. Perhaps she, too, was looking for diversion.

Somewhat to his surprise, she accepted.

Gabriel left Horus to look after the graduation ceremonies and materialized a second skiagénos inside his suite. The animal servants began to deploy automatically. There was a knock on the door, and the otter moved to answer while Gabriel triggered a Kurusu piece from the orchestra.

Zhenling, in the electronic moment between the graduation ceremonies and her appearance here, had changed from a formal suit to summery silk trousers and an embroidered jacket. She thanked the tetrapus for his offer of refreshment, but declined.

Incense began to burn at a wave of Gabriel's thought, spilling from the eyes and mouth of bronze censers formed in the shape of monkey heads. Gabriel offered Zhenling a seat on the sofa.

All this compromised? he wondered. Was anyone listening?

He doubted it.

But he had never heard of Cressida engaged in any intrigue before. None whatever.

(*"Peace and stability stretching over centuries. The frontiers of humanity, and human knowledge, steadily expanded."* Asterion's speech, transmitted by Horus, floated in the back of Gabriel's head.)

"Thank you for transmitting the data on your chemistry," Zhenling said.

"You're welcome. Am I normal?"

"Not really, no."

"I'm pleased to hear it. Your conclusions?"

She smiled. "Too early for that. A context will develop only when other Aristoi contribute their data."

"And will they?"

"No one's turned me down yet."

"That's encouraging." He drew (Augenblick's urging) one foot up under him to encourage informality. "D'you really think you'll find a common thread?" he asked.

"Honestly?" Eyebrows arching. "No."

(*"Mobile, unrestricted populations. Information—all of it— preserved in its entirety for future generations. Information—all save the most dangerous—available to all, and instantaneously."*)

"It seems to me," Gabriel went on, "that you won't discover a great deal about what *makes* an Aristos. We're primates, admittedly, and no doubt we have primate brain chemistry—but we become Aristoi *before* all the people around us became so deferent. So you're charting a process that's aberrant right from the start."

"I anticipate a long-range process by which similar data are gathered for a wide cross-section of Therápontes and the

Demos, some of whom may of course become Aristoi—and then we'll know the difference, if there is one." Zhenling pulled her legs into a cross-legged stance and rested her cheek on a fist. "But for the moment, I'm only gathering data. *All* data is useful, as Asterion just reminded us. It's too early for conclusions, but it's also too early for the questions. I'm studying Aristoi. Why not? One can't claim it isn't a worthy subject for study."

"No. One can't."

"And all our genes are mapped, so that's another solid mass of data . . ."

"They've also been looked at before. No common thread there."

"I'd like to think I have several new approaches."

Gabriel leaned closer. Hundreds of light-years away, in the *Pyrrho*, his palate tingled to her scent. The Welcome Rain purred in his ear. "My own focus tends to be a bit narrower," he said. "I'd like to study but a single Ariste."

"Study all you like. But I prefer not to think of myself as all that narrow."

(*"Hostile environments made habitable. Nature itself become an artifact of the human will."*)

Zhenling cocked her head. "Are you monitoring Asterion's speech? Doesn't it strike you as something of an apologia?"

"He does seem to be reviewing a good deal."

"Perhaps this is the beginning of the reaction."

"The reaction?" Gabriel raised his eyebrows. "Is there therefore a revolution? And if so, are you it?"

She smiled. "You'll pardon me. I should pay closer attention."

"I'll see you at the receptions."

This time she allowed his kiss on the back of her hand. Her skiagénos politely walked from the room instead of merely vanishing, but, he suspected, her consciousness had largely departed.

He returned his focus to the Apadana. Torchlight flickered off the intent faces of the new Aristoi. Asterion stood in a calm, imperial posture and spoke with the authority of absolute conviction.

"It was Marcus Aurelius who said, *'What is not good for the swarm is not good for the bee.'* Nor, I should add, for the queen. Aristoi are granted immense power, verging on the absolute, but the power is not without condition, nor without responsibility.

"Our duty is not to ourselves but to the Demos. Our power is granted for their protection, for their advancement. The tragedy that engulfed Earth[1] was caused by people ignorant of the consequences of their own work. It is our task *never* to be ignorant of consequence. *Never* to be caught off-guard. *Always* to stand between the Demos and that which threatens their peace and development."

Asterion's hands formed Mudras of Teaching and Responsiveness. "Our social classes are hierarchies of service. *Therápōn* originally meant 'servant.' Not a servant to the Aristoi, though that is what is largely assumed, but a servant to the Demos. And *the best*—the Aristoi—more than the Therápontes, are shackled by bonds of service. If we are believed to be the best, it is because we owe our best to others."

Asterion lifted his stance slightly, his center of gravity rising into realms of kinesic uncertainty. "There are critiques of our order. Some believe that the stability and measured growth we have brought to humanity are somehow inhibiting its growth and progress."

Gabriel's electric awareness seemed to fill the room. He perceived the firm, approving glance of Virtue's Icon, Zhenling's skeptical posture, Astoreth's expression of annoyance, the brooding dark presence of Saigo. The awareness that certain lines were being drawn. Power seemed to flicker around the room, weaving a path from one Aristos to the next.

Asterion lowered his stance to one of greater authority, command lancing through his voice. "Progress? Progress, measured progress, is being made everywhere, on every conceivable frontier. Growth? Uncontrolled growth has caused so many problems in the past—it was *uncontrolled growth that killed Earth[1]!*"

Well, Gabriel thought. It was out in the open now. How many tens of billions were watching?

The reaction, Zhenling had called it. Perhaps it ought to be *overreaction.*

"What the critics really seem to mean"—Asterion smiled ironically—"is that they are nostalgic for the past. A past that seems much more adventurous and exciting than the present. Let me remind those who hold this view," forming a Mudra of Authority, "that the past held one catastrophe after another. That the Demos were afflicted with plague and uncertainty, war and neurosis, an endless degrading struggle for sustenance, resources, and a habitable biosphere. That it was this struggle that made the past *interesting.*" He nodded with calm authority. "If it is not as interesting now, we should be thankful. And perhaps it is not the welfare of the Demos that the critics most have in their hearts."

He straightened, took a formal stance. "You nine are chosen foremost in rank, honor, and responsibility. Today, as a reward for struggles made and hardships overcome, each is invested with the title *Aristos kaí Athánatos.* But as your domaines begin to form in your image, as your struggles and hardships intensify and grow in consequence, recall another saying of Marcus Aurelius, one whose burdens and duties were similar to yours. *'Do not waste the remnant of your life in those imaginations concerning others, wherein you do not contribute to the common weal.'* "

He raised his arms. "Ten thousand years to the new Aristoi!"

"Ten thousand years!" All chorused in reply.

"Ten thousand worlds!"

"Ten thousand worlds!"

He held out a right hand formed in a Mudra of Truth. The webbing between his fingers was translucent against the white marble and rich ornament. "I am granted the privilege of administering the oath that will both liberate your minds to fly where they wish, and chain your will to the welfare of humanity. Repeat after me: *With honor we, in taking upon ourselves the imperium of the Aristoi . . .*"

What followed tonight, Gabriel thought, was bound to be interesting.

Colored spheres fell in ultraslow motion from a high, dark, tented ceiling. The music that filled Tallchief's oneirochronic chamber rippled the spheres' plastic surfaces as if the sound waves were become visible within the fluid medium. When they struck the floor, or the gathered Aristoi, the spheres burst and scattered intriguing scents, spice, citrus, and sweetness.

This? Compromised? Gabriel thought.

"Asterion was not forceful enough," said Virtue's Icon. "It is the duty of all Aristoi to protect the Demos from unwholesome revisionist philosophy."

"Absolutely," Gabriel said.

"There should be an explicit denunciation formulated."

"Certainly. Why don't you do that?"

Virtue's Icon was a small, intent woman, plain-featured, with dark hair chopped rudely short at the collar. She wore the plain, unadorned grey tunic that was almost universal within her civil service and very common in her domaine. Like Cressida's, only ugly.

Her eyes narrowed as she looked up at Gabriel. Tonight, for the reception, his skiagénos wore, over ruffled shirt and tight chamois trousers, a sleeveless knee-length cassock-coat designed by Spring Plum. It featured her usual floral motifs—intricate red petals pouted against a leafy green background, seed pearls impersonated anthers, and cunning insects glittered with elaborate beadwork as they climbed about the embroidered stalks.

"You will, of course, sign the denunciation yourself."

"I will have to see the text."

The Icon's expression flattened. "You are insufficiently serious, Gabriel Aristos."

"To the contrary. I am quite serious. I am, however, never solemn."

This particular distinction seemed to elude her. She sniffed, about-faced, and went in search of a more appreciative audience.

Gabriel, back in the *Pyrrho*, smiled a smile he did not permit his skiagénos to display. Offending Virtue's Icon was something of an art—one wished her to go away, but one did not wish to seem rude.

There were penalties for being rude to the Icon.

At least he was not one of her neighbors—she could make them suffer by endless protraction of trade negotiations and bombarding them with endless petitions for the return of the emigrants she persisted in labeling as "fugitives," all because they had decamped without paying back the investment the Commonwealth of Virtue had made in them.

All travel within the Logarchy was theoretically unrestricted. Virtue's Icon imposed not "restrictions," but "taxes." It was a distinction that eluded most of those who tried to leave her sphere.

The Icon's domaine was the largest in terms of size and habitats, if somewhat underpopulated in terms of those who actually chose to live there.

There were reasons for that.

"How can you stand it?" Akwasibo's head floated on the periphery of Gabriel's perception.

Gabriel turned toward her. Her neck, like Alice's, shortened and drew her head back to her shoulders.

"One has practice," Gabriel said.

Akwasibo looked after Virtue's Icon and made a face. "Imagine if Stalin had become Pope," she said.

Gabriel's daimones collapsed in helpless laughter.

"One should consider," Gabriel said, "that nothing said at this reception is entirely private. The Demos and Therápontes are locked out, of course, but any Ariste can review our words from Hyperlogos memory. And no doubt a few will—perhaps the lady concerned." Certainly the lady concerned, if Gabriel knew her at all.

"I don't care. My domain will be well away from hers."

"That doesn't mean you won't have to deal with her. And, unless you expressly forbid them, there will be Temples of Virtue in every habitat of your domain, all proselytizing like mad."

"Gives you a certain sympathy for Tomás de Torquemada's point of view, doesn't it?"

Gabriel decided to change the subject and spare Akwasibo the inevitable, unfortunate consequences of prolonging this conversational topic. Being denounced from every Virtue pulpit, for starters. "Have you chosen your domain?"

She smiled. "Yes. I'm pioneering, as you did. I thought it a shame to waste what I learned from watching you."

"I'm happy to have been of use."

"Just three planets to start—I'll be putting my terraforming team together as soon as we're finished here."

Nostalgia drifted through Gabriel as he recalled his own pioneering days, staking out his new domain on the frontier. Illyricum, Vissarion, Cos, Lascarios, Brightkinde—all planets he had terraformed, adjusted, stabilized, and eventually populated and ruled, along with space habitats and continental shelves. As populations grew, he'd relaxed his direct rule, allowed the Demos to choose their own leaders for all but the most important tasks.

Only Brightkinde was still under a Hegemón, a direct appointed governor. And they would elect their own parliament and premier within a matter of weeks, and the Hegemón would surrender his seal of office.

And that would be that. The last place where his direct authority was still felt. A surge of remembrance filled his soul.

He wasn't nostalgic enough to want to do it all again, however. Building a world from scratch was a lot of work.

Akwasibo went on. "I've already received—good God—almost fifty million applications. Even after I sort out the ones I don't want—"

"You'll get three hundred million more. I did."

Dismay touched her for only a second. "Good thing this has been done so many times. It's all there, in the records—exact numbers of how many electricians and plumbers and able seamen and cosmetician robots I'll need in the first wave." She grinned. "Perhaps if I disregarded the past entirely, and made up my own list, I'd be making my life more exciting, like Astoreth wants."

Well, Gabriel thought. He'd warned her about indiscreet conversation in this setting, and here she was persisting.

Perhaps he shouldn't associate himself with such folly any longer. It wasn't as if she was still his apprentice.

"You'll forgive me," he said. "I see someone I should speak to."

He drifted through the room and grazed on conversation. He spoke to his host, Tallchief, who showed him the design of a new habitat. Tallchief's domaine had no planets, only huge flotillas of space habitats that moved from place to place visiting and trading and then moving on. Tallchief was working his way along the rim of the Logarchy and would be expected in Gabriel's domaine in another seventy or eighty years. Gabriel offered welcome and facilities, and Tallchief smiled and thanked him. Gabriel drifted on.

He encountered Cressida moving serenely through the pack. He greeted her with a Posture of Formal Regard.

She was dressed, as usual, in the simple, practical blue uniform worn by her household. Her skiagénos used a lot of standard programming and did not have the elaborate *presence* of most.

Cressida returned Gabriel's salutation. She assimilated his appearance with her bright, cold eyes.

"Your plumage is bright. As usual."

GABRIEL: On alert, everyone.

"One hopes it reflects the soul within."

AUGENBLICK: Skiagenoi are, as I remind, difficult to

"Ah." Her tone indica- read. The fact that hers is so

ted she had, herself, little hope.

On the whole, Gabriel knew, Cressida had never had much patience with him. Which made her approach via Rubens even more unusual than it might have been.

"I should thank you for the hospitality you've shown my Therápōn," she said. "You've been very kind, and he's learned a great deal simply from watching the Workshop in operation."

"His ceramic might prove very useful to us."

She lifted her chin. "You're the best judge of that, I suppose. For the purposes for which it was crafted, it was a failure."

Rubens was still on Illyricum, taking in the sights. And, Gabriel assumed, spying as well.

"Do you have the specifications for that carbon-carbon-silicon form?" Cressida asked. "Would you like to look at a model now? Some of the thermal interactions are interesting."

Gabriel glanced around, feigned uncertainty. "If you like. I'm not sure—"

standard, without a high degree of individuation, makes it more difficult to read rather than less.

GABRIEL: Tell me what you can.

AUGENBLICK: She is very controlled, though less so than in her recorded transmission. *This* Cressida has not been edited. Her kinesics are civil but restrained. Respiration and pulse slightly elevated, pupils dilated. She is very alert.

WELCOME RAIN: Is it a daimōn we're speaking to?

AUGENBLICK: Probably not. While a limited personality is perfectly capable of carrying on a conversation in this simple, formal mode, an LP would probably show more strain in trying to hold up under the pressure of quite so many Aristoi.

GABRIEL: She may not have been here for any length of time.

AUGENBLICK: In that case it will become apparent before long.

GABRIEL: Conclusions?

AUGENBLICK: None, really. I don't believe daemonic possession is likely.

"It will take only a few moments."

He nodded. "Very well."

Cressida led him to a door in the wall, a door that, Gabriel thought, had not been there a moment before. She opened it: there was a glimpse of bright light, clean, illuminated countertops, functional equipment—a lab. He stepped through and pulsed an oneirochronic cue from the *Pyrrho* to activate Fleta's private tachline.

Gulls called to him. The air had the tang of the sea. He turned and saw the sun nearing the horizon, a falling tide, a wire fence half-buried in the sand. Smoke from a driftwood fire rose in the distance. Soft old planks sagged underfoot.

"Welcome," Cressida said. "Thank you for taking me seriously."

Gabriel turned to her. She was out of uniform, wearing stained old corduroy trousers, scuffed boots, a faded pullover. They were both standing on the screened porch of a building made of logs. Old furniture sagged comfortably, facing the sea. Through a window he could see a flagstone fireplace with driftwood blazing therein.

"This is my parents' vacation place," Cressida said. "I spent much of my childhood here."

"Very nice," said Gabriel, glancing at the rough beams and shabby carpets. He thought it needed about twenty more rooms.

Cressida glanced over her surroundings. "I've been spending a lot of time in this simulation lately."

"I seem to have overdressed for the occasion," Gabriel said, and set Cyrus scurrying through the files for something more appropriate.

She has brought you to a place resonant with childhood memory, commented Horus. **The scene would be comforting for her. I think she is preparing to deliver disturbing news.**

"We won't be here long," Cressida said. "Just enough for me to ask you a few questions."

"How may I be of service to you, Ariste?"

He looked down at the garb that Horus had just materialized on him: canvas pants, flannel shirt with the sleeves rolled up, some kind of floppy hat.

Well. She said this would only take a little while.

Cressida gazed at him intently. "Your domaine is two months away from the Gaal Sphere. Do you know of any activity there?"

Gabriel's reno checked the facts just to be certain. "Yes."

"What do you know of it?"

Gabriel parroted his reno's answer. "A group of several hundred stars, off-limits to settlement due to a supernova. Gaal Ninety-seven, about to cook off in the interior. Saigo Aristos is there, on his yacht, studying the potential nova."

Saigo had been there, off and on, for decades. But then Saigo was an odd sort—asocial, abrupt, brooding, idiosyncratic. Presumably he enjoyed being alone with only the stars for company.

"Saigo initiated the study," Cressida said. "He explored the system with remotes, discovered the potential supernova, brought the situation before the Aristoi at Persepolis, and urged us to forbid settlement. We looked at the data and concurred."

"Well before my time," Gabriel said. His reno confirmed Cressida's details.

"That's the history," Cressida said. "It's also a lie."

Aha! crowed the Welcome Rain. **The daimōn speaks! I doubt it,** said Augenblick.

"The facts are recorded in the Hyperlogos," Gabriel said.

"Stellar evolution is one of my specialties," Cressida said. "It relates to my Chaos Form studies."

"You've discovered a problem with the data?"

"More than that. I recorded Saigo's initial exploration data realtime off the feed, just as it came in from his remotes. It took months, of course, for it all to come in, and I never looked at it. I recorded it because I thought it might be useful someday. I do that with a lot of information—just keep it handy till I need it."

"So do I."

"I never looked at the Gaal data till recently." She licked her lips. "Till just three months ago."

Her physiology is indicative of distress, Aristos, said Augenblick. **Distress and bewilderment.**

Gabriel didn't need Augenblick to tell him that.

"I found an element of Chaos Form that might make sense in light of that anomalous supernova-to-be," Cressida said. "So I turned to the data and looked at it for confirmation." She paused. The silence was filled by a distant gull.

"And?"

"There was no budding supernova. And in its place a normal main-sequence star, with one planet that could be easily terraformed to make it habitable."

Gabriel considered this. "I'm not sure what you mean," he said.

"I cross-checked the raw data in the Hyperlogos, the data that *should* have been identical. And then I looked at the data that Saigo had filed after the raw data had been reduced. *Both* sets of data agree that the potential supernova was in the making."

"Data in the Hyperlogos is inviolate," Gabriel said. "You're suggesting that someone meddled with your recordings of the raw data? Made it appear as if the nascent supernova wasn't there?"

Fire flashed from her eyes. "Don't be such a naïf. *No one* tampered with my data. It was physically isolated the entire time—I put the whole series on one wafer and filed it on a shelf till I needed it. Why would someone tamper with it? It's the Hyperlogos data that's false."

Gabriel and his daimones were struck silent for a moment, and then a tide of babbling protest began to rise in his skull. He told them all to shut up.

"How?" he demanded. "The Hyperlogos was set up centuries ago to preserve *everything*. Special care was taken with the code so as to make tampering impossible. The Seal of the Hyperlogos has a higher priority even than the Seal of the Aristoi. Not even one of us—"

Bitter amusement twisted Cressida's lips. "Are *you*, Gabriel Vissarionovich Aristos, about to tell me what an Aristos can and cannot do?"

Gabriel realized he wasn't and fell silent again. His daimones began to palpate Cressida's revelation with cautious little paws.

"Never mind how," Cressida said. "How isn't important—concede for a moment there's a way to do it. The *why* is what matters. Why did Saigo tamper with the Hyperlogos? Why did he invent a fictional supernova and have an entire sphere of stars declared off-limits? Why is he spending so much time there?" She leaned closer and gazed at him intently. "What is he doing that he doesn't want the rest of us to know?"

The inviolable Seal of the Hyperlogos broken. Very well. Gabriel was willing, at least in theory, to start from that point and reason backwards.

"You've had longer to think about this than I," he said. "What do you think is going on?"

"There is a potentially habitable planet orbiting the star that Saigo says will blow up," Cressida said. "It had occurred to me that there might be . . . another species . . . living on it."

Gabriel thought about that. No complex life-forms other than Earth-descendants had ever been found, but that didn't mean this would never happen. "Do your original data support that?" he asked.

"Not really. The original scan revealed an atmosphere composed of CO, CO_2, and a lot of elemental sulphur. Surface temperature averages over two hundred Celsius and any oxygen seems tied up in carbon oxysulfide. I don't suppose life is completely impossible under those conditions, but if it existed it would be damned unusual life."

"What else could he be up to?"

"There are hundreds of stars in that sphere. Even Saigo's tampered data shows many with planets capable of supporting life once some terraforming is done. I—" She hesitated. "I think he's creating life out there. Completely new life, or experimenting with human genetics in ways of which we wouldn't approve. He's a specialist in human evolution as well as stellar evolution. He's done a lot of publishing on the human genome."

"He could do that sort of thing at home. We might disapprove, but we couldn't stop him."

"What he's doing might be dangerous. He might be using mataglap nano."

A cold chill rose along Gabriel's spine at the very sound of the word.

"Still," Cressida said, "whatever he's doing, he's tampering with the Seal, and that compromises almost everything in the Logarchy. Almost every tachline communication is routed through the switching system in the Hyperlogos. Even our private sealed communications—the Seal of the Aristoi won't hold once the Hyperlogos Seal is broken. He's got access to *everything*, and he can tamper with all of it. Our entire civilization is based on free and unlimited access to data. Even the Seal of the Aristoi fades after the Aristos who sealed it dies or retires. Saigo can change data, communications . . . history itself. And we don't know if he's doing this alone, or with others."

A cold wind blew through the seagrass outside. The sun subsided below the murky horizon. Back on the *Pyrrho*, Gabriel shivered.

"Why me?" Gabriel demanded. "Why are you telling me this?"

"You're nearest to the Gaal Sphere. It occurred to me that you could monitor events in the Sphere without Saigo knowing about it. Possibly from your home system, possibly by sending out probes." She gave an uncomfortable smile. "Besides, I had to tell someone. Preferably someone who hasn't been connected with Saigo."

Gabriel's reno spun him Saigo's life history. The man was almost six hundred years old and the number of people he'd had contact with was phenomenal. He'd only turned reclusive in the last century or so.

"I don't know what to *do*, Gabriel," Cressida said. "I'm not a conspirator, a politician, an ideologue. I only want to know the truth when I see it. And Saigo is *tampering with the truth*."

"You should present what you've learned to the others."

"Which of them are a part of it? What will happen if I send messages through the Hyperlogos to all the Aristoi, and Saigo or one of his hypothetical allies decides to disrupt *all* communications? What if they decide to take possession of the Hyperlogos for themselves—*all human knowledge*, controlled by one man or a small group? What if it means war by one group of Aristoi against another?"

Back on the *Pyrrho*, Gabriel felt his mouth turn dry. "We've never had a war," he said.

"With the potential weaponry we've got available, with gravity generators that can warp space and matter, with mataglap nano that can eat whole planets the way Earth[1] was consumed—what happens to our obligation to the Demos then?"

Gabriel's mind whirled. Daimones cried for attention or driveled hopelessly among themselves. "We need to consider," Gabriel said. "We need to think further."

Perhaps, Horus's coldly logical voice, **a series of private tachline nets, like the one you and Cressida share. A counterconspiracy.**

But who to contact? Gabriel wondered.

"We've been absent from the reception too long," Cressida said. "I never hid the fact that I recorded that data off the feed—my access codes are right there in the Hyperlogos. And once I found the discrepancy I went into the Hyperlogos and checked the data there very thoroughly, along with a history of who's accessed it. So if Saigo was paying attention, he knows that I know."

"If he was paying attention, he knew three months ago."

"As soon as I worked all this out, I withdrew to my orbital lab *Sanjay*. There are only a few people here and I can control access very well. I've been taking care of business through the oneirochronon, but this can't go on indefinitely."

"No." Gabriel was shaken by the thought that Cressida considered herself in danger.

She's *contaminated* us! Augenblick was outraged. **If she's imperiled, so are we!**

She should *not* have taken us here from the reception, Horus said. **This communication should have been private from start to finish.**

Gabriel thankfully replaced his clothing with his Median cloak. "When we speak again," he said, "we shouldn't switch over to our private line from the Hyperlogos comm net."

Cressida's eyes widened. "Oh," she said. "I didn't think—"

"It may mean nothing. It's been centuries since the decisions were taken regarding the Gaal Sphere. Saigo may have assumed long ago that you'd never look at the raw data once he'd reduced it and made it available in the Hyperlogos." Gabriel's daimones felt free to disbelieve this.

"I have no talent for conspiracy. I said that right at the start."

"Find a daimōn who's good at it."

"I've been trying."

"Let's set a time for talking again. I want to be able to digest all of this."

They agreed to speak after the next night's reception. Cressida opened the door to the screened porch, and they stepped through to the reception.

"A total exaggeration of my position!" Astoreth was saying. "Almost a parody!" She was speaking to a pair of gold cat's eyes adhered to one of Tallchief's slowly falling colored spheres. Feathery plumes swayed about Astoreth's elaborate headdress: her skin was a becoming shade of violet. She turned to Gabriel as he stepped through the door. "I'm outraged!" she said.

The falling sphere struck the floor and punctured. Several miniature musical instruments fell out and began to play maniacally, as if trying to get an entire concerto into a three-second burst. They finished, then disappeared with a brief bagpipe honk.

Dorothy St.-John's cat's eyes floated up from the burst of chaos. Gabriel turned to Cressida and set his skiagénos into a Posture of Formal Regard. She returned it.

"Outraged!" Astoreth prompted.

Gabriel turned to her. "I am heartily distressed on your account, Ariste."

"As if I would ever endanger the Demos! My critique is aimed purely at the Aristoi—to urge us to greater and greater exertions! Let the universe ring with the spirit of discovery and adventure, the way that once it did! Where is the spirit of Captain Yuan?"

"Lost on a quest to the center of the galaxy," said Gabriel. "Along with the rest of him."

Astoreth gave him a look. "That wasn't what I meant," she said.

"I beg pardon, Ariste. I seem to be inexcusably literal tonight."

Somehow his heart wasn't in this. Across the room he saw the looming form of Saigo, bearded, dressed in dark colors, locked in an intent conversation with the shimmering sphere of the Platonist Sebastian. He wondered if Saigo was planning to kill him.

(Horus logically evolved a plan in response to this situation. Gabriel didn't feel quite ready to make preparations as yet. Something in him wanted further convincing.)

He wanted to fly off into the night and commit himself to something irresponsible, but he made himself stay at the reception until half the guests had left.

Returning his focus to the *Pyrrho*, he floated out to the shuttle and told White Bear to take the controls. Something was still tugging at him. He went into the oneirochronon briefly to query the Residence's main reno as to Clancy's whereabouts, and found that she'd been in the Carnation

Suite for three hours, presumably sleeping the sleep of the just.

Gabriel wanted something more irresponsible than just sleep. He found himself wanting something delinquent.

He told White Bear to take him to Standing Wave.

Chapter 5

LOUISE: With woolly tongue and throbbing head
        To wake up in a stranger's bed . . .

                (refrain) *Life's an adventure!*

If he were going to be delinquent, Gabriel decided, he might as well do it properly.

He lay on satin in Marcus's pale outflung arms. The Freising Gorge fell away above them, white water glowing in the spotlights and spilling upward into vertiginous black igneous depths . . .

The house he had designed for Marcus was called Standing Wave and spanned the gorge on a site that Gabriel had reserved for himself for the simple reason that he didn't want anyone else's architecture spoiling the scenery.

The building was compressed between two white buttresses that stood at either side of the gorge like giant compacting hands. The name came from the design, which was precisely that of a giant double standing wave, the image of the compacted gravity waves that filled the structure and provided its other dominant feature.

Gravity generators had been built into the buttresses—

Gabriel had granted himself a special waiver to use them on-planet, and they were protected from abuse by ingenious and elaborate security arrangements. Their special compressed waves, imaged in the building's architecture, canceled the planet's gravity within the structure and allowed the unique perspective granted the inhabitants, in which direction was altered, permitting Gabriel and Marcus to lie on a bed on the ceiling and gaze upward to watch, through a transparent floor, the white water thunder and roar and arc away, ever upward, into the blue welcoming pool . . .

The structure had been long since finished. The decoration, plaster and paint and tile, was taking longer—Marcus's living quarters had been finished first and he'd moved in, but the rest was chaos. Every wall, ceiling, and floor was slightly curved, which meant the larger pieces of furniture, all the doors and windows and cabinets, had to be custom-made to conform. Gabriel could have had everything designed and built by CAD in a matter of days, if not hours, but he valued hand-built objects much more than those conceived in the oneirochronon and constructed by autolathe, had founded the Workshop simply to give voice to his prejudice.

An idea crept softly into Gabriel's mind. He turned to Marcus. "Black-Eyed Ghost," he said, "do you have a brush and paper?"

Marcus's drowsing lashes fluttered open. He'd long since grown used to the fact that Gabriel slept many fewer hours than he did. "Next room," he said. "The black lacquer desk."

Gabriel eased from the bed, put on a dressing gown, and walked (gravity shifting subtly at every step) to the small dark-paneled room next door. The rumble of the falls filled the close space. Gabriel could smell the fine rag paper before he found it in the drawer. He made some ink, rubbing the sumi stick into the inkstone, lubricating with drops of water, until the ink was the blackest color imaginable, black as a singularity, with an accretion disk of tiny rainbow bubbles. Gabriel summoned Psyche and picked a large calligraphy brush.

For a brief space Psyche dwelt in his arm and mind. When Gabriel let her soar away, he looked down to find on the paper the poem she had sung, in the Intermediate Ideography, as Gabriel implanted the blastocyst in Marcus. He let the characters sound in his heart once again.

Gabriel's awareness slowly expanded outward from his hand and arm, and he became aware that Marcus was standing behind him and watching over his shoulder.

"Beautiful," Marcus said. "I remember you speaking those words, but to *see* them . . ."

"The contribution of one of my daimones," Gabriel said. He began to clean the brush.

" 'In a nutshell: Shakyamuni.' " Marcus took a long breath, let it out. "I'm very happy to be that nutshell, Gabriel Vissarionovich."

Gabriel turned to look at Marcus over his shoulder. "The other day you seemed full of second thoughts."

"Yes. Sorry. I've always been that way when it comes to big changes, you know. That's why I've been hesitating on retaking my exams. But now that I'm . . . a nutshell . . . I'm happy with it." He smiled. "Last night I was down at the bottom of the gorge, on the little meadow there. And I was dancing for joy. Literally, there on the grass. Your *Divertimento in B* was running through my head."

Gabriel finished cleaning his writing materials, then put them away. The ink on the paper had dried. He took the paper, rose from his chair, handed the paper to Marcus.

"I'll have it framed for the nursery," Marcus said. "Somewhere by the egg you gave me."

They returned to the bedroom. White water soared above their heads, diving into a gorge in deepening shadow.

"It's getting late," Marcus said. "Will you be staying? Shall we have an early breakfast?"

Gabriel shook his head. "I have to go to my father's tomb. I want to be there at dawn."

"May I go with you?"

Gabriel touched Marcus's cheek. "I'd rather not. I want to be alone there."

"I heard that Dr. Clancy is moving into the Carnation Suite."

Gabriel looked at him. "Yes."

A little smile brushed Marcus's lips. "She's a sweet person. I had a call from her the other day, asking if I was well." He reached out, touched Gabriel's cheek. "I hope you will be good for her, Aristos."

"Isn't the normal phrasing usually the reverse?"

"I'm certain, Gabriel, she will be good for *you*."

Gabriel kissed him. "Be happy, Ghost."

"You as well."

White Bear had gone to sleep hours ago, so Gabriel piloted himself. From Standing Wave his shuttle took him on shadowed wings to the tomb he had built of rosy marble high in the Cordillera Oriental, where the rising dawn would find it every morning.

The landing place was on a small plateau two hundred meters below the tomb, and he ascended, breath frosting, via a zigzag path. The predawn air was cold, and he was glad for his warm sheepskin jacket. The stars shone above, along with one rocketing, unwinking ice-crystal moon. Below, spread out over the invisible world, was a layer of opalescent cloud.

The tomb was simple, with Doric pillars and an unadorned lintel leading to the interior. His mother had wanted something far more grand, but part of Gabriel's reason for keeping the place small and difficult of access was so that members of his cult couldn't mob the place.

Still, worshippers were there—Gabriel could hear music, which was cued by a sensor when someone entered the tomb. Since there wasn't any transport in the landing place, these had either hiked up the mountainside or been dropped off by someone else.

Gabriel walked on his soft suede boots to the entrance and activated the IR scanners he'd had implanted in his otherwise organic eyes.

There were two people inside. One weathered-looking woman, clad only in a white loincloth, meditated in a cross-legged stance, and another was wrapped in a sleeping bag.

The music was Gates's *Electronic Diffusion*. Gabriel could remember his father conducting it.

Gabriel moved briskly into the interior, stepping carefully around offerings of flowers, money, icons, and food, and pulsed a command through the oneirochronon to open the interior door.

The weathered woman was deep in trance and showed no sign that she was aware of Gabriel's presence, but a head jerked up from the sleeping bag: Gabriel could sense someone trying to make out, through sleep-ridden eyes, what was going on.

The inner door swung open in silence; Gabriel stepped through, and closed it behind him. Perhaps the person in the sleeping bag would think it only a dream.

Light rose in the cold mountain grotto. Frost rimed the walls, glittered like distant galaxies. The music played here as well as outside. There was a small bench; a simple wooden table, tools, and a piece of bone. The coffin, carved roughly out of the mountain itself, rested in a niche. Above it, in Greek, was inscribed a quote from Aeschylus: "*Sweet is a grief well ended.*"

The grief, in Gabriel's case, had not yet ended.

Vissarion Simonovich Kamanev, Gabriel's primary father, had been a musician and conductor. He had reached the rank of Therápōn Hextarchōn largely through the good-will of Dorothy St.-John, who had promoted him two grades in the years before his death—as, Gabriel suspected, a favor to his son.

Vissarion had not been a lucky man. He had been gifted, but not quite gifted enough. Or, Gabriel suspected, he had always been surrounded by people more gifted or determined than he, one of whom turned out to be his only offspring. Still, his few compositions were interesting, and his interpretations of others' work were, if conventional, at least meticulous and informed.

He had been Vashti's second husband—she had annexed him rather young, at a time when she fancied developing her musical talents. Vissarion lasted longer than any of them, almost eleven years. Gabriel had to give him credit for his well-intentioned, if baffled, attempts to make the marriage work. In the end he's taken Gabriel and fled to another domaine, abandoning his conducting job. The decision had been good for Gabriel but disastrous for Vissarion's career. He'd lost a good twenty years in terms of his own advancement. They were twenty years, as it turned out, he really didn't have to spare.

Gabriel settled onto the bench. Music tingled along his nerves. He picked up the long white bone and placed fingers on the stops he had carved. He thought of his father, dead via Breakdown at the age of a hundred twenty-four.

Gabriel raised the bone to his lips and blew. A high brittle note rose, battled the jagged electronic sound of the recording. Gabriel altered the fingering and blew again. Thoughts of his father rolled through him. Vissarion—gentle, encouraging, loving, slightly bewildered, slightly helpless. Gabriel's doing well had helped him, had given him confidence.

Gabriel blew another note, frowned, blew again. He picked up a little knife, then hesitated as the cold metal stung his fingertips. He should play the instrument until it warmed before he made any alterations.

He told the music in this room to stop playing. He could still hear faint sounds from the anteroom. He played the bone trumpet some more, until the instrument warmed under his hands, and then he took up his knife again and shaved away a fragment of his father's thighbone. He played the note again and was more satisfied.

When the work was done Gabriel would compose music for the bone trumpet, a lament for Vissarion played on an instrument made from Vissarion's femur. Vissarion would be pleased, he thought, that his remains had become music, leaping into life like Athene from the thigh of Zeus.

Memories of Vissarion welled in Gabriel's heart. Unlike the pair in the anteroom, he didn't need to believe he was a god in order to revere his father. He adjusted the stop again, measured carefully, picked up a drill. His work was slow, deliberate, clean. Bone dust sifted gently to the tabletop. The femur was warm to the touch, vibrated to musical tone. Ideas for compositions floated through his mind. He thought of Tunku Iskander's flute music, raised the bone trumpet, and played a fragment. It suits, he thought.

He stayed for an hour. Outside, he knew, it was dawn. He played a few last, long notes, put the bone trumpet down, replaced his tools.

There was, after all, no hurry.

Gabriel rose and bade his father's memory farewell. He opened the door into the interior and stepped out.

The recording had switched to Händel. The weathered woman was still deep in meditation, oblivious both to Gabriel and to the two long streams of snot running from her nostrils. Apparently she was an adept of tumo, the art of keeping warm through inner heat and meditation. The other pilgrim, a young man largely concealed by a hooded parka, was sitting on a bench and eating breakfast out of a self-heating tray.

He saw Gabriel and his eyes widened. He dropped to his knees and slammed his forehead reverently on the marble floor.

"Morning Star!" he babbled, and banged his forehead again. Thoroughly embarrassed, Gabriel cringed. "Child of Glory!" Another bang.

"At ease," Gabriel muttered, before the man could bang his brains out. The poor fellow seemed to have few enough as it was.

Gabriel stepped over the strewn offerings—what did people think his father could do with all this stuff?—and into the dawn. Spilled rice grated on his boot soles.

The rosy sun hung over the layer of boiling cloud. Exemplary black mountain peaks, webbed with white, stood in perfect solitude above the white vapor plain. The call of a bone trumpet seemed to ring a long note in Gabriel's soaring heart.

He had, he thought, done well in choosing this place.

On pulses of snarling, half-tame gravity Gabriel flew to the Illyrian Workshop. Half a continent away, nine hundred Illyrian nautical miles, in ten minutes, counting the time it took to take off, hover, and land. The workshops themselves, yellow buildings with black photoreactive gabled mansard roofs, all set in a mild green valley, had closed for the day, but he left himself in with the Aristos Override. A few craftsmen, working early or late, seemed surprised to see him prowling the aisles. He intended to find a gift suitable for Rubens to take back to Cressida, but he ended up putting a few other items on his account as well.

Cressida's gift was another folding egg puzzle like the one he had given to Marcus, but larger, the size of a pumpkin. Feathered silver Chinese dragons cavorted in relief about its exterior. Gabriel opened the puzzle to its lotus configuration and put inside a small bronze censer. It was ornamented with more dragons, and the incense would pour in a milky cloud from their nostrils. Atop the censer was a large black opal streaked with deep Illyrian blue and swirls of dusky orange. All resonant of ancient myth, little though Cressida would notice.

The flight to the Residence outside Labdakos took six minutes. Once there he changed into his brighter morning silks, ordered breakfast, and queried his reno for Yaritomo. The young Therápōn was, not surprisingly, in the Shadow Cloister. Gabriel made his way there and found Yaritomo meditating in a half-lotus beneath the Shadow Mask.

Gabriel stepped onto the grass and took a position to one side so that he could watch Yaritomo's profile. The boy's eyes were closed and his lips moved in a soundless dialogue with himself. His hands formed Mudras of Alertness and Receptivity. There was a spot of blood on his shirt where one of his wounds had opened. Above him, the Shadow Mask smiled ambiguously in starlight.

The morning wind ruffled Gabriel's hair. Yaritomo's nostrils gave a twitch. His eyes opened, and he looked at Gabriel sidelong. He had smelled Gabriel, or sensed his body heat. A jolt of surprise crossed Yaritomo's features, and he tried to rise into an attitude of respect. Gabriel waved him down as he approached.

"I brought you something," he said.

The gift was a porcelain Workshop miniature of a rearing tiger standing on a bed of leaping flame. The cat's bright bars glowed orange against the dark sward. The clear blue light of Illyricum gleamed off bared fangs.

Gabriel had ordered it from the Workshop after Yaritomo's breakthrough.

"Thank you, Aristos." Conforming to the Third Posture of Humility, chin and eyes lowered. "I don't deserve—"

"Use it as a focus. It may help you visualize the Burning Tiger." Gabriel crouched by him. "Have you brought him out since your rite of chöd?"

"Yes." Yaritomo licked his lips. "Twice now. I've found that being here in the cloister helps."

"Yes. It would."

"I've felt someone else, though. Another." Yaritomo hesitated. "A kind of pressure in my mind."

"How have you tried to bring him out?"

"I've tried the Sutra of Captain Yuan. Posture exercises. Directed meditation. I even tried just talking to it." He shook his head. "I don't think the other is ready."

"Continue what you've been doing for another four or five days," Gabriel said. "If it doesn't manifest, simply return to your duties. Try to see what states of mind or activity bring on the intuition that the daimōn is there. And then try to duplicate those conditions deliberately."

"Yes, Aristos."

"Send me regular reports. I may be able to suggest something."

"Yes, Aristos."

"And your wounds. Are they giving you discomfort?"

"Some." He gave a little grin. "I'm trying to rise above it."

"Mental discipline by all means, but not at the expense of your health. You'll check with a doctor soon? Good." Gabriel stood. "I think you've made the necessary breakthrough. Things should start happening quickly now."

"I hope that will be the case, Aristos."

"I am promoting you to Hebdomarchōn. Your duties of course will be increased."

Yaritomo stared at him. "Sir," he said, "I don't know if I have earned—"

"If you haven't yet, you will before long. Believe me. You'll *need* daimones for the work load you'll have."

Yaritomo swallowed hard. "I'll try to live up to the trust you have placed in me, Aristos."

"You seem a bit nervous. Why don't you try calling up the Burning Tiger? He's a confident sort."

"Ah—yes. Very good."

Gabriel withdrew into the darkness. Yaritomo blinked about him for a moment, then took some breaths, focused his attention on the porcelain tiger, and began his invocation.

Gabriel queried the house reno, discovered Clancy was awake, ordered Kem-Kem to deliver breakfast to the Carnation Suite, then went there himself.

The Carnation Suite didn't have floral motifs but rather floral color, eleven different shades of red, with cream plasterwork and glowing rosewood panels. Clancy was playing the piano he'd ordered delivered to the suite. It was a Workshop artifact, mahogany inlaid with rosewood marquetry and flowering vines in mother-of-pearl, bone, and nanobuilt red coral and ivory. Perfect, Gabriel thought, for the setting.

Clancy looked up as Gabriel entered but continued her procession through a selection of Mozart's ländler. Gabriel approached and stepped behind her. As her fine-boned fingers continued their dance on the keyboard, Gabriel removed her hairpins and slowly sifted her hair through his fingers. He began to braid her hair with ribbons he'd picked up in the Workshop, ribbons holding tiny bells. They were clustered in pale ceramic flower displays, a bell on the end of each stamen. Their sound was clear and distinct, multitoned and right on pitch . . . Each turn of Clancy's head would sound a miniature carillon.

Clancy began to braid the ländler together in the same way that Gabriel was braiding her hair, mixing the statement of one motif with the resolution of another, then progressing to something else, all advancing in stately three-quarter time. Gabriel and Clancy finished at more or less the same time. Chimes rang as Clancy lifted her head to look at him.

"This piano is lovely," she said. "The tone is as fine as the finish. Thank you for sending it."

"You said you lacked practice."

"I said I lacked *time* to practice."

"The piano is yours anyway."

"Mine? Truly?" She put a hand to her throat. "I can't match these gifts, Disturber."

"Not unless you become an Ariste."

She laughed. "It's a plot, then. To get me working toward my exams again."

"Yes."

She narrowed her eyes. "I never know quite when you're being serious."

"Déjà vu." He smiled. "That's what I said to my mother just yesterday."

"Will you join me on the bench? I'll get a stiff neck otherwise."

Silk rustled as he seated himself. "You should try the exams again, you know," he said. "You were in the top twenty percent last time. And there's always need for more Aristoi."

Clancy looked down at her hands, placed fingers as if for

a minor seventh, then let them hover. "You were at Standing Wave last night."

"Yes."

She frowned, looked at her hands again, then crossed them on her chest. Bells tinkled in the key of B flat major.

"I'm still not certain how this is supposed to work," she said.

"It works however we want it to work."

She looked at him sidelong. "I suppose I'm not entirely certain what I want. Two days ago, I thought I knew."

"We have world enough and time."

"Coyness would not seem to be our problem." She took a breath, held out her hands again, laid them soundlessly on the keyboard. "All right," she said. "If I'm to be a part of things here, I want to know what's happening."

"Certainly."

"What was it that threw you off? Was it this Rubens person? That confrontational speech Asterion gave at Graduation? *Something* must have produced that impulse to run off to Marcus. What happened?"

Gabriel found himself more pleased by this burst of perception than he was disconcerted by its content. "It's sort of complicated," he said. "I'm not sure what to make of it myself."

"Don't evade."

"I wasn't evading. I was just pointing out that things are . . . ambiguous."

He explained the hand-carried message, the messenger's bafflement at the suddenness of his mission, then Cressida's revelation.

"Sounds like Cressida's gaga," Clancy said.

"I hope so."

"If she is, what then?"

"There hasn't been a mad Aristos in centuries. Not since the Crackling Prince."

"Sebastian and Virtue's Icon aren't mad?"

"They're . . ." He searched for words. "They're very

eccentric, and their domains have become eccentric places. But no, they're not mad. One doesn't see the kind of appalling civil disorder that the Crackling Prince precipitated. Let alone his plan to use gravity generators to refigure planetary terrain with the population still living on it and supposed to be grateful for the change."

"Not yet, one doesn't."

"Getting back to Cressida."

Clancy nodded; bells chimed briefly.

"An Ariste can only be removed by a unanimous vote of the other Aristoi. We all have to agree."

"It's never happened, has it?"

"The Crackling Prince abdicated, but he probably would have been deposed ere long in any case. A commission had already been formed at Persepolis to look into his behavior." He frowned, reached out to caress ivory keys. "I don't believe Cressida is mad, however. I wish I could believe it, but I don't."

Her eyes held his. "And if you're right?"

He considered the prospects, then shivered. "I'll cross that lengthy and astonishingly razor-edged bridge when I come to it. My turn to play."

His hands moved into a familiar pattern, the duet between Lulu and Louise from his unfinished opera *Louise Brooks as Lulu*—his "long-unfinished" opera, as he now thought of it.

The duet had been intended as a cynical conversation pointing inexorably to a kind of horrible desolation of spirit. The two women—one fictional, appearing in spirit form, the other a real actress assigned to play the first—would compare biographies, share the opinions of the men who used them and their lives that lunged so frantically out of control. The words were sardonic and witty—both women insisted they really didn't care what happened to them—but building behind the lyrics was a motif that suggested the depths of their own tragedy, their horrible isolation, and their ultimate fate, one dying at the hands of a maniac, the other fading over decades through gin and self-neglect . . .

The opera was perhaps half complete, and the duet was the last piece that Gabriel had completed to his own satisfaction. Something in him quailed from completing it.

As he played he called through the oneirochronon for the orchestration: from the room's hidden speakers, strings and stabbing brass tarted up the duet's nasty little conclusion.

He lifted his hands from the keys, looked at Clancy over his shoulder.

"That was sarcastic," she said. "Is it because I asked uncomfortable questions?"

"D flat minor dominant," he said, "with an unresolved seventh superimposed on the A flat minor. That's why it sounds so snotty." He rose from the bench and kissed her. "But it wasn't directed toward you. It's part of something unfinished."

"And what is that, Disturber?"

He told her. "No wonder it's not finished," she said. "That's the most complex operatic structure I ever heard of. Each of the people in the cast is being led to their doom by a spirit of the 'real' characters they're imitating?"

"The phantoms provide an annotation on their reality— or unreality in this case. The same way our daimones provide an annotation for *us*."

"I understand the metaphor, Gabriel."

"It's an annotative age we live in. What's the Hyperlogos but an annotation on all the last few thousand years? Well." He shrugged. "I didn't want merely to recapitulate Berg."

"He's the only one you're *not* recapitulating. Except perhaps in terms of not finishing the work."

"The complexity isn't a problem."

"What is?"

FLASH. Repeat FLASH. Priority one signal follows.

Gabriel held up a hand. A tachline *FLASH* was the highest possible priority signal—one urgent enough to interrupt even Aristoi at their duties. During his fifty-odd years as an

Aristos, Gabriel had received only one such message. Thirty-two years before.

FLASH. **Repeat** *FLASH.* **Mataglap alert—possible casualties.**

A cold river poured down Gabriel's spine. He could feel himself turn pale. The worst—absolutely the worst—had happened somewhere. As it had last happened thirty-two years ago.

Clancy looked at him with wide, concerned eyes.

FLASH. **Repeat** *FLASH.* **Mataglap alert station *Sanjay*, in orbit above planet Painter, domain of Cressida Ariste. Casualties are probable.**

Gabriel was faintly surprised to find that he could still form words.

"No," he said. "I was right. Cressida isn't mad."

Abstractly he watched Clancy put a hand to her throat. "Everything she said is true," Gabriel said.

He wondered what it was he was feeling. Then it came to him: something new.

He had never felt the universe shatter before.

Chapter 6

SCHIGOLCH: 'In Xanadu did Kubla Khan'—
    Oh what the hell—the man is
    gone

P an Wengong took command of the response to the
    FLASH alert, but had to cope with an oneirochronic
    audience of suspenseful, watching Aristoi, ever ready to
offer helpful advice. Fortunately for the Eldest Brother's
peace, response to a nano attack was fairly standardized and
comments were few. Ever since Earth[1] had disappeared beneath the glistening, bubbling black-caviar wave of Indonesian
"mataglap nano," responses had been carefully worked out,
and pre-positioned equipment waited at or near every human
settlement.

At least, Gabriel thought, when *They* decided to kill
Cressida, they hadn't unleashed the stuff on a planet.

It had, he thought, to be a *They.* Saigo was light-centuries
away: he must have had an accomplice near Painter.

Perhaps not, offered Horus. **This could have been set up
many years ago, and operated remotely and in realtime
through a tachline link.**

Somehow Gabriel did not find this thought encouraging.

There could be pre-positioned attack nano on *every* planet, Horus went on. **Just in case the Gaal secret got out.**

You sound like Mataglap, Gabriel said. **I think nano is too dangerous to pre-position it everywhere.**

Not necessarily. One need not pre-position the mataglap itself, but rather nano designed to *create* the mataglap.

Gabriel could do little but hope this was not the case. Things were looking dire enough. He told Horus to commence implementation of the plan that he, Horus, had developed earlier.

Meanwhile, under Pan's command, cameras and sensors rocketed from neighboring orbital habitats and took positions around *Sanjay*. One by one their input was added to the oneirochronic picture of what was taking place.

Sanjay was a hollowed-out asteroid, an irregular potato shape set in orbit by a strap-on gravity generator. Another chill ran through Gabriel as he saw that it was covered with what looked like dirty-white foam. Slow-motion bubbles rose to the surface, burst, left brief hollows soon filled by more glittering nano. Occasionally there was a scintillation, shining six-sided reflective patterns that formed for only a second in sunlight, like a diffraction halo that patterned around a dust speck sitting on a camera lens.

IR scanners showed that the surface was hot. The nano was still active, still working away at something.

They will do this to me, Gabriel thought.

Perhaps there were still survivors. If the nano had started its work from the outside of the station, there might still be livable areas inside into which the personnel could retreat.

The Eldest Brother deployed a solar shield, several kilometers wide, between *Sanjay* and the sun, just in case the nano was absorbing energy from photons. IR readings showed the surface temperature decreased almost immediately.

Pan had slowed the stuff down.

Next came the hunter-killer artiphage, one of several varieties of anti-nano designed to tear apart mataglap and reduce it to inert and harmless matter. It was possible this particular artiphage wouldn't work and another variety would have to be tried, but Gabriel thought not. The little hexagonal gleams that the mataglap had been giving off were indicative of a nano type identical or related to that which had destroyed Earth[1]. That was a clue as to which kind of artiphage to deploy.

Small solid-fuel rockets boosted into view and splashed down into the white boil. Gabriel held his breath for a moment, watching spectrographic readings. Hydrogen lines wavered, then grew stronger. He sensed a cheer welling through the oneirochronon. The artiphages were turning the nano into free hydrogen.

More rockets splashed down. The nano roiled and frothed. Dark streaks spread across it, then widened. Frenetic bubbles of hydrogen burst to the surface. A third wave of artiphages landed in the stew and the dirty-white nano began to break up.

The danger wasn't quite over. Some of the mataglap might, during the bubbling and splashing, have broken off the main body and gone sailing along the solar wind. Its photoreactive properties could keep it active and if it encountered something, a ship or satellite or asteroid or moon, it could run mad just as it had done on *Sanjay*. The entire Painter system would have to remain on a high state of alert for years.

Gabriel listened as Pan Wengong ordered scans of all satellites, habitats, and ships. He also ordered stocks of artiphage to be sent to all distant habitats.

After the nano had all been destroyed there was precious little left of the asteroid, a little stone spine, elongated and fragile, like a squab bone partly eaten by acid.

No survivors. There were fourteen people known to have been on the station, including Cressida Ariste.

Cousins, Pan Wengong broadcast to all Aristoi, **there will be a memorial at sixteen hundred hours Persepolis time, followed by a discussion of the disposition of our late cousin's domaine.**

Had she living relatives? someone asked.

Two children and a sister. Two former consorts. Pan provided names and oneirochronic addresses, then posted the names of the other casualties and their survivors as well.

Gabriel thought of the dragon egg he'd purchased for Cressida, destined never to be delivered. He should contact Rubens.

He left Horus in the oneirochronon to monitor any further business and returned his attention to the Carnation Suite.

He and Clancy looked at each other. He took her hand.

"I'm going aboard *Pyrrho* and leaving the system," he said. "Within the week. That's about the earliest anyone can get any sabotage nano into this system, assuming that Zhenling Ariste, my nearest neighbor, is a conspirator—and that's a very large assumption that I'm willing to make only because I can't absolutely rule her out."

"What about the election on Brightkinde? You're scheduled to attend during the transfer ceremonies."

"I'll have to use the oneirochronon."

Clancy bit her lip, thought for a long moment. "What do you want me to do?" she asked.

"I would be happy to have you with me," he said.

She looked down at her lap.

"But you must decide what is best for you," he added. He squeezed her hand. "There is a nano lab aboard *Pyrrho*, if that helps. Your project to work on packages for rare illnesses can be advanced there, if you can bear to disconnect from your present life entirely."

Her eyelid flickered. "I'm in danger here?"

Gabriel hesitated. "Probably not. Not if you don't behave in a way that will make them suspicious."

She gazed at him gravely. "You seem to be living up to your name, Disturber."

"I didn't mean to. Not this time."

"Yes, very well. I will come."

Gabriel took her other hand and kissed her. Little bells rang their tiny changes. "Thank you, Blushing Rose."

"Where do we run to?"

"The Gaal Sphere."

Her eyes flickered. "I thought we'd fly to someplace *safe*."

"They won't expect us there. And by the time *Pyrrho* arrives, I'll be ready to handle whatever awaits us." He laughed. "It's only Saigo, after all. A gloomy, saturnine gent, unused to dealing with people. I expect we'll have fun."

She bit her lip, kissed him again. He put his arms around her. Tiny bells chimed.

Floating through his senses came a phantom of receding tide, fading sun, distant gulls.

All he knew about Cressida, really, was that she was attached to that specter of her childhood.

That and the fact that, for the crime of contacting him, someone had decided to kill her.

Gabriel contacted Pan Wengong and told him about the weathered log house by the shore. The Eldest Brother used his Aristos Override to locate the oneirochronic environment in Cressida's personal records and brought the Aristoi to the log house for the memorial.

The Aristoi stood on tide-sodden sand while Pristine Way, a former student and friend, spoke a eulogy. White geese flocked overhead, hundreds of them with roaring wings, bright silver against the sky, streaming shadow on the ground. A pillar of smoke rose tall from the stone chimney into the windless air, a memorial.

"*A life devoted to knowledge,*" said the eulogy, "*to the advancement of humanity.*"

The fate of Cressida's domaine had already been decided. She had not been ambitious in terms of domaine, preferring to concentrate on scientific pursuits, and her territory consisted of only three planetary systems. One system would be absorbed by each of three neighbors. A single system would not mean a huge increase in their burdens, and it would spare one of the newly made Aristoi from having to commit himself to taking over a domaine smaller than his aspirations.

"A tragic accident. A moment of carelessness in a nano lab, perhaps on the part of an assistant."

It had been, Gabriel's reno informed him, thirty-two years since an Ariste had died in a nano accident. In the earlies it had been very common, though as the technology developed the accidents settled down to every twenty years or thereabouts. The current safety record was, on the whole, exemplary.

Gabriel forebore from reminding his reno that this had not been an accident.

"Let our Sister's work be carried forward. She has shown others the way."

After Pristine Way came to a close, Pan Wengong made a brief speech about the dangers of nano. Cressida was known as a careful and meticulous researcher, he said, yet even she in a moment of carelessness had made a simple and obvious mistake, or allowed one of her assistants to make one. A mistake that she should have recognized, because the type of mataglap that had killed her was nothing new.

What did she die from? Gabriel found himself wondering. What does it feel like to have something eat you atom by atom? Does it feel like anything at all?

His mood darkened. Blood loss, he decided. She died of blood loss when the mataglap ate a major artery. Or she smothered when a wave of it overcame her. Or died of asphyxia when the mataglap depressurized the station. Or the heat killed her before the nano even got to her—toward the end, when the little micromachines had really got going, *Sanjay*'s surface had been hot enough to boil lead.

There is ample documentation from the Earth[1] catastrophe, Horus reported helpfully. **Eight point four billion died, many of them while transmitting pictures to the satellites above.**

Gabriel hadn't needed reminding.

He told Horus to shut up.

*   *   *

The pattern of Graduation continued—the Persepolis meetings were too important to postpone. Gabriel would have attracted too much attention had he absented himself. He drifted through them, wondering again how much of it was compromised, how much of it really mattered.

The reception of Olympia Ariste was not her usual success. Presumably she didn't mind—she'd died (Breakdown) over four hundred years before. But some of her programs still ran in the Hyperlogos files, and the tradition was that one of them threw a soirée on the evening following Graduation. Each party took place in a different oneirochronic locale; each had different music and entertainment and effects. Olympia must have spent tens of thousands of hours designing new environments, or perhaps an equal amount of time creating a program to do it for her.

There was no sign that she would run out of new scenarios anytime soon. Or that her (possibly electronic) imagination was in any way flagging.

This year's event took place inside a giant hypersphere packed with complex interwoven corridors, large rooms with Escherian stairways on which skiagenoi could walk either downside-right or leftside-up, doors that would take you not to the place next door (Euclidianly speaking) but someplace else entirely.

And the place kept changing. The same door could take you to any number of places, depending on when you walked through it, and rooms kept shifting shape, though never when anyone was looking.

If it hadn't been for a death in the family, everyone would have enjoyed themselves immensely.

Gabriel, carrying a fan, drifted through the place, noting its ingenuity but otherwise distracted by cerebrations of mortality. Horus was compiling lists of objects necessary for the expedition to the Gaal Sphere, and several of his other daimones were engaged in a lengthy appreciation of Olympia's new environment. Neither occupied his attention much.

He walked through a gateway, was abruptly somewhere other than where he intended, and saw Sebastian and Virtue's Icon too late to avoid them.

The two fanatics got along, though their respective philosophies were irreconcilable. Perhaps what they found in common was their utter lack of humor.

Sebastian was again and always in the form of a sphere, one of the Ideal Forms which he had conjured from his Platonic paragon. Although the sphere was eternal, its composition and color were not: tonight it was a reflective silver, which mirrored and distorted the rumpled grey uniform of Virtue's Icon.

"I am more interested in channeling Astoreth's new notions than denouncing them," Sebastian said. "The restless energy she represents should be drawn into a constructive search for the Ideal. Her critique is in essence correct: her solutions are not."

"Her critique," said Virtue's Icon, "is that of a poetasting exhibitionist. She wishes to restructure all humanity to serve her vanity."

"Agreed." Colors vibrated over the sphere, little glowing spectra of approval.

(Spring Plum could not resist pointing out that Sebastian and Virtue's Icon, between the two of them, had done more restructuring of society than the rest of the Aristoi put together; if that wasn't vanity, she demanded, what was?)

Gabriel, concealing amusement, attempted to slip past. "Your pardon, Aristoi," he said.

"I beg your opinion, Aristos," Sebastian said.

(Gabriel told his reno to have the relevant Platonic texts at hand.)

He didn't want—especially now, when he had so much else to think about—to engage himself with these characters. But politeness dictated courtesy.

At least the Welcome Rain would enjoy this.

Gabriel inclined himself toward the floating sphere. "I

have no desire for any massive reconstruction," he said. "The universe suits me well enough as it is."

"What have you done to serve the Demos?" Virtue's Icon demanded.

"For the most part I let the Demos serve themselves. And of course have provided them the biosystems in which they do it."

"It is the duty of the Aristoi to lead, not to merely let things slide along. I spend an average of eighteen hours per day working for the benefit of those who live in my domaine, and I demand those in my service follow my example."

Micromanaging private lives, muttered Cyrus. From the Welcome Rain, however, came the distinct thought that managing other people was not such a bad thing.

"Ah," Gabriel said. (Reno fed him the latest statistics.) "My own bureaucrats spend almost two hours per day at their tasks, although I tend to load my Therápontes rather more heavily."

The Icon's bladelike face brandished itself in Gabriel's direction. "How much of that time is spent teaching the Demos to avoid error? To renounce materialism, walk in the paths of moderation, and serve one another?"

"I thought your system was *based* on materialism?" Gabriel said, and went on to correctly translate (undoing centuries of error) from the original German: " 'From each according to his abilities, to each according to his labor.' And if you work eighteen hours per day, surely by your own creed you deserve a few gardens and palaces."

"It is *false* materialism we renounce. Love of luxury, display, self . . ." She eyed Gabriel in his ankle-length brocade robes, fan, and mandarin hat with its peacock feather.

Gabriel opened his black lacquer fan, displaying the gold arabesques on its surface. "My garb advertises the Illyricum Workshop," he said. "Which advances, if you like, the dignity of hand labor."

"Labor at the behest of luxury is labor without true dignity."

Sebastian's sphere gave a gentle bounce to attract attention. "It would seem," he offered, "that you both concentrate on what in the *Republic* the Divine Platōn called the appetitive element of society—you, Icon, on basic material needs such as sustenance and shelter; and you, Gabriel, on the aesthetics of pleasure. But this concerns itself entirely with sensible appearances, as opposed to indiscernible genuine Being. Where is your concept of society's other goals—the accumulation of wisdom, the metaphysic of the Ideal?"

Sebastian's entire domaine had been ordered along Platonic metaphysical lines. Anyone wishing to advance in Sebastian's system had, at the drop of a hat, to be ready to debate the Theory of Forms as it related to government, technology, education, or the price of beans. Ideal forms, relationships, and harmonies had been relentlessly reduced, catalogued, and subjected to analysis. Endless rhapsodies had been devoted to the Soul and the Good. Temples had been built in ideal geometrical shapes in which proponents of one point of view debated at length with their philosophical adversaries. The Best—the *aristos*—was sought on every hand; the not-Best avoided.

Gabriel disliked Sebastian's style less because of his search for truth than because it had generated a society of fatuous, windy bores.

"Genuine being," said Virtue's Icon flatly, "is nothing *but* the accumulation of sensible appearances. Nothing else can be proven to exist."

"I would disagree," Gabriel said.

The tactics of debating Sebastian, Gabriel had found, were different from those used against the Icon. With the Icon you wanted to offend her into leaving and not bothering you again; with Sebastian, you quoted his own holy writ back at him.

"In *Gorgias* and elsewhere," he said (reno providing him with appropriate texts), "Platōn would seem to argue, through the persona of Sokrates, for an absolute liberty of conscience, the which being necessary for a true discernment of truth and morality—this particularly in opposition to Kallikles, whose theories of the will to power would seem to be echoed by our worthy Icon. Am I correct?"

"Of course," Sebastian said.

Gabriel spoke rapidly while Virtue's Icon was still conferring with her daimones about the *Gorgias,* and before she could raise the objection that Kallikles was a reactionary, Nietzschean scoundrel.

"Following Sokrates, then," he said, "I have ordered my domaine. Each member of the Demos is free to develop his conscience and talents as he wills, save only in the use of those technologies which we all agree are dangerous to the body of humanity."

"You have abandoned your responsibility to lead them to Virtue," said the Icon.

"The Icon and I agree," Sebastian said. "The duty of the statesman is to lead his people toward a revelation of Truth. The statesmen—the Aristoi—direct the executive—our Therápontes—in an effort to bring enlightenment to the Demos. Education is the most important function of the state, as demonstrated in the *Republic.*"

"In the *Republic,*" Gabriel said, "Sokrates is made to confess that he knows no absolute method of proving postulates from an ultimate self-evident principle—why then lead the Demos toward an ideal which cannot be shown to be true?"

(Got him there, the Welcome Rain chortled.)

"The transcendent Ideal cannot be comprehended fully," Sebastian said weakly, "but it may be apprehended by those trained in the paths of wisdom."

"But can such an apprehension be transmitted through dogma? Or should the conscience be free to find its own method of apprehending the Ideal?"

"*I* am the conscience of my domaine," Virtue's Icon said. "I and no other. It is my *duty* to impose virtue on the population."

"Platōn warns of the dangers of autocracy in the *Laws*," Gabriel said.

"Yes." The sphere rippled with color. "He desired a balance between freedom, *eleutheria*, and *monarchia*, authority."

"Platōn made many useful suggestions regarding government and property," said Virtue's Icon, "but his metaphysics are preposterous, and fortunately his system can now be considered obsolete."

"The Ideal is never obsolete!" Sebastian cried. His sphere flushed an angry blue.

Gabriel, having maneuvered the two tedious cranks into debating each other once again, offered a Posture of Respect and withdrew, fanning himself as he went. An oneirochronic gate took him to a chamber in which people were set at all angles to one another on looping paths. Some of them were dancing to cheerful music—one of Evan's *Three Syncopated Dances*.

Something struck him as being familiar about the pattern of the room, and he stopped to think about it for a moment.

A distant radiance, glowing somewhere in his mind, resolved itself into Psyche. The answer rolled from her sunlit spirit and his heart leaped. Psyche withdrew from his conscious mind.

He looked about for someone to share the insight with.

"Care to dance, Aristos?"

Gabriel glanced up and saw Zhenling planted on a pathway above his head. She was wearing a blue-green tartan skirt and a glengarry bonnet, with blue-and-white dicing and the little tails down her neck.

"Does the shape of this room remind you of something?" He gestured with his fan.

Zhenling gave it her attention. "Something is familiar about it," she said. "I can't think what."

"It's the Involved Ideographic glyph for *dance*," Gabriel said. "The room is shaped like a three-dimensional representation of the glyph for movement, and the paths are arranged in the patterns for *joyful, rhythm, music,* and—I'm not certain what that wall projection is supposed to be."

"It's an imperative mark, but you have to look at it from my perspective, not yours."

"Ah."

"Very astute of you, Aristos." She gazed at the room with her tilted eyes, then nodded. "Our environment is commanding us to behave in certain ways."

He looked up at her. "Do you still want to dance?"

"No. It's not as much fun when you're ordered onto the floor by someone who's been dead for centuries."

"Perhaps, in view of the fact that we've all been to a funeral, it's more appropriate than not."

"No. The mood's spoiled." She glanced over the room. "Let's discover what other commands we're being given."

Gabriel made an acquiescent gesture with his fan, then took in the topography of the room once more. "I'm not certain how we'll be able to find one another," he said. "There doesn't seem to be a path from where I am to where you are."

"Perhaps if I jump *very high* . . ."

"Let's set out in quest of one another."

"Very well. An appropriate metaphor," smiling catlike, "at least from your perspective." She turned, bowed, stepped through a doorway.

The door behind Gabriel led to where Sebastian and Virtue's Icon lay in wait for unwary travelers. Calling that room to mind, Gabriel recalled glyphs for *debate, controvert,* and *contend* worked into its architecture.

Gabriel went along a pathway marked by a wine-red carpet. Woven into the carpet, in almost-invisible silver threads, were glyphs for *move, leap,* and *caper.* He chose a door and passed through it.

The entrance hall was *welcome,* the lounge *comfort* and *relaxation,* and the bar *cheer, happiness,* and *indiscretion.* Gabriel found Zhenling in a room resembling a chapel, a room dark and high and solemn, where the walls seemed made of bricks that, with a subtle difference of shade, commanded *reflection* and *thought*. Tatamis were embroidered with the glyph for *invocation*. There was the muted scent of incense and, depending on where one stood in the room, either the faint sound of voices chanting sutras or the solemn, distant sigh of an organ.

Gabriel kissed Zhenling in greeting and told her of his discoveries. The banqueting room, she told him, was *savor*, the sensorium *indulgence*, the game room *play* and *luck*, and another drawing room *joke*, *laugh*, and *make merry*.

"No one there," she said. "I don't think many are in the mood."

"I'm not, either," Gabriel said. "Though I'd like to visit this place again when I'm in better spirits."

"You could call it up out of the Hyperlogos and run it yourself."

"I hope Olympia's program isn't offended by our lack of good cheer."

"Do you suppose she compensates for current events?"

"Perhaps I'll look at the program and see."

"Don't spoil the surprise by finding out what comes next."

"Of course I won't." He looked behind him. "Shall we return to the festivities?"

"I'm not feeling very festive." She turned to him. "There is an opera of yours," she said, "that captures my mood precisely."

"*Mufarse*."

She's familiar with your works, Augenblick noted. **A good sign.**

"And yet when I ask my reno to give me a definition of the word," she said, "I get nothing but—" Her eyes glazed in feigned boredom as she echoed her reno's tedious voice. " 'A quality of melancholy peculiar to the Argentine [Earth[1]/South American] people, particularly those of the Seventh [Blue]

Cultural Epoch [Late 19th-Early 20th Century C.E.].' I can follow references through the Hyperlogos but they all seem to lead to popular songs or bad novels."

"It's one of those compelling, untranslatable words that forces one to use them. I think of Rilke, who had to start writing in French toward the end of his life because he could find no German equivalent for the French *absence.*"

"I don't know what *mufarse* means, but I feel it." Her eyes lifted to his. "Am I a Blue Epoch Argentinian in my soul, Aristos?"

"Possibly. Though on the whole I think you're rather more interesting."

"What was it that made them melancholy? Your opera was about a distant settlement cut off after the Earth[1] disaster, but the Blue Epoch was well before that, and from my understanding of Argentinian history there was no similar calamity."

"The disaster was more of a psychic than physical nature. If you're interested, I think the nuances of *mufarse* are best expressed through the dance I reintroduced in that opera."

"The tango. My reno can give me the steps."

"Would you dance it with me, then? If I risk inflicting tedium via my lecture on *mufarse*, I may at least distract you from boredom through the pleasures of the dance."

Zhenling glanced up at the high, arching ceiling, the muted lighting. "In here? Not that the atmosphere is inap-

WELCOME RAIN: Get her dancing. I think that's the best bet. This melancholy can be used.

GABRIEL: Augenblick— if you can read anything at all . . . ?

AUGENBLICK: Nothing but what she wants us to read, Aristos. She is firmly in control of her skiagénos.

GABRIEL: Her pose remains flirtatious.

AUGENBLICK: Then that is what she wants us to perceive.

MATAGLAP: Why? Why now?

GABRIEL: Load the Autumn Pavilion skiagénos.

propriate to melancholy, but—"

"Allow me to create a more suitable environment."

Gabriel waved his fan and an arched wooden cathedral door appeared in the smooth white wall. Zhenling walked toward it and reached for the door handle. Gabriel made swift alterations in the program as he followed her. She opened the door and stepped into the oneirochronic simulation of the Autumn Pavilion's ballroom. Quite suddenly she was in a blue ball gown, ruffled out along the bottom, Latin-style. Her brows were long and winged; her lips red coral; her hair piled elaborately. Her shoulders and arms glowed dusky gold in candlelight.

Following close behind, Gabriel stepped through the door himself, the shift in oneirochronic perspective, from the Persepolis program to that of the Residence, accomplishing also a change of costume. He was now in extravagant South American Blue Era fashion: tight trousers with silver coins sewn up

Create a Class One portal from the wall on my right to the north wall of the ballroom. Use the gothic door from the Rustic Chapel in the Vissarion Residence.

RENO: < linking through Residence Reno > < linking through Persepolis Master Program > Done, Aristos.

GABRIEL: Door handle: temp ten C. Texture: hammered iron.

RENO: Done, Aristos.

GABRIEL: The ballroom will be lit by one thousand candles. Adjust my costume to Iago's from the second act of *Mufarse*. Put the Latin orchestra from the third act into the band shell. Trigger "Señor Barrasa's Tango."

RENO: Done, Aristos.

MATAGLAP: Let me repeat my earlier question. Why? Why is she being so obliging? She never offered encouragement before.

WELCOME RAIN: The time is right for her. Bonham failed his exams again: he'll never be her equal. And there's been a death among the Aristoi—perhaps she's feeling vulnerable.

MATAGLAP: Merde.

the sides, high-heeled boots, ruffled shirt, high-waisted clawhammer jacket.

The decor was rather severe, with white walls and black parquet floor of equatorial mahogany from Strangeways, though the severity was modified by glowing candlelight. Painted muses, washes of grey, danced on the walls next to trompe l'oeil columns and capitals. The concave band shell at one end was ornamented with diamond-shaped silver mirrors.

Above the main entrance hung Cyrus's self-portrait, black and white like everything else—the face was youthful, the brows a bit skeptical, the eyes a little cruel. The young aesthete, rigorous in his critique of the world as he found it.

An orchestra played a slow tango from the band shell. Gabriel took Zhenling's hand.

She's a part of it—she may have killed Cressida herself. WELCOME RAIN: Preposterous! Do you really think she's naive enough to actually try to seduce us to her cause? Does she think the blandishments of love will turn us simpleminded? Make us give away our plans, our secrets?

CYRUS: It's an interesting point of view, aesthetically speaking. Who's seducing whom? Who's trying to get to the bottom of whose hidden knowledge?

GABRIEL: Children—remember *mufarse*. Remember what's behind it. And let us dance.

WELCOME RAIN: Absolutely! Let's do this right!

GABRIEL: Temperature of hands: 38.5 C. Texture: dry.

WELCOME RAIN: Good. Let's see if we can warm her up.

"The fascination of the tango," he said, "at least the earlier, Argentine version, before the French got hold of it and made everyone dance like robots, is that it combines an extreme sensuality with an extreme emotional distance."

"A rose in my teeth wouldn't be appropriate, then?"

"Behind your ear, perhaps."

One appeared—blue in color, matching her gown, matching the Seventh Cultural Epoch. Its fragrance wafted gently to Gabriel's nostrils, a nice piece of programmatic detail.

(Spring Plum offered an appreciation of her blue gown and blue eye shadow against her pale skin.)

Gabriel took her in his arms, began a step. She followed with cool precision. "Blue Epoch Argentina was a masculine frontier culture," he said. "In some places men outnumbered the women five or six to one. This relative rarity gave the women enormous power, which they didn't hesitate to use."

"Good for them," said Zhenling. Beneath Gabriel's hand he felt her spine stiffen in defiance. Augenblick rejoiced at what was, just possibly, his first real piece of kinesic data.

"You're getting the idea," he said. "*Medialuna* here." He swept his outside foot into a half-moon, then back.

"Argentina was also an immigrant nation," he went on. "The men were isolated not only from women, but from their native cultures. The result was a terrible loneliness, and a terrible melancholy."

"*Mufarse.*"

"*El ocho.*"

He dropped her arms, turned his back to her, and stepped off into the solo eight-pattern, repeating it four times. Zhenling's shoes clicked lightly as she mirrored his movement. (Cyrus swept into Gabriel's feet, maintaining the pattern intact while Gabriel spoke on.) "The old social order had women subordinate, and that was turned around," he said. "Women picked, chose, and discarded—or were perceived as picking, choosing, and discarding—their partners based on standards of momentary advantage. The discarded men consoled themselves with prostitutes, who offered solace but were even more mercenary, stealing whatever they could. And so the tango originated in brothels, danced between people who were desperately lonely but who couldn't trust each other, whose most earnest desire was for intimacy and trust but who dared not offer either."

Gabriel finished *el ocho* and took her in his arms again. (Cyrus admired the smooth curve of her nape.) She looked up at him with perfect coolness. (**Don't trust her,** Mataglap said, so absolutely on cue that Gabriel had to restrain himself from smiling.)

"Tension," he said, beginning a grapevine step, "longing, melancholy, loneliness."

"Manipulation. Secrets. Masks."

"*El corte.*" He swayed her forward, then back, his stance so deep that he brought her, facing him, almost into his lap.

"It's a dance for spies," she said, her eyes near his. "And for people with secrets."

He raised her again and backed her along the dark mahogany dance floor. Their gazes were directed over one another's right shoulders.

"Secrets so desperate," he said, "that only our bodies are allowed to speak them."

"*Our?* I find this shift into the first person plural a bit alarming."

"A tiny death with gross wings," Gabriel said, improvising off Neruda, "entered into each like a short blade, and siege was laid by bread or by knife . . ."

"*Asediado?*" He swept her into *el corte* again. Her eyes cut to his. "You're beginning to frighten me."

Kinesics confirm. The Welcome Rain broadcast pleasure at Augenblick's reading.

It's the skiagénos that's frightened, Spring Plum reminded. **Whether it mirrors her genuine reaction remains to be seen.**

Gabriel raised Zhenling and began backing carefully, drawing her after him, toward the center of an imaginary circle, then moved once more through *el corte.* "Imagine what it must have been like after the death of Earth[1]," he said. "Imagine the isolation, the desolation, the terror—much greater than that suffered by those poor immigrant Argentines, whose old world still existed, even if they were no longer a part of it. And of course our more remote settlements were dependent for survival on the very nanotech that had betrayed humanity."

The dance passed through *mediacorte* to *cruzado*. Gabriel put hands on hips and scissored his steps as he backed away. Leading with her hips, Zhenling stalked in pantherlike pursuit.

"And in your opera," she said, "the men in the settlement outnumbered the women greatly. Which never happened in any of the real habitats, by the way—I checked."

"Dramatic license."

"And everyone died."

"That *did* happen, in a few places."

"I think it's your best work."

He looked at her with mild surprise. "I was very young."

"I find the subsequent work too mannered."

He took her in his arms, spun her, began a scorpion step. "It's a mannered age," he said.

"A mannered age with no secrets."

"Supposedly."

"You keep hinting around something, but I don't know what it is."

Gabriel took her in his arms, backed her away. "Perhaps I hope to fascinate you."

"Perhaps you're succeeding."

Point to us. The Welcome Rain, smugly.

"Ah." Gabriel allowed his skiagénos a small, cold smile. "That brings us back to certain questions related to *mufarse*. Are you someone I can trust, or are you not?"

Mediacorte, heels flashing.

"Why would I not be?" she said.

"You would best know, Ariste Zhenling."

Gabriel, pleased with the conversation returning so neatly to its point of origin, instructed Cyrus to bring the music to a conclusion at the end of the next phrase.

They swept through a final spin, then came to a poised halt as the orchestra brought the piece to a finish. Zhenling gave him a careful look.

"You've succeeded in distracting me from sorrow," she said. "Thank you."

She kissed him, violet petals brushing his lips. Phantom fingers swept his lower spine: a pleasant oneirochronic effect. He sent her a gossamer sensation in reply, silken strands drawn along her neck. A thousand candles fluttered at the touch of his mind.

She stepped back, regarded him. "We will be missed."

"The last person to step into a private space with me died badly."

Her winged brows lifted. "Do you perceive a connection?"

"Do you?"

A thought struck him, chill in his heart: had he endangered her with his hints?

He'd have to closet himself away with a number of Aristoi, he thought. Make Zhenling one of many.

She hesitated, began a walk toward the door, then turned to glance over her bared, golden shoulder. " 'Shadow patterning shadow, dead leaves scattered on ground,' " she said, quoting Cortes, " 'the maze of nature, reflected trembling in a pond.' "

Gabriel bowed in silence, then watched her leave, her azure silhouette framed in the doorway for a moment before she stepped through to another electronic reality.

He had reason, he thought, to be pleased with himself.

Chapter 7

COUNTESS: Will you dance with me?

LULU: At my wedding? In front of all these people?
     Of course!

Under Horus's coaxing, atoms moved. Electrons slotted precisely into place.

Forming a new machine. A new, purposeful machine . . .

The newly graduated Aristoi, nine of them, stood on the crest of the Kuh-e-Rahmat. All were in the traditional Iron Horse posture—bent-kneed, slightly pigeon-toed, thighs at strain—all as described millennia before in the *BaDuanJin* by Yuan Fei of the Sang Dynasty.

Above the Aristoi was another Yuan—the golden image of the First Aristos, commanding the world of Persepolis from atop its golden plinth. Surrounding was the tall cypress grove, the sigh and rustle of wind, the gentle waving of boughs.

Gabriel's skiagénos was leading the Aristoi in exercises.

His students, rooted as the cypress, were following instructions and trying to breathe through their heels.

* * *

"I can offer you employment," Gabriel said, speaking with real breath through lips of Realized matter. "The *Lorenz* can return to Painter with its own crew."

"May I have time to consider your offer?" said Rubens.

"Are you curious concerning the nature of Cressida's accident? I may be able to offer you satisfaction in that regard."

Gabriel was pleased by the shocked flutter of Rubens's gill slits.

The exercises on the Kuh-e-Rahmat, from Gabriel's point of view, were not very interesting. He had delegated them to the Welcome Rain, with Augenblick monitoring the students' vital signs. Gabriel was conducting more important business from his office in the Residence.

The Welcome Rain led the students through arm exercises first, wearying, repetitious punching and blocking and waving, some of it wushu, some dance, some calisthenics designed to exhaust the upper body, stress respiration, and induce, through tedium and exhaustion, a kind of mild hypnotic trance.

The graduates, on whatever worlds their bodies existed, were actually performing the exercises their skiagenoi were imitating in the electronic Persepolis. Probably they were calling up inner resources, including daimones, to assist them in maintaining control of their own flagging bodies. Gabriel and the Welcome Rain were merely manipulating their skiagénos, and had the advantage of not being tired in body.

The Welcome Rain began punching, one-two-three-four, and the graduates mirrored him. After he had set up a long, arm-wearying rhythm, he altered the pattern by thrusting out a hand formed in the Mudra of Domination.

The graduates stumbled, recovered, looked wild. Augenblick monitored leaps in vital signs. The Welcome Rain resumed the exercise, and gradually the graduates fell back into rhythm.

*   *   *

Rubens's shocked form was reflected in the dark jigsaw mirror of Gabriel's Louis Quinze desk. "I'm not certain what you're suggesting," he said.

"I'm not suggesting anything. I'm *telling* you that your former employer was murdered. I'm *telling* you that you and I may be next on the list. Any course you choose may lead to danger—perhaps mine more than most. But such protection as I can offer you, you may certainly have."

No point in mincing words when one was out of the oneirochronon. No one was recording Gabriel's words.

No one heard but Rubens. And Rubens was listening very intently.

The Welcome Rain fired the Mudra of Domination again. Hearts leaped, nerves cried, lungs stammered.

Perhaps none of the graduates knew of this particular mudra's existence. Its theory and practice were under the Seal, and the Aristoi, though not forbidden, tended not to talk about it. But whether the graduates knew about it or not, all their education, all their existence had led them to it.

The Involved Ideography, as with much of Captain Yuan's work, was based on his notion of how the body and brain were wired together. Certain patterns, he thought, could be brought to strike the human mind in very precise ways.

Reinforce, he insisted. Always reinforce. Stance *was* meaning, *was* emotion—someone in a straight-backed, square-shouldered, high-chinned pose *could not* feel sad or depressed; the body-to-brain wiring wouldn't allow it. A slumped, defeated posture *induced* melancholy as well as reflected it.

Words were slippery things, and needed reinforcement. Stance brought clarity, meaning, as did intonation. Mudras could be used to buttress words, or to provide running comment on them, let the audience know what was important, what was vital, what attitude to take to the text.

The Mudra of Domination—the fingers turned just so, and its implication made clear by an appropriate mental attitude and controlling stance drawn from the *Book of Postures*—was among those symbols which Yuan believed could develop universal resonance.

But no symbol is without its context. The mudra would only confuse someone who hadn't been schooled in Yuan's other thought—in the Intermediate and Involved Ideography, in the *Book of Postures*, in symbols drawn from the Involved Ideography and classical literature and dance, the universal culture that the Aristoi promoted throughout their domains . . . The precise jut of the thumb was meant to imitate the ideographic radical for *alarm*, which appeared in every sign marking a hazard, be it traffic or biologic, and the set of the middle two fingers was *authority*, which appeared on every public building, in every classroom, at the beginning of every video instruction or command from a superior, in the seal of every Aristos. The mudra as a whole was supposed to stop people in their tracks, to stun their will, to make them malleable—even if only for an instant.

The Mudra of Domination was the last resort of an Aristos in jeopardy. Humanity had not always enjoyed its present tranquility, and at the beginning of the current era there had been resistance, conflict, small-scale insurrection, assassination. Proper use of the Mudra of Domination could cause an enemy to hesitate, could buy time.

There were other kinds of conditioning as well, mostly societal and more traditional. The Aristoi cloaked themselves in a mystique of invulnerability, of omniscience, and of inexorable if diversified progress toward the greater good. Most people would not think of contravening a direct order or even questioning it, even when the order—like some of those issued by Virtue's Icon—defied sense.

Not even when they knew how the conditioning worked, because many of them did.

"I don't understand," Rubens said. "If there's been a crime, why hasn't this fact been revealed? Why isn't there a formal investigation?"

"If *I'm* doing the investigating, that's as formal as it ever gets," Gabriel said. "The murderer, however, is an Aristos. Or perhaps a group of Aristoi, who may have the ability to seriously disrupt or even overturn the Logarchy. Things are therefore . . . delicate."

Rubens seemed to be trying to decide whether Gabriel had gone mad.

"Allow me to show you the recording you brought from Cressida Ariste," Gabriel said, "and another recording I made of our subsequent conversation."

He touched the mother-of-pearl scrollwork on his desk and called up the recordings.

Which served to convince.

Horus's new machine—a chain of atoms smaller than a dust speck—grew slowly, safe aboard the *Pyrrho*, taking shape under the careful remote prodding of particle beams.

Horus was building a parasite.

"Fleta," Gabriel said. He nodded to his sylphlike Tritarchōn, whose form was wrapped in a red-and-gold-print sari that offset her blue-tinted skin and was mirrored in her vast, wide eyes. "I need a special service of you."

She gave an elegant, insinuant bow, looked up through dark lashes. "I will be pleased to be of any service, Aristos."

No doubt, Gabriel thought.

"I need you to extend the private tachlines you set up between here and Painter. The tachlines can have only a single limited connection with the Hyperlogos or the communal oneirochronon. I need you to devise a series of ciphers that can be changed regularly, all without reference to any already used or listed in the Hyperlogos. I also need an efficient design for a tachline relay satellite." He held out his hand and offered Fleta a wafer. "Here are some suggestions you may find helpful."

"Thank you, Aristos. Of course." One blue-skinned hand rose in a graceful gesture, took the wafer. "Do you require anything else?"

"I thank you, no, Tritarchōn."

In silence Fleta withdrew. Gabriel consulted with his limited personalities: the Welcome Rain was still leading exercises atop the Kuh-e-Rahmat; Horus was working on his machine; Spring Plum and Cyrus were, at a low priority, orchestrating a piece of melody that Gabriel had tossed off some weeks ago and never had time to work with or place within the spectrum of his current work.

Perhaps, Gabriel thought, he'd write some love lyrics to it and dedicate it to Clancy.

Whyever not? He had a few hours.

Gabriel's phantom orchestra played bright music to stimulate wit and aid the digestion. The grave first violinist, a vole in a periwig, took requests. Bipedal badgers and otters, in livery, served oneirochronic treats, complex shimmering gemlike confections that, when placed in the mouth, exploded in a bursting firework of sensation, sometimes triggering a complex pattern of tastes, more substantive, startling, and immediate than real food could ever be, sometimes tweaking the other senses—appearing as a hallucinatory visual shimmer, a lengthy fundamental chord or a scintillation of distant music, a sweet, phantom stimulation of the dorsal hairs . . .

"Eldest Brother." Gabriel kissed Pan Wengong hello. "I thank you for gracing my reception."

The Eldest Aristos wore his usual skullcap and embroidered silk and seemed a little breathless. "Sorry I'm late, Aristos. But I had to go to Sebastian's party—you understand the woeful obligations of my position—and he trapped me into a discussion of Aristotelian heresies. Barely escaped with my life." The Eldest could afford to be rude in public spaces if he wanted.

Pan took one of the treats from a plate, tasted it, looked surprised for a moment. "Cinnamon and fireworks. How interesting."

"I have real food here if you like," Gabriel said. "Just use your seal on the door behind the spirit screen in the banquet room."

"That's kind of you, Gabriel. So many of our colleagues forget that my physical body is present as well."

As a courtesy to his guests, Gabriel had underdressed to his own party—they shone in their finery while he played host. He was dressed in a long open-fronted cassock of black velvet trimmed around the buttonholes with silver embroidery in the form of leafy vines. There was subdued lace trim at his throat, cuffs, and boot-tops. He carried a long walking stick, ebony bound in silver, and his long copper hair was caught at the back with a diamond pin.

He would release pictures of this outfit later, and the Illyrian Workshops would earn a substantial profit selling the design abroad. It wasn't as extreme as a lot of his clothing and would therefore find an audience among those who weren't as certain as he whether flamboyance was a part of their makeup.

Even an Aristos had to have a good sense of the market.

Pan tried another treat from the tetrapus's tray and smiled at the result. Gabriel took Pan's arm and walked with him into the room.

"If you're not hungry at this moment, Eldest," Gabriel said, "and if you've no pressing business, I should like to beg a private audience."

GABRIEL: All of you—on alert, now. I want to see how the Eldest reacts to this.

"Provided the matter's nothing dreadfully serious or long, Aristos. Bear in mind I've just come from Sebastian's."

"I'll be brief. My word on it."

He took the older man to a door, opened it, drew Pan through.

Gulls called in the distance. Worn planks sagged underfoot. There was a scent of marsh and the sea in the air.

Pan looked surprised. "This is Cressida's place, isn't it?"

AUGENBLICK: He has permitted a certain amount of pupil dilation. I would say

"Yes."

Pan's large head cocked slightly as, for a moment, he listened to inner voices. "What have you done? We're out of the Hyperlogos."

"We're in my own AI at the Labdakos Residence."

Pan frowned. "How odd. If you wanted privacy, we could have placed this conversation under Seal."

he's genuinely surprised. He would now appear to be listening to daimones.

WELCOME RAIN: He also obviously doesn't give a damn whether you know it or not.

HORUS: The Eldest has little to hide, I'd guess.

WELCOME RAIN: Don't be ridiculous. Everyone's got something to hide.

Neither case, Gabriel knew, would have guaranteed privacy. The Seal was compromised, and even here, in the Residence reno, Pan was still receiving his own sensory impressions through a link with the universal tachline network.

But privacy wasn't Gabriel's intention. He wanted to gauge Pan's reaction to this environment, that and provide stimulation to his imagination.

"Will you walk with me, Aristos?" He took Pan's arm again and led him into the wide, low-ceilinged main room with its thinning rugs and wood planking, its worn furniture. There was a smell of cedar. A fire burned in the stone fireplace. Gabriel took Pan to the mantel, pointed out the arrangement of silver-framed portraits.

"Did you notice these?" he asked. "Cressida's family— her six parents, her sister. Her two children—she limited herself to two, good citizen that she was—her grandchildren and great-grandchildren."

The portraits moved through their cycle, a series of images of each subject, lost time regained, a variety of poses and themes. Ghostlike, Cressida appeared in each from moment to moment.

"You've put her private electronic retreat in your own reno's memory," Pan said. "You surprise me, Gabriel."

"I felt that I never knew her until I saw this place," Gabriel said, brushing the mantel with his fingertips. The varnish was worn with years. "And by that point she was dead."

"This is very peculiar, Aristos." Pan's brows narrowed. "I understand that Cressida sent you one of her Therápontes before she died, sent him on her own yacht—rather suddenly, it would seem."

"Therápōn Rubens had developed a new ceramic that he calculated might be of use to me. I'm negotiating the use of it now."

Pan nodded slowly. "That's in the Hyperlogos, yes."

"Cressida was someone we could not afford to lose."

The Eldest made a Mudra of Reverence. "That is so, Aristos."

"Her death seems uniquely strange and upsetting. The reason I called you here was to tell you that I am going to embark upon a quest to make such deaths impossible."

AUGENBLICK: A good deal more control has just entered his skiagénos. We've aroused his suspicion. His reno is combing the records.

WELCOME RAIN: Fob him off, but only with truth. He'll know otherwise.

AUGENBLICK: His look is alert, but passive. He is very controlled. He is waiting for us to make the moves here.

HORUS: Be cautious with these hints. The Eldest has been doing this for centuries longer than we. He may be lazy, but he is also acute.

AUGENBLICK: He is totally controlled. I would judge we have his interest now.

"Indeed?"

"I am going to isolate myself on my yacht for a period of months. During that time I will be working exclusively with nano in hopes that I can work out a new safety mechanism."

"Your dedication is commendable, Gabriel. But such a mechanism has eluded us for centuries."

"I have some notions that may be of service. And I will

have a handpicked crew of assistants, including Rubens Therápōn."

Pan bowed briefly. His eyes scanned the mantel again, the
framed images of Cressida's family moving through their sequence.

"I wish you every success, Aristos."

Gabriel prolonged the conversation a bit, but the Eldest
offered only conventional responses. Pan had seen, had drawn
his own conclusions, had said nothing. Gabriel's daimones
were disappointed—they always enjoyed it when an Aristos
let his mask slip—but Gabriel hadn't expected anything but
what Pan gave him.

No doubt Pan Wengong's daimones were busy in the
oneirochronon, however. Where, if Cressida's surmise was
correct, her murderers would be able to keep track of everything he did.

Still, it would be a brave Aristos who would attempt the
assassination of the Eldest. And a foolhardy one, to attempt
it so soon, and by the same means.

And were they going to kill everyone with whom Gabriel
spoke privately?

He was going to make a point of speaking privately to a
great many people.

He was going to bring them all here, to Cressida's place.

But for the present, he took Pan's arm and led him back
to Persepolis.

Horus's machine, in the silence and safety of the *Pyrrho*, had
been completed.

It awaited only a proper test.

Gabriel's reception was a success. People enjoyed themselves
and Gabriel managed to speak with a startled few in Cressida's
house, learning very little other than that some considered the
gesture terrible taste. Han Fu had given a start as he'd stepped
through the door, but Gabriel couldn't tell whether it was
because of a guilty conscience or because Han had just noticed

that Dorothy St.-John, disguised as a jeweled scarab, had slipped in clutching his arm with tiny emerald talons—the communications software had sounded the alert the instant they'd all passed through the portal.

Gabriel realized that Dorothy St.-John may have picked up some useful information, and decided to speak with her when the opportunity presented itself. At that moment, however, he was too amused by his guests' shocked flutterings.

After he showed the last guest to the door, Gabriel left the oneirochronon and took flight for Standing Wave, which he found rose-pink with dawn light. Below, in the shadow of the gorge, he found Marcus sitting in a half-lotus on the sward below the falls, his eyes closed, lips moving silently. Gabriel didn't disturb him and instead watched sunlight slowly move down the walls of the gorge, the strong clear light illuminating in turn strata of red, grey, and green, imaging as well the ever-lengthening rainbow in the hanging mist of the falls. He let Spring Plum rise inside him and call his attention to detail—he hadn't noticed the tiny pink buds on the mosses at the foot of the falls, or the spray of white flowers high on the gorge wall, drenched in sunlight and dew.

He and Spring Plum quietly absorbed the scene. Somewhere in his mind a stray melody flowed, the one he would dedicate to Clancy.

"Thank you for letting me finish," Marcus said. He had risen and assumed, from conditioning and habit, the Second Posture of Formal Regard. He grinned and walked toward Gabriel.

"I was working on a design for a tour bus with a three-hundred-sixty-degree view, all transparent. The problem is the solar panels, which have to be opaque in order for them to work at all, but I realized that if I made the seats transparent I could put the solar panels underneath—" He kissed Gabriel hello. "The passengers would block the sunlight, but not too much, I think, and they won't mind overmuch if their view of the road is hindered. Would you like breakfast?"

"Yes. Very much."

Marcus wore a sleeveless shirt, loose trousers, and his feet were bare. Gabriel followed his footprints up the damp marble stairs to the house, then watched as Marcus prepared omelettes flavored with morels, lean bacon, and shallots from the kitchen garden he'd planted out back.

Birdsong floated through open windows.

"You seem to be settling in," Gabriel said.

"At least the cabinets are finished. I've got a place to put my pots."

Marcus had designed all his own cooking gear and earned royalties on licensed commercial versions. He slid an omelette onto one of Spring Plum's "morning garden" plates—another of her floral patterns—placed it in front of Gabriel, then sat opposite him at the table.

Above their heads the water fell away into its own mist and rainbow.

"I'll be leaving soon," Gabriel said. "Perhaps for a year or more. A lengthy space journey for purposes of research."

"You *hate* space journeys. You're the worst traveler I've ever met."

"I'm not that bad."

"Yes you are. You hate being confined." Marcus considered and ate a bite of egg. "I'll come along, of course."

"I'm not certain it would be appropriate."

Waterfall rainbows reflected in his eyes as Marcus leaned back in his chair. "Why not? Because Clancy will be along? I *like* Dr. Clancy. We've been talking every day. We get along famously."

"On the ship we'll be working with nano. You're not a nano specialist."

"It's precisely nano I need to work on for my exams— you convinced me to try the exams again, remember? And when study gets too strenuous I can do my own work."

"There is also—I beg you not to speak of this—there is also danger. It may not be safe where we'll be going."

"There's danger here as well."

A cold hum settled into Gabriel's nerves. He regarded Marcus carefully. "What have you heard?"

Marcus smiled. "Nothing. But you're proposing to leave me here on Illyricum with your *mother*, Gabriel. She's been calling me two or three times every day, trying to get me to move to the temple where she can take charge of me and our child."

"I asked her not to bother you."

"The pressure started almost the hour I returned to Standing Wave. She's not going to give up."

"Well." Eating the omelette. "My other children escaped her, and ours will as well."

"I've told the house reno not to take her calls. But now people are starting to leave *offerings* at the front gate. What am I supposed to do with the stuff?"

"Have the sanitation robots take it away, I suppose."

"Some of it's valuable."

"Donate it to some worthwhile cause. Or send it to my mother."

"I think what I would rather do is fly away till the baby is born. With my doctor, and the child's other parent."

Gabriel gazed at Marcus. Birdsong hovered in air.

Gabriel always had a hard time refusing people who had a claim on him. And Marcus was right—Gabriel hated space travel, hated confinement, and the unreal comforts of the oneirochronon, being unreal, were of little genuine comfort. Marcus might make the time go faster.

And Marcus's most recent apprenticeship had been under Saigo, and his insights might be useful.

"I will try to keep you very, very safe," he said.

Gabriel floated through the limitless velvet depths of oneirochrononic space. Above him, atom on giant atom, stretched the long linkèd fabric of Horus's machine. Electron shells glowed like luminescent planets, color-coded as to energy state; photons buzzed like hornets as they exchanged electromagnetic force; quarks rearranged themselves, like dancers exchanging places, at the hearts of atoms.

A new and parasitic form of nano was about to be unleashed throughout human space, and Gabriel was going to release it. But before he did so, he wanted it to be as free from danger as possible.

It was the part of his job he took most seriously. Every six months or so he announced a Nano Day, in which he would review the efforts of every nano designer in his domaine prior to approving licenses and patents. Gabriel ran the simulations himself, watched the materials grow, then dived into the simulations to watch the nanomechanics themselves at work, the atoms rearranging, recombining, assembling. He forcibly intervened, imposing quantum fluctuations that compelled the nano to mutate into less tractable forms. He found weak points in each design—usually the changeover point where one set of nano had finished its job and was scheduled to alter itself into another form or dissolve—and then forcibly altered the schedule, prolonging the nano well beyond its term or turning it berserk. He assaulted each structure with the special artiphage attack nanos that had been designed, since the death of Earth[1], to prevent the stuff from running amuck. And he compared their results with other nano already designed, on file, of proven safety margins and capable of doing the same job.

Relatively few of them actually ran wild even in the event of massive tampering—weaknesses had been recognized long since, and safeguards were built into the software that manipulated the nascent nano as it rested in its Kam Wing containers—but other weaknesses and flaws were often revealed.

Gabriel was particularly careful with this design. The nature of Horus's machine was that it was going to be constantly exposed to intense solar radiation from which it had to be properly protected—both to keep it in operating order and to keep the stuff from mutating into mataglap.

As a further protection, Horus had carefully built a fail-safe into the design. He had made critical parts of the machine very happy to bond with oxygen.

In the event that any of the machines were actually dropped into the pressurized environment of a habitable biosphere, the machine's active parts would oxidize in a matter of minutes and render themselves both safe and useless. No working nano would long survive outside of the vacuum of space.

Gabriel, floating through the simulation like an angel through some newly hatched cosmos, was very pleased with his handiwork.

His next step would be to test it on the *Pyrrho*.

Gabriel was pleased to tell his mother that neither he nor any of his daimones would be coming to the Rites of Inanna. He was going on a voyage, and the pressure of work would be intense.

Vashti disapproved of the voyage, its timing, its suddenness. She was clearly suspicious that some plot was afoot, that Gabriel, flying off with Marcus, Clancy, and his unborn, was trying to put something over on her.

It was equally clear that she was going to be driven mad until she figured out what it was.

Vashti would be disappointed, Gabriel knew, when she finally found out that, instead of engaging in some plot with herself at the center of it, Gabriel was instead off on some insignificant task regarding the fate of the human race.

"The most generally held view, Flame," said Dorothy St.-John, "is that you're cracked."

St.-John, on walking through the portal into Cressida's retreat, had assumed a form more-or-less her own: a compact, muscular woman, black-haired, copper-skinned. A jeweled scarab—the one she'd once impersonated—was pinned to her gown. She leaned against the mantel and regarded the portraits as she spoke.

"Astoreth, for example, is convinced that some daimōn

has got you. Or that being worshipped has turned your head and that you think you're in one of your own operas. Or that you've managed to go mad all by yourself. Actually she seems to hold all three views at once—which, I must say, is typical of her." She smiled. "Perhaps she's just upset that you—and Cressida—have stolen attention from her dramatic plans for reform."

"And your own view?" Gabriel said. He was reclining on the soft, scratchy cushion of a cane chair.

"I think you're up to something, though I have no idea what it is. And I can't tell whether Cressida really has something to do with it, or whether she's just someone you've dragged in to disguise what you're really doing. If the latter—" She gestured at the unadorned room. "It's in terrible taste, Flame. I wish you'd stop."

Gabriel simply looked at her.

"It's known that Cressida sent someone to you," St.-John said. "But you and she weren't close—no one can figure out what the connection can be. The ceramic story really doesn't make any sense, does it? Rubens could have made his presentation through the oneirochronon."

"What do people say about Cressida?"

"I'd rather you answered my questions for a change."

Gabriel smiled at her. "Indulge me. Please."

"You can look through the Hyperlogos recordings. All the meetings and receptions are on file—you can follow everyone around and eavesdrop every word if you like."

"I prefer realtime communication." Because, he thought, the recordings could be edited if the Hyperlogos Seal was compromised. Not that he wouldn't look, anyway, when he had the time.

St.-John was looking at him skeptically.

He adopted a Pose of Humility. "*Please*, Ariste?" he said. "My time is valuable."

"And mine isn't?" She looked at him, then shrugged and walked over to sit on the couch. She leaned close to him. "No one wants to talk about Cressida, Flame. People just *don't*. I suspect *they* suspect Cressida's death *might* have been arranged. But no one knows why or who, and no one wants to go on the record about it—so instead they talk about *you*. Why you're behaving this way, why you're leaving your domaine."

"Did I say I was leaving my domaine?"

"You're not?"

He shrugged. "Not necessarily."

"You're the worst traveler in the Logarchy. Why are you doing this?"

"What else are people saying?"

"That's all they'll say in public. What they're saying in private conversations under Seal I can't speak to."

Someone could, the Welcome Rain reminded.

"Tell me," St.-John said. "What do you suspect?"

Better, Gabriel thought, if they started digging around themselves. If he intrigued enough people into conducting their own investigations, the truth might come to light without his having to put any of them in danger.

"I think Cressida's death was needless and stupid," Gabriel said. "And I think I owe it to her—" He repeated St.-John's gesture, taking in the rustic surroundings. "I owe it to her to do something about it."

"And?"

"And?" he repeated. "That's all."

"Flame." Chiding. "How did Cressida lay this obligation on you? You barely knew her—don't think people haven't gone through the records looking for some connection."

Gabriel simply shrugged.

"And how did you know about this place? The Hyperlogos would have a record of it if you'd been here."

"Therápōn Rubens told me about it."

She looked at him closely. Her expression was concerned. "I hope you know what you're doing, Gabriel Aristos Vissarionovich."

"So do I." He rose from his chair and offered his arm. "Shall we return to Pristine Way's party?"

She rose, took his arm, failed to change her expression.

"I thank you for your candor," he said.

"And I don't thank you for yours."

He smiled, bowed. "I suppose you'll have to do some more hovering around."

"I would in any case. At least now I've got more of a reason to hover than usual."

"You will tell me if you hear anything interesting?"

"I will if you will."

"If I find out anything for certain," he said, "you will know it. I promise."

Pristine Way's party enveloped Gabriel, and Dorothy St.-John turned into a seal dangling from Gabriel's chain-link belt. He glanced back at the portal before he sealed it and repeated the last words.

"I promise."

The words were directed behind him, not forward. To the woman who had so carefully constructed the oneiro-chronic beach house on the waterfront, who had, in her passion for truth, set him on this quest.

I promise.

> "*With ravished ears*
> *The Monarch hears*
> *Assumes the god,*
> *Affects to nod*
> *And seems to shake the spheres.*"

Gabriel spoke the words, watched them disappear into Fleta's transmitter. He purged them from his implant reno, made sure there were no copies of them on file anywhere.

Another backup, another safety.

He hoped he'd never have to use it.

Yaritomo had begun to wear a bare spot in the grass in front of the Shadow Mask. Gabriel, hovering behind one of the turquoise-studded arches, watched as the young Therápōn performed wushu.

Burning Tiger was rather obviously in charge. The movements were aggressive, wrathful, angry. The daimōn growled at each attack, and his eyes glittered with fury.

And then his movements altered. A different spirit seemed to pervade them—cranelike, Yaritomo held himself more erect, on the balls of his feet, his neck more elongated, chin lifted. His hand and foot movements became more precise, more delicate, almost fussy.

Clearly another daimōn had entered the picture.

Gabriel entered the Shadow Cloister and walked toward the young man. Yaritomo froze for an instant as he saw Gabriel, his face pursed in an overnice look of suspicion, and then the look dissolved and Yaritimo's presence returned to his body, which relaxed into the Second Posture of Formal Regard.

"Someone new, I see," Gabriel said.

"They're coming quickly now, Aristos," Yaritomo said. Sweat gleamed on his skin; his chest heaved with exertion. "This was the third—I call him Old Man Ali, after the character in the story."

"Very appropriate."

Gabriel regarded him. Once Yaritomo discovered the personalities that lived within him, he would have started a partial encoding of their personalities on his implant reno, which would make them easier to access. Space in the reno would also be reserved for the daimones' own activities, so that they could undertake the prioritized duties Yaritomo assigned them.

"I have instructions for you, Therápōn."

Yaritomo shifted to the Primary Posture of Formal Regard. "I hear you, Aristos."

"In order that you might undertake a special assignment," Gabriel said, "you are hereby relieved of all your normal duties as demiourgós. You will take appropriate belongings and any materials you may need to continue your studies, and bring them to Loading Area Seven of Labdakos Port at oh-nine-hundred in two days' time. You will join other Therápontes in a lengthy space mission aboard the ship

Pyrrho. You may expect to be in space for a period of one or two years."

Yaritomo struggled to master his thoughts. Gabriel had thought him a suitable candidate for the voyage—he was young, unattached, and therefore free; and a year or two of training directly under an Aristos would do him good.

Gabriel assumed a Posture of Authority. "I will leave you, Therápōn. No doubt you have preparations to make."

"Yes, Aristos."

Gabriel turned and walked from the Shadow Cloister. As he passed under the giant white face on its pillar he glanced up at its ambiguous pneumatic smile, and he hoped he was achieving, in his own business, as masterful an inscrutability as this.

Gabriel watched through remotes as Horus's machine assembled itself on the skin of the *Pyrrho*, which he had moved to an orbit near the bustling orbital habitat Rhodos. He would test it on his own craft first; if something went wrong, he would be the one to pay.

The machine was only a few molecules deep and, saving the antenna, less than a centimeter across. It was a low-energy tachline transmitter, solar-powered and capable of reproduction.

Wherever the ship went, passive sensors would search the horizon for other ships. When they detected one, a small piece of the machine—a long molecular chain, a seed, sitting on top of a chemical booster so tiny it was almost invisible to the eye—would break away and fire itself toward the target. Once it arrived, the seed would construct a copy of itself.

As months passed, the transmitters would be carried to other star systems, then reproduce and be carried further. Gradually they would cover all human space. Gabriel calculated this would take eight or nine months.

By use of the machine Gabriel intended to build himself an alternate tachline communications system. He would not have to depend on the compromised system of the Hyperlogos, a system that might conceivably be shut down if he tried to warn the other Aristoi.

He would not go on his mission without backup. Fleta's engineering had created a central communications center capable of handling an enormity of realtime communication. Nano had converted the interiors of two asteroids and was in the long, slow process of turning one moonlet into data storage modules, the same way that Earth's moon had once been converted. The storage capacity was vast. At any moment he could activate his alternate system and establish tachline contact with whatever star systems his molecular machine had infiltrated.

And it would happen automatically under certain conditions. If he didn't pulse a coded message to Illyricum at regular intervals, a prerecorded *FLASH* alert would be transmitted, both on the regular communications channels and his own private system, and all Aristoi would become aware of their danger.

Gabriel watched as the machine completed its reproductive task. He activated it briefly, tested its systems, told it to go back to sleep.

Its monitor showed that it had already detected several of the other ships docked at the Haydn habitat. The tiny seed-carrying boosters were already being constructed.

Gabriel let them proceed.

Graduation, and its ceremonies, receptions, and meetings, had at last come to an end. Everything, once again, had been postponed till next time.

Gabriel and Zhenling, sharing the oneirochronon, paced along the scarlet-veined marble floors of the Red Lacquer Gallery. Works of art—oneirochronic versions of the molecule-perfect copies that occupied the real wing of the real gallery—gazed at them from the dark-red walls. The facsimile heritage of Earth[1], the originals long ago destroyed.

This wing offered various exhibits, but at the moment was devoted to Flemish works, and this side gallery to Peter Paul

Rubens. Silenus belched blearily from ahead, and next to him Greeks and Amazons, swirls of violence, battle back and forth across an arching bridge. The small and large *Last Judgments* threatened on either side, cascades of the pink-skinned Damned tumbling down to Hell. There seemed to be acres of rosy flesh.

"Do I sense a moralist at work in this grouping?" Zhenling asked, and pointed from one picture to the next. "Judgment, war, insensibility?"

"The good old days," Gabriel said. "I thought you wanted to bring them back."

"Nobody wants that, Gabriel. Not at all. I want a transcursion of the good old days through the present and into the future. I want the old adventurous spirit transformed."

Her skiagénos wore a version of the harness used when she raced submarines: a strapped black bodysuit that left the arms, shoulders, and legs bare, with a utility belt and soft black booties. Her hair was held up with a tall mother-of-pearl comb; a pair of gloves was thrust though the belt. Gabriel was delighted by the revelation of flowing sculpted muscle in her shoulders, arms, and legs: Augenblick was overjoyed by a superabundance of kinesic clues.

She would not, the Welcome Rain reminded, **be wearing this outfit unless she wished you to offer more than admiration.**

Gabriel put his hands in the big pockets of his embroidered day robe and pretended to study the large *Last Judgment,* contrasting the precise articulation of Zhenling's frame with Rubens's pink-fleshed tumblers. "Half these people are damned," Gabriel said, "and the others seem more relieved than happy with their lot. Such a waste—I think we Aristoi have done better than Jehovah, all things considered."

Zhenling stepped in front of him, looked at the painting. "He had less to work with in terms of human material."

"Appreciated," Gabriel said. He stepped behind her and did what the Welcome Rain had been urging for some time; he slid arms gently around her waist and kissed the juncture.

of neck and shoulder. The unreal experiential flesh was warm to his lips, not forbidding, and so he repeated the kiss, diving over her shoulder into the inviting shadow of her clavicle, telling Spring Plum to send little oneirological nerve-pulses along the sensitive slopes of Zhenling's neck.

Zhenling gently detached herself. "Patience," she said, "if you please."

"My vegetable love shall grow vaster than empires, and more slow."

She gave him a look over her shoulder. "That was a bit commonplace, don't you think?"

He shrugged. "Apt enough, though. At least I didn't go on about time's wingéd chariot."

She padded toward the next room. "Besides, I need to know whether or not you've gone mad."

The Welcome Rain tugged at Gabriel to follow; he didn't resist. "I understand that's Astoreth's theory," he said.

"You've been very busy since I last spoke to you alone," Zhenling said. Allegorical peasants roistered around her, genre art by Brouwer in tans and browns. "Your private ship readied, a crew standing by, lots of little quiet meetings, private tangos danced with one partner or another . . ."

"I want to say proper good-byes."

"You're not Magellan, for heaven's sake," she said. "You're still going to be hooked into the oneirochronon." She lifted an eyebrow. "Aren't you?"

"Yes."

"Then why the—" She paused, chose words. (**Her meta-linguistics are indicative of frustration,** Augenblick reported pointlessly.) "You're setting up your own tachline network," she said. "Why?"

"How did you find that out?" Gabriel was mildly surprised.

Her brows narrowed. "It took some digging—I had to track the raw materials around. But that sort of thing is what renos are for."

At this revelation a paranoid howl from Mataglap was suppressed, and Mataglap with it.

"And you started setting the thing up before Cressida died, just to talk to her, but now you're expanding it. Your current capacity is beyond description. How many channels are you expecting to have to use?"

"I'm not sure."

Zhenling stepped close to him, looked levelly into his eyes. "A claim could be made that your moves are seditious," she said. "The entire Logarchy is based on free and complete access to information. Every transaction, every communication is recorded in the Hyperlogos. Even the data placed under Seal is made available sooner or later. For someone to establish private communication links outside the Logarchy could be thought subversive. You're withdrawing from the civic life of the republic."

Gabriel held her gaze, gave Horus control of his face so that nothing could be read into his expression. "Is that the only interpretation that occurs to you, Ariste?"

Zhenling gave a little nod. "No," she said. She bit her lip (or allowed herself to be seen to bite her lip—in any case Augenblick gave a little spasm of joy).

"I'm setting up my own tachline rig," she said.

"As you wish, Ariste." His words went carefully uninflected.

"When I do, we can have a genuinely private interchange."

"Yes."

"Will you tell me what's happening?"

Gabriel allowed himself to drift away from her, toward the next gallery. His silk trousers whispered as he walked, a nicely subtle oneirochronic effect.

"I won't," he said.

"Because you think I'll be in danger."

"No. Because I don't know what's going on."

"Do you know where you're going in this excursion of yours?" Following him. "Any destination in mind?"

"A tour of the neighborhood. Perhaps I'll go visit Earth[2]—I've never seen it in person."

"Perhaps you could visit me."

"I'd like that." Noncommittally.

He didn't think she was a conspirator, but he couldn't absolutely rule her out. He couldn't tell her too much.

The next gallery opened around him. He had drifted back in time, to Breughel the Elder. He paused in front of the *Land of Cockaigne*, where a knight, merchant, and peasant lay tumbled on the ground, stunned by their own gluttony in a land in which the food walked onto their plates and lay down to be eaten.

Zhenling approached, spoke softly from behind. "That's us, isn't it? That's the Logarchy. Everything perfect, everything known, everything easy, everything abundant. And there's no reason for it to change."

"If everyone chooses to be happy," Gabriel said, "why should you interfere?"

"There are degrees of happiness. Why should you choose one over another?"

"I don't. The choice is left to the individual. And in the domaines where that doesn't happen, we condemn the Aristoi in charge."

She frowned. "*Condemn* is a little strong. We *disapprove*, in our own quiet and unobtrusive way."

"Your alternative?" A number of these passed through his mind: institutionalized intolerance, pressure of the muscle-flexing sort, responded to by militarization, cold war, proxy war, hot war. Legions of brainwashed clones advancing with gravity weapons and the latest in attack nano . . .

It was all too possible.

"I'd like to expand the human gene pool, for starters," Zhenling said.

Gabriel was surprised. "But we're doing that," he said as he turned toward her. "Adapting humans for different environments—space, the ocean, even mountain and lowland adaptations. Eliminating hereditary diseases, boosting intelligence, making the human body more efficient . . ."

She held up a hand. "Listen to what you're saying, Aristos. Yes, we're making functional adaptations for specific environments. But on the whole, human genetics is far less diverse than it was two thousand years ago."

"Much was lost with Earth[1], yes."

"That's not what I mean. One of the constant features of human genetics is that *we never choose our own genes.* In ancient times the genetic mix was haphazard; since then our parents, or on occasion the state, choose our genetics for us. We can retroactively alter them with nano, but that's complicated and hazardous and expensive."

Breath and speech are more forceful than strictly necessary, reported Augenblick. **Eyes slightly dilated, jaw and neck muscles tautened, head thrust forward like a weapon. She is speaking with deep conviction.**

The real Zhenling at last, exulted the Welcome Rain.

"I follow you, Ariste," Gabriel said.

"But now that parents can choose the genes of their own children, what are they choosing? Intelligence, yes, always. We can't guarantee genius, we can't guarantee an Ariste, but we can make them bright. Resistance to disease, general physical vigor, specific physiognomies regarded as aesthetically pleasing or interesting. That's all well and good, but what are they leaving out?"

Gabriel responded quickly. "Genes for Huntington's chorea, schizophrenia, Tay-Sach's, sickle cell, arthritis . . ."

Zhenling impatiently waved her hand. "All that's to the better, granted, though an argument could be made that all these exclusions aren't necessarily good—some forms of schizophrenia can result in genius."

"I will be saved from such genius, thank you."

"Conceded—my point being that some genetics are associated with both positive and negative features. Some genetics, for example, can create a very impulsive personality. That's wonderful for an athlete, say, or an explorer, or a stunt pilot—but impulsivity can also result in extremes of emotion, including rage and violence. The same genetics that produce a champion athlete can, with different circumstances, also produce a vicious criminal. Or a great soldier."

"Which is why attempts have always been made to divert budding criminals into athletics or the army," Gabriel said.

"Absolutely. But what is more important to my thesis is that impulsive genes make for difficult children. Aggressive, impetuous, disinclined to sit still. Active, dynamic explorers of their environment, prone to tantrums . . . What parents would choose *that* list of characteristics for their offspring, particularly if they see a sidebar associating that genetic pattern with criminal behavior?"

Gabriel looked at her. "It isn't as if those genetics aren't available. People simply don't choose to have such offspring. How many explorers, stunt pilots, and soldiers do we need?"

"More than we've got, I think. The Demos is composed of bright, polite, scholarly, well-behaved, unaggressive, rather unenterprising people—they're very pleasant, but they're not world-class fire breathers. And the Therápontes and Aristoi are drawn from the population of the Demos."

"We all have aggressive, enterprising daimones. Shouldn't that compensate?"

"Firstly, most of the Demos and many Therápontes have limited control over their daimones, and therefore don't get the best use out of them," Zhenling said, "and secondly, although you have aggressive daimones . . ." Her gaze was penetrating. "How often do you let yours loose?"

Mataglap, Gabriel thought, never. The Welcome Rain only rarely, because he was utterly manipulative and a sociopath—but sometimes it served Gabriel's interest to be manipulative.

The others, whose interests were a bit obsessive but on the whole more amiable, were given more free rein.

"In your silence I deduce an answer," said Zhenling.

"I restrict some of my daimones because it is for the

general good," Gabriel said. "But you would unleash their material counterparts on society?"

"Daimones are Limited Personalities. They aren't well rounded, they're just component aspects of a larger psyche. But children *can* be brought up well, with fully developed personalities. In a society such as ours, particularly with our multiple-parent institutions, we could raise a host of such children and turn them into a positive force."

"And how would you convince parents to host these difficult children?"

"Financial incentives, tax relief, medical and counseling assistance . . . there's a host of ways. One declares a certain genotype desirable, and supports it with state assistance."

"This isn't something that Persepolis needs to do. You can do it yourself, in your own domaine."

"I am."

"Oh."

"It happens I think I shouldn't be alone in this endeavor."

"Do you think you'll produce more Aristoi?"

There was a hesitation in her expression. "I don't know. Expanding the population of Aristoi may turn out to be a separate problem. But if you look at the genetics of the first generations of Aristoi, there was certainly more diversity than there is now. And diversity, whether in Aristoi or the Demos, would seem to be a good thing."

"A lot of the early Aristoi died badly, taking chances that we know better than to take today. Look at what happened to Shankaracharya and Ortega. And we still don't know what happened to Captain Yuan—he just went off on his quest and vanished, disappeared from the Hyperlogos."

Zhenling shrugged. "They took chances—that's what Aristoi were *for*. They were the cutting edge, and they experimented on themselves as much as on anything else. Casualties were high."

"We honor them," Gabriel said, "but do we emulate them?"

She drew back, regarded him. "I don't know," she said. "Is that what *you're* doing, Gabriel? Setting yourself on some glorious, private adventure, fraught with hazard and enterprise?"

Gabriel allowed himself a smile. "Modesty," he said, "forbids an answer."

Her tilted dark eyes hooded, Zhenling was silent for a moment, and then she gave a brief, decisive nod and stepped toward him. She hooked a forearm behind his neck and drew him to her lips.

Her kiss was fierce. Gabriel fell in love at once. He put his arms around her and (through his reno) ordered the Red Lacquer Gallery dissolved. A bright exuberant scintillation of colors bled through the walls, evaporating them, and then surrounded the embracing pair, buoyed them up. He felt sculpted, catlike muscle shifting beneath her bodysuit. She seemed content to let him choose the surroundings; he called up the Autumn Pavilion, Psyche's high-arched bedchamber. Zhenling in turn chose music, a pulsing, racing electronic piece whose origin he couldn't place.

Strands of silk seemed to move delicately up his spine. He let a warm mist of musky scent fall from the ceiling, called phantom feathers to brush her neck. He ordered the chrysanthemums on his embroidered day robe to blossom, blossom, blossom, a riot of floral brilliance emerging in time to the music.

Lovemaking through the oneirochronon was sufficiently unreal that dullness and monotony were a genuine danger. Sensation had to be instilled, sharpened, focused. Made better. The Realized World had to be improved upon.

Gabriel ordered the unreal palms of his hands to grow warmer, peeled away the black bodysuit. Her soft booties, to save anyone's awkward bending, simply dissolved away, one of the advantages of the incorporate sphere. The light fell, turned to rose twilight—Zhenling's work. Shadows contrasted with her glowing skin. Gabriel ordered warm puffs of wind, like a lover's breath, to touch her back, breasts, belly.

Invisible hands, an entire harem of caressing, impatient hands, tore away Gabriel's clothing. Zhenling seemed to float out of his arms, her still, poised body moving backwards without visible impulse. Suddenly the room streamed with silken banners, blue, red, yellow, all strong colors that flooded through the air, crackled in a sudden wind. The silks absorbed her body, flowed around it. Soundless lightning played overhead, strobelike flashes that illuminated the chiseled form of Zhenling's body, her pointed breasts, her intent, hungry expression.

Gabriel plunged into the flood of bright banners. Their texture was warm and moist. They flowed over his body in a thousand caresses. Lightning flashed again and again, revealing Zhenling just ahead. He threw himself high and flew through the storm of color. The journey seemed to take centuries.

He found her, only a few feet away, on the bed. Jewels glowed softly in her unbound hair. She wore a long string of pearls that trailed along her body, outlined her breasts and abdomen, then dipped between her thighs.

Gabriel hovered over her for a long, appreciative moment. He altered the nature of the banner storm, creating a tempest of color that whirled around them, the bed a calm eye in the bright rainbow hurricane. Lightning flashed again and again. Gabriel called rain into existence, a silent Heliogabalian cascade of flower petals that fell in thick profusion and spilled off his arms and shoulders.

Amid the rain of flowers he descended. Zhenling rose off the bed to meet him, heaped petals sliding off her skin.

Her strong arms grappled him; her legs wrapped round his thighs. Individual pearls imprinted themselves on his flesh. Her laugh seemed half a snarl. There was a ferocious quality to it all that surprised him; but the Welcome Rain growled suggestively in his ear and he responded, his arms compressing her waist, bending her backward under the power of his kiss. They tumbled suddenly, landed in a blizzard of petals. Fire kindled in Gabriel's heart.

One smile from her, he thought, recalling Li Yien-Nien, *would topple a city—two smiles, bring down a nation.*

Her hips rolled up against him, demanding pleasure. He provided it, took his own. Lightning flashed, colors swirled.

The rain of petals buried them long before they were finished.

With kisses and promises for the future, Gabriel eased himself out of the oneirochronon. He was lying sprawled on blue-and-gold cushions in his own private apartments. To judge by the state of his clothing, at least one of the oneirochronic orgasms he'd awarded himself had been imitated by nature.

He called Horus to his mind, checked the recordings of the last few hours of the nanomachine. The transmitter had been functioning as designed. Neither *Pyrrho,* nor any other ship, had disappeared in a devouring tide of mataglap.

Things were going as planned.

He checked the time and recalled that he was scheduled to have a private dinner with Clancy tonight, their last in the Autumn Pavilion before embarkation. Anticipation sent pleasure tingling through Gabriel's nerves.

He called up Spring Plum and Cyrus and reviewed through the orchestration of the melody he intended for Clancy. Cyrus's minimalist elegance clashed in places with Spring Plum's lush, fruitful intimacy, and he reconciled the two, adding touches of his own until he was satisfied.

He went to his wardrobe to change. As he tossed his trousers to the clothing robot, he considered that he'd have to pick up some hormone supplements from his private cabinet.

He could still taste a phantom scent of flower petals. The melody ran through his mind.

All sorts of adventures were beginning, he thought.

Chapter 8

PABST: I will be the mastermind,
I will set the stage,
In their weakness I will find
The truth, the word, the rage.

Miracles happened, one after another. A furious miracle of gravity transported the *Pyrrho* and its crew of thirty-five through several star systems, leaving Fleta-designed communications buoys behind. It was possible, though difficult, to trace tachline communications, and Gabriel intended to make the trail as confusing as possible.

For a four-day period the *Pyrrho* settled into an orbit around a sun forty light-years from Illyricum, in Maximilian's domain. The star system was uninhabited by humanity, and that's what Gabriel wanted.

Pyrrho dropped into a matching orbit next to an uncharted asteroid and there Gabriel created another miracle.

Seeding the asteroid with a careful sequence of nano, Gabriel built a large and powerful warship.

In doing this, Gabriel used nano designs already available to him—other than making certain the right sequence of micromachines was dropped in the right order, he didn't have to work at all. All the basic work had been done generations ago—any drug, any raw material, any substance at all, could now be manufactured cheaply and in quantity—so the chief alternative for the ambitious designer was to combine the basic research in ever more elaborate and imaginative ways. Gabriel's Therápontes, over the years, had handed him carefully tailored designs in which nanomachines were designed to manufacture, from piles of dirt hauled onto the property, entire office buildings, down to power, water, and sewage connections. Other designs featured asteroid material reassembled into huge space transports, capable of shuttling tens of thousands of passengers all happily housed in individual staterooms with nanobuilt paneling and sculpted gold nanofaucets above the nano-gold sinks.

A large percentage of these designs were never intended to be employed—much as Gabriel's closet music was never intended to be played—but rather served to demonstrate the creators' mastery over the form, and to provide solid grounding for the exams.

One of Gabriel's students had, as a kind of whim (or possibly as a comment on how pointless these exercises were) sculpted nano to build a battleship. Since her work was theoretical to begin with, she'd designed it to its limits. There was room for a full brigade of combat-ready troops, with shuttles to carry them. The crew quarters were a marvel of Olympian comfort. Camouflage was provided by the fact that the exterior of the asteroid would remain the same: the battleship, except for the odd hatch or antenna, looked just like a piece of rock. The gravity generators on board, once powered, had enough potential power to dismember a planet and possibly even a star.

Gabriel liked the idea of a huge ship. It would seem less confining than the *Pyrrho*, spacious and comfortable though the *Pyrrho* was.

No doubt, Gabriel thought, his student would be surprised to discover her impressive exercise in theory was actually being deployed.

If Gabriel were going into hostile territory, he was going to pack suitable firepower.

And then the miracles were really going to start.

Gabriel's quarters on the *Pyrrho* were cozy, rather tentlike. The walls were hung with wine-colored felt hangings covered with appliqué of gold and bronze-green; the soft Persian rugs were piled layers thick. Tasseled pillows were tossed around to sit on; there were bronze censers and wrought-iron light fixtures. The overall effect was of being in the interior of a very large yurt.

Spoiling the illusion were the glowing ebony piano Gabriel had shipped upwell from the Autumn Pavilion, and the buffet table just brought in from the kitchens. Clancy was late for dinner—her studies and duties were driving her hard. Gabriel struck random chords on the piano and considered answering a < Priority 2 > call from Zhenling.

While he waited for Clancy, Gabriel filled the room with voices, bits of his *Lulu*. Song balanced and harmonized, clashed and spat, wooed and denounced.

As he played he became aware that Clancy had entered the room and was listening. He waited for the conclusion of a phrase, then banished the sounds. He rose to kiss her hello.

"Your unfinished work again?"

He nodded. His silk-clad legs made little singing sounds as he led her to the buffet, life imitating the art of his skiagénos in the red lacquer gallery, that first time with Zhenling. Clancy put cold noodles and pickled vegetables on her plate, then sprinkled them with sesame oil. He filled his bowl with stuffed-cherry soup.

"Complex," she said. "I wouldn't want to attempt it."

"The complexity isn't a problem—it just gives me an opportunity for more interesting harmonic arrangements." She sat on a pillow; he curled up at her feet. "Mozart has eight people singing at once in the 'Pian pianin le andró piú presso' section of *Figaro*—all singing different tunes, more or less, but harmonizing wonderfully—but he didn't have the advantage of a reno programmed with harmonic and music theory. Still, he kept the record until Sandor Korondi managed ten. I've got *twelve*, and it's going to be lovely, and very strange. Listen."

He ordered his reno to call up the finale to Act II, the whole cast singing at once. The music was synthesized, because it had never been recorded live, and constituted an ideal a live performance might reach only in dreams, albeit a somewhat sterile one. Clancy glanced up in wonder at the eerie highlights that pervaded the music. Gabriel smiled to see her nape hair rise as if with a charge of static electricity.

She looked down at him, eyes wide. "That's the strangest thing I ever heard. How do you get that effect?"

"Some of the voices are up in the ultrasonic, above the range of normal hearing. I call them ultrasopranos, which I suppose is a very obvious name."

"A good trick. But if I can't hear them, why do I perceive the effect?"

"It's a harmonic. Although you can't hear the singers themselves, the ultrasopranos' voices are generating harmonies with the other singers, a kind of intermediate voice that floats from place to place. So even if you can't hear them directly, their influence still wafts about the stage. You can feel it in your toes when they shift into a minor key."

"You're planning a live production eventually?"

"When my singers come of age, yes."

Clancy put her plate down on the cushion beside her and leaned forward to look intently at Gabriel. "Tell."

Gabriel bowed. "As you command, Blushing Rose. When the idea proved out in simulation, I sculpted some genetics to produce the singers capable of performing my music. It involves a second set of vocal cords just above the first—quite tiny ones that are only deployed on command. Breath control is very important, so I strengthened the diaphragm, altered the lungs to efficiently absorb more oxygen, and . . ."

"How do they hear their own voices?"

"Ear implants."

"And there are how many of these?"

Gabriel smiled paternally. "Fifteen adorable little girls in the first generation, all between the ages of eight and eleven. The extra set of vocal cords will form during early adolescence, so they're not really in training yet. Their guardians all come from musical families with very little seniority on the childbearing lists, and were happy to have an early start on child rearing. The girls are all being given intensive musical educations courtesy of the state. When they mature they'll have their choice of careers, but a career in the musical field will be assured for them should they choose to accept it."

"But you haven't finished the work for which they were intended."

"No. But when the girls get a little older I'll toss off some choral pieces for them to train on." He looked up at her and thought about Zhenling's reaction to his scheme. "Some, I suppose, would consider the business decadent."

Clancy thought for a moment. "What's decadent about it? People have been choosing their children's genetics for hundreds of years. If you want some specialized singers, why not build them? You won't have your security forces standing over them *making* them become singers; you merely make the opportunity very attractive."

"So I thought." He relaxed against her legs and took a spoonful of cherry soup. The cherries had been stuffed with ham to balance the sweetness, and the taste was exquisite. Kem-Kem had achieved another wonder.

"Still," Clancy pointed out, "their function will become decadent, or at least useless, unless you finish your opera. If it isn't the complexity that's stopping you, what is?"

Gabriel dropped his spoon into the soup, watched as red cherries and pale bamboo shoots floated through the emerald-green lily-leaf broth.

"It's the hideous people I'm writing about," he said finally. "The entire cast is headed toward self-destruction without a thought for themselves or one another. And I don't know what makes them work."

Clancy leaned forward again, began playing with her long, curling red hair. "You have a fine grasp of psychology," she said. "I've seen you use it. You've used it on me, for that matter."

"Have I? I hope you don't mind overmuch. But whatever knowledge I have is of contemporary psyches. Disciplined minds, well educated, with a common culture, a society that provides for the material and mental welfare of its members . . . I've got that aiding me here.

"But these people are primitives. Savages. Their drives are alien and destructive. Their parents and their culture bred them, tortured them without mercy for years, then threw them away. I have a theoretical knowledge of their motivations—Louise Brooks was sexually abused when young, therefore grew up with little self-esteem, threw herself into compulsive alcohol abuse and negative sexual impulses in order to escape her real problems, et cetera . . . I can write a psychological profile of her without trouble, but I can't get into her head. There are demons in there, and the demons aren't our sort. And in order for the music to be true I've got to crack her skull and get inside, and that goes for the rest of the cast, too."

There was a moment of silence. "It occurs to me," Clancy said, "that those little girls will have their work cut out. Perhaps you should write something a little lighter for their debut."

Gabriel smiled. "Perhaps I should."

"Something with fairies singing at the bottom of a garden. No suicides, no throat-cutting. Okay?"

He kissed her hand. "As you wish. You can compose it, if you like."

"I have quite enough to do. You talked me into going for the exams again, remember?"

"You still need to work toward the Humanitas part of the exams. Composition is as good a way as any."

He finished his soup and returned to the buffet for some curry. "Tomorrow," he said, "I'll have to tell the crew what we're really doing out here. I've implied that building the battleship was an exotic nano experiment—which I suppose it is—but when we actually move into our new flagship, I'll have to explain why we're making the shift."

"Ah." She picked up her noodle plate, started eating again. "A chance to exercise your powers of contemporary psychology."

"I'm going to have to censor their communications," Gabriel said. "No realtime tachline chats with loved ones back home. They're not going to like that."

"No." Frowning. "We're not."

"I hope you understand the necessity."

She sipped some noodles and frowned. "It will cause talk among the loved ones in question."

"Good."

"If that's what you're after, then."

"I want people to wonder what we're doing."

"So long as they don't actually guess."

He curled up at her feet again. "So long as they don't actually guess," he said. "Correct."

"Forward," he said, and thrust a fist into the air, *"to the heart of the mystery!"*

He had the crew cheering, stamping, clapping their hands, jumping atop tables in the *Pyrrho*'s lounge. Amid the din, White Bear sang the "Excelsior March" from Gabriel's *Knights of Shinano* in a fine, light tenor.

Amid all the enthusiasm the censorship decrees passed without comment. One miracle among many, Gabriel thought. He must have outdone himself.

He named the battleship *Cressida.*

The parade of miracles marched on. *Pyrrho* was grappled to *Cressida* and, as gravity waves beat time, the expedition set out for the supposed supernova Gaal 97, the heart of the Gaal Sphere, at ninety percent of its maximum speed. Obedient robots and implanted chimpanzees transferred personal belongings to the flagship. *Pyrrho*, with a much-reduced crew, separated every so often to drop more communications buoys in out-of-the-way star systems, catching up by boosting its own speed to the maximum.

Robot probes leaped ahead, accelerating to the limits of gravity drive. Gabriel was of two minds about them—if they arrived too far in advance and were discovered, they could give away his intentions. But small probes were difficult to detect, and if Saigo and any other conspirators could find them, they could surely detect *Cressida* as it came storming in. Intelligence concerning Gaal would be very valuable, Gabriel thought, and even if Saigo discovered one of the probes, it wouldn't necessarily prove that Gabriel was coming himself— he could have sent it from Illyricum.

The voyage out would take four long months.

Gabriel anticipated boredom. He knew he was a very bad passenger.

He would require diversion ere long.

"The hell with you," said Louise Brooks. She was drinking bathtub gin straight from the bottle. "The hell with everyone." She smiled, the famous beautiful sparkling smile on the famous beautiful sparkling face. She slammed back another load of gin, wiped her mouth, smiled the famous smile again. "And the hell with *me*," she said.

Gabriel froze the simulation. He had built Louise Brooks and the others in the oneirochronon, using modern psychological modeling programs and techniques. Looking for answers, finding none.

He could talk to Louise and Lulu and Pabst and the others—even the fictional creations would stay in character, would act scenes with one another.

What they couldn't do was surprise Gabriel.

He had gone back to *Lulu*, hoping that he would have

developed greater insight. He hadn't; he was just finding another way to occupy himself when bored.

He banished Brooks and the others. No music sang in his
head. Manfred snored in his lap.

Gabriel looked at the felt wall hangings and realized that
he was sick of them.

Reconfiguring his suite took another half-day out of the
trip.

The troika sped across a rolling plain of white. The sky was
an illumined azure; evergreen forests cut graceful curves
across the landscape. Cold air nipped Gabriel's cheeks as if in
teasing love-play, but under his fur coat and hat he was perfectly warm. Runners growled lightly over the snow, and
harness bells jingled—Gabriel recalled the beadlike bells he'd
strung in Clancy's hair.

Zhenling wore a coat and hat of glossy sable fur and
shared with Gabriel a bearskin comforter. The hand that Gabriel held was warm as toast. Gabriel never saw the face of the
driver perched on his box out front, but the man had white
mustaches flaring wide on either side of his ears.

"Thank you," he said. "I got so tired of my quarters that
I had them completely redone, just so I have something different to look at."

"You could visit me at Schloss Eiger," Zhenling said.
"I'm planning a classical ascent of Mount Trasker—you could
join me."

"I'm dedicated to conquering the mountain of quantum
uncertainty at the moment, Madame Sable. Perhaps another
time."

"Madame Sable?" She brushed her sable hat with her
free hand and looked pleased. "I rather like the name."

"Take it. It's yours."

The troika's runners grated over hard snow. A wide frozen lake was visible ahead, a white dacha with an onion-
domed tower visible on the far side.

"I hope you're enjoying the entertainment," Zhenling

said. "This is presumably something indulged in by your Kamanev ancestors."

"Those that survived *your* ancestors when they came up out of the Gobi, yes." He looked out over the white low hills. The sun was so bright it seemed the snow was on fire. "Getting out into the country was a splendid idea," he said. "We seem to spend all our time together in one or another simulation of the indoors."

"Bedrooms are getting too small for us," she said. Zhenling's dark eyes glanced up from under her long lashes, and Gabriel felt an answering pulse of flame up his spine. She took his hand and drew it into her sable coat. He felt heated flesh, taut muscle, a pointed breast that nestled like a bird in the hollow of his hand.

He resisted the impulse to glance at the silent figure of the coachman. Let that oneirochronic figure, he decided, stand for Saigo or whatever other eavesdropper had broken the Seal . . .

"I'm in need of diversion myself," she said. She stretched luxuriously against the pressure of his hand. "Greg left this morning to take up his apprenticeship with Han Fu."

"Is that so?" Gabriel said. His hand slid down her sleek flank.

He was prevaricating. He knew perfectly well that Gregory Bonham, Zhenling's consort, had left the Violet Jade labs and Tienjin and taken out an indenture with Aristos Han Fu. Bonham remained her legal consort, but had committed himself to living apart from Zhenling for years.

"Should I offer congratulations," hand moving, "or condolences?"

She looked up into his eyes. "Would the condolences be sincere?" His hand dipped low; she gave a sudden gasp.

"No," he said.

"Then say nothing at all." Her lips brushed his. He tasted orange and spice. She drew herself away and closed her coat about her.

Gabriel, savoring his brief taste, returned his attention to the landscape. The dacha on the far side of the lake was covered with lacy white gingerbread and the onion dome was painted crimson and gold.

Vanity wanted him to claim credit for Bonham's departure, but Gabriel judged vanity to be mistaken. Zhenling and Bonham had, he thought, been coming apart for years, ever since Zhenling had passed her exams and he, with two tries, had not.

"It's difficult for an Ariste to find an equal, isn't it?" she said. A bright wink of snow-covered landscape was reflected in her eyes.

"There are only other Aristoi."

"And that doesn't work out very often, does it? In the past Mehmet Ali and Castor, and now Maryandroid and Maximilian." The troika grated over ice as it began moving over the frozen lake. With the flat terrain the wind speed rose, carried tiny grains of ice that raised tears in Gabriel's eyes. She turned toward him. "Have you ever loved an Ariste, Gabriel?"

"Twice before you."

"Dorothy St.-John, yes?"

"When I was indentured to her. But I was a Therápōn at the time. And then again with Pristine Way, but that was more of an aesthetic collaboration—we were working on a play—and it didn't last long."

"Why don't we Aristoi stay together?"

"We're very busy people."

"Greg and I were busy, too—we're pioneering, remember. Four new systems to be terraformed and populated. It's something more than merely being busy. I suppose we Aristoi are too intense, too dominating, too self-willed to succeed very often with one another . . ." She turned to him suddenly. "Do you find our time together a strain?"

"No. Of course not." Gabriel declined to smile at the question.

"Of course you won't see me as often as I'd like. Too busy with your conspiracies."

"The longer the interval," he said, "the sharper our desire."

"As long as it's not *too* long, Gabriel."

" 'Sweetest love,' " he said, " 'I do not go/For weariness of thee.' "

She sighed, took his hand. The troika grated briefly over bare ice, then rose smoothly onto snow again. "Forgive these questions. It's been such a long time since I've had to wonder about any of these issues. Since I've been involved with anyone new."

"There is no need for me to forgive you anything."

"Whereas you," continuing the former train of thought, "seem to find someone new at every turn."

"I love easily."

Her eyes turned to his. "You fall in love with all of them? Truly?"

"I do. It's not hard." He smiled. "They're good people. I don't choose badly."

Her gaze turned suspicious. "And where do I fit into this seraglio? One among the many?"

"You're different. Sharp as a sword, brilliant as diamond, challenging as one of your mountains . . ." He smiled, looked into her eyes. "I wanted you the first time I met you, at your Graduation."

"Greg and I were new then. Your attentions were obnoxious." There was a secret glow in her eyes; the wind had burned her cheeks, a nicely done effect. "But most flattering," she added.

"I like it when I can flatter someone and do it with such absolute truth and sincerity."

Zhenling had the modesty at least to pretend skepticism. The troika lurched as it rose onto the lake's opposite bank. On the unreal air floated the taste of woodsmoke. The dacha rose on the right, all onion dome, glass, and white gingerbread. Icicles hung from the jigsaw tracery.

"Stop here, Gury."

Though strictly speaking unnecessary, the words maintained the illusion. The troika jingled to a stop. Steam rose from the horses' muzzles. Zhenling threw off the lap robe and stepped out of the vehicle. The lightly built conveyance swayed as Gabriel swung himself out; she took his hand and led him into the building.

The entry hall was paneled in light wood. The window-panes and a marble entryway table glittered with rime. Zhenling led Gabriel through a room with a long table set for a banquet, white tablecloth, white china, crystal glasses etched with frost. Another room had plush, fussy Yellow Epoch furniture, all in shades of white, silver, and ice-blue, and an ornate iron stove in which was a flickering ivory flame, like ice afire.

The programming skills displayed were splendid. Gabriel's mind buzzed with pleasure.

Zhenling led him to a second-story bedroom illuminated by a pale sun that shone through wide French windows scored with fractal curves of frost. Outside was a gingerbread balcony. Icons gazed down from the corners, saints and madonnas with unearthly eyes, their images partly covered by sleeves of gold brocade set with white pearls. Delicate lace hangings wreathed the bed. Frosty mirrors hung on the walls.

An ermine coverlet was stretched over the bed. Zhenling turned and opened her arms wide, sable against white. Gabriel stepped toward her, slid his arms inside her coat, and kissed her.

The only warmth in the room was hers. He placed her on the bed, black hair on pale body on sable on ermine. The mirrors reflected his movement through distorting mist. The opposites, hot and cold, black and frost, sent a memory of the Black-Eyed Ghost along Gabriel's spine, and then a hunger for more contrasts.

A notion drifted through his thoughts, solidified there.

Something he hadn't done since he was very young. He had mastered the art, then lost interest.

Like riding a bicycle, he thought, one shouldn't forget.

(GABRIEL: Reno, location of Dr. Clancy. < Aristoi Override, Priority 1 >

(RENO: Dr. Clancy is still asleep in her quarters, Aristos.)

The ship's schedules were complex and at variance with Zhenling's day in Tienjin in any case. It was fortunate under the circumstances that Gabriel needed only two or three hours sleep per night.

He stretched out alongside Zhenling, stroked her skin that was stippled with cold.

Gabriel needed to delay this until he got the second feature in place. He tongued Zhenling's nipples, then called a warm breeze into life that played over her skin, evaporating the saliva his tongue had left on her, turning the nipples first cool, then hot.

He felt a hand on his cheek. "Stop," she said. "This is my fantasy, built for you. No extraneous effects, please."

"As you wish, Madam Sable."

He rose up above Zhenling and tented his coat over both of them. He kissed the hollow of her left clavicle, let his lips browse down the length of her body until he

GABRIEL: Cyrus, navigate my body to Clancy's quarters.

He rose from his couch, cinched on his dressing gown, and strolled to Clancy's quarters. The doors parted for him.

It was morning for her, as near to her normal time of rising as no matter. Clancy was curled on her disordered bed. She sighed as she felt Gabriel's presence, turned her head blindly toward him.

Cyrus's astringent, youthful perceptions floated through Gabriel's mind. Cyrus moved Gabriel's body into the bed, slid close up behind Clancy, gently kissed her throat.

"Behold how goodly my faire
*   loue does ly*
In proud humility."

pressed his lips to the high, fine arch of her instep.

Warm human smells rose. Gabriel's lips grazed upward, slid along the smooth inner thigh. He felt an involuntary muscle twitch, heard a startled gasp of laughter.

Carefully Gabriel tasted her.

Her oneirochronic liquor awarded him a taste of fire.

His consciousness slid from the oneirochronon to his body. Cyrus was perfectly capable of handling this part.

Zhenling gasped, shuddered. Strong fingers clutched at Gabriel's scalp. Liquid nitrogen cold flowed from her fingertips, pierced his skull with daggers of ice; then they turned warm, sources of light that licked at his senses with laser fire.

Energy flooded along his nerves.

Gabriel moved Cyrus aside, overlapped one set of perceptions on the other. He rose, threw off the fur tent, regarded Zhenling's pale body against the midnight-colored sable. Mirrors echoed her in infinite image. The ghost of Blushing Rose

Spenser's words, Cyrus's choosing, Gabriel's voice. Pleasure shimmered through Gabriel at the interwoven perceptions.

"Disturber?"   Sleep grated in her voice. "What time is it?"

"You were scheduled to wake soon, Blushing Rose," Cyrus said. "I thought I'd try to make your waking more . . . arousing."

Clancy drowsily considered this while Gabriel's consciousness slipped into the waiting glove of his body. He slid a hand into her embroidered bed jacket, cupped one warm breast.

Clancy turned toward him, raised a hand to stroke his hair. He bent, kissed a nipple, tongued it until it swelled and turned rosy with blood.

He knelt over Clancy and pushed Cyrus from the oneirochronic body, ordering the ghost body, in the unreal dacha on the edge of the unreal lake, to take its cues from his shell of flesh.

The contrast, rose flesh superimposed on old yellowed ivory, struck his mind like a poem.

overlapped his perceptions, a warm-colored image in his mind.

He entered her and felt a warmth enclose him followed by a surprising sensation of cold that gripped him at the root, then traveled down the length of his engorged focus like a deliberate caress.

The sensation paralyzed him for a moment, then it was repeated and took his breath away. He ordered a slight decrease in the intensity with which he was receiving the sensory input, found he could tolerate the sensation.

He let his physical body set the pattern and rhythm. Zhenling adapted effortlessly to his lead. Pleasure floated through him at the success of this, the precise art of simultaneous pleasuring. The swift alteration of warm and cold caresses continued, like the alteration of black and white, ivory and rose . . .

A rose blossomed in his heart, his mind.

He entered her, felt her pelvis lift to welcome him. Supporting himself on his hands, he looked down into her drowsy peridot eyes, felt as well the glittering touch of Precious Jade's slitted, calculating glance.

He gasped. She touched his cheek. "Something wrong?"

Gabriel shook his head. "Overcome with poetry," he said, which was true enough.

Love continued in its fond, fanciful way. A few times he had to gasp from what the oneirochronon was doing to him; other times found him slowing in order to prevent sensory overload or a premature explosion.

White heat rose up his spine, touched his brain with daggers of ice.

Roses pierced him with thorns of frigid cold and tore his mind asunder. His cries seemed to echo through a million mirrors.

Zhenling rolled away, laughing, wrapping herself in

Gabriel was still propped above her on his

her sable coat. White mist floated from her mouth and nostrils. Gabriel reached out with his mind and the frost traceries on the windows and mirrors expanded, uncoiled, traced the images of vines and roses on the pane. The rose petals were red-tipped with snow-white centers, Snow Queen and Red Lady in one.

"My fantasy, remember?" Zhenling said. "You're not supposed to do that." She reached to the pane, translated a rose into three dimensions, plucked it and held it in her hand. She inhaled its bouquet and smiled.

"But still," she said. "Very nice." She glanced up at him, her eyes intent. He heard the sound of dripping water. He looked at the mirrors and saw that the frost was melting, water drops, as they descended, outlining the frostpatterns on the glass.

Warmth rose in the room like a flush rising to a young girl's cheek. Colors, green and red and blazing orange, began to blossom through the white-and-blue wallpaper, turning the walls springlike. Outside, through the window, Gabriel could see spring roll over the landscape

arms. Clancy reached up, touched Gabriel's forehead. It was dotted with sweat. Sensations of heat and cold were still shooting up his spine.

"*That* was very intense," she said.

He couldn't quite locate any words of answer and stretched out beside her in the bed, nestled close to her, inhaled her scent. He wished he could work her a miracle here, in the Realized World, as he could in the oneirochronon.

Clancy was silent. There was a thoughtful glow in her eyes.

" 'Our love white as snow on mountain peak,' " she quoted, " 'Brilliant as moon between clouds.' "

White as snow, Gabriel thought. How appropriate. As if the spirit of the thing, the superimpositions, had somehow communicated itself to her.

Clancy rose and stepped toward the bathroom. He heard water gush from the tap.

Gabriel turned his body over to Cyrus and faded entirely into the dacha.

like a carpet. Another miracle, he thought. Birds began calling from the eaves. He turned to Zhenling, saw her dressed
in a long Yellow Epoch spring dress, covered with beadwork in floral patterns. The sable fur had vanished from
the bed, replaced by a scattering of the white-and-scarlet
roses.

Zhenling rose gracefully from the bed. "Shall we drive?"
she said.

Spring Plum chose a costume for Gabriel, a white linen
suit, cravat, straw hat with floral ribbon. "Certainly," he said.

He took her arm, led her down to the entrance. The soft
carpet was plum-red, a brilliant fire blazed in the cast-iron
stove, the plates in the dining room held ripe fruit, and the
goblets brimmed with wine. Zhenling took an umbrella from
the stand by the door.

Outside, Gury the coachman stood next to a berline
drawn by four horses with flower plumes nodding from their
forelocks. The top of the coach had been folded down.

The sun was low on the horizon. Presumably it was
morning, since there was a heavy dew and the scent of freshly
mowed lawns. In a far-off valley Gabriel could see a brush-
stroke of mist.

Gury took off his top hat and opened the door of the
coach. Gabriel got a look at his face for the first time, saw that
behind the spreading white mustachios, beneath the bald
crown, Gury looked as much a Tatar as Zhenling. There was
a familiarity to the visage, but Gabriel couldn't place it.

Gury bowed and Gabriel handed Zhenling up into the
coach, then joined her. She unfurled her parasol and held it
gracefully over one shoulder so that its lacy fabric cast sun
dapples on her skin. Gury took his place on the box and took
the reins.

"Your fantasy is peerless, Madame Sable," Gabriel said.
She put one arm through his.

"I hope I have distracted you from your cares. Whatever
they may be."

"You've succeeded most wonderfully."

"You're a wonderful lover," she said, "even if the oneirochronon gives you certain advantages that nature may not. Not that Gregory wasn't fine in bed," she added dutifully, "but there's a difference. More in style and texture, I suppose, than technique." She nestled closer to him; Gabriel felt warmth stir in his loins. "I would like to meet you in the flesh, Gabriel," she said.

"You will. When my current task is over."

"The matter of style intrigues me." She looked up at him. "May I ask a question?"

Gabriel smiled indulgently. "If you must."

"You love men, too, don't you?"

"Yes."

"Is that a matter of style and texture as well?"

"I suppose. Mostly a matter of love, I'd like to think."

"But you've never been involved with any of the male Aristoi, even though some are inclined that way."

"They don't attract me."

"Not Salvador? With those eyes, that skin? A man who has to appear as a hawk in the oneirochronon to protect himself from unwanted attention? He certainly attracts *me*."

Gabriel shrugged. Zhenling looked at him again, eyes narrowed. He smiled.

"You're going to analyze me again, aren't you?"

"Forgive me, yes."

" 'Why then should I accoumpt of little pain, that endlesse pleasure shall vnto me gaine.' "

An amused light sparkled in her eyes. Her hands were warm on his. "I'll try to keep the pain at a minimum."

"And the pleasure?"

"I think it's your brain chemistry."

"Determining sexual preference? Of course. That's not news."

"Not that. You're so buffered, you see, and deferred to and so on."

Gabriel permitted a tiny degree of impatience to settle into his expression. "I believe we've been over this."

A forceful enthusiasm had entered her tone. "But it's significant, isn't it, that your partner selection is different with Aristoi and non-Aristoi? When you're involved with what for the sake of argument we will call your equals, you choose only women. With your inferiors, men and women both."

Clear enough where this was leading. "I would say your database is a little small, isn't it? Besides, I didn't wait till I became an Aristos before I started jumping into bed with boys."

"But how many of the boys became Aristoi? Whatever their social class, they were still your inferiors, and with your inferiors, gender doesn't matter to you. You don't distinguish between men and women, because what makes them desirable is that they're in a subordinate position."

"I'd say there is more to it than that."

"I'm sure there is. I never said there wasn't." She laid her cheek on his shoulder.

"I don't know whether that's a compliment or not."

She looked off into the horizon for a moment before a reply rose to her lips.

"I don't know that I meant it either way."

An hour or so later the ride was over and Gabriel was in his bath musing over his morning. *Our love white as snow on mountain peak,* he recalled—Clancy's words after love, taken from an old Han Dynasty poem by Jo Wenjun. *Brilliant as moon between clouds.*

I'm told you have another lover.

The next line. He'd forgotten it till now.

A chill went up his back. Jo's poem had been about a woman saying good-bye to her faithless partner.

For a moment he considered the possibilities. Gabriel wondered if Clancy had meant it as farewell, or if the poem had merely been meant as a signal that she knew of his other involvement, a little reminder to call him back to the Realized World.

FLASH < Priority 1 >.

A jet of terror shot through Gabriel. Someone else, he thought, had been killed.

He hoped it wasn't Zhenling.

Aristos, this is Rubens Therápōn. The probe sent to Gaal 97 is halfway through its in-system pass. I've been monitoring the feed, and the data is unmistakable. Forgive the *FLASH*, but the matter is important.

Gabriel calmed himself. This wasn't another mataglap strike. **Report, Therápōn Rubens.**

The fourth planet around Gaal 97 has been terraformed. Preliminary data indicates that it's inhabited by tens of millions of people, though their level of technology would seem to be rather low. Orange Epoch or worse. There's a lot of burning biomass down there.

Surprise rolled through Gabriel's mind.

Where did he get them? Gabriel wondered. Where did Saigo get all those *people*? He couldn't have exported them from the Logarchy without both immense logistical problems and other Aristoi discovering the fact.

He made them. The answer came with awesome force. Gabriel felt his mind stagger with sickness and awe.

Saigo had built these people, the same way he'd built the ecosystem off which they lived. Built the atmosphere, the trees, the life in the oceans and on the land. Built the entire population—*tens of millions*—and then left them here to struggle at a barbarized level of technology.

Totally at odds with the Aristoi's ideal of service to humanity. The most loathsome thing of which Gabriel had ever heard. The greatest crime in all history.

Release the nano to build more probes, he told Rubens. **Including those with interatmosphere capability. We're going to need a lot of them.**

At your service, Aristos.

I will see the data now.

At your service.

Gabriel was going to have to come to the rescue, and fast.

Chapter 9

ANIMAL TAMER: Madness kindles madness in the
                    people
                  Madness kindles madness in
                    the heart
                  The animals will rage when the
                    meat is in the cage
                  And blood drives them
                    together, then apart.

The probe was shooting through the Gaal 97 system at about one-fifth the speed of light. Its gravity generators were off, to avoid detection, and Gabriel ruled against a change in course this close to an inhabited area. The gravity waves might be observed.

Still, such data as the probe revealed was compelling. The planet had been half shadowed when the probe shot by, and the lit side showed bright swirls of blue ocean and silver cloud, white upthrust mountain ranges and green vegetation, all a far cry from the sultry, sulfurous atmosphere reported by Saigo's first probes.

There was a continuous respectful babble in the oneiro-chronon as more and more of the *Cressida*'s crew came on line to observe. Gabriel asked for a list of those currently in the oneirochronoic environment. Clancy was among them.

Dr. Clancy. Will you make an estimate of the public health and sanitary conditions on the planet?

I will do what I can, Aristos. But the status of hospitals and sewers is difficult to estimate from the data available.

I ask only what's possible.

Yes, Aristos. I'll do what I can.

Gabriel sorted the rest out into teams and gave each team an assignment, then busied himself with his own speculations until the team reports began to roll in.

The night side showed a scattering of light, faint spots that marked human habitations. Spectrography revealed that it was biomass or oil that was burning, not gas or electric light—but even with that limitation, some of the glows were quite substantial, revealing cities with populations in the hundreds of thousands and enough sophistication and wealth to light their streets at night.

This was confirmed by another look at the daylit hemisphere. Following the glittering tracks of rivers from the oceans Gabriel came upon more cities, marked more often than not by the grey-black smudge of chimney smoke. Where visibility hadn't been degraded by pollution or weather, individual people could be seen in streets. Rubens quickly wrote a program to estimate the population of the cities by applying an algorithm to the number of streets and a density sampling gained by counting individuals.

The largest of the visible cities seemed to be in the vicinity of a million people. Apparently at least some social systems were working well.

Other areas, arid or covered with jungle canopy, seemed to have little population at all, although whole civilizations could in theory be concealed beneath the treetops.

Gabriel's observation teams provided more detail: wind- and oar-powered vessels on the water, the largest in the neighborhood of eighty meters from stem to stern; draft animals at work in the fields; wagons, riders, and coaches moving on primitive roads. Castles overlooked rivers, star-shaped fortresses guarded cities and invisible borders, regiments marched on drill fields.

Saigo apparently allowed his creatures to fight one another, world-sized gladiatorial games. Thousands could die, shot or hacked to bits by primitive weaponry, and collateral casualties among civilians would be even more appalling. Gabriel was staggered by the brazen callousness of it all.

There was no sign of any engine more powerful than a windmill. These poor nanobuilt inhabitants had been deliberately barbarized.

While Gabriel and the crew of the *Cressida* were examining the data, their probe had swept through the Gaal 97 system and was now on the opposite side of the sun from the inhabited planet. None of its data indicated any further habitation of the system. Gabriel issued it orders to swing around on a long curve and return. Its course correction would be timed to coincide with the probe's eclipsing a distant quasi-stellar radio source in another galaxy: if there were detectors set up on Saigo's planet, perhaps they would believe the burst of gravity waves came from the quasar instead.

Other probes were being readied in *Cressida*'s nano chambers, being linked together atom by atom.

Gabriel withdrew from the oneirochronon, leaving the Welcome Rain behind to monitor any further developments. He found the Realized World uncomfortably damp: while he'd been focused on Gaal 97 he'd left his bath and thrown himself on his bed without toweling himself off. He seemed hyperalert; his brain was racing faster than *Cressida*. His pulse and breathing were elevated. He realized he was dehydrated and hungry.

He rose, toweled, put on a day gown, poured fruit juice, and sent a message to Kem-Kem to prepare food.

NOW IT BEGINS. The imponderable voice rolled through his mind, leaving (to his surprise) no sense of surprise behind.

There was a taste of metal on his tongue.

Gabriel paused, waiting for another pronouncement, sensed nothing. The Voice (capitals coming to his mind) had Spoken.

Silly Voice.

He was going to have to do a lot of thinking, and he hoped the Voice would shut up while he was doing it.

And despite what sense and thought recommended, Gabriel knew he would have to put that planet under his feet. Taste its air, drink its water, watch its inhabitants struggle with their appalling lives.

He wouldn't be able to stop himself. However hideous, Saigo's planet was still the greatest marvel of the age. Gabriel *had* to experience it.

But all in good time.

Backup, always backup. The data was shot via tachline to Gabriel's new communications setup: it would be held in simultaneous storage in several of Gabriel's data banks. Nothing but an all-out mataglap strike would destroy it, and a strike of that dimension would give away the conspirators far more decisively than anything Gabriel could do.

Nothing but Gabriel's sending Fleta a code, once every seventy-two hours, could prevent the data from being released.

The probe's return floated more data to the *Cressida*: it only confirmed the first. The planet's population was estimated as being between 1.1 and 2.0 billion, a number that would be more fully refined as more information came in.

After sending the data packet and the preliminary team reports, Gabriel returned to the oneirochronon, listened for a moment to the hyperintelligent murmuring of his crew.

Gabriel Aristos? Marcus's voice.

Good morning. I was about to ask you to evaluate the design potential—

May I see you?

Now? He made an Olympian survey of the study teams

he'd set up, concluded his presence was no longer strictly necessary. **If you like,** he said.

He welcomed the Black-Eyed Ghost into his redesigned quarters—Palladian-style pillars and plasterwork, sixteen shades of apricot paint, all applied by implanted chimpanzees working meticulously to Gabriel's design. Marcus offered a Posture of Formal Regard, then kissed Gabriel hello. Gabriel pressed his hand over the omental fetus.

"You are well?"

"A little crazed with unaccustomed hormones, but all right. And very happy."

"I'm pleased, Black-Eyed Ghost. Does my mother still plague you?"

"Increasingly. Vashti Geneteira questions your sanity, and mine, with increasing frequency."

"I believe it's now the fashion in many quarters."

Manfred trotted up: Marcus knelt to greet the terrier and let Manfred lick his face. Gabriel dropped onto an apricot-and-silver sofa and offered tea. Marcus asked for orange juice and seated himself.

"I've come about Clancy," he said. Manfred jumped onto the sofa next to him.

"Ah," Gabriel said. "She is displeased?"

"At some point she recognized what you were doing. She had a former partner who was prone to the practice, and she feels software sex partners are hideous bad taste."

Enlightenment descended upon Gabriel. "No wonder she's upset!" he said. "A software partner would have been poor style indeed. But my partner was real, linked through the oneirochronon."

"Ah."

"My performance was more than adequate, far as I can judge. As long as both were pleased, where's the harm?"

Marcus considered this. "Perhaps you should ask Clancy. She's afraid you've grown bored with her."

Gabriel was surprised. "I'll have to set that right. She is," tactfully, "one of most interesting and accomplished partners I've had in a great while, and I adore her utterly."

Marcus looked at him for a moment, then nodded. "So do I, and I hate to see her upset."

"She was monogamous for a number of years—perhaps old reflexes came to the fore."

Marcus permitted a severe look to cross his face. "Tastes in these matters differ, you know. And no doubt the realization was an unpleasant shock, coming as an unpleasant reminder of a former relationship that did not end well."

Every so often, Gabriel reflected, he had to be reminded that though Marcus chose to *look* eighteen he really was thirty-odd years older than that.

"True," he conceded.

"You should have asked, Gabriel."

"I should. I will ask her to breakfast and beg her forgiveness."

"I hope you will." Marcus gave the terrier a final pat, then rose from the couch. "You wanted me to analyze something?"

"Industrial capacity and design, such as it is."

"As you wish, Aristos."

Marcus offered Formal Regard, then left. Gabriel floated back into the oneirochronon, checked the progress of his teams. Among the messages waiting in his stack was a note from Clancy that her preliminary report was ready.

Have you had breakfast? he queried.

Coffee and a plum.

That sounds an adequate first line for a poem, but insufficient for a meal. Will you join me?

She hesitated, said yes.

When will the river run dry? he added, a line from Li Jiyi, the poem that began *I live at the riverhead, you at the mouth.*

Drinking the same water, but apart.

He ordered something digestive in the way of music. Kem-Kem's assistant delivered the usual banquet under heavy silver covers, and Clancy arrived shortly thereafter. Gabriel

fed Manfred some boar sausage, then helped himself to wood-
cock in pastry and a shirred egg flavored with thyme and sweet
basil. Clancy had fruit, cold salmon in aspic, more coffee. He
admired her skillful hands as she peeled a kiwi with a little
curved knife.

"Have we been speaking overmuch in poetry?" he asked.

"Prose, then." She studied the kiwi, raised both brows.
"Are you bored?"

"No."

"Three hours ago?"

"Restless. Frustrated. Not bored."

"I don't want to be part of something you continue with
because you're having a dull time, and there's no other adequate diversion."

"That's not the case." Gabriel could feel the pressure of
the Welcome Rain in his skull, wanting to manipulate this
situation in his usual capable, inhuman manner. He always
tried to keep the Welcome Rain away from anyone he cared
about; but the Welcome Rain was a part of him, as much a
part as any other component of his personality, and the part
couldn't be banished totally.

He threw himself to his knees before her and took both
her feet in his hands. She looked down at him in well-bred
surprise.

"You aren't a diversion," he said, "or something to fill
empty moments in time. You're someone I need."

"And the other? The thing?"

"Not a thing. Zhenling Ariste."

The knife hesitated in midpeel. "I'm impressed," she said
finally.

"She's an impressive person."

"The lives of the Aristoi are so intricate," she said. "I've
watched you for months now, but I can't begin to comprehend it all. I only have a part of you."

"An important part."

"Can she share more than I can?"

"Probably not. The Aristoi are too territorial to make good partners."

Slices of kiwi began to fall onto her plate. "I'm surprised you're still interested in me at all. I can't hold a candle to an Ariste." She looked up at him. Her voice softened. "Rabjoms couldn't hold a candle to you."

"Will you come to the planet with me?"

She hesitated. "Which planet?"

"The one we just found. Saigo's planet."

Astonishment blossomed in her face. "We're actually going to land on it?"

"I am. And a few others."

"Why?"

"There will be things to discover." Vaguely.

"You can't resist, can you?" She smiled. "You want to see it."

"I don't think it will be any more dangerous than what we're already doing. Nothing an Aristos can't handle, in any case."

She pointed the knife at him. "That thought is perfectly delusional. Are you so eager to get out of this shell that you'd deliberately endanger yourself? But still." She allowed herself a smile. "Yes, I will come to Saigo's planet with you."

He removed her slippers and kissed her feet. "Thank you, Blushing Rose."

She lifted an eyebrow. "And if you wish to cast me in any more orgies, Disturber, you will inquire first."

"I will."

He took her hand, the one without the knife.

"There is music I've composed for you," he said. "Would you like to hear it?"

An Aristos, he thought, could have *everything*. Lovers, diversion, adventure, the glory of uncovering the greatest and most fearful conspiracy in history.

Boredom sailed away on grail-shaped clouds of glory.

* * *

Self-replicating probes, every one a miracle, raced toward Gaal 97. The initial probe looped back, passed around the fourth planet again and again, provided more data. Population estimates stabilized at around 1.3 billion, the final number depending on how many people were actually living under the vast tropical canopies. All lived at Orange Epoch levels of technology or worse.

Windmills, wind-powered ships, oxcarts, and flatboats, but most work seemed to be done by brute human muscle alone. Primitive firearms existed in large number—cannons were picked out on the ramparts of castles and star-forts, and musketeers were seen drilling next to other soldiers carrying swords and pikes. Apparently Saigo's creations slaughtered each other with great frequency.

Clancy's report on public health: open sewers down the middle of every street and open cesspits everywhere, some in alarming proximity to wells and cisterns. A few of the larger urban areas had some proper sewers, but only in a few neighborhoods and in any case inadequate for the observed population. A few aqueducts existed here and there to guarantee good water, but most water was acquired from rivers, streams, or public wells.

The public health situation, in short, was horrifying. If Saigo had provided his people with as many microbes as he had firearms, disease and plague were bound to flourish.

There was no direct evidence of widespread disease, but Clancy's report dryly noted that the cemeteries were full to bursting.

Reports began to appear from the other stellar probes sent out in the first wave. One encountered a planet that was in the process of being terraformed—gigantic automated terraforming ships hovered overhead, seeding the planet with a constant rain of nano.

Then a second inhabited planet was found, one much resembling the first in its ecosphere, population levels, and level of barbarism.

Then a third.

Saigo was building himself a population base independent of the Logarchy. But why?

If he wanted to challenge the Aristoi directly, he could have given his creatures powerful technology and welded them into a barbaric fighting force.

No, he was up to something else.

"It's a philosophical experiment," Rubens ventured. "He's throwing people together in various ways to see what happens. Perhaps he wants to confirm some theory or other concerning human nature."

"Or political dynamics." This from Yaritomo.

The setting was informal, a terraced garden-amphitheater in the heart of the battleship *Cressida*. Fountains played, fronds waved, robots delivered refreshments. Chimpanzees slept heedlessly among ferns. People sat on benches of soft-crystal ceramic.

Gabriel, dressed in monkish white cotton, walked barefoot on green grass in the center of the group. He wanted his people to meet in actuality as well as in the oneirochronon—group brainstorming to send thought in unexpected and worthwhile directions.

Remember the green-skirt girl. Delicate memory rose as Gabriel knelt on the moist timothy. *Everywhere be tender with the grass.*

"The simplest explanation is that he's a sadist," Clancy said, not in the humor to play green-skirt girl at the moment. "He's letting people die in hideous ways, and from what I can see every single death is preventable."

The others blinked. Even Gabriel recoiled from the thought.

None had been trained to think of Aristoi in that fashion. The Best were the guardians of humanity, and their chief credo was service. Even the most excessive and wrongheaded, like Virtue's Icon, had human betterment at the heart of their obstinate political philosophy.

"I haven't observed that in him," said Marcus. "Though

when I served him I saw him only rarely." He gave a laughing smile. "He was *here*, I suppose, most of the time."

"He's a serious man, often a gloomy one," Clancy said. "Perhaps this supposed dedication to his work was an attempt to sublimate vicious tendencies."

There was another small silence as the others absorbed this additional unwelcome thought.

"With all respect, Therápōn Tritarchōn," Marcus said, "I think not. Saigo's closest associates were serious, dedicated individuals like himself, clearly consecrated to the philosophy of truth, science, and betterment. Saigo might have been able to hide or sublimate his own wicked inclinations, but if his associates were similarly disposed, complete concealment would have been impossible. It would have just been too big."

"And if his inner circle were *not* so disposed," Gabriel pointed out, "Saigo wouldn't have been able to gain their loyalty."

"Possibly not," Clancy said. "But there are many kinds of sublimation, and many more kinds of denial."

"Our first goal is to know ourselves honestly and truly," Yaritomo protested. There was a little of the Burning Tiger's insistence in his voice. "Can so many be deceived?"

"I would say it is not without precedent." Calmly. "Look how far the Crackling Prince got before he was stopped. And many of his circle gave him trust and loyalty right to the very end."

Rubens turned to Marcus. "Therápōn Hextarchōn," he said, "why didn't you become a part of Saigo's inner circle?"

Marcus shrugged. "Perhaps I wasn't serious enough for him. Or talented enough. His closest Therápontes were all ranked Tritarchōn or better." He gave a little nod. "But I think I may have helped him, in a way. Saigo's specialty was change and evolution—human and biological evolution at first, then cultural evolution, and lastly—supposedly—stellar evolution, hence his interest in the Gaal Sphere.

"But he and the people around him were supposed to be running simulations of theoretical cultures. Designing fictional human societies, then using up vast reno capacity to observe how they evolved."

Gabriel was delighted. "The societies were *real*, then? They disguised their real project under the cover of a simulation?"

"I was asked to contribute some designs, by Therápōn Deuterarchōn Gulab, who was my supervisor during one stage of my training. He wanted a compact furnace design capable of turning out wrought iron with less than one-point-five percent microscopic slag particles, which normally wouldn't be a problem except that he imposed some curious restrictions—I had to use natural materials and Orange Epoch technology. No compressors for the air, not even the most primitive blast furnace."

"You didn't think this odd?" Rubens asked.

"It was part of my training." Marcus shrugged. "I thought it was an exercise, a test of creative problem-solving. I was always being asked for designs, some with equally odd restrictions—it wasn't unusual, and I didn't think any of it. Gulab also asked me for a winch design that would use the iron produced in the furnace, and later he wanted a design for an eight-horse draft wagon—he wanted a rational arrangement for controlling the reins, I recall, but not one that had been used historically."

"How many other people were involved in these design projects?"

"Hundreds. Thousands, perhaps."

So Saigo had been able to tap the brainpower of his most brilliant subordinates, and all without telling most of them that their inventions would have an immediate use.

Other theories rose, were debated, were shelved until further data arrived. Gabriel called an end to the meeting and rose to his feet. The others saluted him and began to leave. Clancy called out to him.

"Yes, Therápōn?"

"I wanted to tell you I've finished the search-and-destroy nano for the meningitis virus," Clancy said. "It's a much more elegant version of the one I cobbled together when Krishna was ill, far more efficient and less dangerous for the patient—it sweeps up all the bacteria DNA instead of just exploding it and permitting it to foul the patient's bloodstream. Shall I wait for the next Nano Day to submit it for approval, or will you want to look at it before that?"

"I'll look at it within the hour," Gabriel said. "Congratulations."

"I'm also well advanced on a package that may be useful in case of Lodestone's disease."

Gabriel took her in his arms and kissed her. "I'm obviously not giving you enough work."

"You'll make up for that soon. Assuming the plan to land on Saigo's planet is still in the works."

"It is."

Her look turned reflective. "I'm learning a great deal, and you've awakened such stirrings of ambition . . ." She sighed. "Life was once so simple, Disturber."

"Blushing Rose," Gabriel smiled, "I've always found simplicity overrated."

Cressida sailed on, aimed like a bullet for the heart of Gaal 97. The meningitis cure, and later the Lodestone package, were patented under Clancy's name and released to the Logarchy. Two more inhabited planets were discovered, along with another that was still in the process of being terraformed. Back in Gabriel's domaine, on Brightkinde, the election campaign was in full swing.

The second wave of probes hit Gaal 97. Some perched on asteroids to replicate themselves, others dived straight for Saigo's planet. Of these, some orbited at a respectful distance, sensors deployed, while others dove into the atmosphere. Most looked like ordinary objects, very often a simple nail or paving stone that could burrow into a building or roadway and record everything it observed for transmission later. Information was sent in short, unobtrusive bursts, each packed with data, each directed to relay satellites on the far edge of the system. It was hoped they would remain undetected, even those that dropped straight into population centers to sample the inhabitants.

Some of whom turned out to speak something related to Latin, a descendant about as far removed from its original source, though in another direction, as Provençal. Others spoke a Khmer derivative. Others something else that sounded like a Navajo dialect.

The replicant probes followed and with them came more data on languages. There were several hundred language families, fully as many as had been present during the Yellow Epoch of old Earth[1] precedents.

The broadcast images showed that existence, even for the better-off, more than justified Thomas Hobbes's remarks on life being nasty, brutish, and short. Heads were observed stuck on pikes above city gates; bodies that showed signs of pitiless torture swung in cages over city streets. Filthy children slept in gutters while disinterested oligarchs in their finery were carried in chairs over the starving bodies. Diseases were various, unimpeded by rational treatment, and often fatal. Disfigurement was even more prevalent: seemingly healthy individuals were often revolting *ugly*, a fact that disturbed *Cressida's* cultured, gene-enhanced observers almost as much as anything else.

In the country, wandering families of laborers and gleaners slept under haystacks while those with property largely slept with their animals. Famine seemed fairly commonplace—banditry, much of it under the guise of warfare, even more so.

The style of warfare destroyed whole provinces. Campaigns were under way in many corners of the globe, and economic despair, rising populations, and the collateral effects of war itself seeded the armies with more volunteers than could be fed. The primitive firearms available in the more civilized countries increased the soldiers' abilities to terrorize and extort the population, but gave little power to the civilians' abilities to resist. Only those who could afford large and costly fortifications could guarantee any degree of safety to the local populations, and this was almost everywhere a king, emperor, or despot.

The result, everywhere, was tyranny, a tyranny as total as the tyrants' limited grasp of technology permitted. Not a breath of political freedom was to be discovered except in very isolated rural populations, or most often in neolithic cultures living in areas of environmental extremity, polar chill or tropical jungle.

It was mass chaos, mass hardship, mass death. The lives of the aristocracy were enviable only in comparison to those of the Demos. The cumulative impact of the probes' images staggered *Cressida*'s crew. Rubens and Yaritomo took to spending several hours each day in tranquil meditation; others buried themselves in work or sport; Clancy took refuge in unremitting fury.

"Sadist, did I say?" she said. "De Sade was a piker by comparison! Hitler was a trifle maladjusted, Stalin a blunderer, and Chingiz Khan a mere amateur!"

She pushed her half-eaten breakfast away. "If you see any sign of Saigo," she said, "I want you to sterilize his location to half a solar unit."

Probe images floated through Gabriel's mind. Red-armed washerwomen, drunken young men carrying weapons, a legless beggar with a coating of artfully applied filth. All speaking plausibly derived variations of Earth[1] languages—Saigo's design was fascinating in its baroque complexity.

"This is the end of him, you know," Gabriel said. "Once these images are seen, Saigo's finished. Even his own people will be appalled—he'll face a revolt in his own domaine."

"It can't happen too soon." She reached out, took his hand. "You can't release the data now, can you?"

He shook his head. He remembered another scene: a marketplace, pop-eyed merchants arguing over the price of vegetables while a wide-eyed girl-child expertly filched a cabbage behind their backs.

"We've got to be absolutely safe," he said. "The communications setup won't be complete for another five or six months."

"The amount of human suffering down there is so appalling . . . Can't something be done?"

"By all appearances it's been going on for hundreds of years. Another six months won't make much difference in those poor people's lives."

"Except in the number of their dead."

Gabriel recalled a scene of naked children playing some kind of game, screaming as they ran through the streets, ducking under the hooves of carriage horses. He had never in his life seen children play with such abandon, or as dangerously.

They are daimones, he thought. Not complete personalities at all. That's why everyone on the planet seemed so intense: it was as if they had the Burning Tiger in them, along with Kouros and Mataglap, and no overarching personality to control them, just switching from one to the other, reactive.

Not really self-aware. Just essences. Strong perfumes, bitter, sweet, or heady.

"Disturber?" Clancy's voice was tentative.

Gabriel snapped to the present. "I beg your pardon," he said. "I was thinking of something I'd seen on the planet."

"So was I. The cemeteries."

"We've become redundant, it occurs to me," Gabriel said. "We've got the data in our comm network, we've got a communications system growing throughout the Logarchy. If we and the *Cressida* disappear now, the data will be released— not to everyone, not completely, but to enough of the Aristoi to result in effective action. Our task from this point is to gather more data, and to make certain that the timing is right for its release."

Clancy smiled thinly. "And to stay alive, I presume."

"Yes," Gabriel agreed. "That, too."

The oneirochronon, the ballroom, the dance. *Mediacorte, demiluna, cruzado.* Apologies.

"Apologies," Gabriel said. "I'm neglecting you."

Distantly she moved within the circle of his arms. The stack of messages from Zhenling had grown to alarming proportions. He had wanted to construct an oneirochronic fantasy for her, like her troika ride, but he hadn't the time. The best he could do was repeat himself, take her here.

"The work is taking all my time," he said. "I've made a breakthrough."

"Congratulations." Her eyes were focused at a point somewhere behind his right shoulder.

"And you?"

"I'm in a base camp halfway up Mount Trasker."

"You're doing well?"

"Got over a couple of moraines successfully, but the hard part's yet to come. You know—where the mountain turns vertical."

Gabriel thought of a mountain range he'd seen on Saigo's planet, volcanic tuff soft enough that the inhabitants could dig in it with their primitive stone tools, building themselves eyries halfway up the mountainside. The way humans seemed to adapt to every ecosystem even without the technology available in the Logarchy.

"That was humor," Zhenling said. "You might have acknowledged the attempt, even if it wasn't that amusing."

"I'm sorry, Madame Sable," Gabriel said. "I must be the worst of companions."

FLASH. Screaming in his head. *FLASH.* **< Priority 1 > Gabriel Aristos, we have detected a tachline communication from Saigo's planet.**

"A poor companion," Gabriel said, "and I'm about to be a worse one."

Her tilted eyes turned to his. "No kind of companion at all," she said, "if I'm any judge."

"You are, madame, the greatest and wisest of judges," Gabriel said. "And I crave your pardon."

Zhenling smiled, a bit coldly. "I'll pass sentence later," she said.

* * *

A coded tachline burst had been intercepted by one of Gabriel's out-system satellites, which through sheer coincidence had just happened to pass between the transmitter and receiver. Apparently the transmission was aimed at Earth^2, right for the data store that was Luna.

Saigo was using the Hyperlogos without anyone knowing. Cressida's suspicions had been proved absolutely correct.

Gabriel ordered one of his satellites to hover perpetually between Saigo's planet and Luna and intercept any further communications.

The burst's origin was very precisely pinpointed: a large mansion in one of the largest cities centered in a temperate zone of one of the two southern continents. The city had a population of around three-quarters of a million people and was the capital of a large, thriving, expanding kingdom, ruled by the typical vainglorious despot with, in this case, more-than-typical efficiency.

It was also the only place that had shown any evidence whatever of modern technology.

Concentrate the next generation of probes there, Gabriel ordered. **We'll want data on language, customs, dress, social organization.** He called up the aerial survey maps of the city and smiled.

That's where we'll go, Gabriel said.

Chapter 10

PABST: I will pit the actors one against another
I will drive them mad with my demands
What reaction will I get from this savage,
half-tame pet
When I lash her with my whip and my
commands?

Welcome new scents rose gloriously to Gabriel's senses: leather, damp soil, horse sweat, vegetation thriving after recent rain, and always manure. Red wildflowers flashed past the windows, were reflected in the silver butts of bandit-deterring snaphaan pistols, hopelessly awkward and long as his forearm, stuck in embroidered, tasseled window-side holsters. The uncovered wheels flung up little rainbows of spray as they thundered through puddles left in the two-rut highway. The sensation was all of a complexity that only the most careful oneirochronic programming could hope to simulate. Even Zhenling's dacha hadn't been this good.

Gabriel's heart soared at the reality of it all. He was off the *Cressida* at last, and moving across the surface of Saigo's

planet—Terrina, as it was called locally. Gabriel squeezed
Clancy's hand and laughed out of sheer exuberance.

This was going to be a glorious adventure.

It had started out adventurously enough, slamming
through the atmosphere in a glowing aerodynamic shell that
streamed fire from its trailing edges as it battled with thicken-
ing air . . . Rubens's new heat-shield ceramic performed as
advertised. Gabriel hadn't dared bring *Cressida* too far into
the system, so he and his party had shifted to *Pyrrho*, sending
the smaller yacht on a looping trajectory that would pass near
Saigo's planet without having to use its gravity generators
while in-system.

The shell, once free of *Pyrrho* and braked by the atmosphere to a subsonic velocity, altered its shape to permit a
slow glide to the target, a pasture near what passed locally for
a major highway. Backup chemical rockets were provided in
case an abort proved necessary, but they weren't used: there
was no gravity generator to emit detectable waves. When the
glider had disgorged its passengers and cargo, little nanos
dissolved the structure, turning it within minutes to crum-
bling, windblown powder.

The coach was a careful copy of the most advanced version on Terrina's roads—unsprung, dangerously top-heavy,
but gorgeously ornamented with landscape paintings on the
rear and sides (copies of Canalettos from the London period),
and otherwise covered with elaborate wood carvings, glowing
nymphs, and fabulous beasts, all covered in gold leaf. The
four horses were matched black "modern" Friesians—as all
old equine stock had perished with Earth[1], modern horses
were re-creations, based on old records and creative reinter-
pretation. The four were absolutely matched in this case,
since they were identical quads, grown in vats from the same
genetic design and implanted with renos so that White Bear,
the inexperienced coachman, could better control them
through the oneirochronon. The massive horses, with their
synchronized high-stepping gait, were an awesome prologue
to the gold-leaf coach that followed.

Therápōn Yaritomo sat next to White Bear on the top, a musketoon standing upright between his knees. Two riding horses, genetically "modern" Polish-Arabs, trotted behind the coach for use in town and country. On the bench at the rear of the coach, legs dangling over Canaletto's view of the Thames near Hampton Court, was the lean form of Quiller, a cloak and wide-brimmed hat protecting his servant's livery. A sheathed sword and a pair of pistols were ready near his hand.

The ancient weapons were just for show. Gabriel and his company were well protected by other arms that were neither as clumsy nor as apparent.

The five adventurers called themselves the Surveyors, as opposed to the thirty Synthesists who remained behind in *Cressida*.

Manfred thrust his head out the window, sniffing the air, and Gabriel followed suit. Anvil-shaped cumulonimbus floated distantly, threatening a late-afternoon drenching. A thatch-roofed half-timbered farmhouse pressed against the side of the road, its narrow bulls-eye windows thrown open. Barley stood breastbone-high in the early summer fields, most of it probably destined for the brewhouses.

Occasionally White Bear exercised his fine tenor. A ruined castle, covered with ivy, stood on a nearby hill, over-looking a group of grazing sheep.

Saigo had gone so far as to populate his world with *ruins*, ruins supposed to belong to earlier civilizations that had never actually existed. He had given his cultures an artificial past.

The carriage slowed as it topped a rise, then gained speed as the road descended into a valley. There was a gap in the foliage, and Gabriel caught a view of a wide, tranquil vale, a silver-blue river winding as gently as the Thames in Canaletto's view, small towns—suburbs really, of the capital beyond—clustered on either side of the broad, placid river . . . a view as perfect, peaceful, and symmetrical as any of Canaletto's *capricii*.

The road dropped, met another, and widened. New

gravel crunched under the wheels, and a gibbet passed by. Hanging from it, in a rusty cage of iron straps, was a decaying bandit transfixed by the rusting cleaverlike sword that had disemboweled him. An old greybeard in a pot helm, armed with a long staff, stood guard over the body.

No, Gabriel thought. Not Canaletto. Not quite.

Stop at an inn for luncheon, Aristos? An oneirochronic inquiry, relayed through the reno and transmitter concealed in—built into, really—one of Gabriel's trunks.

Very well. Gabriel missed Kem-Kem's cooking already.

Perhaps it was better to test the impersonation in a small town before they attempted it in the city.

The town smelled of manure and consisted of neat white-washed stone houses, narrow and tall on either side of the narrow road, each with flowery window boxes. White Bear pulled the team into the courtyard of the inn; ostlers bustled to feed and water the horses; a grey-bearded servant in some vague sort of uniform opened Gabriel's door and placed beneath it a stepstool.

"*Grazame.*" Gabriel hitched his sword around and stepped out. His small stiff shoes balanced awkwardly on cobbles. He suppressed an urge to repair the scars and wens on the greybeard's face, and turned to give his hand to Clancy.

The basic feminine costume consisted of oppressive layers of skirts over perfectly adequate pantaloons, but Clancy had practiced aboard *Cressida* and now moved as gracefully as if born to it. She wore a wide hat with the brim rolled fore-and-aft and decorated with silk flowers. Her breast was flattened by a kind of polished hardwood stomacher on which was usually painted some prototype of feminine accomplishment—a flower arrangement, for example, or the tools of a lacemaker.

Clancy's was a flute.

Gabriel was dressed in the same open-fronted black velvet cassock he'd worn, oneirochronically, in his Persepolis party. The fashions were close enough—his own distinctions just marked him as a foreigner. All he'd needed to add was a wide hat with the brim pinned up on one side.

And he'd altered his appearance. His hair was now jet-black, longer, and straight, his eyes brown. He'd left the epicanthal folds—they weren't entirely unknown here, and he was supposed to be a foreigner anyway.

Clancy exited the coach without mishap, and she and Gabriel glided toward the entrance to the inn. The servant looked up at Gabriel and smiled with pitted brown teeth.

"*Sas ekhselencias requirn refresco?*" he asked.

Gabriel favored him with a gracious inclination of the head and spoke with an aristocratic drawl.

"*Pet' merendas solement'. No mi impelero frettero bar la capital'.*"

Odd use of the reflexive, that, Gabriel thought. *We are myself-driving in haste to the capital.*

The greybeard affected to be impressed. He turned to the ostlers and shouted "*Gitme-gitme*" to speed them about their work.

Above the door of the inn were plaster reliefs of horrid monsters that glared at incomers with red basilisk orbs. Inside, the whitewashed walls were painted with an appetizing religious allegory of sinners being dragged to Hell. While their "little luncheon"—*pet' merendas,* as opposed to the more elaborate *gran merendas*—was being prepared, Gabriel and Clancy were served a sauce of garlic, onions, and peppers on little round slices of bread. White Bear, Quiller, and Yaritomo dined in the servants' hall. The beer was toasty and rich; the luncheon, when it came, was simple but hearty. The Damned in Hell gazed at the food with longing eyes.

Gabriel was disappointed that no one asked him who he was. He had his story all ready.

The country was officially called Beukhomana, but its inhabitants usually referred to it as Ter'Madrona, Motherland. It was one of a number of nations in which a Romance language was spoken—if not for the supposition that the whole bio-

sphere had existed for, at the most, a few centuries, this could
have been taken as evidence for a large Earth[1]-style Latin
empire in the planet's history. Instead it merely demonstrated
design economies on the part of Saigo and his team, who had
simply grafted variants onto already-existing language stocks.

Saigo's economies also meant that Gabriel's microprobes
could listen to the Beukhomanan language and have an excellent chance of understanding and analyzing it.

The inhabitants of Ter'Madrona were largely dolichoce-
phalic Caucasians, though according to their own history they
had been overrun three or four centuries previously by Tur-
kic-speaking brachycephalic Mongolian conquerors. These
had only recently been ejected in a series of wars of liberation
that had, once Beukhomana had been united and militarized,
evolved into wars of conquest and religion. The Latinate language now included a number of Turkic phrases and gram-
matical turns, and there were Mongolian genes in the
population, especially in the ruling classes.

Gabriel and Yaritomo, with their epicanthal folds, were
not out of place, and they were impersonating foreigners in
any case—Beukhomana held commerce with any number of
nations inhabited by "Asian" types.

Despite the economies of race and language, Gabriel
found any resemblance between this Terrina's "Latins" and
"Turks" and the "Europeans" and "Asians" of Earth[1]'s own
history to be largely coincidental. The Caucasians inhabited
an area larger and less well-defined than "Europe" ever was,
and lived in the southern hemisphere; the Mongolians lived to
the north and west of them, and straddled three continents;
the Negroids had two smallish continents all their own, both
equatorial, and monopolized the thriving ocean trade between
them.

Still, with all the changes, Terrina was the most recogniz-
able of Saigo's inhabited worlds—perhaps it had been the
first, and the designers felt freer to experiment with subsequent creations. Another planet featured one neolithic culture that lived in pyramid-shaped concrete-and-stone

apartment blocks and spoke a completely artificial language, one with no referent in human history. The reno aboard *Cressida* was using much of its massive capacity to analyze its structure, so far without great success.

Another of Saigo's worlds featured both aquatic humanoids with gills and high-mountain peoples with superefficient lungs. Yet another was inhabited by humans with genetically boosted intelligence. All these creations were at low levels of technology, ranging from Grey Epoch neolithic to Orange Epoch savages-with-guns—the more intelligent ones didn't seem to be faring any better than their brethren in that regard.

Nine planets altogether, at least as far as Gabriel's probes had reached. And of those, there had been one single intercepted signal—here, from Terrina, from the capital of Beukhomana, the city called Vila Real.

The capital.

Are you realistic? That's how the rental agent's question came across to Gabriel. *I wouldn't want to lease to anyone not realistic.*

The word was actually *realistico*. From *real*, Gabriel realized, "royal." As in Vila Real, Royal City. But the agent wasn't asking if Gabriel was a royalist; instead he referred to Iuso Rex, Jesus the King.

Are you a Christian? That was what the man meant.

The Christianity he referred to, and its basic documents, were specific to Terrina—it was Christianity without any reference to the Jews. Saigo, or whoever had developed this culture, had apparently concluded that Judaism was so unique to its original setting that it couldn't be transplanted—at least not without more work than he wanted to undergo. Gabriel's electronic spies had got a good look at the Beukhomanans' Bible and found that, except for some highly altered texts anticipating the arrival of the Messiah, most of the Old Testament had been expunged. The fundamental New Testament was much the same, with references to Jews, Pharisees, and Romans altered to fit the planet's phony history.

Sloppy work, Gabriel thought. He could, given the opportunity, have done better.

There were Muslims on Terrina, too, but their holy book had fared better in translation, came almost straight across. Such was the advantage of inspiration over history.

The Realisticos had no Pope to set doctrine—or rather there were too many, in too many nations, and none of their ecclesiastical writs ran in Beukhomana, which had instead its council of bishops appointed by the king. Variant faiths and schisms sprang in profusion, some authorized and some not. Heresy was punishable by death, but it was difficult, in this confused background, to tell who was heretic and who merely confused.

"Of course I'm realistic." Gabriel drew himself up, pretended to slight offense. "The Gospel has long reached our shores. I'm as Christian as the day is long."

The agent had a stiff neck that tilted his head at an angle, and a strange, masklike cast to his face that kept flitting on and off. "I beg Your Excellency's pardon," the agent said. "The Argosy Vassals are ever active within the confines of the city. You'd do well to stomach it out in church."

"I shall," Gabriel said. His reno failed to provide him any clear data on the Argosy Vassals, but the stomach business seemed clear enough.

"Take care to be seen." A warning.

The agent eyed Clancy—across the room looking at the plasterwork—then sidled closer to Gabriel. His voice was pitched low. "If you should wish to rent a small, discreet cabinet in Santa Leofra's quarter of the city, I'm your man."

Gabriel steeled himself against the man's breath. He had yet to make the acquaintance here of anyone with good teeth.

"I do not believe such a place will be required," Gabriel said, "but if I see the need, I shall inform you."

"You will need servants. I can make the arrangements."

"Tomorrow." Gabriel took the man's arm, steered him toward the door. "I thank you, senator. My man Quil Lhur will pay you."

In fine coins of solid nanobuilt gold, not the debased
wreckage that passed for Beukhomanan coin of the realm.

"Tertiary syphilis," Clancy said, after the man had gone.
"The stiff neck? The parkinsonian mask flitting on and off?
You saw?" Before leaving *Cressida* she had loaded her reno
with data on extinct diseases.

"I saw and wondered."

"Fourth case I've seen today. Saigo has blessed Terrina
with so much . . ." Her voice trailed away. She strolled to the
window, crossed her arms, looked out. "Saigo would have
had to recreate it—the original spirochete died with Earth[1].
We've seen smallpox in the hospitals, and cholera, and typhus. All reinvented, so that he could inflict it on the people
here." She took a breath, let it out slowly. "Such loving
work."

Gabriel approached from behind, put his arms around
her. He could feel the tension in her. "Another few months,"
he said, "we make them all go away."

"Perhaps we could invite him over along with the servants he's sending," Clancy said. "I could drop an antibiotic
into his beer."

"At least we're protected." With rebuilt immune systems about two thousand percent more efficient than the local
variety, and that was just for starters.

"Into all their beers. Into the vats at the brewery. *All* the
breweries . . ." Her voice, and the fantasy, died away.

Gabriel swayed back and forth with Clancy in his arms as
he gazed down at the cobbled street. Their apartment was in
a wealthy suburb called Santo Georgio, halfway between the
royal palace and the capital city, and the street was fairly wide
and fairly empty. Only a few servants were seen, some pushing barrows as they headed to the market on behalf of their
masters. Beggars perched unobtrusively in doorways, each
assigned a place—so the agent had said—by the beggarmaker,
their syndic, who often altered them with crude surgeries in
order to make them more pitiable and worthy of charity.

Gabriel's eyes rose from the streets to the rooflines. The

district was fairly new, built of a gold-brown stone that woul
glow a fine shade of red at sunset. The buildings feature
gracefully curved gables and false fronts, vaguely baroque i
style, that somehow suggested their plump, wealthy, satisfie
inhabitants.

Over every door and window was the carving of a fabu
lous beast, fangs and talons bared, threatening anyone in th
street below. The symbol was universal—even the poores
hovel had a crude painting of a snake or dragon above th
door.

Gabriel's eyes sought a particular silhouette of dorme
and chimney on the horizon. *There*—five gables, leaded roo
brick chimneys twisted artfully into spirals.

The only place on Terrina, so far as he knew, that pos
sessed greater technology than that of the Orange Cultur
Epoch. The precise location from which the transmission ha
occurred.

He needed to see it. That was why he had chosen Sant
Georgio as a place to live.

"I should present my credentials down at the Saffro
Monopoly," he said. "Would you wish to accompany me?

Clancy sighed. "You're supposed to be the foreig
lord—I'm just a glorified servant. Won't this saffron perso
think it a bit strange if I'm with you?"

"Perhaps. But foreign lords are *supposed* to be strange.

"I think I will occupy myself with domestic matter
today. I want to check the kitchens and cisterns to mak
certain we're not going to be poisoned the second we have
sip of water or bite of supper." She sighed again. "And I'
want to spray the bedding to make certain we're clean o
bedbugs, lice, and fleas."

He knew her reluctance wasn't simply an uncharacteristi
fit of domesticity: she simply didn't want to go out into th
streets and encounter the disfigured hordes whom Saigo ha
inflicted with the diseases she knew she could cure if she ha
the chance. Her gaze was fixed down in the street. Looking, h

knew, at the beggars, the ones who had chosen mutilating surgery in order to guarantee a secure living.

Today was their second on Terrina. The previous night, in the midst of the promised rainstorm, they'd stayed at an inn across from the Martyrs' Cathedral, a gloomy half-built church, built on the site of a famous massacre, that hulked over its district like a vast grey beast squatting on its haunches. From their tiny oval upstairs window Gabriel and Clancy could see the church portals, around which clustered gory bas-reliefs of barbarian quasi-Turks slaughtering Beukhomanan zealots. The supposed bones of the zealots in question (pilgrims informed Gabriel over dinner) were wall-mounted in artful geometric designs and displayed in a side chapel. Praying to them was supposed to be good for a number of ailments, including (if the cause was just) ridding oneself of troublesome neighbors.

Gabriel wanted to see the bones, but in the morning there just wasn't time.

He looked down from his apartment window and saw the agent hurrying away, his neck still tilted at that odd angle.

A cure in his drink, Gabriel thought: good. Though his wife or mistress would probably reinfect him before the week was out.

He kissed Clancy's cheek and left the apartment after strapping on his sword—the straight double-edged "female" broadsword used in wushu, not the longer, heavier instrument brandished locally. The stable boy (employed by the landlord) saddled an Arab for him. He dropped a coin into the lap of the legless beggar on his doorstep and rode away.

The beggar wore a steel helmet, meant to imply that he'd lost his legs in one of the king's wars, but as he rode past Gabriel couldn't help but wonder if the stumps were the work of the beggarmaker.

"Prince Ghibreel?" The monopolist in his darkened room looked at Gabriel with eyes rheumed by cataract. "You are a relative of the Nanchan king?"

"I am a Kinsman of the Twenty-Third Degree," Gabriel said. "His Omniscience the emperor and I share a great-grandfather."

"Emperor, not king. I beg your pardon."

"Nanchan is far away, Highness. There is no reason why those here should concern themselves with its court etiquette."

Or so Gabriel hoped. The twin islands of Nanchan were on the other side of the planet, in the northern hemisphere, and Beukhomana had little contact with them.

The monopolist's look was sharp, though a little eerie since his cataract-ridden eyes were focused over one of Gabriel's shoulders. The man was in his forties and looked much older. His hair and iron-frizzed beard were white, his cheeks reddened with rouge applied over a white-lead cosmetic that was probably doing unspeakable things to his liver. His eyebrows were shaved and redrawn halfway up his forehead in quizzical half-circles. His teeth were black, possibly the result of syphilis. His lips were reddened with betel—he imported the stuff and was trying to make it fashionable. Heavy crepe was drawn over the windows to keep the room dark, so that his pupils would widen around the cataracts and permit him a degree of vision.

"We receive Nanchan nutmeg and cloves," Adrian said. "The crop was abundant, last you knew?"

"The signs favored a good harvest. But I'm not in that business—I'm from the northern island, and my family's fortune is based on the salt trade."

The monopolist gave a little rightward jerk of his chin, an affirmative gesture. "Always reliable."

"That is the case, Lord be praised."

Saffron House was deep in the heart of the city, on the Royal Canal. There the great monopolist Prince Adrian spent his afternoons overseeing the trade awarded his grandfather in return for forgiving a loan to the then-king. Adrian's wealth and title were based on commerce, not royal descent.

Gabriel had been faintly surprised that the business

wasn't left to deputies, but apparently the prince was obsessive about the family business and, despite decaying vision, kept his nose in the books.

Prince Adrian glanced at the (perfectly forged) letter of introduction allegedly written him by a family member in Kundzara, a saffron-trading station five long months away by sea. He put it down next to the gift Gabriel had presented him, a small silver chest decorated with enamel inlays of mythological scenes—a copy of a fine work done originally, eons ago, by Cellini.

Gabriel was disappointed that Adrian hadn't paid much attention to it. Perhaps it was *too* exquisite, he thought—maybe he just should have covered the thing with crudely cut hunks of precious stone.

"You wish an introduction to society, my prince?" he said. "Very well. There is a reception tomorrow evening at Count Rhombert's, in honor of the engagement of his niece to old General Baiazd—another voice in favor of Rhombert's reentry to Court, you see."

"I'm afraid not, Excellence."

"That isn't necessary." Sharply. "What *is* necessary are the conditions of my presenting you."

Gabriel leaned forward. "I am all attention, Highness."

"You will shun the party of the Piscopos Ignatio. We support Peregrino in doctrinal matters—you are *realistico*, are you not?"

"Of course, Excellence."

"You had better be, and orthodox, too." Adrian pointed a heavy-ringed finger at him. "You will also avoid the ex-chancellor's party, the so-called Velitos. They will all be wearing copper mourning medals, as His Majesty decided, at my recommendation"—the monopolist smiled—"to have the old bastard disemboweled. And thirdly, you will refuse to acknowledge so much as the existence of the Old Horse Faction, particularly Duke Tenzin. Since Ladimero's death, they've become the real threat."

Gabriel considered this. Another of his forged letters of

introduction was to this selfsame Tenzin. But still, he reckoned, Adrian would do.

"How shall I know them, Excellence?" he asked.

Adrian gave a satisfied smile. "They shall be the ones to whom I shall *not* introduce you."

Gabriel started to nod, but his reno reminded him to give the little rightward jerk of the chin instead.

"I understand, Excellence."

"These terms are acceptable?"

"Of course, Excellence."

Adrian took the letter of introduction, glanced at the seals again, then put the letter in a pile of other correspondence. "Come to my house in the Via Maximilianus tomorrow at the third gong of the evening watch, and we will proceed from there. Do not bring your own coach or companions—tomorrow night *I* will introduce *you*, and at some future date you may introduce them."

"Yes, Excellence."

"Very well, my young prince." Adrian smiled with his strong black teeth. "You may take your leave."

Gabriel rose from his padded leather chair into a Posture of Formal Regard, then went to one knee—a servant had earlier provided a pillow for this purpose—bent his head, and placed the palm of his right hand to his forehead.

Adrian jerked his chin. "Good afternoon, prince. God speed you."

"And you."

Saffron House was in the oldest part of the city, the commercial district. The ancient streets were clogged with wagons, handcarts, and barrows. Life bubbled all round Gabriel, eccentric, driven, and ferocious.

"Hey!" some broken-nosed old woman hailed. "That horse got any brains, with that dished-in face?"

Gabriel laughed in delight at this—the woman was as colorful as a character in a romance. Scowling, beribboned men, carrying swords and stepping right out of the same fantasy, offered to beat the woman for a consideration: Gabriel, who noted that their right wrists, used to dandle swords, were twice as big around as the left, declined. Drunken, dirty-faced children reeled after him, begging for coins—"for beer," one said, as if Gabriel was supposed to approve of this ambition. He decided not to feed their appetites. They abused him in vile terms and bent for cobblestones to throw.

Gabriel accelerated and crossed over a bridge. Below, narrow canal barges brought commerce to the warehouses. The cobbles fell short.

Yet just a short distance away from these scenes, past a decayed old city gate now used as a jail, was a pleasant quarter of large houses and old tree-lined avenues, among them the Via Maximilianus on which Adrian had his house. Here were the ancestral mansions of many of the old families of the city.

Gabriel rode through the district on his way home. Like his own suburb, the area was strictly residential and the streets were largely empty save for messengers, servants, and beggars. He considered what such a district would be like in his own time: there would be restaurants, boutiques, parks, galleries, perhaps a concert hall or theater.

Here there was nothing. The streets were dangerous at night, even here, so there was no night life, nothing approximating café society or even a good restaurant. Polite society dined at home, at the home of a friend, or (if traveling) at an inn, behind a stout door bolted against intruders.

The nobility who controlled the country, court appointments, and the civil administration belonged to fewer than three hundred families. A stranger wishing to move in their circles would have to provide letters of introduction from one of their number to another.

Hence Gabriel's forged introductions. It appeared that, simply by presenting one of them, he'd involved himself in the hopeless puzzle of court politics, an intricate maze so convoluted that even *Cressida*'s omnipresent eavesdroppers failed to make much sense of it.

Velitos? Old Horse Faction? Was that the same as the Old Court Party, of which the eavesdroppers had also heard?

Perhaps it was best, in the event, to be guided by Prince Adrian. The monopolist had, after all, survived and prospered amid all this.

He returned to Santo Georgia, to a fine if improvised vegetarian dinner—the meat at the market had not enticed—some flute music from Clancy, a privy of unspeakable vileness, and a bed big enough for both a king and a fair-sized harem.

His reno reviewed everything the eavesdroppers had learned about local politics. There were listening spikes in Adrian's office and home, and Gabriel was interested to know what the monopolist thought of his visitor.

Nothing at all, apparently. Once Gabriel took his leave, Adrian never mentioned Prince Ghibreel to any of his associates.

Gabriel was disappointed. He would have thought an Aristos was worth at least a mention.

"Count Gerius," Adrian said, "the Knot Secretary. Countess Fidellia. His Excellency Prince Ghibreel of Nanchan."

There wasn't room enough at the packed reception for formal bows—people were jammed together in a sweating, reeking mass, with new arrivals still packing themselves in. Gabriel was the tallest person present: his view of the Beukhomanan elite was largely confined to views of long, carefully curled hair and sweating foreheads. Prince Adrian's enormous prestige created a respectful distance around his armchair, and only this allowed Gabriel to cross his palms over his breast and incline his torso respectfully toward Gerius and his lady. The countess was heavily pregnant and looked about sixteen years of age. The Knot Secretary had a grey-streaked beard and wore more cosmetic than his wife. He had the heavy shoulders and thick wrist of a swordsman, and the sword as well.

"Is that a toy sword you've got?" he asked.

"It is the sword of my country," Gabriel said.

"Looks light enough for a woman."

"It is—that's why it's called a 'female sword,' or sometimes 'scholar sword.' "

"Which are *you?*"

Gabriel looked into Gerius's eyes and saw a savage daimōn, perhaps a little drunk, glowing there.

"Female," Gerius prompted, "or scholar?" In case Gabriel had missed the point. It wasn't clear to Gabriel why either category was supposed to be insulting, but in context it clearly was.

Gabriel inflated his chest with a breath, straightened his legs to raise his center of gravity above that of the count, to the First Posture of Esteem. He used the Principal Inflection of Command.

"I am a prince of my country," he said, "and a master of the Eighteen Warlike Techniques." He glided forward slightly, intruding subtly into the count's space, and ended in the catlike Second Posture. His voice lowered to diminish the threat. "Which of these are *you?*"

Gerius swayed back slightly. He hadn't actually taken a step back, but even that slight retreat had lost the battle, and his only option at this point was to overtrump, to escalate all the way to violence.

Which, Gabriel was fairly certain, he wouldn't do here.

(But Mataglap made his preparations, just in case. They involved the classic *O-Lo-Dzai* of the Mantis Style, Hook-Grapple-Pluck, ideal for close confines, but Gabriel wasn't really paying attention to the specifics.)

Gerius blinked. Then he smiled—took, rather, a conscious decision to smile—and clapped Gabriel on the shoulder. "Bravo, my bull!" he said, making a joke of it. "We must practice together one time. My sword master is Senator Osano in the Old Sailmaker's Courtyard. I am in his loft on Mariaday afternoons."

"I will be honored, Excellence."

"In three days' time, then!"

Gerius smiled, clownlike in white-lead cosmetic with

rouged cheeks and painted-on eyebrows; he bowed to Adrian and towed his pregnant wife away.

The countess's vacant expression had not changed throughout the encounter.

Gabriel was pleased with himself. An Aristos, he thought, can do *anything.*

If he stayed here, he thought, he'd be running this kingdom in three years.

Prince Adrian laid a hand on Gabriel's arm and smiled with betel-stained lips. "That was well done, princeling," he said. "Though it wouldn't have come to a fight—Gerius's fighting days are over, if he wants to keep his court appointment. He was merely testing the size of your stones."

"His wife seemed charming." A suitably neutral change of subject.

"That vacant-eyed heifer? His fourth. He married her for the dowry: her father's a bourgeois anxious for court influence and a corporate exemption from taxes."

"Will he get it?"

"Probably not—Gerius has the dowry now, and other schemes with which to plague the king. He can afford to let his countess die in childbirth, as the others did, and go in search of another bourgeois father with another dowry."

Another pair approached to pay their respects to Adrian, a little baroness and her pale-faced duenna. The younger of the two had not shaved her eyebrows: Gabriel had noticed that in this matter the young did not always follow their elders. Gabriel was introduced, and bowed, and filed their names away in his reno so that he would remember them.

It was becoming his job, and on the whole a tedious one.

The only thing that was keeping this interesting was the thought, however improbable, that he'd meet Saigo. And if that happened, he was ready.

The room was well lit and Adrian couldn't see much through his rheumy eyes: he had a nephew standing next to his chair, whispering names to him on each person's approach.

Gabriel found himself beginning to like Adrian. The monopolist was the closest thing to a whole person he'd met— Gabriel had the idea that there was more in his skull than a bunch of unruly reactive daimones.

But still, the standing and bowing to one group of strangers after another was dull. Gabriel wondered whether the reception would amount to anything else.

Still, it was probably better than watching the election results on Brightkinde, the other task to which duty called him.

At some point an inner door was thrown open and the crowd surged toward a buffet. A distant orchestra began to tune. Adrian waited for the room to clear and then rose from his chair and let his nephew lead him toward refreshment. "Now business will begin, my prince," he said. "You will find this tedious—by all means seek out some of your new acquaintances and spend a few pleasant hours."

Gabriel was happy to slip away.

The buffet had been laid out in a ballroom, though there was no dancing going on as yet. The fine hardwood floor glowed in the light of brass chandeliers. The walls were "gold paint," which meant a gold varnish over a white base, without actual gold. Plasterwork allegories stalked pompously across the ceiling. People juggled plates and cups while candles in the chandeliers dripped scented wax down their necks. Overhead punkahs, manipulated by invisible servants, stirred the air in a haphazard way. A twelve-person orchestra began to play— isorhythmic polyphony, fortunately, but there were odd discordant bits thrown in that were, in Gabriel's opinion, either too much or not enough. He wandered the room, eavesdropping.

"Sir Leo took the sausage in grip; sawed it, but caught horn in flank." A grizzled, one-armed noble to a young cleric, the oldster's remaining hand making gnashing movements. It took a few moments for Gabriel to realize they were describing the disemboweling of a bull by a pack of dogs. By that time the oldster had become aware of Gabriel's presence.

"Are you keen, Excellence? D'you keep a pack?"

"I'm afraid not, Excellence."

"The finest sport on God's earth, at any rate this side of the Loiontan frontier, where cutting neck's the thing." The single hand made a slashing movement. "Curse the king's unholy peace, anyway."

Gabriel said something noncommittal and drifted away.

The orchestra finished its tune and a pudgy man stood up on a box and began to sing in a clear, shivering soprano. Gabriel had never seen a castrato before and wandered over to have a look. No one seemed to find it incongruous that a man incapable of physical response was nevertheless singing a passionate love ballad. The singer wrung his plump hands while sweat popped out on his forehead, his eyes leapt out of their sockets, and hopefuls of both sexes stood in a half-circle around him and gazed at him with daimōn-ridden lustful eyes.

Gabriel disassociated himself from this company and floated back toward the buffet. Boredom swathed him in its muffling cloak. What passed here for cultured society compared unfavorably with being stuck on the *Cressida*. And the guests of honor had yet to arrive, so this would probably go on forever.

He glanced up and above the crowd of heads saw someone nearly as tall as he—or perhaps as tall, but for poor posture. The man was young, twenty perhaps, clean-shaven, with red-gold hair, deep green eyes, long delicate fingers at the ends of powerful arms. He wore a deep green cassock embroidered with gold thread, and had kept his eyebrows. He was talking with a man Gabriel had just met through Adrian, the king's Master of the Theater, Duke Orsino. (Gabriel, at the introduction, had been pleased to meet a character from Shakespeare.)

The young man's eyes rose from Orsino, met Gabriel's, blinked, and looked away.

Perhaps the evening would turn interesting.

Gabriel glided toward the pair. Augenblick and the Welcome Rain analyzed stance, blush response, pupil dilation.

Indeed yes, said the Welcome Rain.

Orsino blinked. "Prince—Ghibreel, is it? This is Lord Remmy, second son of Duke Maximilian of Zhagala."

Remmy had good skin—for this place—fine gold hair on the back of his hands, and miraculously good teeth.

Gabriel crossed his hands over his breast and made a formal bow.

"Pleased to meet you," he said.

Chapter 11

SCHÖN: What is the meaning of this?

LULU: The meaning? The knife and your death!

B y morning Gabriel was in love. The remorseless Welcome Rain had stalked Remmy through the reception like Vronski pursuing Anna through the train—wedging through chinks in armor, provoking, proposing, turning away softly every repudiation, consistently inferring, through the haze of Remmy's denial, Remmy's own nature . . . Gabriel had left the reception in Remmy's coach, driven to his cabinet in Santa Leofra's quarter, the Welcome Rain savoring his triumph in Gabriel's skull.

All because Gabriel knew how the psyche worked, how it was mirrored by the body. How to trump every stance, every pose, every physical mode; how to pursue an inevitable course through another's mind.

These people, with their fragmented psyches, could not resist a whole human being who wished to direct his entire force against them.

An Aristos could do *anything* here. Gabriel wondered if

Saigo had discovered this, and had found it to his liking—a small cosmos where he would find nothing but victims.

Lucky for everyone, Gabriel thought, that he, Gabriel, had no real vices.

Remmy slept. Gabriel finished his usual two hours' rest, then drew on his cassock and went prowling through the apartment.

The place was small, only three rooms stacked vertically around the building's corner staircase, bedroom on top, parlor in the middle, entryway and servant's room on the bottom. It was elegantly decorated in green and apricot, with glossy hardwood floors. There were icons, crosses, and a small shrine—Remmy had amused Gabriel by kneeling and saying prayers before sleep. Hand-colored prints shared the walls with musical instruments. A kind of cembalo stood on four stout legs in the second-floor parlor.

Gabriel peered out the window into predawn, saw only workmen heading for their jobs, the usual poor sleeping in the usual doorways, and one fashionably dressed man, cloaked, hooded, and very well armed, leaving a rendezvous. The buildings were a curious mixture of stately, imposing buildings and crowded tenements.

Santa Leofra's quarter. This seemed to be where the various classes of the city came together.

Still, even if they were here they weren't doing anything interesting. Boredom settled onto Gabriel again. He considered trying to contact the *Cressida* and deal with correspondence and matters from his domaine, but he decided he was too far from the long-range relay transmitter in his luggage. Not that he couldn't reach it, but the transmission would have to cross too many city blocks: Saigo or his minions might detect it.

Gabriel looked at the instruments again. They didn't seem of high quality, but then this wasn't Remmy's official home, either. He took a five-stringed guitarlike instrument from the wall, strummed it, found it needed tuning. There was fine mother-of-pearl inlay on the face, but otherwise it was rather battered. Gabriel sat on a sofa, tuned, and played. There were no frets on the neck, but Gabriel experimented, built reflexes into and through his reno, and soon managed (Cyrus transcribing for the new instrument just ahead of Gabriel's fingers) a competent Bach sonata.

He heard a creak on the stair and looked up as Remmy stepped through the door from the stair. He was in a satin dressing gown covered with appliqué embroidery in the local "Turkish" style. He looked puzzled.

"What is that music?"

"From my country."

"But on an instrument of *my* country." Remmy entered, then hesitated. The Bach sonata wound on undeterred. Remmy assumed a stern expression.

"I apologize for the poor quality of the instrument. Everything in this cabinet is cheap, because sooner or later it will be stolen." He looked disapproving. "You're not even looking at it when you play."

"I'm concentrating very hard."

"You've tuned it in a strange way." Severely. "And you're supposed to play it with a slide." He walked toward a commode, opened it, genuflected to the little shrine set therein. "There's a slide here, in the top drawer."

Gabriel's fingers ceased their motion. "Have I offended you in some way?"

Remmy opened the drawer, hesitated again, closed it. His back was still toward Gabriel. "You've encouraged me to surrender to a weakness," he said. That reflexive again: *you are myself-encouraging* . . .

Gabriel put the instrument down, rose from the sofa. "I'd like to think that I'd allowed you to express your heart," he said.

"My heart." Remmy turned, leaned back against the commode, looked down at the polished floor. His words came in an affected upper-class style, mocking himself and the style both; there was a context to it all that Gabriel couldn't read. "My heart is in one realm; my duty as a man in another.

I had sworn a holy oath to Santo Lorenzo that I wouldn't use this place for anything but—'' A spasm ran across his face. "The accepted vices," he finished. "Good God! I wasn't even drunk."

Remmy's tone sank in: Gabriel realized that the phrase about his heart and manly duty was a quote.

Gabriel wondered if he was dealing with a young man's overexaggerated sense of guilt, or whether people in this set were actually intolerant. Historically (his reno informed him) the upper classes were usually fairly liberal in matters of preference.

"It's a large . . . world," Gabriel said. He'd almost said *universe.* "It's only here that such things are a vice."

"It's only here that I live." Remmy looked stern. "And I'm a loyal son of the Church."

How to explain, Gabriel wondered, that in another year or so this wouldn't matter—there would be Logarchy ships filling the skies, engaged in freeing these people from their prejudices, their unhappiness, their murderous habits.

Gabriel approached Remmy, lifted a hand, touched his neck. The other man wouldn't look at him.

"You are who you are," he said. "Suppressing one's inner nature is torture and bitterness."

Remmy looked up at him. "Perhaps it's different in Nanchan. But here sodomy's considered a Ketshana vice, not something a true Beukhomanan would do." Ketshan was one of the pseudo-Turkish kingdoms that, in that possibly illusory past, had once been established here.

"If it matters," Gabriel said, "what we did wasn't technically sodomy."

Remmy gave a little laugh. "That's significant, you know. The difference between prison and burning. Perhaps."

Gabriel drew the other man close, embraced him, then to the sofa and picked up his instrument again. His fingers browsed along the strings. "I'm a foreigner," he said. "These local prejudices are incomprehensible to me. Why interfere between a human being and his happiness?"

"Happiness rightly belongs only to true Beukhomanans, not half-breeds, not half-men. Not heathen Ketshanese, or the damned." He peeled back one sleeve of his dressing gown. "See? Evidence of a few too many dark-skinned ancestors, of heresy and degeneracy. The veins aren't blue enough."

"I thought they were very nice veins," Gabriel said. Programmed fingers shifting key.

Remmy flushed. "There are political reasons as well," he mumbled. "Would you like to hear?"

"Of course."

"My father may be a duke, but he's not a rich one. The family needs money, but the Old Court Party is out of favor and my father with it. My elder brother is the heir, but I'm important to Dad's schemes—I'm to marry some poor child with a dowry rich enough both to advance me in the army and provide sufficient display so that royal favor may be directed my way, at least once the Orthodox Party oversteps and our faction comes back . . . Meanwhile the Orthodox will be looking for someone to discredit in order to keep themselves in power—look what they did to the chancellor. And my getting cooked on a griddle would not do me, my family, or my party any good." He looked up at Gabriel from under his brows. "Does this make any sense to you?"

"Yes. A question: is the Old Court Party the same as the Old Horse Faction?"

Remmy gave a faint smile. "Yes. That's what our rivals call us."

Remmy straightened, took a breath. "There are other reasons, too. I'm to marry soon—my father tells me—and I don't want to bring a life of misery to my bride, as my father did to my mother for altogether different reasons. I'm perfectly capable of finding pleasure with women. So I will love this girl if I can, and try not to bring some horrid disease to her wedding bed, or—" He turned, fingered a crucifix on the wall: Christ dying, half naked, swanlike. "Habits too ingrained to break."

Let me handle this, the Welcome Rain suggested. **I'll have him adjusted in no time.**

Gabriel considered for a moment. He stopped playing, damped the strings, put the instrument down. He rose deliberately from the sofa, approached Remy, clasped his hands behind the other man's neck, and told the Welcome Rain to vanish.

"Your duty to your family and your party and your God and your bride is clear," Gabriel said. "But what duty do you owe yourself? What contentment is your lot?"

Remmy looked thoroughly miserable.

"I will offer you this thought," Gabriel said. "You owe yourself happiness, not misery. What you owe your family, or family-to-be, is caution and discretion. But they owe *you* something as well, and that is understanding."

Gabriel dropped his arms, returned to the sofa, began to play again.

Remmy looked unhappy. He sighed, walked to the sofa, sat down, and stared at the ceiling. "Where did you learn to speak Beukhomanan like that?" he asked. "You have an accent, but you're far too eloquent for anyone's good."

"I learned it on board ship, sailing to this continent."

"Sailors don't talk like you do."

"I'm a good mimic. I picked it up somewhere, just like I picked up this instrument."

"It's called a larozzo."

"Tell me about the Old Court Party. And the Orthodox. And the Velitos."

Remmy made a flipping gesture of the hands that signified a kind of stylized bafflement, like a profound shrug. "Once the labels meant something. The Old Court Party was the nobles, and the Orthodox the church, and the Velitos were the . . . hard to say. They're the ones left over. But none of that means anything anymore—it's just who's in power, and who's not. The Orthodox are in power right now, but when they overreach, or if we get into another war, the king will have nowhere else to turn but to us."

"So the Old Court is pushing for war?"

"We're *always* pushing for war. It means employment for us, and plunder." He smiled thinly. "And a job for me at the head of a squadron of cavalry, perhaps a regiment."

"And Piscopos Ignacio?"

"Ah." He smiled faintly. "Father Ignacio is Piscopos to the Chapel Royal. I like him—he's counseled me now and again. A great mind to whom no one listens. He believes Christians should prove their loyalty by following the teachings of Christ instead of slaughtering those whose perfection might be suspect. He's widely respected, but no one in power can afford to follow his advice."

The Erasmian wing, Gabriel thought. Ignacio might be someone with whom Gabriel Aristos could deal once responsible people started dealing with the Gaal holocaust.

"Peregrino?"

Remmy straightened, shuddered, crossed himself. "He's the fellow who'll burn the both of us if he catches us. Piscopos of the Martyrs' Cathedral and head of the Argosy Vassals."

"Who are the . . ." Gabriel hesitated. He wanted to use the phrase "church police," but realized the word for "police" wasn't in his vocabulary. His reno cast back to the Latin *politia* and he made a guess. "*Polizia dominica?*" he finished.

"*Politicia*, you mean." Remmy smiled. "You know, that's the first error I think I've heard you make. Still—" He laughed. "*Police.* What an odd notion. There aren't any police here—there are only gangs who serve important people. The Argosy Vassals are the murderers and ruffians who serve the church *and* the royal authority. They root out subversives and heretics—one and the same, in Peregrino's opinion—and have their headquarters and prison at the Old Temple. In front of which the late chancellor had his bowels ripped—the Orthodox used Peregrino to do their dirty work."

"I saw Peregrino's Martyrs' Cathedral. It's not finished."

"Anyone wishing to stay on Peregrino's good side will donate a reliquary or stained-glass window." The thin smile came again. "It's been known to hold off an investigation. Most people feel the investment well made."

There was a screeching from outside the shutters. Gabriel rose from the couch and peered out the window. A half-dressed woman, hurling abuse, was pursuing a harassed-looking swordsman down the street. The swordsman was trying his best to ignore her. Passersby annotated the dispute with their own comments. The swordsman said nothing but increased his pace.

Just like a scene in a comic opera. Gabriel watched, thoroughly entertained, then turned from the window.

"Tell me about Santa Leofra's quarter. Someone offered to rent me an apartment here."

"Many people with a reason to be discreet have cabinets here. Santa Leofra's quarter is part of the Principality of Pontanus, which is a royal domain mostly in the northeast, but with little additions here and there. The civil authorities have no authority here unless they're serving a Yellow Warrant with Knot and Seal, which can only come from the king. So the place is full of foreigners, criminals, whores, fugitives, debtors, heretics—" He made the flipping gesture with his hands again. "And well-off people like me who probably ought to know better."

"It seems to be the most intriguing district I've seen thus far." Gabriel turned back to the window and looked out, hopeful of seeing something interesting. He hadn't ever seen anyone behave as had the woman and the swordsman, and the whole episode was tinted with a theatrical quality he found delightful. Not, he admitted dutifully, but that there wasn't probably some horrid tragedy at the bottom of it.

The predawn street had returned to normality. Disappointed, Gabriel returned to the sofa and sat next to Remmy.

"I think I like your country," he said.

Remmy gave his tight little smile again. "That's only because you don't know it well."

Gabriel put his palm over Remmy's gold-backed hand. "I

know some parts well, and still like them enough to want to know them better."

Remmy sat up on the couch, looked at the hand that covered his own. A smile twitched at the corners of his lips.

"Well," he said. "If I'm to be burned, I may as well thoroughly deserve it."

Remmy's carriage returned at the appointed hour of mid-morning, just as the fourth gong of the forenoon watch was being struck. Gabriel told Remmy where he lived in Santo Georgio, and was told that Remmy lived there as well, in his father's house with the rest of his family.

As they entered the suburb Gabriel pretended to lose his way and directed the carriage down the street from which the transmission had originated. He called up his daimones and watched as the big house moved past . . . big gables overhanging the walled yard, fluted chimneys, the bas-relief monster over the door. Shuttered windows, so perhaps no one was home.

"There's a fine house," Gabriel pointed out. "I admired it yesterday."

"Duke Sergius's place." Remmy didn't seem interested.

Gabriel, feigning confusion, leaned his head out the window. "I seem to have misled you," he said, trying to keep the building in sight. "Perhaps—" He raised his voice for the coachman. "If we turned left at this next street."

He turned to Remmy again. "Tell me about this Sergius," he said. "I've heard the name somewhere."

"I don't know much about him," Remmy said, "though he's well-placed enough. A philosopher and friend of the king, and of the Piscopos Ignacio. I've hardly ever seen him— he spends most of his time at his estate in the country."

Or in another part of the Orion Arm, Gabriel thought.

"He has a fabulous house out there," Remmy said. "Quite unlike anything ever done."

"Perhaps I've seen him," Gabriel said. "What does he look like?"

"A big dark man. Older. Slant eyes, like yours. Rather gloomy looking."

Saigo, clear enough.

Remmy looked up at Gabriel in some surprise. "And now that I turn my mind to him, I find he reminds me of you. Why do you suppose that might be?"

"I've no idea. We don't seem to look anything alike."

"Do you think you and he might," Remmy hinting delicately, "share certain tastes?"

Gabriel concealed his amusement at this idea. "Why do you think so?"

"Because—" Remmy turned puzzled. "No idea, really. He's unmarried, but I've never heard any hint of—" He frowned. "He always struck me as standing and moving in an interesting fashion. Stylized, posing almost, like a dancer. And you carry yourself in a similar way."

The Book of Postures, Gabriel thought. Further confirmation, were it needed. "And he knows the king, you say?"

"Oh yes. He's said to be one of the king's most intimate advisers. He's fabulously wealthy, and he's made it known he'll never accept office and will never join a party, so for the most part there aren't any knives out for him."

Fabulously wealthy. Easy enough when you can assemble gold from base matter.

Like a clockmaker god, Gabriel thought, Saigo had built this place and set it running. But once he had it going he hadn't been able to resist interfering.

Wealthy and prestigious. Advisor to the king. Grey eminence, most likely, to the whole damn planet, if not the entire Gaal Sphere.

Gabriel was thrilled to have a genius of Saigo's caliber for his enemy.

Nothing else could ever be more flattering.

One of Gabriel's half-dozen new servants opened the door for him. He hadn't realized he would need so many servants in the house: Clancy required two maidservants just to lace her into her formal clothing.

Gabriel wrote a short apology to Prince Adrian, then sent one of his new footmen to Adrian's place to collect his horse. He climbed two flights of wide, creaking wooden stairs to his apartment and entered. He found Clancy in the parlor, sitting in an armchair and staring vaguely at the rooftops visible through the open window. She was dressed in a native blouse and her own baggy trousers.

Doubtless the new servants were scandalized by this ensemble.

She rose as he came in and kissed him hello. Her face had a fluttering kind of gaiety in it, and she moved with a lilting, tossing motion unlike the Clancy Gabriel knew. A daimōn.

"Hello. I'm Falling Water." The voice was bright, the light in her eyes flirtatious.

"Is Dr. Clancy busy?"

"Yes, she's working on a project. I can call her if the need is urgent."

"No. I'll wait."

"Would you like breakfast? I can ring."

"I'll do it." Ringing.

"There is a message for you, an invitation to a reception this evening at Count Bertram's."

Gabriel found the invitation waiting on a tray; he'd met Bertram last night, a smiling porcine predator in white-lead cosmetic.

He'd go, he thought. He could introduce Clancy to some of these people. If it was boring they could simply leave.

He wrote an acceptance and sent it with the servant he was sending to Adrian.

"Would you like me to play the flute for you?" Falling Water asked.

"If you could do it without bothering Clancy, that would be nice."

Falling Water tilted her head, smiled, and fluttered her lashes at him. "No problem at all," she said.

Gabriel had a *gran merendas* of some forcing-house fruit along with an egg dish that seemed a benevolent, if bland, combination of pancake, omelette, and custard. He then closed his eyes and listened to Falling Water play a Sher Bahadur sonata while he contacted *Cressida* and used the ship as a relay to his domaine. He dealt with correspondence and administrative matters, and postponed (again) contacting his mother.

There was another stack of messages from Zhenling. He decided to postpone answering that as well.

Lastly he sent his encrypted password on to his new communications net, giving him another three days before the news of the Gaal Sphere was released.

Disturber? I'd like you to look at something, if you're not busy. The voice was Clancy's, but the contact oneirochronic rather than in the Realized World, where Falling Water's flute continued without missing a note.

If you'll hold a moment.

He concluded the most important matter—certifying election results on Brightkinde—and told Horus to finish the rest.

Clancy was waiting in a comfortable oneirochronic office: padded leather chairs, shelves with reference works, three-D projectors, facsimile printer, beautifully calligraphed diplomas, a shelf that held a collection of ancient seals.

"I need you to tell me if I'm on the right track," she said. Gabriel's oneirochronic ghost kissed Clancy, then sat in one of the chairs and heard a pneumatic hiss as the chair adjusted itself. A nice touch, that.

"What are you working on?"

"A holding container for nano, with built-in stepped artiphages in case the nano goes bad."

"Like the Kam Wing container."

"Yes and no."

He smiled. "Tell me more."

A safe container for nano had been a goal for centuries. A container that somehow held a counter-nano artiphage had been an obvious idea, but had been subjected to a number of limitations. Artiphages were fairly carnivorous themselves—they were designed to eat mataglap, and they could devour other things while they were at it. And no single artiphage was good for all species of mataglap.

Kam Wing, known as the Aristos Knight for his elaborate courtesy, noble behavior, and singleminded dedication to human betterment, had centuries ago designed a container for nano that featured multiple liners, with artiphage nano sandwiched between layers of neutral substance. If the nano went mataglap it would eat through the neutral lining to the artiphage, which would then be liberated to destroy the mataglap in turn. If the first layer of artiphage didn't stop it, the second might, and so on.

But there had always been limitations. The process could produce so much heat and/or gas that the container would rupture. The neutral substances had to be carefully chosen so that the artiphages wouldn't eat them but the nano could, further so that the artiphages wouldn't devour each other, and additionally so that the neutral substances would bond properly with their neighbors. Stable artiphages had to be chosen, so that they wouldn't mutate to undesirable forms. So thorough had been Kam Wing's design that, although it had been altered for different conditions or different varieties of mataglap, the basic work had not really been improved upon.

"This morning I was doing what I hoped was the last work on the Lodestone hunter-killer," Clancy said. A model of the Lodestone virus appeared over her shoulder as she spoke, a nasty little bundle of sugar-protein that could lie dormant for years in the parenchyma of the pancreas before emerging to interfere disastrously with secretion of amylase, a process that, by fatal coincidence, produced a waste product that was itself a vicious nerve toxin. The patient could die either from nerve shutdown or wild swings in blood-sugar levels. Usually a doctor wouldn't look for both.

The disease itself was so rare that the vector was completely unknown. Probably Lodestone was a slow-motion mataglap, a bit of mutated nano that had somehow escaped into the human environment.

"The easiest way to attack the Lodestone is when it's shed its protein sheath and invaded the parenchymal cells," Clancy said. "Before that stage, no one looks for it anyway."

A strand of the Lodestone uncoiled and enlarged so that Gabriel could see individual molecules arranged in their long strands. The ends stretched out into infinity. Another long molecule appeared, an array of lithium atoms arranged along its length like fangs.

"I've devised a hunter-killer that will steal the hydrogen bonds from the target DNA," Clancy said. "It's smaller than the virus, a kind of pseudo-RNA, and it should be nonpolar until it actually encounters the Lodestone."

The hydrogen-hungry lithium fangs quietly absorbed the hydrogen atoms holding the target's nitrogenous bases together; bits of the Lodestone strand began to fly apart. "In order that the fragments won't recombine into something equally deadly, I've added little functional groups that will attract fragments of the Lodestone DNA." The Lodestone fragments bounced through the simulation, then discovered the sections of the hunter-killer meant to attract them. The hunter-killer's functional groups slotted into the Lodestone's nitrogenous bases like keys sliding into tumbler locks.

"Very nice," Gabriel said. "What happens to the hunter-killer then?"

"The simulation says it should be passed with pancreatic fluid into the digestive tract, and thence from the body. At that stage it should be completely inert. But of course that's only what the *simulation* says. Further testing is needed."

Gabriel ran the simulation back and forth several times. Dimly he was aware of Spring Plum's approval of both Sher Bahadur's adagio movement and Falling Water's interpretation of it. The hunter-killer performed as advertised.

"I'm impressed, Blushing Rose," he said. "This is admirable. Do you wish to submit it formally?"

There was a hesitation in her reply. "I think so. Give me a little more time."

"As you like. But what does this have to do with the Kam Wing system?"

"As part of my double-check routine I combed the Hyperlogos to find whether this particular cut-and-lock system had been used before. It hadn't—not quite—but what I found out was that the *target*, the Lodestone virus, had qualities similar to Brilliant Emerald-type mataglap."

"Indeed?"

"Perhaps one is a mutation of the other. I checked, and with a small adaptation the hunter-killer could be turned into an anti-Brilliant Emerald artiphage."

"There already are Brilliant Emerald artiphages. Romance[1] and its descendant, Romance[2]."

"Yes, and Romance[2] was used by the Aristos Knight as the centerpiece of his container system." A glowing model of Kam Wing's container, red and green and gold, appeared in place of the first simulation. Clancy demonstrated how the Romance series worked by subverting the target like a virus does a target cell, an obviously attractive feature. But, because Romance[2] degraded under high temperature, Kam Wing had to include a heavy insulating layer in his containers to keep the Romance artiphage from being destroyed by the heat-producing Devouring Web mataglap.

"That's not a problem with my design," Clancy said. Simulations blossomed over her shoulder. Her ghost voice turned rapid. "I started by modifying the Lodestone hunter-killer into a Brilliant Emerald artiphage. The result—" She smiled. "I've had the temerity to call it Blushing Rose[1]."

Blushing Rose[1] was less efficient than the Romance series—its destruction of the target was less elegant—but it was stable at higher temperatures and didn't require heat shielding. She could therefore sandwich it between a resinous polymer that would react well with the Summer Surprise artiphage, and a doped $Carbon_{60}$ fullerene of sufficient slickness so that the Big Kiss artiphage couldn't get a grip. Between the three artiphages, seventy-nine percent of the known mata-glaps were covered.

Gabriel absorbed the displays, had Horus and Cyrus run simulations, received their reports.

"It's nothing short of brilliant," he said finally. "You've gone back to first principles and produced a marvel."

"The Aristos Knight didn't have the advantage of knowing about the Summer Surprise artiphage. It would have simplified his work."

"Still, this is staggering. How long has this taken you?"

"Since a little after dawn."

"Dawn . . ." Gabriel repeated. His skiagénos held out his cupped hands, palms up. A glow began there, a shining rose-hearted gold radiance. The glow lifted from Gabriel's nesting hands, crossed the room, settled onto Clancy's head. A halo surrounded her; dazzling laserlike beams shot from her brow.

"The dawn is in your eyes, Blushing Rose," Gabriel said. "This is magic itself, and a wonder."

Gabriel handed over the control of the halo to Cyrus: immediately it became more formal, a silvered neoclassical rainbow.

Clancy permitted scarlet to touch the cheeks of her skiagénos. "Thank you, Aristos," she said. "But I remind you that this system is untested and incomplete."

Spring Plum floated Gabriel a joyous echo of Sher Bahadur's triumphant finale, *la réjouissance*.

"You have done the most complete and elegant design in decades," Gabriel said. "The rest is details."

Gabriel gazed at Clancy's shining skiagénos and evaluated her in terms of its new light. Without doubt she would achieve the rank of Ariste: the long-latent synthesis, the tumbling-together of ideas, had begun. The integrative thinking of the Aristoi, wherein each thought, each skill and idea, began to expand and multiply and reinforce the other.

Psyche sang in his heart, a wordless poem of joy.

"Watching you has been of great benefit," Clancy said.

"I'd never been close enough to see how these things were *done* before."

"I doubt there's anything left for me to show you," Gabriel said. "I think, after this, you will find the technical part of the exams no mystery. The humanitas sections are the only ones that need give you concern—you should probably try to develop a daimōn to help you with composition or civic design or some other creative art."

She frowned. "I don't know if I'm creative in that way."

"Creativity is a resource that can be applied to any art, once the art itself is sufficiently understood."

She lowered her lashes. "Yes, Aristos. But—"

"You don't know if you want to be an Ariste?"

Clancy's eyes rose to meet his. "Correct."

"Blushing Rose," he said, "once the thing happens, you won't be able to stop yourself."

"Ah."

"We dominate humanity because we can't help it, and because the others couldn't stop it even if they wanted to. When the form of the new container created itself in your mind, could you stop yourself from working the thing out?"

"No. But that's a little different."

"You'll find that it's not."

Gabriel felt his heart lift, soaring with Psyche, with *la réjouissance*. His mind was already working with Clancy's innovation, daimones plodding at low priority, taking over unused portions of his reno to run simulations and test new innovations.

He could sense other ideas, notions unrelated to Clancy's project, fluttering at a lower level. Clancy's burst of inspiration had started a long, complex pattern of association running deep in the less organized portions of his mind, conceptions formed by things less organized than daimones, vague elements of ideation buried deep below conscious thought.

He'd have to undergo deep meditation to bring it all out.

This was shaping into a very creative morning.

Gabriel would concentrate on the less formed ideas for the moment, since he didn't want to disturb Clancy's work until she was finished. He wanted her synthesis-burst to run itself out, and then perhaps he'd help with the final details.

"This is all absolutely right," he said. "I don't think you need my assistance at this point."

"I suppose I wanted reassurance."

"You have it, and my honor and admiration as well. You also have your fortune made—you'll be able to afford your own asteroid lab when we return. Finish the work, Therápōn, then contact me."

He bowed his head in a Posture of Humility, then faded from the oneirochronon. Falling Water had commenced another flute sonata; her eyes dallied with him through fluttering dark lashes.

Gabriel's left hand was drawing with the point of a knife on the breakfast table in front of him. He looked at it in surprise. The hand kept drawing.

Gabriel leaned forward for a closer look. There was a peculiar metallic taste on his tongue. The knife's dull point had impressed a character into the fine linen tablecloth, the Intermediate Iconography glyph for *Beware*.

The hand shuddered and dropped the knife. It rang against porcelain with a clang. Gabriel ordered the hand to make a fist and move off the table: the orders were obeyed.

Gabriel used his reno to provide a quick mental inventory of his daimones. His primary personality was right-handed, as were most of his daimones; Cyrus and Augenblick were the only exceptions. Both denied being responsible for the glyph.

Spring Plum had been controlling his body while she listened to Falling Water's flute, and she was right-handed. While her attention was diverted, some Limited Personality had taken control of the left side of the body.

Beware. The style, the one-word ominous message, was familiar enough. Silly Voice.

Resourceful Voice. The Voice had been ingenious

enough to take control of his body when he was otherwise engaged. This deserved some thought.

But not now. Gabriel rose from his seat, locked his hands behind his back, paced the room.

His mind was in ferment, and he had no desire for further distraction.

"Welcome, Prince Ghibreel. What a lovely companion you have brought. From your native country?"

"My personal physician," Gabriel said. "Dr. Okhlanu-Sai."

This was, unfortunately, the nearest phonetic Nanchan equivalent to "Clancy."

Count Bertram's eyebrows, had they not been painted high on his bald forehead, would doubtless have risen. "A physician? Have they female physicians in Nanchan?"

"At least one, my lord," Clancy said, and dipped gracefully into a long formal bow, hands crossed on her breast.

Bertram was amused at what he presumed to be an unusual affectation. He smiled with tiny predator teeth: another diverting animal for his petting zoo. "Splendid! Excellent! Welcome to my house, Dr., ah . . ."

"Perhaps Clansai would suit your tongue better," smoothly.

"You do not mind if I shorten it? Santa Marcia bless you, child." He turned to Gabriel. "You are lovers, of course?"

"Of course."

Somehow, for Bertram, that explained everything.

Gabriel presented a gift to his host, an enameled gold perfume bottle that contained a glorious scent, and he and Clancy entered Bertram's hall. People, standing in front of old, murky landscape paintings, gazed at the newcomers with well-bred curiosity. At the far end of the room a young girl sang in a fine mezzo voice to the accompaniment of a cembalo. Voices murmured; the room glowed in candlelight.

This wasn't a formal, public reception, as last night's at Count Rhombert's had been—this was a more intimate occasion, a gathering of friends and people presumed to be interesting.

Perhaps it wouldn't be dull, after all.

Gabriel had been reluctant to go: the day's cascade of invention had been too exciting to leave behind. But he had sworn to investigate things here, and he'd already told Bertram he'd come.

Horus was still laboring away on new designs, along with Cyrus and a high-priority call on the reno. Clancy's daimones were equally busy—her bolt of inspiration had bogged down in a nasty mass of detail that would require hard slogging before they were dealt with.

The journey of the *Cressida* had been justified by this last day alone, never mind what happened in the Gaal Sphere.

The soprano's voice echoed interestingly off the paneled walls. Gabriel made his way along the large room, introducing Clancy to people he'd met at Rhombert's. Prince Adrian's nephew was among them, the young man who had stood at Adrian's elbow the previous evening and whispered the names of those come to pay their respects.

Gabriel looked at him, and the nephew cut him dead.

The servant sent to collect his horse from Adrian's house in the Via Maximilianus had returned both with the horse and with the silver Cellini chest, the gift Gabriel had presented to the prince. It appeared that Adrian had severed his relationship with his new client.

Gabriel felt a touch of regret at the loss. He had quite liked the cynical old man.

Pity. But that didn't seem to affect his relationship with anyone else in the room, all of whom received him quite civilly.

He set about the business of making himself interesting.

The task was easy enough in this circumstance: he floated about the room and made comments. For the most part he simply cribbed from the great wits of history, safe in the knowledge that his audience hadn't heard Sheridan or Wilde or Ben Jonson.

The mezzo—some lord's daughter, Gabriel discovered, demonstrating her accomplishment by way of searching for a husband—bowed and withdrew to general applause. Her performance, Gabriel thought, deserved a better audience, one less diverted. A quintet replaced her—they were quite good, given the wretched quality of their instruments: Count Bertram either had a good ear or good taste in advisers.

Clancy, introductions having been performed, moved about the reception on her own. Young men loitered around her, absorbed in her flawless face and hands, her rose complexion. From what Gabriel could hear, she seemed to be keeping them at bay by discoursing on medical topics.

"Experience," said Gabriel, sampling the buffet and paraphrasing Oscar, "is the name people give to their mistakes."

His audience, two young men and a cynical old lady, laughed. A man standing behind them, tall and long-armed, face made cartoonish with cosmetic, seemed absorbed in his own business.

Gabriel lifted a pastry from the buffet, sampled it, put it unfinished on his plate. Too sweet.

He found himself wishing they had coffee here. Even the teas were insipid. He reached for a glass of wine he'd placed on the table.

"Mock me, do you?"

The voice was drawling, heavy with menace, almost a parody of itself. Gabriel's audience gasped audibly. Gabriel looked up and gazed into the eyes of the long-armed man who had been standing contemplating the buffet.

Gabriel collected his daimones, drew himself into the First Posture of Esteem. The tall man met his gaze levelly.

"Mock you, sir?" Gabriel said. "I do not mock you. I do not even know you."

The man stepped forward. Gabriel's audience made way for him, all save the old woman, who held her ground. He had to make a small detour around her.

Heavy use of cosmetic had made the man's face dead-white. His beard and long hair had been frizzed with curling irons. His lips had been painted on in red, and two red spots formed perfect circles on his cheeks. His painted eyebrows narrowed in a ferocious, scowling expression.

"You deny that you bit the pastry and put it down?" he said.

"I deny that I did it with any intention of mocking you."

Something peculiar here, Augenblick reported. **He's not interested in this—it's like a recitation.**

Mataglap advised Gabriel to draw the right leg back and take the Third Posture of Confidence as a ready stance. Gabriel concurred and did so.

Silence grew in the room. The quintet played on, eyes focused on Gabriel's drama instead of their music.

"I ate just such a pastry a moment ago," the man said. "You picked up the pastry and put it down after taking a single bite. Such an action can only be a mockery."

"It was not."

The man smiled with delicately painted lips. The smile was soulless, disinterested. "You have just called me a liar, foreigner."

He's *not* interested, Augenblick said. **This is all pro forma. He doesn't care about the pastry; that's just an excuse.**

This man is committing suicide, remarked the Welcome Rain. He didn't seem repulsed by the notion.

Gabriel, without real hope, attempted to turn the situation away from where it was headed, trump the man's behavior by raising the level of the dialogue to another level.

"Why are you provoking this?" he asked frankly.

Instead the man hawked and spat on the floor. He put the toe of his right shoe into the blob of saliva, then drew an X with it.

There were gasps from the onlookers. Out of the corner of his eye, Gabriel saw Clancy drifting closer, her attention locked on the painted man.

Shall I take him out? Clancy's voice, over the oneiro-chronon.

**Not unless he attempts violence. Thank you, Ther-
ápōn.**

Gabriel rose into the First Posture of Esteem. He turned
away from the man and addressed the bystanders.

"I'm a foreigner, I'm afraid, and don't understand these
customs," he said. "What do I do now?"

"Name your friend," the man said. "My friend will call
upon him."

Gabriel feigned a moment's thought before naming
Count Gerius, the Knot Secretary. The most useful name he
could think of.

The man jerked his chin. "Very well."

Gabriel glided forward another few inches, taking the
Second Posture. "May I ask your name?" he said.

"The Knight Silvanus."

The word was *Equito*. There were more gasps from the
crowd: apparently the name was known.

Silvanus smiled. A daimōn, hot and aroused, glowed in
his humid eyes. **There's feeling in it now,** Augenblick said.
He's not just reciting.

"Never heard of you," Gabriel said.

The daimōn vanished without a blink. Silvanus's face
turned blank. He turned to the host, Count Bertram, and
bowed.

"I thank you, my lord, for a delightful time."

Bertram gave a short bow in return. Silvanus made his
way out, and Gabriel frowned after him.

Who set him on us? Clancy wondered.

Gabriel wondered if it was Saigo. He hoped it wasn't
Adrian.

Beware, he thought.

Bertram was at his elbow. "I would not invite such a man
here," he said quickly. "He must have come in company."
His face was flushed under its layers of cosmetic; the encounter had made him breathless. And it had made his party a
social success, since people would be talking about it for days.

Gabriel took his arm. "Think nothing of it, my lord," he said.

His mind was turned to other things.

He had no doubt that he would survive any encounter. The problem was to find out why it was happening at all.

Chapter 12

ANImal TAMER: In their visage you will see
Animals like you and me

"Silvanus? Are you serious?" Count Gerius frowned. "You must flee the country, Highness."

"Flee from such a fellow?" Gabriel patted the man's arm. "Don't be absurd."

"He'll kill you. He's been the victor in over two hundred fights."

"So many? No wonder, if he fights over pastry." Gabriel found himself mildly impressed. He made the local hand-flipping gesture. "Has nothing been done to stop him?"

"There are laws, but who will enforce them?"

"Perhaps I shall."

Gerius folded his arms. They stood in his parlor, illuminated only by a single candle brought in by a servant. Gerius was wearing his Turkish-style dressing gown and an embroidered pillbox nightcap with tassel: Gabriel had interrupted him after his official *débotter*.

"He chooses his fights very carefully," Gerius said. "He knows you don't have a chance. You *must* flee."

"Shan't." Gabriel smiled. "I will show him a thing or two, and spare his life if I can."

Gerius closed his eyes and shook his head sadly. "You'll make a brave corpse, Highness. Unless you run."

"All men would be cowards, if they dared." After Lord Rochester—his index of wit was still on the surface of his reno.

Gerius jerked his chin. "I can't have anything to do with this," he said. "My position at court won't allow it. But I'll give you an introduction to a martial nephew of mine—he'll do you well."

"I thank your lordship."

Gerius picked up the candle and walked to his writing desk.

"Pity I won't have a chance to know you better, Highness," he said.

Gabriel smiled. "I'll win, you know."

Gerius did not answer.

Clancy, seated thoughtfully in the corner, watched as Gabriel climbed back into his coach and sat next to her. He took her hand, kissed it, and sent an oneirochronic message to White Bear to take the route to the rooms in the waterfront city where Gerius's nephew had his lodgings.

"I'm fascinated by this country," Gabriel said.

"You were out all night," she said. "Clearly you found something worthy of fascination."

"Someone, rather."

She looked at him sidelong. "I assumed so. But I haven't seen anyone here appealing to your taste—the people are so unattractive."

"Not all of them."

The coach lurched as the four black Friesians stepped out in unison. Iron-shod wheels growled as they rolled over cobbles.

"The intensity here is bewitching," Gabriel said. "Such people!"

"Their lives are so brief. Perhaps they must live intensely in order to live at all."

"Yet they're so careless with their existence. Sacrificing their lives for the most trivial of reasons."

Clancy knit her brows. "That's because they're *mad*, Aristos. They can't control themselves at all—they have no more knowledge of their own minds than a newborn child. Did you see that daimōn surfacing in Silvanus?"

"Yes. His personality has been fragmented, but not like ours—shattered, not dissected. He doesn't know how to control his daimones." He shuddered. "It was strange, facing that nameless *thing* I could see in his eyes. I *knew* it, and it couldn't know me. I wonder if it wondered what I was . . ." His voice trailed away. A tune was floating through his mind.

Clancy frowned. "Probably the result of abuse in early childhood. Or paranoid schizophrenia."

"Or syphilis. Or all three." Gabriel shook his head. "Yet the man survives. As does the race, from generation to generation. Look at Adrian—all those handicaps, cataracts, bad teeth, whatever the lead-based cosmetic's done to his liver, possible syphilis . . . Yet the fellow functions, and dominates most of those around him."

"In the country of the blind, the one-eyed man is king."

"Or the man with cataracts." The carriage lurched; White Bear shouted at someone blocking the narrow street. Clancy clutched at a strap to avoid pitching forward.

"What will you do?" she said.

"Defeat him, I expect." The mental tune shifted into a minor key, turned ominous.

"I know *that*. What I meant was, how?"

"Using what weapons, you mean? I expect I'll have to fight him fairly—our own weapons, the real stuff, would produce results the locals would think pretty peculiar."

"Can you do it without hurting him?"

"I'll have you there, should surgery be necessary. But if I can injure that sword arm of his, he won't be provoking many more fights."

"He'll probably just turn to murdering people in alley-ways."

Gabriel recognized the tune still floating through his mind: the "Ripper" theme from his own *Louise Brooks as Lulu*.

Yes, he thought.

Exactly.

Count Gerius's nephew was called the Knight Gerius, one of several in the family: he called himself Gerius of Retorno to distinguish himself from the others. Gabriel found him awake and half-drunk in his attic lodgings. Four of his friends were with him, all cadets in the Elira Foot, a not-very-fashionable regiment quartered, to its luck, in the capital.

The army did not extend to anything quite so formal as uniforms, but there was nevertheless a kind of regimental *style* that ran, as far as Gabriel could see, to supple brown leather and dirty linen in about equal proportions. It was equally clear that the style did not encompass either sobriety or bathing.

The *Equito* Gerius scanned the letter his uncle had written, then sadly shook his head. "A fight with Silvanus? I'd run for it."

His comrades booed. Gabriel wanted to crack with his thumbnails the lice he could see running in Gerius's collar.

"I'm not leaving," Gabriel said. "I'll fight him." The cadets cheered and poured him a drink. Gerius looked at the sword hanging at Gabriel's waist.

"You're not planning on using that thing, are you?"

"Certainly."

Gerius shook his head. "No, Highness. Against the rules. You'll have to use one of ours."

"I'm a foreigner, and the challenged party. Don't I get choice of weapons?"

"Choice of weapons, Highness? A foreign notion, surely. The weapons—weapon, rather—is specified in the published rules." He reached for a sword that hung from a rafter by a nail and drew it from its battered leather scabbard. "Longer

and heavier than yours," he said. "You'll do more damage
with it, I think."

The weapon was a kind of backsword, the bottom edge
sharp along its length, the top edge sharp about halfway.
There was an egg-shaped pommel, a simple crossguard, and a
hilt long enough to be used two-handed. The point was perfectly serviceable.

Gabriel hefted it dubiously. The thing hung like a bar of
iron at the end of his arm. Gerius watched him with small
keen eyes.

"You'll be able to afford a better, Highness," he said. "A
little lighter, and of better temper."

"It seems very awkward."

"Not as awkward as the heavy broadsword we use in
battle." Gerius smiled and took the weapon in his own right
hand. He made a few clumsy passes in the air, his thick
swordsman's wrist straining under the weight of the blade.
"You see? It's for fine work. A gentleman's weapon."

"Oh yes," Gabriel said. "Absolutely."

Gerius drew his arm back, let the point drop to the
floorboards. It landed with a thunk. "Tomorrow, after I see
Silvanus's friend, I'll call on you and arrange with my sword-
master to give you a lesson. Will that suit?"

"Yes," Gabriel said. "I think it had better."

He drained the drink they gave him and went on his way.
On the stairway, going down, he heard them toasting both his
bravery and his inevitable death.

The Knight Gerius's sword master was a giant Turk named
Brutus, a professional attached to the regiment. His upper
body was round-shouldered with heavy muscle, and he had a
ferocious scar that ran from one eye-ridge to his chin. He had
won over forty combats, some against professional opponents
of his own class. He taught in a long attic above a military
barracks, with skylights open to the air. He eyed Gabriel's
slim frame and said, well, he would do what he could.

Gerius's fellow cadets had heard of the encounter; a

group of them hung on the fringes, commenting and cheering the action.

The duelists' garb was specified in the rules, a copy of which Gabriel never actually saw. Both arms were clothed in iron chain, and both hands wore gauntlets backed with metal but with a leather palm. A chain-mail skirt covered the thighs and groin, and heavy leather boots protected the shins and feet.

The trunk, throat, and head were open to attack; the rest of the body protected. Any successful strike was likely to be a fatal one.

That seemed to be the point.

There was also, Gabriel discovered, a specific prohibition against wearing amulets and charms.

In action, the combattants were turned about forty-five degrees from their opponents, sword arm at near-full extension with the hand pronated, the armored off-hand held near the face, ready to parry. The combattants carefully circled each other until they saw an opening. The weapons were too clumsy to admit of much play, which mostly consisted of a cut made in conjunction with the front foot stepping forward to put the weight of the body into the strike. In order for the cut to be effective, the whole arm and shoulder had to be engaged. Thrusts were for finishing off an enemy after a cut or slash had staggered him.

Brutus went through a repertoire of guard positions, strikes, and footwork: Gabriel's reno memorized the lot. Gabriel pleased Brutus by repeating the movements very precisely, including the slight exaggeration the master added by way of effect.

Afterwards Brutus and Gabriel fought with blunt weapons. Gabriel did well enough until his arm got tired of holding the heavy weapon at guard position: at that point Brutus sliced in and dropped his edge on Gabriel's shoulder.

"You'll have to end it quickly, Highness," he said. "You're simply not used to holding a sword out for a long amount of time. Most fights are lost when one man's point drops."

Gabriel rubbed his sore shoulder. His daimones were involved in a long analysis of the fighting style.

"Is it permitted to strike Silvanus with hands or feet?" he asked.

Brutus jerked his chin. "It's not good form—people will say the blow was foul—but in a real fight, what's that matter? You've got armor on your free fist, after all. May as well use it if you can." He shook his head. "I'd make a real swordsman out of you, given time. Pity your career will be so short."

Gabriel flipped his hands. "Why does everyone seem to think I'll lose?"

Brutus clapped Gabriel on the shoulder. "That's the spirit, my bull! Never cry mercy!" A glint entered his eye. "Pity there's no time to teach you some more of my secrets."

"And those would be?"

"Tricks such as are too good for *them*." Jerking his head towards the cadets. "Masters' secrets. Taught only to my best clients." He jerked his chin. "They can run into money."

"Really? How much?"

Brutus smiled—he'd lost several teeth in front, possibly to fists in armored gloves—and rubbed his chin with one swart hand. "Secrets like these have been sold for as much as ten thousand crowns."

Gabriel smiled and called on Augenblick and the Welcome Rain. "Ah," he said, "but consider how your reputation is involved."

"Yes. If you lose, my reputation goes down."

"Hardly. I'd be considered some ignorant foreigner who lost to a master swordsman despite your doing your best in a few hours' lessons. But should I *win*, all credit will of course go to you, and your secrets will be all that much more valuable."

Brutus pretended to consider. Augenblick dissected pupil dilation, pulse rate, respiration. **Push a little more,** said the Welcome Rain.

"Reckon it, senator," Gabriel said. "Your price would rise to the heavens once it became clear that one of your students beat Silvanus after only a single day's instruction."

Brutus settled for a hundred fifty crowns—gold, unclipped currency—for each of his three secret thrusts. Gabriel sent a note to Clancy for the money, and when it came Brutus chased the cadets from the loft and got to business.

The first secret consisted of a drop to one knee in conjunction with a two-handed upward thrust. The second was the notorious, uncouth, but practical *botte du paysan*, converting the weapon into a bayonet by seizing one's own blade halfway down with the free hand, batting the opponent's guard out of the way, and plunging the point, spearlike, into the enemy's vitals.

Gabriel was perfectly familiar with these attacks. He just needed to know whether they were known in Ter'Madrona.

The third technique was ridiculous, based on a complex pattern of footwork designed to mirror the Six Realms of Heaven, intended to call angelic forces to aid the downward hack that followed.

Gabriel could only hope that Silvanus would try to use it.

"Tell me, master," he said. "Are these parries known?"

His blade-tip sketched two half-circles in the air, the French semicircular parry. Brutus frowned.

"Known, yes. But too weak—a brisk bang with the forte's better. And with your little wrists, I wouldn't even think of it."

"Perhaps this?" He drew two diagonal lines, the "destroying" parry of the Hungarian school.

"Never seen that. Can't see why you'd use it, either, though I suppose it's stronger than that other."

"I thank you, master." Gabriel flashed his blade in the salute. Brutus stepped to the table were Gabriel's gold crowns, stacked neatly, were waiting. He scooped them into a bag. "Where'd you get money like this?" he said. "I haven't seen this many unclipped crowns in my life."

"I suppose my secretary would know," Gabriel said, all offhand. "From the king's treasury, I suppose."

"It's the treasury that's clipping the money," Brutus said. "It's His Majesty's idea of thrift."

"Well." Gabriel flipped his hands. "I'm afraid I don't know where they're from, then."

How to report that he owned a philosopher's stone, a portable nanomachine that knit gold coins at the atomic level? Perhaps, in order not to stand out, he should instruct it to make debased currency instead.

Brutus accompanied him down the stairs that led to the courtyard. As Gabriel placed his new dueling gear in his saddlebags, he looked up at the coiled, snarling serpent placed over the doorway.

"Why do your people put those creatures over their doors?" he asked.

"That?" Brutus looked over his shoulder at the sinister figure. "It's a ward against demons, Highness."

"Does it work?" Gabriel asked, as the Welcome Rain chortled in his head.

Brutus grinned with his broken teeth. "It must. I haven't seen a demon yet."

You'd be surprised, Gabriel thought.

Chords thundered in his head as he rode home. His opera was taking shape.

Music filled Gabriel's dreams.

He woke early but remained in bed, music and microphages assembling themselves in his thoughts. His consciousness floated between one set of daimones and the next.

Fierce chords thundered through part of Gabriel's mind, where Cyrus and Spring Plum were supervising the climactic end of his *Lulu*'s third act, where Lulu and Louise declared their independence and their dedication to self-destruction by murdering the Animal Tamer who had tried to turn them into exhibits in his menagerie of human folly. Their macabre, chilling duet afterwards, in which they toasted each other with champagne, voice and ghost-voice exultant and uncaring, was a piece of matched malice that held Gabriel's spirit in thrall. He kept returning to it, rearranging it, making it even grander, even stranger.

He kept trying to describe, in musical terms, the daimōn he'd seen in Silvanus's eyes.

At the same time Reno and Horus were working on Clancy's container. She'd finished her work late last night: now Gabriel had to apply every test he knew to see if it would perform as planned. So far it had. He'd found a few minor improvements he thought he could add, and he had to test those as well.

The matter of Silvanus was third on his list of priorities, and he returned to it reluctantly. Just in case the thing went wrong he sent his work to *Cressida*, where it would remain on file. Clancy could find another Aristos to give his blessing to her project. And with luck someone, perhaps Clancy, might wish to finish the opera . . .

Gabriel rose, dressed, and had some plums for breakfast, enough calories to feed his muscles, but not enough bulk to sit heavily in his stomach. At the appropriate predawn gong he woke the household and had the carriage readied. Clancy pinned his hair back and out of the way with finely worked silver-and-enamel clips in the shape of rearing lions. While White Bear and the local servants readied the horses he went to the courtyard to stretch and warm his muscles. The Knight Gerius arrived on horseback, looking cold and martial with his hair tied back and his dueling skirts jingling, and watched with surprise as Clancy, clearly female despite a heavy cloak, and Manfred, in a studded collar, climbed into the coach along with Gabriel.

"Faith, is this wise?" he asked. "I would wish to spare the lady—"

"Clansai is a Nanchan doctor," Gabriel said. "I wish her to attend any wounded."

"I have arranged for a local doctor," Gerius reminded. He pulled his cloak tighter around his body.

"I prefer to have my own on hand," Gabriel said. "You look cold, sir. Would you like a warm drink before we depart?"

Gerius raised a silver flask. "I brought brandy in case you needed some."

"I thank you, but it won't be necessary."

Gerius looked at Clancy again with his small eyes. An expression of annoyance crossed his face. He turned his horse about and set out at a slow trot. The Friesians followed at their high-stepping machinelike pace. Gabriel covered his warmed limbs with a blanket to keep out a chill, then looked out at the predawn sky, stars and mother-of-pearl and chimney soot, and felt a sudden fierce longing for his own Illyricum, his World of Clear Light.

"This is pointless," he said, without quite knowing why he said it.

"Wrong, Aristos," Clancy said. "It is a point against Saigo. And there are millions more."

Gabriel jerked his chin in agreement—the local gesture won over the more accustomed one—and closed his eyes. He turned control of autonomic systems over to Spring Plum, who kept the blood flowing through his warmed muscles, kept the body alert and ready. He placed his fingers in Mudras of Concentration and deepened his breathing, setting a rhythm that lulled him into a mild hypnotic trance. He brought to his mind, one by one, all Brutus's attacks and parries, his foot movements and tricks and gestures. He rehearsed them all mentally, trying to feel the heavy blade in his hand, the power of an opponent transmitted through impure low-carbon steel, the circle, defined by radius of arm and blade, into which he could project his power. He slowed and rehearsed all the single-sword forms he knew from wushu, refining the abstraction from them, uncovering the practical techniques hidden by millennia of symbolism.

The coach slowed, and he opened his eyes. A ruddy sun was battling with cloud on the eastern horizon. Cowbells clanged in the distance. Tall ash trees stood like spears on the other side of the road.

Gerius came to the coach door and peered in. "There is a clearing just inside that grove," he said. "Frequently used for encounters. If you would step out, Highness? The . . . *doctor*," using the term dubiously, "may remain until called for."

"Certainly not," said Clancy.

"As the doctor wishes," Gabriel said. Gerius scowled.

Gabriel threw off the blanket and stepped out onto wet gravel. Dew clung to thick grass on the road's verge. Birds called tentatively from the trees.

"You should don your mail now," Gerius said. "Sometimes there are ambushes at these moments, and although I don't believe Silvanus will see the need, it's best to take precautions."

"Very well."

Gabriel took off his coat and let Gerius ease the heavy mail sleeves up his arms and strap them across his chest and shoulders. Clancy handed him his armored gloves and he put them on while Gerius belted the chain skirt around his waist.

Gerius reached under his cloak. "I took the liberty of visiting a sorceress," he said. "I bought a charm for you."

Gabriel looked at him. "I thought they were forbidden by the rules?"

The soldier lifted a big hand that held a small opaque bottle. "Only the kind you wear. This is a sort of oil that I touch you with. May I?"

Gabriel blocked himself from shrugging and flipped his hands instead. "If you like. It's very kind of you to think of it."

Clancy watched suspiciously as Gerius took oil on his finger and dabbed Gabriel on the forehead, the eyelids, the ears, and (reaching into his shirt) his breastbone. Gabriel detected a spicy scent, like cinnamon. "The saints bless you," Gerius said.

Gabriel opened his eyes. "I feel quite invincible," he said. "Let's get on with it."

Jingling and treading heavily under the weight of the iron, carrying his sword sheathed in one hand, Gabriel followed Gerius into the wood. Clancy followed, and behind her, Manfred.

I have my gun, Clancy reported, **just in case.** She had her medical bag in one hand, and the other was hidden in her cloak.

Very wise, Gabriel replied. **Take command of Manfred, will you?**

As you wish, Aristos.

Dew sparkled from Gabriel's boot-toes as he walked through the spring grass. He began a careful series of stepped meditations, his hands again in Mudras of Concentration, all designed to fire his glandular system, to increase the ACTH supply from the hypothalamus that would in turn trigger the release of epinephrine, adrenaline, cortisone. Blood poured out of his constricting digestive system, was diverted to major muscles. He narrowed the capillaries of the skin, both to reserve blood for the muscles and to prevent excessive bleeding in the event of injury. His skin would look pale and clammy—perhaps the others would think him afraid—but his muscles would swell with power.

The trees parted and revealed three men standing by picketed horses. Gabriel shuddered as his muscles reacted to the onslaught of blood and chemistry.

Silvanus stood among the three, his face a fierce cosmetic scowl. He waved his sword two-handed in big circles, warming his shoulders.

"Wait here," Gerius said, and stepped forward into the grove. The two strangers, one casually hefting an axe, approached him and the three conferred for a space. Then they began to pace the ground, clearing small spring growth away with the axe, kicking stones away.

Gabriel began to stretch again. Birds sang in the trees: chemical awareness sang in Gabriel's blood. The three walk-

ng men managed to scare up a half-dozen startled quail. One
of the men cursed loudly in surprise.

The last bush hacked away, the three approached Gabriel
and Clancy. One of the strangers was a middle-aged, grey-
haired man in a black cassock with a red pinstripe. The other
was young, wearing the skirt and mail sleeves of a duelist. He
had a pointed face and a sneering smile.

"Your Highness," Gerius said, "may I introduce the physician Lavinius, and Silvanus's friend Lord Augustino."

Gabriel crossed his hands over his breast and bowed. "I
would like to confide," he said, "that I have never had any
intention of provoking the Knight Silvanus to this quarrel."

Augustino flipped his hands. "Hardly matters," he said.
"The offense existed whether the prince meant it or not."

The physician sighed, and dabbled at his mouth with the
ends of a kind of neckcloth he wore about his collar. There
was old blood on the cloth that had not entirely washed away.
Gerius turned to Augustino. "Bring your man to the mark,"
he said, "and so shall I."

Gabriel turned to Clancy as the others marched away. He
drew his sword, tested its weight. The sunlight rippled along
the silver blade. His consciousness seemed to swell through
the wood, encompassing the trees, the dawn, the weaponed
men, the waiting horses. Words filled his heart.

> "The dawn runs like blood on the steel,
> Yet my heart is at peace.
> Why must the trumpets disturb the stillness?"

Clancy stepped forward, took his arm, kissed his cheek.
As she stepped back he saw that she was in a Posture of
Respect, her hands at the salute, right fist in left palm. Gabriel
returned the posture, the gesture, cupping his left hand
around the sword hilt.

He dropped the scabbard to the ground and walked to
the center of the clearing. His soul still swirled through the
woods; he called his daimones to heel and deliberately nar-

rowed his focus to the figure of Silvanus, seeing him intently, as if through the wrong end of a telescope. His daimones heightened his awareness of sight, touch, and hearing, then dampened the rest. Adrenaline-fired blood sang in his ears. Chain-skirt jingling, the long-armed Silvanus was walking toward him, a daimōn lying in his eyes like a glint of dull, soulless steel. He carried his sword in his left hand, and a sinister smile was painted on his face with red cosmetic. He'd drawn his eyebrows in a ferocious, woolly scowl, and outlined his eyes in glaring red.

Gabriel had been undecided whether to fight right-handed or otherwise, and the sight of Silvanus made up his mind: he gave his body to a left-handed daimōn and shifted the sword to his left.

Silvanus saw it and a hint of a frown touched his painted lips. Otherwise there was no reaction at all.

Augustino and Gerius placed the two combatants in the center of the clearing. The rising sun was to the side, on Gabriel's right, so that it didn't shine directly into anyone's eyes.

Before a word was spoken Silvanus dropped into stance, a low crouch, sword extended at the end of his long left arm. His ferocious, red-rimmed eyes stared into Gabriel's own. His sword-tip pointed at Gabriel's face.

Gabriel answered with

AUGENBLICK: He's left-handed, Aristos.

GABRIEL: Take command of my body, Augenblick. <Priority 1> He won't be used to left-handed opponents.

AUGENBLICK: At your service, Aristos. <Priority 1>

AUGENBLICK: His daimōn is very purposeful, Aristos. He is as focused as I have seen any of these people.

MATAGLAP: Kill him and get it over with.

WELCOME RAIN: Imitate him at the start, Aristos. Mirror him.

GABRIEL: Bear. Commence a strengthening meditation for the left arm. <Priority 1>

BEAR: <Priority 1> You are breathing through your heels. Feel the qi rise like a

his own stance, an exact copy of Silvanus's. When dealing with an unknown system, mirroring the opponent was best.

He didn't return Silvanus's stare—the *Equito* could trick him by staring at one place while striking for another. Instead Gabriel kept his focus lower, on Silvanus's belt buckle. That way awareness would encompass all of his opponent's body and weapon, and he could perceive physical cues from any part of Silvanus's body.

river from the earth, along your legs, up your spine, and out along your left arm and along the sword. A river of power runs through you and along your arm . . .

WELCOME RAIN: Careful, Aristos!

GABRIEL: I am responding.

WELCOME RAIN: He seeks to intimidate you before we even start. He may intend an impetuous attack to overwhelm you right at the beginning.

AUGENBLICK: < image of the pulse beating in Silvanus's throat > His pulse is only 95, Aristos. He is not afraid of you, and he is not out of control.

WELCOME RAIN: He's deep in psychosis.

Gerius looked from one to the other, mildly surprised that they had readied themselves without his instruction. "Might as well begin, my lords," he said, and quickly stepped out of range of the blades.

Silvanus did nothing for a moment, apparently waiting for Gabriel, and then began a careful sidling move to the left. Gabriel imitated him, circling to his own left. Chain skirts jingled faintly.

The hawk flies with the sun at his back, warned Spring Plum.

As the sun took him in the face Gabriel narrowed his eyes, exaggerating slightly in hopes of convincing Silvanus he was blinded. His focus was total. In the lower part of his focus he saw Silvanus's left foot shift back half a centimeter, a slight forward tilt in balance . . .

The warning was sufficient. Silvanus came out of the sun, blade slicing for Gabriel's head. Gabriel took the strike on the back of his armored right glove and extended his left arm in a stop-hit directed against his enemy's body.

"*Tzai!*" he shouted, tightening the abdominals.

KILL! roared Mataglap.

Silvanus batted the strike out of the way, parried the blade up over his left shoulder. Letting gravity help him, Gabriel dropped the forte of his blade on Silvanus's foible, then (hand in supination) stepped forward in hopes of getting his point in Silvanus's shoulder. Silvanus drew his lead foot back in a nicely judged *rassemblement* and Gabriel's blade fell a thumb's width short.

Silvanus was obviously ready for him.

Gabriel slid to his left again and got the sun out of his eyes. Both went on guard once more.

Silvanus began to circle to his left again, his strong side. Gabriel imitated him. Silvanus narrowed his eyes as the sun began to shine directly on his face.

Gabriel waited until it was the turn of his left foot to move, then stepped toward Silvanus instead of maintaining the circular creep. He tried to make the move absolutely spontaneous, without giving it away by any balance shift or minor adjustment of foot position.

AUGENBLICK: His daimōn has absolutely kept his head. He will not be stampeded or rushed.

BEAR: Breathe. A river of qi runs up your spine . . .

WELCOME RAIN: He may expect an attack out of the sun. Can we use the expectation to trap him?

GABRIEL: Yes. < Visualization of technique >

WELCOME RAIN: Absolutely.

MATAGLAP: Don't warn him.

BEAR: Inhale.

AUGENBLICK: He'll counterattack if he's expecting this. A stop-hit most likely. < visualizing >

MATAGLAP: He's lost you

in the sun. Destroy him!

His sword hand went high, up into the sun, in hopes that Silvanus would lose sight of it. His right hand parried the expected stop-hit off to his right. Instead of bringing the sword down from above, Gabriel dropped the point down behind him, then looped it upward with the intent of catching Silvanus under the chin with a rising cut.

"*Tzai!*" he shouted. **KILL!** came the echo.

Silvanus stopped the point just short of its target with a cupped right hand. Gabriel shuffled back with a "destroying" parry, prime to low tierce, that beat off Silvanus's expected counterattack, then went on guard again.

As if they had all the time in the world, Gabriel and Silvanus continued to feel one another out—little flurries of bladework, neither committing fully to an attack. Silvanus's concentration seemed total: his daimōn might be a single-minded murderer, but it was also a patient one, content to bide its time. Perhaps it felt, with Silvanus's massive wrists, shoulders, and long arms, that it had only to wait for Gabriel to grow tired before finishing him off.

Gabriel devoted himself to cold-eyed analysis of his opponent's style. Silvanus favored edge over point, circular movement over linear, and he was tricky—he tried stomping to distract Gabriel from an attack, or deliberately rang his chain skirt to draw Gabriel's attention down and away from his blade; he stared furiously at one part of Gabriel's body while attacking another; he made intelligent use of the sun and attempted a long series of sly feints and stop-hits.

But Gabriel, at each exchange, found himself growing in confidence. Silvanus gave his attacks away by tiny shifts in balance, breathing pattern, and footwork. Gabriel's footwork was superior—Silvanus took full steps as he moved, but Gabriel used a faster shuffle, moving swiftly without having to alter foot position. His preferred use of the point was in his favor. He had the use of the circular and destroying parries and he had any number of tricks he hadn't used yet.

Time to finish him off, Mataglap said. **Look at those arms and shoulders! He still may tire before you.**

Fatigue toxins are high, reported Gabriel's reno.

Kill him and end this. Mataglap seemed pleased by the thought.

Not kill. Not if I can help it.

He's a barbarian and a murderer. He will never adjust to the new order we'll have to impose here. Dust beneath our shoes.

Concur, said the Welcome Rain.

Nonetheless . . .

Gabriel and Silvanus continued their careful crabbing circle. Gabriel prolonged the movement until the red dawn turned Silvanus's white cosmetic to rose, until the sun was almost in the big man's eyes . . .

Perhaps Silvanus would relax then, anticipating that an attack, if it came, would come right out of the sun. Instead Gabriel moved just *before* the most favorable moment. And the move, when it came, was to the right, not the left. Directly into Silvanus's sword, and therefore not to be expected.

WELCOME RAIN: The sun is about to come onto his face, if you're considering a move now.

GABRIEL: Not then . . . just before, rather . . .

WELCOME RAIN: < applause >

AUGENBLICK: His pulse is 110, breathing regular.

BEAR: A river of qi flows from your arm. Breathe.

GABRIEL: < visualizing technique >

WELCOME RAIN: You're stepping into his blade— make sure you neutralize any conterattack.

He stepped in with the right, gliding the back of his armored glove along Silvanus's inside line while he swung his pronated left hand inward to launch a backhand *("Tzai!")* cut at Silvanus's body. The move was weak, but he could launch it without warning, and in any case it was a prelude to something more interesting.

Silvanus parried the first strike, tried to grip the blade,

failed. He spent a fractional second of time supinating his sword hand in preparation for a powerful cut, was blocked. The blade rang: Gabriel felt stunning impact on his gauntlet. Gabriel swung his left foot inward and ended in crane stance, left leg cocked high, right supporting. His sword point dropped, came around in a vertical wheel to drop straight on Silvanus's head from above.

That was the strike that Silvanus was intended to see. The other was a side kick launched out of the crane stance, the heel of Gabriel's boot aimed at Silvanus's solar plexus.

"*Dai!*" he shouted.

Silvanus somehow knew he was in trouble and took a blind leap to the rear, landing balanced and on guard in a breathless jingle of mail. Gabriel's sword whistled as it sliced air in his wake, point grounding in the sod. Gabriel's foot contacted Silvanus's chest, but it was at full extension and couldn't drive through.

Gabriel's daimones screamed: he was one-footed and off balance and his enemy was ready. Silvanus came back in, lunging with the point as Gabriel was trying to retrieve his balance. Gabriel got his sword up in time to beat the blade aside, took his hilt in both hands, swung it around on his right side as he stepped forward with the right foot once more, as Silvanus was trying to recover from his lunge.

The blade swung up, then down, its power shifted to the right hand. Gabriel hoped to bring the edge down on Silvanus's left shoulder just inside the chain sleeve and cut the muscles controlling the sword arm.

"*Dai!*"

The big man blocked the strike with an X-guard made up of blade and parrying arm. His daimōn glared red-eyed at Gabriel as his hand rotated, took Gabriel's point in his fist as he dropped his own edge on Gabriel's head. Gabriel blocked up with his left glove, kicked out with his left foot, drove the pad of his left foot ("*Dai!*") into Silvanus's solar plexus.

The kick drove Silvanus back and freed Gabriel's blade. The red-eyed daimōn never blinked, but Silvanus was gasping for breath. Gabriel began a figure-eight pattern with his sword as he advanced, a pattern that would enable him to shift back to the left hand whenever he needed to. Silvanus fell back, content to give ground while his dead eyes tracked Gabriel's sword point, analyzed the strange attack pattern, timed the movements.

In the distance, well outside his focus, Gabriel saw other figures scattering, getting out of the way of the fighters.

When Silvanus moved it was an all-or-nothing lunge over Gabriel's arm, aimed at Gabriel's tierce just as Gabriel's sword was descending to a low quarte, on the other end of the figure-eight pattern.

Gabriel was ready for it: he knew the figure-eight's weakness as well as anyone. His left hand crossed his body and parried the lunge outward with his palm. His arms were now crossed in front of his chest. As Silvanus recovered from his lunge, Gabriel stepped forward and scissored his arms together, the left aiming a back-knuckle punch at Silvanus's face, the right slashing at his body with the edge of his sword. Silvanus, probably confused about right and left, chose to block the punch—the sword sliced a neat line of red down the big man's flank.

Silvanus kicked, a vicious stomp aimed at Gabriel's groin: Gabriel pivoted, raised his left knee, took the strike on his thigh. Pain crackled, muscles spasmed—Gabriel dropped the raised leg close to Silvanus, too close for either sword to have play, and (with his good right leg providing the power) drove his left elbow into Silvanus's face while wolves of pain howled up his thigh. Silvanus was knocked back and way, his sword slashing out in a blind strike that was probably as much defensive as a genuine assault. Gabriel parried and let him go: the Welcome Rain told him that the injured leg might not support a follow-up attack.

Gabriel pursued cautiously as he tried (Bear chanting in his inner ear) to master his protesting leg. No more crane stances, he thought. Silvanus, sniffing blood from a broken nose, fell back and tried to circle. His shirt was turning red.

The sun was high and bright, and no longer conferred an advantage to anyone. In the distance, outside of his focus and in someone else's body, Gabriel could feel drops of sweat coursing down his forehead. He decided to keep the sword in his right hand: his left arm and shoulder were tired.

"Knight Silvanus," Gabriel said, "this does not have to continue."

Silvanus said nothing. His blood spattered the grass.

"We may end it here," said Gabriel.

Silvanus's chest inflated with air, let it out. Air whistled out of his mouth.

He has set up a breathing pattern, Augenblick said, **flushing his tissues with oxygen to support an attack. His heart is about 125.**

Finish him, said Mataglap.

Concur. Welcome Rain. **Best to attack him before he has time to think his next attack through.**

The two moved simultaneously, each with a step and a slash. Blades clanged, Gabriel's on the outside line. He used a circular parry to bring his point above his opponent's blade for a thrust at the shoulder, but Silvanus shrugged his massive mailed shoulders and the deflected point pierced only sky. His own point dove low, for Gabriel's abdomen: Gabriel parried it away with his left hand.

Then Silvanus charged forward, his armored shoulders slamming into Gabriel's chest, driving him back. The wind went out of him in a rush. Pain shot up his leg. Daimones wailed at his loss of control. He heard a cry from one of the onlookers.

Gabriel was carried back by Silvanus's body rush, his injured leg unwilling to support him in a contest with the larger man. Blades were useless at this range. Gabriel tried to drive the stiffened fingers of his left hand into Silvanus's eyes while Silvanus smashed at his face with an armored fist: the hands hit each other instead, grappled.

Oppose hardness with yielding, suggested Spring Plum.

Gabriel sidestepped to his right, onto the strong leg, and smashed the pommel of his sword into Silvanus's kidney. The big man grunted, spun, raised his blade high to bring it smashing down. Gabriel blocked with his armored glove, made a cut of his own. *One . . .*

Both fell back slightly, panting for breath, but their swords kept moving, a series of cuts and thrusts. *Two, three . . .* Blood covered Silvanus's side, drooled down his face. Spittle and blood flew from his mouth at each gasping breath.

His inhuman eyes were as focused and intent as ever.

Silvanus's blade arched high, sliced down. *Four, five . . .* Gabriel caught the strike on his forte, directed it away as his point described a neat descending semicircle. He waited a heartbeat, then drove forward.

. . . and a half!

"*Die!*" Gabriel cried.

The point took Silvanus under the left arm and drove deep into the body with all Gabriel's weight behind it. There was a hideous sucking

GABRIEL: *Yes!* < visualizing movement >

BEAR: You're forgetting to breathe!

WELCOME RAIN: < stepping out with right foot > < shifting weight to right foot > < pommel strike >

GABRIEL: < breathing >

WELCOME RAIN: < block/cut >

GABRIEL: Built a rhythm. One-two-three.

WELCOME RAIN: < parry/thrust >

GABRIEL: We'll half-step him at the end of this.

WELCOME RAIN: < parry/cut >

BEAR: Breathe.

AUGENBLICK: He's coming in high.

GABRIEL: Circular parry with the blade, high-low. Shift into broken time.

WELCOME RAIN: < circular parry >

GABRIEL: Wait . . . *now!*

VOICE: < lunge >

BEAR: Kiai.

VOICE: *DIE! DIE! DIE!*

MATAGLAP: *DIE!*

HORUS: Who the hell . . . ?

GABRIEL: I didn't want to kill him, damn it!

AUGENBLICK: The . . .

sound as air followed the blade into the pleural cavity.

thing . . . it took control.
WELCOME   RAIN:
< withdrawing blade >
GABRIEL: I'll take my body back, if you please.

The *Equito* dropped to the ground like a sack of stones, transformed in an eyeblink from a formidable mass of weaponed brawn into a nerveless hull incapable of even a twitch. Astonishment floated through Gabriel's mind at the sight— Silvanus had turned to nothing when he was punctured, like a balloon—then Gabriel flung his sword away and dropped to the blood-spattered grass next to Silvanus's body. A bubbling sound came not from Silvanus's throat but his chest. Sucking chest wound, therefore . . .

It was possible the lung hadn't even been pierced. The rushing air that followed the blade into the pleural cavity might have collapsed the lung or moved it out of the way. If Gabriel hadn't cut a major artery then Silvanus might yet survive.

Gabriel heard feet drumming as the witnesses raced to the scene. His reno gave him swift access to medical data. He tore Silvanus's shirt away from the wound, pressed the palm of his hand over the wound to seal it. A flap wound into the pleural cavity could cause a mediastinal shift, the lungs and heart moving away from the wound, making it impossible for the blood to circulate.

"Get away!" The cry came from Lord Augustino, far off on the other side of the field but coming on the run. "Get away from him, witch!"

"I'm trying to *help* him!" Gabriel shouted. Boots thumped behind him as Gerius ran up. "Clancy, we need a chest tube!" If he'd sliced an artery, he might have to open the chest wound wider to get a hand in, put manual pressure on the artery to shut it off . . .

"*Chest tube!*" Augustino screamed. "Keep your foreign sorcery away from him!"

It occurred to Gabriel that he might have difficulty explaining to Augustino the necessity of widening the wound in order to get the chest tube in place.

Never mind explaining, he thought. Just do it.

There was a rattle as Clancy opened her medical bag on the run. A couple of sandbags, Gabriel thought, to put pressure on the chest, and once the tube was in place a water drain.

Look out behind! The Voice again.

Unwilling, Gabriel turned just as he heard the sound of a blade drawing, saw Gerius's point clear the scabbard and swing toward him . . .

"Aristos!" A scream from Clancy.

Gabriel rolled to the side as Gerius's downward thrust pierced the sod. Gabriel came up on a three-point balance, hands and one foot, then reversed his direction by lashing out with the remaining foot, the classic Monkey Style sweep called "Whipping with the Dragon's Tail."

Gabriel's lashing straight leg took both Gerius's feet out at the ankle. Gerius landed heavily on his shoulder blades, the wind going out of him in a *whuff*.

The local doctor, Lavinius, stood open-mouthed, astonishment freezing him.

Augustino was drawing on the run as he neared. Gabriel's own sword had been thrown far out of reach, and Gerius had kept a grip on his, but Silvanus's sword was

MATAGLAP: We're on the ground, damn it!

GABRIEL: *Use* it! Monkey Style!

WELCOME RAIN: Whip the Dragon's Tail?

GABRIEL: < !!! >

BEAR: Kiai.

VOICE: *DIE!*

GABRIEL: *DIE!*

MATAGLAP: Get the *sword!*

BEAR: Breathe.

VOICE: Augustino's coming!

WELCOME RAIN: We can't wrestle for the sword now. Where's a free weapon?

CLANCY: < via oneirochronon > I hid my pistol again, damn it, but Manfred's coming!

HORUS: The nearest sword is Silvanus's.

MATAGLAP: Augustino's going to be standing over it

lying on the ground halfway between Augustino and Gabriel.

Gabriel did a forward somersault toward the sword, covering ground faster than Augustino's lumbering run. There was a snarl and a scream as Manfred savaged Gerius's sword arm with his razor diamond teeth. Gabriel came up on one knee with the sword held awkwardly reversed in his two fists, point down.

in a second.

HORUS: Tumbling is the fastest way of covering ground . . .

GABRIEL: Monkey Style! < somersault >

VOICE: Give me your body! I know what to do!

GABRIEL: < affirmative >

HORUS: < !?! > Aristos! I question this!

GABRIEL: He's been right so far . . .

Gabriel's mind filled with purposeful fury as he gave control to the Voice. A strong metallic taste flushed his tongue. He parried Augustino's thrust, then screamed *"Die!"* as he sliced upward into Augustino's abdomen with the reversed blade. Blood and tripe spattered Gabriel's face, and he felt the sword-edge grate on Augustino's spine. There was a horrid smell of bowel.

Gabriel rose to his feet, clearing his sword from Augustino as the man fell. Augustino's mouth was open in a scream that, with a slashed diaphragm, he didn't have the power to utter.

Fiery triumph raced through Gabriel's body like a welcome dose of liquor. He spun, sword at the ready, to see Gerius staggering to his feet. The torn right arm hung limp, and Gerius hacked unsuccessfully at Manfred with a sword transferred to his left hand. Then Clancy's pistol cleared her costume and she took out Gerius's left knee with a smart explosive homing bullet. Gerius crashed to the ground again.

Gabriel spun once more, turning to the only stranger still on his feet, the doctor Lavinius. The doctor had picked up the axe, held it uncertainly. Lavinius stared for a long moment, then dropped the axe, turned, and clumsily began to run.

Clancy's pistol blew bone fragments out of his shoulder, and he spun and fell.

I will have my body back now, Gabriel said.

Get the truth out of Gerius. The Voice was implacable. **I will.**

The Voice faded away, and with it Gabriel's sense of fierce exaltation. He staggered for a moment—the Voice's ferocity seemed to have been holding him upright—then walked toward Gerius.

Gerius looked both dazed and terrified. Manfred circled him, uttering menacing growls. He raised his sword to protect himself.

"I apologize, Aristos," Clancy said, speaking Demotic, the principal language she and Gabriel shared. Her pistol, a little blue-black thing that protruded between the second and third fingers of her right fist, was held steadily on Gerius. "After the fight, I hid my pistol away. I didn't think I'd need it."

"Stay away," Gerius panted. "I'll kill you, I swear it!"

Gabriel ignored him, knelt by Silvanus, found him dead and staring. He'd cut an artery after all. Gabriel supposed it was possible to revive him, but radical techniques would be required, and there existed in this world no way to keep the patient alive after his renascence.

There was a sharp cry from Dr. Lavinius. Gabriel looked at him, saw him trying to crawl away on his three functional limbs, a panicked, grunting animal leaking a trail of red.

Clancy moved toward Augustino, knelt, plunged her free hand wrist-deep into the wound. "Iuso Rex!" Gerius screamed. "Get away from him, you butcher!"

Methodically Clancy searched for the abdominal aorta that Gabriel was fairly certain he'd slashed. She leaned in, putting pressure on the torn vessel. Augustino died anyway.

"You must have got the spleen," she said. "Nothing I could do about it."

Gerius screamed threats, waved his sword. The others ignored him.

"See to Lavinius," Gabriel said. "We have no certainty that he had a part in this."

"Just a high probability," Clancy said. She withdrew her hand, gory to the elbow.

"Yes. Only that."

Clancy, weapon still in her right fist, trotted toward Lavinius. Gabriel rose from his crouch and looked at the dead Silvanus, the dead Augustino. Two more little data points for Saigo's great experiment, two more people murdered by their creator before they were ever born.

He could feel Augustino's blood drying on his face. He wiped it with a sleeve.

"Iuso help me!" Gerius shouted. He tried to brandish his sword, but toppled backward and the point stuck in the ground. "What is this witchcraft, you foreign bastard?"

Gabriel took a step closer to Gerius, took up a Posture of Confidence, spoke in a calm voice. "What witchcraft is that?"

"You're stealing my limbs from me. I can't feel anything on one side, damn you." He raised his face to the sky and screamed. "Heaven and the saints protect me!"

Manfred's hollow hypodermic teeth had pumped the man full of a paralyzing anesthetic. Gabriel smiled.

"Yes," he said. "It's witchcraft. You'll be completely paralyzed before long. I'm employing a spell meant to get the truth out of you."

There was a desperate light in Gerius's small eyes. "I believe in God the Father," he began, "and Iuso His Son, and the Saints of Heaven . . ."

"Why should they help you now?" Gabriel pointed out. "You've engaged in a conspiracy to murder a stranger."

"*God help me!*" The voice was an agonized scream. Gerius's hand lost its grip on his sword and he fell completely on his back, his limbs paralyzed. Gabriel advanced to stand over him, his sword hanging loosely from his hand.

"The only hope of earning the Almighty's help," Gabriel

said, "would be a full and complete confession. I'm eager to hear it."

"Go to hell!"

"Mercy, mistress!" That was Dr. Lavinius. Gerius frantically looked in the direction of the cry, but there were too many bodies in the way.

"What is she doing to him?" he demanded. "She's worse than the king's torturers!"

Gabriel pulsed a short oneirochronic suggestion to Manfred, and the terrier trotted forward and began licking in the face. Gerius turned his head away. "Get him off me!"

"Mercy!" Lavinius shrieked. "It's none of my doing!"

"Do you know why dogs lick a person in the face?" Gabriel asked. "It's thought to be affectionate, but it's not. It's to find out if you're warm or cold. Because if you're cold, then that means you're dead, and the dog can eat you. Are you feeling cold yet?"

Manfred licked Gerius's ear. Gerius screamed.

"You'll start to feel cold in a minute or two," Gabriel said. "That's the next stage of my sorcery."

"Get the dog away!"

Gabriel smiled. "Are you cold yet?" he asked.

I'm working on Lavinius, Clancy reported. **Sterilization may be a problem here—do you know, I don't think he's bathed in weeks?**

"Adrian was behind it!" Gerius shouted. "Prince Adrian, the Monopolist. He put Silvanus on to you."

Gabriel called Manfred away and analyzed Gerius with care. The man seemed desperately sincere.

"Adrian wanted to kill me?" he asked.

"Not kill you, just make you run away. You'd offended him in some way. He didn't think you'd actually fight Silvanus, not when you didn't have anything at stake here and could easily leave. But once you accepted the fight, Adrian was afraid you'd become too popular if you won, so he decided to make certain you were killed."

"And your uncle Gerius, the Knot Secretary?"

"He didn't know about Adrian's plot, I don't think. I don't really know, but I don't believe so. It was all Adrian's doing."

"And whose idea was it to involve you?"

"Silvanus, Adrian—I don't know! But Adrian was a party to it."

"And your role?"

"We were to make sure you died. We didn't seriously think you'd win the fight, but there was a possibility you might be only wounded. So we were commissioned to make certain the wound was fatal."

"We?"

"Lavinius and me."

No wonder Gerius had been unhappy that Gabriel had brought his own doctor. There might be an argument over the poison soaking the bandages or the extra sword thrust in Gabriel's chest . . .

"And your little magic potion?"

"It was a bad-luck charm. It was to make certain you'd lose."

"Luckily for me my own magic was superior," Gabriel said.

"Help me!" Despite lying in the bright sunlight, Gerius's lower lip had turned blue. His limbs shivered. The power of suggestion, Gabriel reflected, was truly marvelous.

"I'm freezing!" he whimpered.

"Not quite yet," Gabriel said. "What were you offered in return for murdering me? Money?"

"No. An appointment in the Yellow Cavaliers."

"A fashionable regiment."

"*The* fashionable regiment." Tears spilled from Gerius's eyes. "I could attract royal favor there. Patronage is the only way to advance when there's not a war."

"And your uncle Gerius can't get you into the Cavaliers?"

"He *won't!*" Gerius spat. "He doesn't give a damn for any of us—not if we can't earn him money!"

Gabriel looked down at Gerius's bloody knee. So much for the Yellow Cavaliers, or any regiment—his career as a soldier was clearly over. Gabriel wondered if he would be pathetic enough for the beggarmaker.

Clancy appeared at his elbow with her medical bag. "I've patched up the doctor," she said. "He admitted to a plan to have you killed. He said Prince Adrian was behind it."

Gabriel looked down at Gerius. "It's unanimous, then."

"For God's sake help me!"

Gabriel took a quiet walk about the glade as Clancy tended to Gerius's injuries. His muscles twitched in reaction to surges of adrenaline.

The two bodies lay in the sunlight, already attracting flies.

> The glade is at peace,
> And birds dart overhead.
> Why is there blood on the grass?

Partly, he considered, because the Voice had put it there. Gabriel hadn't meant to run Silvanus through, just puncture him enough so that he couldn't continue the fight. But when the moment came, he'd found the matter out of his hands. The Voice had called for a lunge, and the body had obeyed. When had he lost control?

The Voice was left-handed, and Gabriel had started the fight in a left-handed stance. The Voice might have been able to gain a foothold in Gabriel's psyche that way.

Carefully he replayed the fight blow by blow. He remembered his kiais, his "cries of the spirit," the yells delivered with each blow. He'd started by shouting *tzai*, a formation he favored because uttering the *tz* sound efficiently tightened the diaphragm for increased strength. But partway through the fight he'd started shouting *dai* instead, and then at the end of the homonym *die*.

Die, he thought, *die die die*.

The Voice had come at him, appropriately enough,

through his voice box. From control of utterance he had proceeded, stealthily, to control of the entire body.

And possibly saved Gabriel's life. The Voice had known, or suspected, Gerius's treachery.

It was time to talk to the Voice, Gabriel thought. And by now he had a very good idea how to do it.

Chapter 13

ANIMAL TAMER: Back to your cages!

LULU: You give me orders?
   The bloody knife is still in my hand!

Zhenling's domed pavilion stood in the snow atop Mount Trasker, an orange-red billowy fantasy out of the Arabian Nights, sunset-colored, surrounded by flagpoles with swallow-tailed banners. Sprawled around the summit were wide blankets of snow, grey-black fortresses of granite, eloquent flowing rivers of translucent glacier-ice. The wind boomed, cloud roiled, and ice particles skimmed, with a serpent's hiss, through the violet sky.

The cries of nature, inside the tent, were subordinated to the cries of music. Gabriel, thighs locked by Zhenling's legs, moved in time to the impelling rhythm of his own orchestration. Ghost voices blended with the wail of wind, the crack of flags, the throaty song of the two lovers. A series of climaxes, only one of them musical, occurred in perfect synchrony.

Afterward Gabriel stepped outside the pavilion. The cold burned his bare feet; flying ice stung his skin. He gazed down from the summit, wind tearing at his long coppery hair. Far below him, in some little valley, he saw flashes of lightning illuminate the clouds from below.

Zhenling padded out of the pavilion wearing only the long sable coat and hat she'd worn in another fantasy. She put an arm around his waist, gazed down into the flickering lightning below. "Do you see why I climb?" she said.

"Perhaps."

"Flying up here is nothing, nor getting it on remotes. I wanted to *earn* this view. It deserves nothing less." She tilted her head, closed her eyes, let the fierce white sun shine on her sculpted features.

"It was a magnificent climb, Madame Sable. I watched an oneirochronic recording of it."

Zhenling threw her arms out, circled in the snow like a pinwheel.

"That music was amazing," she said. "And unpublished, my reno tells me."

"The 'Blood Aria' from my *Lulu*. Where Lulu kills Schön."

"Magnificent," she said. "But hardly the sort of thing one usually makes love to."

"It's the only thing I've done lately that I can make a gift of. The most passionate thing I've done."

"Did I hear the word *knife*? In the earlier versions of the story Lulu shot Schön with a pistol. Why did you change it?"

Gabriel thought for a moment about blood drying on the grass, about Augustino falling with his mouth opening to a scream he could not utter.

"I didn't want it to be impersonal," he said.

". . . *and siege was laid by bread or by knife*. Neruda. I remember you saying that once." She slitted her eyes, looked at him sidelong. "But everything Lulu does is impersonal. She's an engine of destruction for herself and everyone around her. Isn't that the point?"

"Then the horror is all the greater," Gabriel said, "if the

weapon she uses so impersonally is an intimate one. And of course it echoes the knife that kills her at the end."

"Ah. I see." She stepped back and regarded him. The wind tore at her sable coat, revealing flashes of leg, belly, breast. "You've been doing a great deal, Gabriel. Returning to a long-abandoned epic work, taking a quixotic journey to the stars, helping your Dr. Clancy, I suspect, with her massive container project—"

"She didn't need much help."

"Really? She hadn't done anything that original before, so I assumed you had a hand in it. In any case, it must have taken *months*—" Gabriel restrained a smile. "And you've done some related publishing yourself. When do you return to your domaine? Or visit mine?"

"I'm not done. All that other stuff was by the way."

"All those accomplishments happy accidents? What project encompasses all that as a side effect, I wonder?"

Gabriel allowed an enigmatic smile to touch the face of his skiagénos.

"That sphinx act of yours is getting a bit timeworn, Gabriel," said Zhenling. "But I've been doing research and discovered a few things."

"Ah. Tell me, Madame Sable."

He was beginning to get cold, even though his body was safe and warm in Remmy's cabinet in Santa Leofra's quarter. He took Zhenling's arm, returned with her to the pavilion. Warmth enfolded him like a velvet caress. He wrapped himself in a silk-lined quilt and took a seat on the gleaming silver-rimmed sofa. She paced up and down in front of him, strong toes gripping the white fur carpet.

"Cressida's Hyperlogos records have been unSealed now she's dead," Zhenling said. "I've dug through it for the three-month period previous to her death, and concentrated on the time span immediately before the time she sent Therápōn Rubens to Illyricum."

"Indeed." Cautiously.

"The only unusual traffic at all was to access and reaccess all Saigo's data on the Gaal Sphere."

"Perhaps it related to her Chaos Form studies."

"Then why, O Sphinx, did she go back and reaccess the data for a second time? As if she wanted to be certain of something?"

"Perhaps she put the first copy into portable hard storage and misplaced it."

"It was never downloaded into hard storage, Sphinx, just copied into her RAM and left there, where I found it. And the second copy also. And when I looked next, both copies were gone. Erased. Along with about fifty backups scattered in redundant storage throughout the Logarchy."

Gabriel felt the cold touch of danger on his nape. Why would Saigo and his cohorts erase those copies? he wondered. They were just duplications of their own phony data. The very act of erasure was suspicious.

Had someone panicked? he wondered.

"When did you do this?" he asked.

"Some weeks ago."

Terror wailed deep in his psyche. It was all that he had feared, through his actions to put someone else in danger. "I think—"

"No, wait." Her smile was teasing. "I've danced a little tango with this data. Conclusions have offered themselves."

Gabriel bit down on his protest. "Go on."

"Saigo's in the Gaal Sphere. Cressida was poking into Gaal Sphere data just before she started acting peculiar. Within days of your getting a message from Cressida, she's dead and you've changed all your plans and taken off in your yacht. Not much is heard from you until a few weeks after you *could* have reached the Gaal Sphere, after which we have this sudden burst of activity from you, all these projects completed or resumed or otherwise dealt with. As if you're clearing the decks before commencing something major."

"Madame Sable—"

"Conclusion, Gabriel"—her tilted eyes danced—"you're

in the Gaal Sphere, and something's going on there. Is it something Saigo's up to, or one of Cressida's projects, or something you're doing all on your own?"

Gabriel rose to his feet, took her hands, looked gravely into her eyes. "Run for your personal yacht. Get away from Tienjin, away from anywhere you've ever been. And keep running."

Her look was pure control, pure oneirochronon. All blazing enigma. "Am I then in danger, Sphinx?"

"Yes. And I've put you there. My apologies, Ariste. I can't tell you how sorry I am."

A slow fierce smile rose on her face. Like dawn, he thought.

"Good," she said. "I'm where I want to be. With you, in the center of this mystery."

Gabriel's heart leaped. Love and admiration stirred in his blood. "True Sound!" he said. "Get away. Now. If you want to avoid happening to Tienjin what happened to the *Sanjay*."

"My Realized Body is already on the move," Zhenling said. "And daimones are unlocking the necessary gates."

"Good."

"Shall I come to the Gaal Sphere?"

He hesitated. He thought of enemies listening to every word. "Your chronology is a little inexact," he said. "If I wanted to come to the Gaal Sphere, I could have been there over a month ago."

"The Hyperlogos is compromised, I realize, otherwise all Cressida's data wouldn't have vanished. So you can't give me directions."

Gabriel said nothing.

"I have built my own communications setup, as you did. Can we link our networks?"

He thought for a moment. "Get clear of the system," he said. "Then aim a tachline receiver at Illyricum and tune to Channel Three Thousand. I'll send you a cipher."

She nodded. "I am pleased to be with you, Aristos."

"And, in spite of the danger, I am glad to be with you."

He kissed her, and at that instant she, the pavilion, Mount Trasker, all vanished, and Gabriel was sitting in Remmy's cabinet, fingers idly bringing chords out of the cembalo.

He looked up in wild alarm.

Someone had pulled the plug.

Gabriel called Fleta in the Illyricum Residence and was told that communication seemed normal throughout the Logarchy. Apparently only the one channel to Tienjin had been cut. Gabriel gave orders for Zhenling's receiving her cipher, then rose and paced back and forth as he gazed through the unshuttered second-floor windows. The day was gloomy, with a constant low drizzle.

For once, trapped in a small space and away from everything, Gabriel wasn't afflicted by boredom.

His fight with Silvanus had been yesterday. He and Clancy had returned to their apartment after having received assurances from the two conspirators that, whatever story they told to justify the wounds and bodies, it would be one favorable to Gabriel.

After his return, Gabriel sent a message to Remmy at his family's house a few streets away. Remmy answered the message in person, arriving wild-eyed and under the impression the duel had yet to be fought. He'd been interrupted in the midst of some private devotions, and wore a plain white shirt on which religious medals had been sewn with blue and red ribbons. More medals hung around his neck and had been tied to his four limbs by their ribbons. After being reassured that the fight was over and Gabriel had won, a perfectly astonished Remmy agreed to hide Gabriel in his Santa Leofra cabinet, then make inquiries to determine the position of the authorities.

Gabriel made the experience bearable by setting up a tachline relay directly between the cabinet and his Santo Georgio home, and from there to *Cressida* and the Hyperlogos. The relay antennae were directional and shouldn't result in any leakage that could be detected from Saigo's Santo Georgio house, at least not over this short distance. It was possible, of course, that the whole planet was wired, that everything that happened here was recorded and that the Surveyors had been spotted the second they'd arrived, but Gabriel could think of no reason why the conspirators would do such a thing, and in any case there was nothing he could do about it.

Except for a few hours' sleep Gabriel had been pacing the floor ever since his arrival, working on his music and his new nano patents while Horus dictated sociological analysis into the *Cressida*'s official record of the journey.

A gust spattered drizzle over the windowpane. The streets were empty save for a few beggars who viewed the weather with professional disregard.

The conspirators had done some very dangerous things. Cutting communication for someone not otherwise under their control was as reckless as erasing something already in the public record was stupid. Gabriel wondered whether Saigo had made these decisions, or whether it was one of his disciples who had panicked unreasonably. Perhaps, he thought, Saigo'd let a daimōn take him, a daimōn with considerable force of will but with little common sense.

Perhaps Saigo had a Voice of his own, a subtle monster capable of working its way to power.

Hmmm.

Gabriel considered the Voice. He hadn't made an attempt to contact the Voice again, largely because his thoughts had been too turbulent, and his rush of creativity too overwhelming, for the deep meditation he suspected the contact would require.

But still, the Voice knew something. Perhaps it was time for Gabriel to compose himself and make the attempt.

He made another call to Fleta first, was told that Zhenling hadn't made contact. Then Gabriel sat at the cembalo, pulled the lever that, with an unmusical thunk, dropped its complicated mechanism into the key of B-flat, and struck a few soothing chords while he tried to settle his thoughts. His spirit began to float off on a musical tangent, and he took his hands off the keyboard and forced his mind back to the task at hand.

Gabriel closed his eyes, took a long breath to the count of ten, held it for ten seconds, let it out for ten seconds more. "*Tzai*," he said, a whisper invoking his cry of the spirit. His left hand, the Voice's hand, began to trace the Involved Iconography glyph for "beware" on the top of the cembalo. His other hand adopted the mudra for "dialogue." He let the character "beware" trace itself in his mind, writing it inside his eyelids in characters of fire. "*Dai*," he said. He imagined the character floating in void, the sole inhabitant of the universe; he changed its color, rolling through a bright electric spectrum; he moved it away to a pinpoint-distance, then brought it up close, overwhelming. Gabriel dissected the character, calling its meanings to his mind, invoking the modalities for "threat" and "vigilance," the claustrophobic trapezoid that surrounded the character, like walls leaning in, the imperative mark that gave it all a sense of urgency.

"*Die*," he said, and then a cold, faint whisper tracked along his spine.

Gabriel Aristos.

Gabriel's heart lurched. A keen electric cry sang in his nerves.

An inexpressible sensation of distance filled Gabriel's senses. He had the impression of a long, darkling plain, a distant, half-heard cry from an unknowable distance. There was a strong eddy of melancholy, of loneliness.

The Voice seemed light-years away.

The taste of metal tracked strongly down Gabriel's tongue. He focused his attention down the unearthly distance that separated him from the distant Voice and sent his message wailing down into the darkness.

What is your name?

I have no name. Names are dangerous.

Name a thing, Gabriel thought, and you control it. The daimōn was determined not to be controlled.

What are you?

I am the thing you need now.

What do I need? Gabriel would play Sokrates with the thing, ask it questions until it revealed its nature.

You need a . . . There was a hesitation. **You need a navigator.**

A navigator? Do you know where I am going?

You are going into dangerous places.

And you will see me safe?

Do not trust them. Shifting to warning mode again. Gabriel's strategy was too transparent: the daimōn would not play question-and-answer.

Who should I not trust?

Remmy. Zhenling. The Black-Eyed Ghost. All on this Terrina.

Why should I not trust Remmy?

Remmy will not withstand.

He is weak?

Zhenling is driven. Who is her coachman?

Possibilities tumbled through Gabriel's mind. **Do you mean a daimōn has her?**

The Black-Eyed Ghost is a servant. But whose?

Gabriel's mind whirled. The strain of communicating across this cold, unspeakable distance was beginning to tell. The Voice's loneliness chilled his bones like a cold wind.

How do you know these things?

I don't know. But I know that I know.

Riddles. A mystery wrapped in an enigma . . .

How long have you been in existence? Gabriel asked.

I am recent. I came into being as the result of a threat perception so subtle that you never noticed it. I noticed. But I could not tell its nature.

Could a part of his mind have intuited the corruption of the Hyperlogos? Gabriel wondered. Was the Voice then its response?

Some dreadfully distant mind-part, this. Possibly the buried lizard brain, perceiving somehow a threat to itself.

You became aware of me only through accident. I have learned not to make that mistake.

Fagit. That peremptory burst had not been intended to be overheard, had only made itself apparent because Psyche had united the daimones in a moment of transcendence.

I will name you Navigator, Gabriel said.

That is not my name. There was a sensation of terrible isolation in the far-off cry, a sound like interstellar hydrogen freezing in the void.

If you give me your name, I will give you access to my reno. You can use the reno to make yourself more powerful.

I do not trust your reno.

Gabriel was surprised. **But it is mine—my implant. A part of me. It can enhance you.**

Your reno is not necessary.

You will find other daimones there. You do not need to be so lonely. Why must you hold yourself apart?

Sadness flooded Gabriel's senses. He felt tears stinging his eyes.

I must be alone. It is needed.

I will help you. You are Navigator. You will come when I call you.

I will not come. And that is not my name.

The Voice faded, leaving Gabriel alone on the dark dreaming plain. His skin was sheened with sweat and his breath rasped in his throat. Tears fell down his face; there was an ache in his sinus. Never had he felt such isolation.

The sense of aloneness slowly faded, replaced by quiet foreboding. The Voice had given him a list of people not to trust. And the Voice had been right about Gerius.

Zhenling? He had never intended that she come to the Gaal Sphere—she would arrive too late to be useful in any case—but the notion that someone, or thing, was "driving" her was startling. *Who is her coachman?* A daimōn, insinuated into her consciousness? Did *everyone* have a Voice somewhere? A stealthy terror began to creep along Gabriel's nerves. What if *everyone* had a Voice, what if the Voice was like some virus creeping through the Hyperlogos, infecting every healthy mind . . .

Gabriel shook off the wave of paranoia, recognizing it as a psychic remnant of the Voice's visit.

He remembered the long hissing journey over snow, the troika driver with his long snowy mustachios. His name had been Gury. *The coachman?*

That mustached character hadn't said anything, hadn't acted as anything other than a coachman. There was no evidence he was anything other than an oneirochronic artifact.

Still, there had been a different quality about the character. Gabriel recalled a flash of something like recognition when he'd finally seen Gury's face.

He wondered what that was. He would seek the answer within meditation again, when he wasn't quite so drained by his contact with the Voice.

The Black-Eyed Ghost is a servant. But whose?

Somehow this allegation was the most disturbing. Marcus had served under Saigo, of course, and had, he admitted, contributed to the design of the Gaal Sphere's primitive technology without realizing it. But could he be Saigo's plant within Gabriel's organization? Or worse (the Voice's paranoia oozing again through his veins) a kind of (seeking the right word) *psychomorph*, a plastic artificial personality created specifically to appeal to Gabriel's tastes and get close to him? And Marcus had *insisted* on accompanying Gabriel to the Gaal Sphere—perhaps as a spy.

Gabriel contemplated this thought for a long, horrid moment before he concluded that the scenario was far too unlikely. Marcus had been on Illyricum for years, and Saigo hadn't had any reason to spy on Gabriel until a few months ago.

Unless, Gabriel thought (paranoia smothering him again like damp cotton wool), Saigo had done it to *every one* of the Aristoi. Created hundreds of psychomorphs, one for each . . .

But wouldn't that be awesomely difficult?

How hard could it be, Gabriel thought in sudden despair, for someone who had created whole planets from scratch? Whole *civilizations?*

His ricocheting mind bounced again to the coachman. What if the coachman was Zhenling's psychomorph? Someone with access to her Sealed files in the oneirochronon?

Gabriel blinked, calmed himself, slowed his breathing. This kind of thinking was perfectly insane. The Voice was getting too firm a grip on him.

Gabriel heard a bolt working on the floor below, then the door opening. "Ghibreel?" Remmy's voice. Gabriel played some chords on the cembalo to let Remmy know he was on the second floor, and continued to play as he listened to the sound of Remmy's shoes on the stair.

Incoming cipher tachline communication from Ariste Zhenling. Reno's voice. Gabriel thought for a moment, then called up Bear and gave the daimōn control of his body and voice before telling Reno to proceed.

Springtime blossomed in Gabriel's mind. A brisk wind ruffled the surface of the once-frozen lake, stirred Zhenling's unbound hair.

She stood on the sward in front of the onion-domed dacha, her slim body enclosed in a Yellow Epoch gown, high-collared, broad at the shoulder and hips, narrow at the waist and ankles.

Seeing this, Gabriel gave himself an English walking suit from the same period, with a four-in-hand scarf and a white carnation, its petal tips touched with scarlet.

Faintly, through Bear, Gabriel felt the the ivory cembalo keys through his fingertips, heard the sound of music, Schön's love aria from Gabriel's *Lulu.* He felt the touch of Remmy's lips on his cheek, Bear's answering sensation of warmth and abiding goodwill.

"Good news," Remmy said. He sat on the bench next to Gabriel. "You're famous."

"Famous in what way?"

"As the killer of Silvanus. People live in terror of those sorts of people—everyone thinks we're well rid of

Gabriel embraced Zhenling, kissed her.

"I'm upwell and out-system," she said. "I'm on my own, alone in my ship. I didn't have time to order anyone to go with me."

"It's wise you didn't delay," Gabriel said.

"I need information, Gabriel Vissarionovich," Zhenling said. "I need to know what to do, where to go."

"The cipher changes every six hours or so," Gabriel said. "More if there's a lot of traffic." He took her arm, walked with her up the drive. Gravel crunched beneath their feet. "It's best if we save the private tachline only for the most important and confidential communications—the less traffic, the more difficult it will be to break any of the ciphers."

"Understood."

"I am sending you now"—(Horus pulsed a message to Fleta)—"plans for a communications satellite network." (**Transmitted,** said Reno.) "This way you can relay communications with a near-certainty of not being traced."

him. And when Gerius and the doctor revealed the treachery—"

"Treachery?" Bear's pity for Gerius and Lavinius filled Gabriel's soul—poor, benighted puppets. His fingers continued the aria.

"They said that Silvanus asked for a moment to refresh himself, and that he and Augustino drew sword and attacked without warning. That's how Gerius and the doctor—what's his name?—that's how they were wounded."

How sad, Bear felt, that they needed to invent such falsehood.

Remmy looked at Gabriel closely. "You haven't said anything, Ghibreel," he said. "Isn't that how it occurred?"

Bear looked up. "They . . . underexaggerate their own part."

Remmy gazed at him carefully. "What really happened?"

"It doesn't matter," Bear said. "It's over."

"You haven't even said what the fight was about."

Bear struck a few

"I see." She straightened slightly as a thought struck her, stopping in her tracks, then looked at him sharply, gloved fingertips tightening on his arm. "Our communications—? All of them compromised?"

"I believe so."

"All our . . . tangos? Our private moments?"

"Yes."

"And you knew?"

He looked at her, touched her cheek. "I could not behave otherwise without putting you in danger." He kissed her; the oneirochronic lips were moist. "And I am not ashamed of my art. Let them envy us if they will."

Zhenling thought for a moment. A shimmer of defiance flashed in her dark eyes. "Yes." She kissed him fiercely. "We have privacy now," she said. "For the first time ever. We should take advantage of it."

Lust bubbled happily up Gabriel's spine. "Indeed yes," he said.

"I want to take advantage of it in reality," she said. They began walking up the chords, let his hands rest for a moment on the keys. It would be dangerous, he thought, not to let Remmy know.

"It was about you," he said. "Adrian wanted revenge for my running off with you the other night, and he created a situation in which I would either flee or die. He thought."

Remmy looked at Gabriel for a long moment, one jaw muscle twitching. Bear's heart melted with pity. "I'm sorry," Remmy said.

"It's not your fault. I made choices, and I'll live with the consequences. But in case the consequences include an attack on you, I want you to be prepared."

Remmy gave an incredulous laugh, then flipped his hands. "Consequences? Remember what I said—you're *famous*. Everyone wants to know you. My father heard from the Grand Chamberlain that even the king wants to meet you." He laughed again. "Who would dare attack the hero of the hour? You're safer than His Majesty among the Yellow Cavaliers."

drive again. "How can I meet you in the flesh? And where? The Gaal Sphere?"

"I think you must head for Earth², " Gabriel said. "Speak to Pan Wengong. The Eldest needs to be informed. The conspirators are panicking and taking hasty action, and he will need advice close to home."

Zhenling shook her head. "It will take me months to get there—longer than it will take to get to where you are, I suspect." Her hand, once again, tightened on his arm. "I want to be with *you*, Gabriel."

"You would not be able to help me," Gabriel said. "Either I will succeed in my actions or I will fail. Putting another at risk would not increase my chance of success. The best thing you can do is to keep yourself safe."

She dropped his arm and whirled to face him. Passion colored her cheeks, flamed in her eyes. "What does it matter at this point?" she cried. "The entire Logarchy is about to blow up! *Everyone* will be at risk—and I'd rather die with you than alone!"

Admiration surged

"All I had to do to achieve fame and celebrity was kill someone?" Bear was astounded.

"Someone no one liked, anyway." A thought came to Remmy, and he smiled with his fine teeth. "Adrian must be terrified! If his part in this conspiracy is revealed, there'll be prosecution—we Old Horses will insist, and the Velitos are spoiling for revenge after he killed the chancellor. Together we could have his head."

Adrian would be disappointed, Gabriel felt, if he knew how little Gabriel cared for his little plots, how insignificant the Monopolist seemed next to Saigo's Sphere-spanning intrigue . . .

Bear played some triumphant chords and grinned. Remmy looked down at Gabriel's hands. "I didn't know you played," he said.

"I learned last night, after you left."

Remmy paused for a moment, then shook his head. "I don't know why you expect me to believe something so preposterous," he said. "Nor do I know," sigh-

through Gabriel's heart. He was about to give his assent when he was stabbed by a cold needle of paranoia, an aftertaste of the Voice. He looked at her, felt the gravel drive under his feet, remembered the gravel crunching under the wheels as they drove off in the carriage with the reins in Gury's hands.

"Who is your coachman?" he asked.

There was a stricken look on Zhenling's face—terror? guilty knowledge? sudden realization?—in any event something so genuine, so surprising, that she couldn't conceal it even in the oneirochronon.

And then springtime vanished in an eyeblink, and with it Zhenling, and the dacha, lake and gravel drive and all, and Gabriel was alone in his own mind.

Terror skittered around the fringes of his consciousness on fast rodent feet. **Reestablish contact with Zhenling Ariste,** he ordered, but the tachline signal had gone—and not the signal from Zhenling to Illyricum, but from Terrina to *Cressida*.

It was as if the battleship

ing, "why I somehow find myself believing you."

Bear took one hand off the keyboard, then took Remmy's hand in his own. "I'm talented that way," he said. "I have a kind of . . . spirit . . . that can learn things."

"Instruments. Languages." Remmy's voice was slow, thoughtful. "Swordsmanship, too?"

Bear jerked his chin.

Remmy seemed not to know how to respond. He stood up abruptly, moved to a chair. He seemed not to know what he wanted to do with his big hands.

"May I advise you not to say such things in front of people?" he said. "They'll misunderstand. They'll think you're possessed by demons."

Bear couldn't prevent himself from smiling. "I'll be discreet."

"You could get yourself burned. You could get *me* burned. I'm being very serious."

"I shall be cautious. Please be at ease."

Remmy didn't seem comforted.

had ceased to exist. Carefully Gabriel suppressed any outward sign of alarm. He sent a *FLASH* alert to Clancy.

See that everyone is armed. We've lost telemetry with the *Cressida* and I'm afraid Saigo may be making some kind of move.

Where are you, Gabriel?

I'm still at Remmy's. I'll be as safe here as anywhere.

If telemetry wasn't regained, Gabriel knew, things would happen automatically. In another (**47.3666 hours,** Reno informed), after Gabriel failed to renew his password, the prearranged *FLASH* alert would be transmitted across the Hyperlogos and through Gabriel's own private communications network, which (by now) should cover at least half human space. The Aristoi would become aware of their danger.

The problem, for Gabriel, would be reduced to one of surviving here until someone arrived from the Logarchy to pick him up.

Aristos. Clancy's voice. **All attempts to reestablish our tachline have failed.**

"There are some things I don't understand," he said. "May I ask some, ah, personal questions?"

"Of course." Bear's tender heart was moved by Remmy's evident distress.

"May I ask about Clansai?" He licked his lips. "Is she really a doctor?"

"Oh yes. I'm sure Gerius and Lavinius owe her their lives."

Remmy looked thoughtful. "I think this also deserves care and discretion. Women aren't supposed to do that sort of thing. Some local physicians may try to get her arrested as a witch if they think she's actually practicing medicine. It's happened before."

Anguish flooded Bear at the fate of these unlucky women. "I'll tell her not to practice."

Remmy appeared to steel himself. "And your personal relationship with her?"

"We are lovers," Bear said.

"Does she know about you and me?"

"Certainly."

An icicle of foreboding leaked from Gabriel's

Desist. *Cressida* knows where we are. If they are in a position to resume communication, they will do so.

Shouldn't we continue ourselves?

No. Someone else may be there, and listening. We don't want to alert others to *our* presence.

There was a moment of silence, long enough for a thought to loom unspoken between them: *has* Cressida *been destroyed?*

Clancy's voice, when it came, was brisk.

As you wish, Aristos. Fini.

Gabriel thought about the crew of the *Cressida*, Marcus and Rubens and the others, all here on his orders, his mission. He had thought he, Gabriel, here on Terrina, would be in the most dangerous role.

Perhaps he had been wrong.

He could think of nothing else to do. Either *Cressida* was safe or not. Saigo's forces would burst in the door in a few minutes or they wouldn't. Precious little Gabriel could do either way.

Gabriel wasn't used to thoughts into Bear's personality. Alarmed, Bear sent a query to Gabriel; Gabriel told him things were under control and to continue.

Remmy was looking thoughtful. "She's a remarkable woman," he finally decided. "She feels no . . . rivalry?"

Bear took hands from the keyboard, clasped them, leaned forward toward Remmy. "She's very secure in herself, and she knows me quite well. Jealousy progresses from insecurity, and she is not an insecure woman."

"I wish I were as secure." Remmy's face twisted as if in pain. "The jealousy is hurtful. She was even present at your duel, and I was not."

Poor child, Bear thought. Tortured from birth, improperly raised, divided from his own nature. He rose from the bench, approached Remmy's chair.

being helpless. He found it
not to his taste.

What was there left to
do, he wondered, but con-
tinue to play Ghibreel the
Foreigner?

He might as well.

Gabriel widened his focus to include Bear's perceptions,
then encompassed them. Awareness of his body filled his
mental image of himself, filling a chasm he hadn't entirely
realized was there.

Remmy sat before him, his tall body hunched miserably
in a chair. His posture, Gabriel thought, was really deplorable.
Gabriel squatted on his heels in front of Remmy and looked
up at him.

"How can I help?" he asked. "How can I assure you that
you are precious to me?"

Precious to Gabriel, who had just, he suspected, lost so
much. Who needed every loving soul he could find.

"Suffer my company, I suppose," Remmy said, and tried
to smile. He slid forward out of the chair, put his arms around
Gabriel. Gabriel kissed him.

"You frighten me, Ghibreel," Remmy said. "Why is
that?"

Mirrors can be frightening, Gabriel thought.

"I will try to be very careful," Gabriel said, aware of the
absurdity of what he had just said. *Careful*. As if the word
applied to anything he'd done in the last several months.

Recklessly, then, he took Remmy upstairs, and tried to
take momentary comfort.

It didn't help him forget.

Gabriel returned to Santo Georgio later that afternoon. His
companions were solemn, already half in mourning. Dinner
was a silent business. Later that evening, at the appropriate
time, they all took the carriage out to a field near where

Gabriel had fought his duel, stood in the cool of the evening, and waited.

Cressida was a little over nine light-hours out from Terrina, hiding from detection far on the edge of the star system. Gabriel's company knew precisely where in the sky the battleship would be, assuming they had the instruments to see it.

The instruments weren't available—Gabriel's group depended entirely on the tachline that connected them to the battleship. Tachyon generators were bulky: their own equipment wasn't powerful enough to generate a powerful enough beam to carry the distance to Illyricum or anywhere in the Logarchy.

Stars glittered frostily; what the locals called the *Via Lactía* stretched like a celestial blanket across a far corner of the sky. Moths fluttered beneath Terrina's distant violet moon. Clancy and White Bear set out such detectors as they had.

They had an escape route planned, but it would only take them so far. A complex nano had been built into the coach, ready to drop onto the ground and create, within forty minutes or so, a chemical-powered rocket capable of boosting half a dozen people into low orbit, from which *Cressida* or *Pyrrho* could then rescue them.

Useless, if *Cressida* and *Pyrrho* were gone.

Thirty seconds, reported Reno.

Gabriel held Clancy's hand.

As if a knife had torn away the black velvet arch of night, the sky bloomed with sudden light. **X rays,** Clancy reported from the invisible spectrum. **Alpha and beta radiation. Neutrons.**

The debris that formed when spacetime itself was ripped apart. There were gravity guns being used out there.

He wasn't the only one who could use nano to build battleships, Gabriel thought. The plans were on file and available to anyone with the license to use nano.

The Aristoi. Saigo. Saigo's minions.

The enemy. He hadn't thought of them that way before.

The brightness faded quickly, leaving cold bright flowers printed on Gabriel's retinas. His breath caught in his throat.

"Oh Gabriel," Clancy breathed. She rested her head on his shoulder. Stricken to the heart, he put his arms around her.

Marcus, gone, he thought. The unborn child, gone. Rubens y Sedillo, gone. Kem-Kem, gone. Twenty-six others, drawn from the most talented of Gabriel's Therápontes, gone.

He could rebuild the girl-child, he thought fiercely—her genetics were on file. For that matter he could rebuild the Black-Eyed Ghost, rebuild all of them.

But even if they were genetically identical, they wouldn't be the same. The girl-child would not be the same child that Marcus would so lovingly raise; Marcus's genetic double would mature into a different, if equally tender-hearted, young man.

They were all lost, their very atoms torn apart by the murderous force of unleashed gravity. It was precisely this sort of tragedy, this hideous misuse of technology, that the Aristoi were sworn to prevent.

From a distant, grieving part of his own soul, Gabriel heard the plaintive sound of a bone trumpet mourning the dead.

And the dead that were to come.

Chapter 14

LOUISE: Why do I feel that ghosts are more real
Than these creatures of substance and matter?
Why does their song seem to drive me along
More than humanity's drivel and pratter?

Manfred rested his head in Gabriel's lap on the return to Santo Georgio. Clancy held his hand. In his head a bone trumpet mourned.

He could close his eyes and still see the bright flashes that marked the violent death of friends. Friends, his thoughts remorselessly insisted, that he had brought here to die.

"In thirty-odd hours," he said, "when the *FLASH* alert is sounded, all humanity may be at war."

"And we're on the sidelines." Clancy sounded as if she regretted it.

"We'll be picked up sooner or later."

She looked at him. "Is there anything we can do?"

"Try to jury-rig a tachyon beam to Illyricum, I suppose.

Perhaps if we scavenge some of the spikes we've been dropping in the capital we can use their parts, but I don't think we have the right tools to make use of them." He assigned Horus to work on the problem and see if there was a way to jury-rig the proper equipment.

Her voice was level. "I meant, is there anything more direct that we can do?"

Gabriel sighed. "Direct? Probably not."

"Saigo is here, we think. On Terrina. If we can seize his person before the alarm is given, we might seriously affect our enemies' plans before the war even starts."

"Even assuming he's on the planet, which is by no means certain, he's not in Vila Real, he's at his country estate. And we don't know where that is."

"We could find out."

"He'll have guards."

"He'll be guarding against low-technology Terrinans, not us."

Gabriel closed his eyes, saw violent blooms of light. "All this has occurred to me," he said. "I want nothing more than to take some kind of desperate action. But if I do something, I want to make certain that it will be proper and effective. I don't want to make this move out of a kind of despair, out of a misplaced mourning for our friends. Adding the Surveyors' names to a long casualty list won't be of service to anyone."

Clancy's voice was earnest. "What do our lives matter, Aristos? Within a year, half humanity may be gone."

Five thousand soldiers lost, Gabriel thought, after Chen Tao, *Cold fur, cold silk, lying on an alien world . . . bones with wives who dream of them still.*

Five thousand. Five thousand dead was a bad break for the Tang Dynasty, but now the casualties could number five thousand million. Fifty thousand million. More.

"White Bear, Quiller, and Yaritomo will have to consent," Gabriel said. "I want unanimous agreement on it. But if they're willing, we'll break into Saigo's house tonight, and see what we can find."

* * *

White Bear, Quiller, and Yaritomo agreed, but the Surveyors found nothing.

The Santo Georgio house of Lord Sergius, as the place from which the tachline burst had originated, had been under discreet surveillance since before Gabriel's arrival on the planet. For fear of detection Gabriel hadn't dared put listening spikes inside.

The eavesdroppers reported the place shuttered and uninhabited except for three servants—apparently locals—who lived in the basement and who looked after the place in the absence of its master.

Under the cold light of the *Via Lactía*, Gabriel, Clancy, White Bear, Quiller, and Yaritomo went over the outside wall—twelve-foot-high iron spikes—and then crept beneath the carven beast-ward above the front door and examined the lock. The mechanism was simple but huge: it would require a key two feet long to open it, and the intruders simply didn't have the specialized equipment necessary to pick it—"high-tension crowbars," White Bear suggested.

Gabriel took off his shoes and, daimones whispering sutras to his inward ear, climbed up the exterior of the building, finding finger- and toeholds in the mortarwork. Smoke scented the air. In his concentrated state time seemed to creep by: there seemed an eternity between each of his heartbeats. Hanging like a mantis on the wall, he inserted one of Clancy's surgical instruments through the gap in the shutter and lifted the crossbar holding the shutter in place. From there he slipped easily into a dark room that smelled of mildew and dust.

For an endless moment Gabriel waited in case a hidden alarm had been tripped. Clancy's detectors sensed no sudden pulse of energy. His expanded vision revealed a third-rate guest room—dusty draperies, a threadbare carpet. Gabriel closed the shutter behind him and padded out into the hallway, then down a curving flight of polished marble stairs to a window on the ground floor. He opened the window, and the heavy shutters.

Carefully the Surveyors crept through the building. Intricate tapestries hung in silence on the walls; paintings in carved, gilded frames were covered by white sheets. Gabriel ghosted over cold marble and parquet floors, slid silently through carved wooden doors, looked behind tapestries. The library contained several thousand volumes and gave off the scent of fine leather. There was a room of thick bound volumes filled with accounts: Gabriel set Yaritomo to reading and memorizing all of them, a simple enough task given the capacity of his reno. Clancy found the master bedroom and adjacent study, and carefully picked the lock on the master's desk. Once opened it unfolded, like a Chinese puzzle, into an extravagant cherrywood secretary of sliding leaves, silent drawers, niches, and shelves for different sorts of paper, all embroidered with ivory and gold-wire inlay. When Gabriel arrived he recognized the design as a product of the Illyricum Workshop.

He was not amused.

Gabriel read and memorized the stacks of correspondence thus revealed—letters to Lord Sergius from all sorts of people, mostly either tradesmen's matters (the imported marble for the new fireplace seemed to have generated a lot of trouble for everyone), or notes from acquaintances about who would be home to visitors, and when. The copies of Sergius's correspondence, neatly annotated by his secretary, were equally mundane. A search for secret panels or drawers failed to turn up anything.

Saigo's secret drawer was in his reno, of course. He didn't need to put anything in writing.

No energies were displayed, no alarms went off. Nothing of importance was discovered save that Saigo played his Sergius role with as plodding a thoroughness as might be expected of him. Gabriel and his party left the house, leaving a scattering of eavesdropping devices behind—fear of detection at this juncture seemed beside the point, all things considered.

It was near dawn when Gabriel and Clancy slid beneath the embroidered coverlet of their bed. The raid on Saigo—perhaps it had been little more than a gesture—had failed, leaving behind a weighty residue of despair. Gabriel and Clancy kissed, clung, made love. Gabriel tried to achieve utter tenderness, utter delicacy. The fact of love should not, he thought, interfere with the fact of mourning. The bone trumpet should harmonize, with grace, sadness, and care, with the pipes of Pan.

Two people, Psyche wrote in his mind, *bereft, and far from home.*

Gabriel slept briefly, then left Clancy in the huge bed, put on his brocade dressing gown, and, because local custom did not permit otherwise, woke one of his servants to make tea. He drank it and gazed out the window, watching as his neighbors' fine brown stonework turned gold in the rising sun, as red sunlight glowed off diamond-shaped windowpanes.

Daimones prowled through his thoughts, argued courses of action. He could find out from Remmy, he supposed, where Sergius's country place was, at least roughly.

The location of Sergius/Saigo had always been one of his goals, but until a few hours ago it hadn't had a high priority. He had been content to wait in Vila Real until his own plans had matured.

Now he was working to someone else's timetable. He desperately needed to know whether he could reach Sergius's county seat within the thirty or so hours before his *FLASH* alert went out, and there was no obvious way of doing it.

He restrained himself from sending Remmy an urgent note. He had caused that young man enough agitation in his few days here.

Perhaps, he thought, he could pretend he needed to send Sergius a letter, and wake up the servants in his town house.

Within the range of his sight he could see soot rising from a dozen chimneys. Stoves were being lit, servants' breakfasts prepared. Masters and their mistresses clasped feather

pillows in their feather beds. Soon the daily wave of beggars
would be taking up stations in doorways.

Soon, far away, the rest of the human race might be in a
war on a scale inconceivable to any of these people.

Sharp hoofbeats pounded the air. A man turned the corner a block away, lashed his horse with a whip, came flying
down the road. By Gabriel's gate he pulled up, looked around
wildly, then gave a brutal jerk to the reins and rode under the
arch into Gabriel's courtyard and out of sight.

Gabriel waited for a moment to hear whether the bell
rung would be one of the other lodgers', but knew in his spine
it would be his, and so it was. He sent a half-awake servant to
answer the bell, then waited patiently for the stranger to be
introduced.

"Count Magnus of Constantina," the servant reported.

Count Magnus was a tall, thin young man with a long,
slim razor-cut mustache that stretched to meet his sideburns
just below the ear. Cosmetics couldn't disguise his bad skin.
His wrists were knobby, and his flaxen hair fell in one eye. He
had kept his eyebrows, but dyed them henna-red.

"You are one of Lord Remmy's relatives, I take it?"
Gabriel said. The family resemblance was clear enough.

"His older b-brother, Serenity." A slight stammer presented itself on the plosive. "Do you know where he is?"

Gabriel sent an alert to his daimones. "I last saw him
yesterday afternoon, in Santa Leofra's quarter. He had been
kind enough to put me up for a few days, and—"

Magnus waved a hand. "I know all that, Highness. But
he's not to be found, and we've word that he's been arrested.
One of our n—" He stopped, his blue eyes blinking fiercely.
Gabriel realized his tongue had stalled on the word *neighbor*.
"—one of our acquaintances thought they saw him taken
away, early yesterday evening, on Via Real between here and
the city."

Aimed at you, Mataglap said.

Concur, said Horus.

It's connected to everything else, Mataglap insisted.

Cressida destroyed, Remmy arrested the same night you were playing burglar in Saigo's house . . .

"Taken on his way home," Gabriel clarified.

"Yes, Highness. But our n—" Blink. "—our witness—said that he couldn't be certain if it was Remmy he saw. Just a man fitting his description who was overtaken by some riders, then carried away. One of them waved what he said was a warrant."

"Was it a Yellow Warrant with Knot and Seal?"

Magnus seemed surprised that Gabriel would know of this detail. "Not likely," he said. "If it were a royal warrant, it would have been served by members of the *Guardia Real*, the Cuirassiers, or the Cavaliers, and they would have identified themselves. Also they could have taken him in Santa Leofra's quarter, instead of waiting for him on the highway."

"Who else would have done it, then?"

Magnus's look was a little defiant. "I was hoping you could tell me, Highness."

Daimones' frantic speculation filled Gabriel's head. He told them to shut up. "I'm afraid I don't know," he said. "Who has the authority to make such an arrest?"

"Anyone who could persuade a magistrate to sign a warrant. And there are over a hundred magistrates in the city."

"I would suspect Prince Adrian, if anyone," Gabriel said. "He has made himself my enemy."

Magnus's eyes widened slightly. "Iuso," he said. "And my father's out of town."

FLASH **< Priority 1 >**, Gabriel sent. **Coach to be readied, horses saddled. Prepare to evacuate.**

"Which magistrate would Adrian use? Which prison?"

Magnus flipped his hands. "Santo Marco's. The Caverns. The Old Gateway. Any of them." A look of apprehension entered his eyes. "Unless the takers were Argosy Vassals. Peregrino has magisterial authority, and Adrian's an ally of his. In that case Rem's in the Old T-temple. No one gets out of there. And very possibly he's under t—" He stammered to a halt, eyelids twitching.

Torture. Magnus didn't have to say it.

There was movement in the back of the room. Dr. Clancy appeared silently in the doorway, behind Magnus's back. She wore only her nightdress. Gabriel could see a pistol in her fist.

We are not in immediate danger, he broadcast. **But have the ostlers shut the street gate.**

Clancy ghosted away.

"Can you send people to find out?" Gabriel asked.

Magnus jerked his chin. "I can send servants to the prisons, but they might not come back."

"In that case," Gabriel said, "you'd know which prison Lord Remmy was in, wouldn't you?"

A businesslike smile crossed Magnus's features. "Aye. So I would. And I'll send them with coin, to put the jailers in a less severe frame of mind."

"Are you in funds, my lord? Can I give you money?"

"My lord the D—" Blink. "—my father—left me adequate, thanks."

"Have you allies? Can you send word to the members of the Old Court that one of their number has been imprisoned, possibly by another faction?"

"Ah." He licked his lips. "Yes. I could do that."

"Who could order Lord Remmy released over the magistrate's warrant?"

"The king, of course. The new chancellor, but he's Adrian's man. The Assembly of Magistrates, though they won't meet till autumn. The chief j-justice, but he's old and mad and locked in his own attic."

"You and your allies must petition the king, at once."

"Y-yes." He sighed, brushed hair out of his eyes. "There is so much to do, and I'm n-not used to . . ." He shook his head. "I thank you for your attention, Highness."

"Do you know where Sergius's country place is?" Gabriel asked.

Magnus was startled. "Duke Sergius? The king's friend? I—he—he lives in Ocarnío. In that fabulous house of his."

"How far is that by the fastest.express post?"

"A week. Perhaps five days."

So much for a preemptive strike. Horus, sourly.

Gabriel thought of billions dead. Remmy languishing in some cell.

One of these, at least, was a matter he could do something about.

"Do you think Sergius would intervene?" Marcus asked.

"I will write him and see," Gabriel said. "He and I . . . know each other. But perhaps it would be best to approach the king first."

"Ummm . . . yes." Trying to reach a decision.

"Can you introduce me to him?"

"Ah . . . if you like."

"First I'll have to find a place in Santa Leofra's quarter in case these takers are after me as well. Why don't you send out your servants to the various prisons, and then meet me in the city? Around the second gong of the forenoon watch?"

A decisive look came into Magnus's eyes. "Yes. Very well, Highness."

"At an inn called the Eagle. Do you know it?" Gabriel had seen it on his travels to and from Remmy's cabinet.

"In Santa Leofra's quarter? No—but the q-quarter's small. I'll find it."

"Are you certain of this, Aristos?" Clancy asked after Magnus took his leave. She and Gabriel watched from the windows as White Bear, Yaritomo, and Gabriel's servants packed the carriage with belongings—a visiting prince and his mistress, of course, being above doing it themselves.

"Though I understand your reason for wanting to get Remmy out," she said, "time may be critical if we wish to intervene in Saigo's plans. And if you leave the country the Vassals won't have reason to hold Remmy."

"They won't have a reason to keep him alive, either," Gabriel said. He thought of the Black-Eyed Ghost torn to bits and given to the Void, of the others who had died with him, whose very atoms had not survived. Remmy suffering under tortures without any of the tools that Gabriel, or any of his people, possessed, tools that would enable them to withstand the pain.

Yaritomo, with his rite of Kavandi, had even tortured *himself* in search of enlightenment. Even someone as young as he, with his conscious control of capillary dilation and mental states, could survive torture better than could Remmy.

"No," Gabriel said. "From now on we all stay together. To triumph or die."

Clancy looked at him. He knew that she disagreed, that what compelled her was the logic of one torn life—a life condemned to barbarism at birth—against the possible lives of billions.

Perhaps they were both being irrational. He wanted to rescue a friend even though it meant postponing the meeting with Saigo; while her reaction to the crisis had been to burglarize an empty house.

"I understand," she said.

She would be an Ariste, he thought, if she lived. She was developing her own style of decision, of execution. If, that is, there were Aristoi left to administer the exams.

The Eagle served beer flavored with raspberries and hard bread that tasted of sawdust. Gabriel left both untouched on the table and listened to Count Magnus's report.

"It's the Old T-temple, Highness," Magnus said. "The officer on duty denied it, but after a few coins unshackled his t—" Blink. "—his *speech*—one of the guards reported that someone of Remmy's description had been brought in yesterday evening, along with two other men."

"Two others?" Gabriel repeated. "Have you any idea...?"

"None, Serenity." Magnus's look turned accusing. "You don't know either? Because if he's not arrested in some connection with you, Highness, I can't think what this could be about."

Gabriel composed his face in an expression of intent sincerity. "I swear to you I do not know, my lord. I know so few people here, and no one else of my acquaintance has been arrested, at least to my knowledge."

The place smelled of spilled beer and garlic sausage. Laughter echoed from the low roofbeams. The patrons were a mixed lot, down-at-heels aristocrats rubbing elbows with workmen. All male, except for Clancy, who was in male clothing. It wasn't considered a suitable place even for the most dubious of females.

Clancy, Quiller, and White Bear sat on benches at Gabriel's table, keeping between Gabriel and eavesdroppers. Yaritomo kept watch outside and made certain no one hovered in the street.

Gabriel looked into Magnus's eyes. "What goes on in these interrogations? What is Remmy going through?"

Magnus paused, apprehension clear in his face, then steeled himself. "It depends on how much time they think they've got. Usually they show the . . . instruments . . . to the prisoner and explain how they're used, then let him sit in a cell for a while and think about them. Many will ask to c-confess right then. But if the Vassals are pressed for time they'll commence with Extraordinary Justice right away."

"How would they approach it in this case, do you think?"

Magnus shook his head. His hands were trembling. "I don't know, Highness. They took him on the highway without anyone knowing, and they brought him in with two other people. He often spends the night in his cabinet, or with friends, so they may have assumed he wouldn't be missed—at least until my servant showed up asking for him. Even so they may choose to interrogate the others first, or . . ." Tears filled his eyes. "I don't understand it, Highness! Our family has never been members of an irregular sect, and Remmy is a pious boy who's never expressed any unorthodox r-religious opinions. Why would the Vassals even be interested in him?"

Gabriel put a hand on his arm. "Courage. We'll have him out."

Magnus blinked, shuddered. "Thank you. Though I don't know how."

"You must tell me." Earnestly. "You say the king must order Remmy released. How would that be done?"

Magnus wiped his eyes, frowned. "A simple order of release relayed through the chancellor's office. Or a Yellow Warrant with Knot and Seal could transfer the prisoner to a royal prison."

The chancellor's office would take too long, Gabriel thought. "What does a Yellow Warrant look like?" he asked. "Is it actually yellow?"

"In old times it was, a special parchment dyed with saffron. Only the king was permitted to have such paper. But then the old king gave the saffron monopoly to Adrian's grandfather, and now the warrant is written on ordinary parchment and wrapped with a yellow ribbon."

"The Knot and Seal?"

"Are you considering a forgery, Highness? N-not possible. The Seal is the royal seal, of course. About the size of a small plate, pressed into wax by the Seal Secretary. The Knot is a special knotted string partly hidden under the wax. The Knot is, oh, a finger's span in length, with little beads worked into it. There's a different pattern for each king. Only the Knot Secretary and the king are supposed to know how to tie the knot—it's very complicated, like macramé."

"But of course other people know."

"Other p-people *think* they know."

Gabriel leaned back, crossed his arms. "Think carefully, my lord. Are there any documents in your house with the royal seal on them?"

Magnus bit his lip. "Yes. Two or three, royal proclamations thanking my father for his services. But they don't have Knots—only royal orders bear the Knot, not letters or proclamations."

"Bring the documents. We'll lift the seals. I'll work out a way to make a Knot, then I'll need you to make certain that the language is correct."

Magnus's eyes were wide. He slowly shook his head. "This won't work, Highness. Forging a royal warrant is death."

"Your name will not be mentioned. I'll deliver the warrant to the Temple myself, and then either bluff it out or die." *Or bring the Temple down like Samson*, he thought, but didn't say it.

Magnus's look was sharp. "With all respect, Highness, if you're captured, it may not be up to *you* whose names you give them."

The stammer had gone away now that Magnus was caught up in the plot. Gabriel leaned in close, lifted his center of gravity above Magnus's, summoned daimones to blaze intently in his face.

"The naming of names may not be up to Remmy, either," he said. "It is precisely the restoration of choice to Remmy that I wish to affect."

Magnus thought about it. "I will petition the king this afternoon," he said. "If that fails, I will do anything you suggest."

"Can you send me the seals in the meantime?"

Magnus sighed as he gazed into a horrid world of unknown consequence. "Very well," he said.

"Any Yellow Warrant would be delivered by the Yellow Cavaliers, you say? The Cuirassiers? Who else?"

"The *Guardia Real*."

Gabriel turned to Clancy. "You have the steadiest hands, Doctor. I want you to buy some wax and large seals in the marketplace, then practice moving them."

"Yes, Prince Ghibreel."

White Bear and Yaritomo could find uniforms, he thought. And he knew the Knot Secretary.

Things were coming together.

By the first gong of the second evening watch, the document was ready. Gabriel had paid a visit to Gerius the Knot Secretary to thank him for his assistance in the duel. He had brought a gift—the same silver Cellini casket Adrian had rejected—and over a glass of mellow wine had brought up the subject of the royal knots. Count Gerius amiably showed him some samples from his locked strongbox, and Gabriel's reno promptly memorized the stitches and constructed a mathematical model that worked out how the knot was made. Later that day, Gabriel's fingers followed the pattern and produced a copy.

Yaritomo and White Bear, claiming they were going to a masked ball, had investigated the matter of uniforms. The Yellow Cavaliers wore a saffron-dyed buff coat that could be acquired only from Prince Adrian's outlets—too dangerous—and the Cuirassiers wore armor on duty, equipment available only from the royal armories.

They had returned as facsimile Guardsmen. The uniform was nothing more than a plumed hat and a sky-blue coat and trousers, with sunset-colored braidwork—linen, style of boot, and even the cut of the coat were left to the wearer.

Clancy, after a little practice, lifted all three seals with a hot surgical knife. One of them came up a little wrinkled, but the other two were perfect.

Quiller, his old-fashioned secretarial skills coming to the fore, did a beautifully calligraphed parchment with the synthetic royal command on it.

Magnus returned from the royal palace in disappointment. The king spent most of his spring days hunting in the royal park, and in his remaining time worked fast. He had given Magnus only a few seconds, but had promised to undertake an inquiry through the chancellor's office. "Either the king will forget the promise, or the chancellor will," Magnus predicted.

Gabriel passed the parchment across. "Will this draft do?" he asked.

Gabriel stepped out of the coach, felt the light touch of drizzle on his skin. It was a chill spring night and the air was heavy with woodsmoke. He straightened the white officer's sash he

wore over one shoulder, glanced up at Clancy sitting next to
White Bear on the box of the carriage, and touched the rolled
Yellow Warrant to his hat brim in salute.

Good fortune, Aristos, she broadcast.

Horses stamped impatiently. This was a carriage rented
for the occasion, Gabriel's own being too conspicuous—it
was lighter and faster, but the horses weren't as good, nor as
responsive to White Bear's inexperienced hands.

If I fail to return, Gabriel said, **do as you think best. You
are in charge.**

Quiller on one side and Yaritomo on the other, Gabriel—daimones snarling in his head—made his way across
the drawbridge to the closed gate of the prison. They all wore
heavy cloaks that floated out behind them, a device intended
to make them more imposing. Each was disguised with artfully applied white-lead cosmetic; each had shaved his eyebrows, drawn them on again in expressions of fixed hauteur.

The Old Temple, Gabriel had been told, was a temple
from ancient pagan times turned into a fortress by the conquering Ketshanese. There wasn't any hint of a temple remaining, though, no fluted columns or graceful high arches, only
a lowering fortress of grey stone, with brooding round towers
on each corner. It was surrounded by a dry moat partly filled
with refuse and human waste.

Bootheels echoed hollow on the drawbridge as Gabriel's
party crossed. No one challenged them. Massive hardwood
gates blocked Gabriel's entrance, with a smaller human-sized
door inset into one of them. A bellpull—actually an old iron
stirrup on a chain—hung from the darkness above. Gabriel
tugged on it, heard a clatter overhead, and waited for a response.

"*Que vá?*" The question boomed down from a cross-
shaped window above the gate.

Gabriel stepped back, allowed arrogance to dictate the set
of his chin and stance. "Open in the name of His Orthodox
Majesty!" he called. He brandished the warrant. "We have a
Yellow Warrant."

There was a moment's cold unease. "I'll call the officer of the guard."

"You'll open the door first, man! The king's business will not wait. *Gitme-gitme!*"

There was no answer. Gabriel stood in a wide stance with his arms crossed, the parchment and its ribbons dangling.

There was a thump, and the door opened. A guard—long mustachios, earrings, polished celata and breastplate—appeared briefly, then stood back to allow Gabriel's party to enter.

The door, Gabriel noticed, was held with a simple wooden bar reinforced with iron. Quite easy to open from the inside, should he need to do it.

The inside of the gateway was illuminated only by starlight that filtered through from the open courtway beyond. Gabriel's improved vision could see fairly well, the burning infrared image of the red-hot guard superimposed atop cooling moist stone. There was the smell of damp straw and manure. "I'll take you to the cornet," the guard mumbled.

"The king's business will not wait," Gabriel reminded.

The guard walked into the courtyard, turned, shuffled toward a door, banged on it. The interior of the Old Temple was an untidy, complex huddle of buildings that leaned against the walls of the old fort. Gabriel looked for landmarks, noted the sharp-cornered main building bulking opposite the gateway—the keep, he supposed—a pitch-roofed chapel that looked as if it were added to the structure at a later date, other rooms that looked like barracks. He could hear loud male voices coming from the guardroom, then one louder voice.

"Who is it?"

"Messengers from the king! Yellow Warrant!"

There was a moment of silence, then sounds of shuffling and the clank of armor. Gabriel gathered that the officer of the guard and his companions were trying to make themselves presentable.

Somewhere ahead a horse whinnied. It was good to know

where the stables were, just in case an extrafast getaway was indicated. Or if straw needed to be set alight by way of diversion.

The door opened on a breath of hop-scented air and a spill of yellow light. The cornet was in his midteens, with a pimple on his chin and a faint mustache. Gabriel ghosted forward out of the darkness and tried to loom over him.

"Senators?" the cornet said.

Gabriel pointed the warrant at him as if it were a sword. "Yellow Warrant with Knot and Seal," he said. "The king wants the prisoner Lord Remmy transferred to his own prison at Fort Makan."

The cornet looked at the warrant and did not take it. Behind him, his friends—other young officers—peered out of the light. "I've been instructed to say that Lord Remmy is not here," the cornet said.

There was an impatient growl from Yaritomo. The Burning Tiger, Gabriel judged.

Gabriel narrowed his eyes and lowered his voice, glided forward into the Second Posture of Esteem. "Do you want to inform the king of that personally? I will take you to the *Palaccio Real*, if you like, and you can explain your . . . *instructions* . . . to His Majesty."

The cornet's eyes went wide. Gabriel jabbed the warrant at him. "Take the warrant," he said. The Principal Inflection of Command rang in his voice. "Read it. Then either obey the king's express command, or not." His voice turned silky. "What did you say your name was, senator?"

"Ah—the *Equito* Pontus, senator." Pontus took the warrant, stepped inside, slid the wide yellow ribbon off the end and let the parchment fall open. As he held it to the light of a lantern, Gabriel entered the room, followed by his seconds.

Pontus's companions shuffled to their feet, smiled affably. Gabriel gazed back with a chill in his eyes. The room was small and the fire smoked badly, filling the upper part of the chamber with blue haze. There were four men, all young, all more or less drunk. Pontus, as the officer on duty, wore a celata helmet, breastplate, and gorget, but the others did not. All, however, carried swords.

If it becomes necessary, Gabriel broadcast to his companions, **take them out bare-handed. Their defense will concentrate solely on their weapons, and we have many more weapons than that—hands, feet, elbows, knees, wit, and daimones. They will take time to draw, and also have no room to swing. Go for their throats, to keep them from crying out.**

Acknowledged, said Yaritomo.

As you wish, Aristos.

Pontus frowned at the text of the warrant, then began moving toward the door. "I will have to consult the captain," he said.

Gabriel blocked him with an arm. "Did His Majesty *order* you to consult your captain?" he asked.

Pontus looked at him. "No, senator," he said.

"Then," the Principal Inflection again, "I suggest that you do as His Majesty *orders*, and nothing else."

"Yes," said Quiller.

"Absolutely," said Yaritomo.

The chorus of assent was meant to reinforce Gabriel's suggestion. Pontus took a step backward.

"It's complicated," he said. "The Lord Remmy is being interrogated now, and—"

"*Bring him,*" Gabriel intoned. "*His Majesty wants him. What else is there to know or do?*"

"Now," said Quiller.

The Burning Tiger growled.

"Especially if you don't want your head brought to a place where it won't want to go," Gabriel added.

Uncertainty fluttered in the cornet's eyes. "Yes," he said, and jerked his chin. "Right away."

Gabriel let him scuttle off, and only too late realized he'd left the Yellow Warrant behind. Gabriel folded his hands and looked at the others and waited. They shifted uncomfortably. One spat betel into a cup he held in his hand.

"Will you drink with us, senators?" one asked.

"We have no time," Gabriel said.

They looked at each other. One cleared his throat. "Early duty tomorrow," he said.

"Yes," another chorused.

"You will excuse us, senators?"

Gabriel stood away from the door and let them leave. *The Lord Remmy is being interrogated now.* Anxiety jittered up and down his spine. Operatic fantasies chorused through his head, the rescue party charging into the dungeon, waving the warrant and crying, *Stop the proceedings!*

Well. That was more or less what he was doing, come to think of it.

He waited, and let Horus send an objective description of their progress to Clancy atop the carriage.

The fortress, cold stone and colder iron, brooded around him.

There was a boom as a door was thrown open, and then Gabriel saw the bright infrared images of people emerge from a kind of tunnel beneath the square keep. There were about a half-dozen, including two carrying a third on a stretcher.

Mataglap's cries for vengeance throbbed in Gabriel's blood. A steady drizzle began to fall in the courtyard.

The party was led by a thin ecclesiastic who wore a pointed beard and sober black vestments over immaculate lacy linen. He wore an odd felt hat shaped like a truncated pyramid, with flaps cocked up over his ears like blunt and uncertain wings prepared for takeoff. Following was the Knight Pontus in his armor, a pair of blue-jowled bruisers who wore leather aprons and carried short swords—precisely Gabriel's image of two torturers—followed by the pair with the stretcher.

Remmy was dressed in a shirt, with a blanket covering his lower limbs. Even in the poor light Gabriel could see the vivid abrasions on his wrists, the cuts and welts on his forehead. As his two bearers put him down, there was the sound of a chain

ringing on the wet cobblestones that testified to Remmy's
shackled feet.

"What's this about a Yellow Warrant?" the priest de
manded.

"It's here, Father," Gabriel said. He pitched his voice
low, made it as soothing as possible in hopes Remmy
wouldn't react—but even so he saw Remmy start, saw him
lean violently out of the stretcher, bruised eyes wide and
staring.

In hopes of drawing attention to himself, Gabriel
whipped off his hat and made a flourishing bow.

"Lord Miletio of Samandas," he said. A real person,
Magnus had told him, a new appointment to the Guards not
yet arrived from the provinces.

The priest gave an irritated look over his shoulder, first
at Remmy, then at Pontus. Raindrops glittered on his shoul
ders. "This fellow," he said, "didn't get your name."

"He was in haste to obey His Majesty, I'm certain,"
Gabriel said.

Remmy had calmed, but astonishment was still plain on
his face. Gabriel gave him a neutral look (compassionate Bear
wailing in his head), then reached for the parchment. "If you
would care to read the warrant?" he said.

Yaritomo, he called, **mark the stretcher bearers.**

Gabriel wanted all his pieces in place in case there was
unpleasantness.

Yaritomo let the priest and the first two guards step
inside, then slipped out into the night. He feigned interest in
Remmy, then politely nodded to the nearer of the stretcher
bearers.

The priest held the warrant to the light of the lamp. "I
had been given to understand," he said, "that His Majesty was
willing to let the interrogation take its course."

"Apparently His Majesty changed his mind," Gabriel
said. "Such are the privileges of royalty, I suppose."

"We were making progress." Taking his time with the
warrant. "I would hate to interrupt the business now." He

lifted an eyebrow, looked at Gabriel. "Perhaps if Your Honor would consent to wait until we have extracted a full confession?"

"The Governor of Fort Makan can continue the interrogations, at the king's pleasure."

Something cold entered the priest's eyes at Gabriel's words, a daimōn not accustomed to being thwarted. A thrill of recognition hummed along Gabriel's spine.

Here, he thought, was the *real* enemy. The intent, predatory *thing* that glowed from the priest's eyes as he watched the interrogations, as he read his questions and heard the screams echo from the grey stone walls.

"There will be a delay in arresting this one's accomplices," the priest said. "And I hope you brought your own stretcher, as we dislocated this one's knees."

Augenblick dissected the priest's daimōn in a minute. **Only superior force will budge him,** he said, **and the retreat will be grudging. Try to save him as much face as you can.**

Gabriel glided forward to stand over the man. *"Rex vult, pater,"* he said, in Latin: the king wills it. If he couched his commands in another language, perhaps the priest's embarrassment in front of his servants would be minimized.

A grudging smile twitched its way across the ecclesiastic's face before dying in his inhuman eyes. *"Bene dicis linguam doctam,"* he said; you bless the learned tongue. Not very good Latin, Gabriel judged; *Latine bene loqueris* would have been closer to the language of Cicero.

"Magister meus diligentissimus erat," Gabriel said: my tutor was most exacting.

The priest blinked and the daimōn went away. There was something human in his manner as he straightened and put the warrant on the table. *"Multarum linguarum peritissimum esse videris,"* he said: you must be quite a linguist. "In fact," thoughtfully, "the sorcerer we're after speaks many tongues brilliantly . . ."

He halted, shock widening his eyes.

Kill, Gabriel ordered simply.

The daimōn had returned to the priest's eyes by the time the edge of Gabriel's hand sliced upward to crush his throat. Gabriel spun, saw a guard reacting, mouth opening to shout, chin tucked in and denying access to the windpipe—he drove the heel of his right hand into the man's philtrum, knocking his head back so that the left could crush the trachea with a Y-hand.

The *Equito* Pontus, armor rattling as he stumbled back from Quiller's onslaught, jostled into Gabriel's back: Gabriel reached behind him with a hand crooked Monkey-style, found Pontus's jaw, planted his other hand on the armored shoulder, and snapped the boy's neck with an effortless motion.

There was a moment in which the only sound was the thud of falling bodies. Quiller had accounted for the second guard before going for Pontus, and Yaritomo had as efficiently taken out the two stretcher bearers.

In unruffled, objective tones Horus reported the encounter to Clancy. A hard, cold rain began to fall outside the door.

The priest, choking to death, tried to crawl for the door. His daimōn was a most determined one. Gabriel put a foot on his back and slammed him to the ground. **Bring the two stretcher bearers in, he ordered.**

The two bodies were lifted inside. Remmy watched in awestruck silence. Eventually the rattling and twitching ceased.

"We'll make them look as if they killed each other," Gabriel ordered, and pulled a guard's short sword from its scabbard.

Such a deception wouldn't last long, but it might sow confusion for a few hours.

A few moments later Gabriel, the forged warrant under his arm, closed the guardroom door and locked it with a key he found on Pontus's belt. Quiller and Yaritomo picked up Remmy's stretcher and began carrying it toward the gate. Cold rain beat on their shoulders. Gabriel broke character for the length of time it took to squeeze Remmy's hand.

"I'm sorry, Ghibreel," Remmy whispered in a voice hoarse with screaming. "I told them everything."

"No matter," Gabriel said, and then turned into Lord Miletio again and marched arrogantly to the head of the party. They were let out of the fortress, without comment, by the same guard who had let them in.

Remmy was made as comfortable as possible in the carriage, with Clancy to tend to his dislocated knees and lacerations.

White Bear snapped the reins, and the carriage rolled away into the night.

Gabriel was already forgetting Vila Real and its inhabitants. His real business, the war with Saigo—the private, undeclared war—would begin in a matter of days.

Chapter 15

LOUISE: You love me? Are you serious?
Why should you give a damn
when I don't?

Gabriel's party switched to Gabriel's own carriage in Santa Leofra's quarter. Count Magnus, swathed in a shiny rain cape, waited there on his horse, two pistols stuck in his sash in case either robbers or inquisitors descended. He embraced his brother, kissed him, and—quite practically—gave him a sack of money. "All we had in the house," he said.

"We'll take him out of the country," Gabriel said. "You may yourself wish to hide at the house of a friend—though we managed to keep it quiet and I don't think there'll be an outcry till morning, we had to kill some people at the end."

"That was the Piscopos Peregrino you killed," Remmy said. "The head of the Argosy Vassals."

Magnus stared in shock and crossed himself.

"Was it?" Gabriel said. "Good." He turned to Magnus and gave him the forged warrant. "Here's your seal. You may wish to reattach it to the original document, just in case anyone wants to look for it."

"I'll b-burn the rest."

"Good idea," Gabriel said. He embraced Magnus. "Thank you," he said. "We'll take care of Remmy until he can return."

"If ever," Magnus said. "My God! You killed a P-piscopos!"

"Remmy and I shall be back, I think," Gabriel said. "And before you expect us."

He launched himself into his coach and pulsed a command to White Bear. The Friesians commenced their awesome march and the carriage began to move.

When he returned to the Vila Real, Gabriel thought, he would bring enlightenment and civilization to this place, tear down the Old Temple, and use its stones to build something useful.

And then do the same for the rest of the planet.

In silence, as the coach rolled through the night countryside near the city, the deadline passed. Gabriel's private communications rig was presumably activated. Most of the Aristoi, perhaps two-thirds, were alerted to the crimes being committed in the Gaal Sphere.

War, perhaps, was declared. In Gabriel's nightmares, preemptive strikes were launched by the conspirators, mataglap flung against every Aristos.

In silence, far away.

Gabriel let the moment pass, and tried to sleep.

"They were building a case against you," Remmy said. "Peregrino believed you had beat Silvanus through sorcery—" He bit his lip and stifled a cry as the carriage lurched through a pothole, and then his look turned amazed at the lack of pain. Manfred had given him a very thorough anesthetic through one of his hollow fangs, one that eliminated pain but left

Remmy lucid, and then Clancy administered other drugs that began the job of reducing swelling and knitting torn tissues.

He had held out for a long time, Gabriel could see. They had used thumbscrews first, then a clamp that squeezed the head. In the end, they'd had to wedge his kneecaps to the outside of his knees before he confessed.

Carefully, after anesthetic, Clancy had massaged the kneecaps back to where they belonged, then wrapped the knees to keep them there.

"I am not interested in what Peregrino thought," Gabriel said. "Rest yourself."

There was a scratching sound, Manfred's toenails as he shifted position on the carriage floor.

"It's important," said Remmy. "Because you'll want to know what charges they intend to lay if you ever come back."

"I expect killing a Piscopos will take precedence over whatever else they've got in their files," Gabriel said. He put a hand on Remmy's shoulder. "It's not of real interest to me."

But Remmy had been made to confess once, and now he seemed compelled to do it again. "They interrogated Gerius and Dr. Lavinius first," Remmy said. "They made me watch. Gerius said you had used sorcery on him. That you had a demon with you in the shape of a dog. And Lavinius said that Clansai had shot him with a magic bullet, then healed his shoulder with witchcraft."

"Why would I do both?" Clancy asked sensibly.

Gabriel wondered if Peregrino would have issued a warrant with Manfred's name on it. "Did they admit to a plot to murder me?" he asked.

"Yes. And they named Prince Adrian as the man behind it."

Peregrino and Adrian were allies, Gabriel knew, but situations could change, and Peregrino had probably intended to insure Adrian's future cooperation by holding the depositions over his head.

Now—with bodies discovered—there might be a thorough royal investigation, and the dossiers might be made public. Things might be quite different in Vila Real by the time Gabriel returned.

He could only hope.

The carriage jounced again. Remmy braced himself, then looked surprised once more. "Your medicine is a blessing, Doctor," he said.

Clancy looked down at him. "We have much to teach people here," she said.

"I didn't tell them much about you," Remmy said. "I didn't know very much. But I know they thought your practice of medicine was unnatural."

She smiled grimly. "I'm sure they would."

Remmy looked up at Gabriel, reached for his hand. "Forgive me, Ghibreel," he said. "I admitted to . . . committing acts with you."

Gabriel smiled indulgently. "As long as you told the truth."

"I told them you could play instruments you'd never seen. Learn languages, skills . . . that you'd said you had a spirit in you that taught you such things."

"It was only the truth," Gabriel said. "Why must I forgive you for speaking the truth?"

"Because it was *our* truth. One it was a betrayal to share."

Gabriel looked down at him. Peregrino had shattered him, broken his body, mind, and pride. He was a cripple now, and not just a physical one—for the rest of his life he might have a daimōn in his head, calling him worthless, no friend, a betrayer. Calling him something unnatural, foul, and Ketshanese. Speaking every time he felt a twinge in his knees or saw a priest on the street.

Gabriel would have to rebuild his body, exorcise the daimōn, fire the spirit. Make Remmy more powerful, he swore, than before.

"We will repair your body, Remmy," he said. "And then we will teach you things. Beginning with simple things, like how to stand, how to walk. How to understand what others are telling you even when they're not saying it."

"That's simple?" Remmy said.

"Yes, once you know how. You know most of it already, but you don't know that you know. And then, once you've learned that—" He tightened his fingers on Remmy's hand. "Great things." *Hegemón of a continent, perhaps.*

"This is a fantasy, Highness," Remmy said.

"Great things," Gabriel repeated.

But first he had to win a war.

The horses were rested and watered at a roadside inn; the Surveyors ate their luncheon on tables, in the open, with one or another of them sitting by Remmy in the coach to keep him company and to make certain he ate.

Gabriel looked at his Therápontes, saw Yaritomo and Quiller eating in silence, each withdrawn into himself. Too much death, he thought: each had killed with his bare hands, and that less than a day after colleagues had died in a holocaust.

Not enough, he thought, had been said about it.

The journey resumed. The horses marched along the road at their lockstep trot. Remmy dozed, his head swaying lightly with the motion of the coach. Gabriel called on his daimones, heard them sing sadly in his mind. One hand made a mudra calling for attention.

Friends, he broadcast. **There has been too much death of late.**

Through his reno he received their silent agreement.

Gabriel's hands made teaching mudras. **Our comrades have died, and we have not had time to mourn,** Gabriel said. **I propose that we do so now.**

Their approval passed before him.

Let us name them, Gabriel said. **Stephen Rubens y Sedillo, Therápōn Protarchōn. A stranger to us, who left his home on an underwater reef to bring us warning of the danger now facing all humanity. A man of brilliance, of dedication, who became our friend. All humanity should mourn him. In the name of humanity, let us do so.**

We mourn him, they choroused.

Therápōn Marcus, the Black-Eyed Ghost. Lover and friend, warm-hearted, ever youthful. He carried a child of promise. Let us mourn him.

We mourn him, they called.

He named them all, imagined them, invoked their shorn lives. If there was one he didn't know well, he called on one of the others to give the name and speak the invocation. Eventually all the crew of the *Cressida* had been named.

There are others we should mourn as well, Gabriel said. We do not know all their names. But the first known to us was the *Equito* Pontus, a young man of good family. He sensed the surprise in the others at the mention of Pontus's name. We do not know why he served the Argosy Vassals, whether it was from belief or ambition or mere chance. But in order to preserve a friend and to keep us free to complete our mission, I myself had to kill him. I regret the necessity, and in the name of humanity I mourn.

We mourn him.

The Piscopos Peregrino was a man of years, Gabriel said, but he had not achieved the wisdom that comes with years. There was an irresistible compulsion in him, a daimōn of sorts, that made him hurt and destroy. He committed evil, but the fault may not have been entirely his. He had been brought into life on this place, and raised without proper guidance. I regret the necessity that called me to kill him with my hand, and in the name of humanity I mourn him.

We mourn him. Words choroused in Gabriel's mind.

The others I do not know. Four men, anonymous, brought to maturity in this brutal place, where for reasons unknown to us they chose a brutal profession. I regret the circumstances that forced me to order their deaths. In the name of humanity we mourn them.

We mourn them.

There was a moment's silence. Gabriel reflected for a moment, listened to the voices of his daimones. **These deaths**

may not be the last, Gabriel said. **Already there may be war among the great population of humanity. We must rededicate ourselves to our attempt, however desperate, to prevent further loss of life. If we can affect the course of the war from here, we must do so. We may be able to strike the enemy an irrecoverable blow.**

Let us hope that it is so, Clancy said.

Let us hope, Gabriel repeated. **Let us hope that we can prevent further mourning.**

We will hope.

Gabriel let Cyrus speak, his voice a bone trumpet playing Gabriel's dirge. Cyrus's spare, unmannered rendition was perfect, letting the notes, the trumpet, the somber mood speak for themselves.

Afterwards there was silence. Gabriel made such plans as he could.

That night, a few leagues from an inn where they hoped to rest the horses for the night, the coach was attacked by a group of horseback robbers, all brandishing swords and pistols. There was no reason, with these people, to conceal the party's true abilities; Gabriel and the others disregarded the ridiculous snaphaan pistols they carried for show and used their own weapons instead. Darkness did not conceal the menacing figures to humans equipped with infrared sight. The party drew as one, marked their targets, and homing bullets hissed through the air. The bandits had their horses shot out from under them within three seconds, and were too busy coping with suddenly being unhorsed to retaliate. Soon they were left behind. Manfred's excited barks mocked them from the window of the coach.

Gabriel could feel morale improve somewhat. It had been an inconsiderable triumph over some ridiculous opponents, but still it was a victory.

Remmy, a silver-butted snaphaan half-drawn in his hand, looked at the others for a long moment, then returned the pistol to its holster.

"Are those weapons?" he asked. "I heard no noise."

Gabriel looked at him, showed him the little palm-sized gun, the stubby barrel that protruded from between the second and third fingers of the fist, the magazine that fitted the barrel like the crossbar of a T, intended to be held crosswise in the palm.

Remmy held out a hand. "May I?" he said. "I'll be careful."

Gabriel handed it to him. Remmy looked at the featureless implastic mass, the smooth black curves that matched corresponding curves in Gabriel's hand. He turned it over, shook his head.

"I've seen pocket pistols," he said, "but nothing akin to this." He looked up. "Why did it make no noise?"

Gabriel gave thought to the question. "The propellant—the kind of gunpowder we use—has been attached to the bullet, and it burns more slowly than the sort of powder you're used to. The bullet is fired more like a firework rocket than the kind of projectile you're familiar with, and makes the same sort of hissing noise."

Remmy looked at the pistol again, hefted it. "Your rockets must be tiny. How can they do damage?"

"They have a small explosive in them," Gabriel said. "They enter the target, then blow up."

Gabriel decided not to mention the sensors in the rocket, the oneirochronic triggering system, linked to his reno, that fired the weapon on mental command, the targeting systems in his reno. Nor the fact that the pistol contained two magazines, one with explosive rounds, the other with a fast-working anesthetic.

"Why didn't you use them against Peregrino?"

"It would have caused too much comment," Gabriel said. "Bodies with wounds that no one could understand would have intensified the search for us." And the anesthetic used in the drugged darts required several seconds to take effect, even if fired right into the carotid artery, time enough for the Vassals to call out in alarm.

Remmy looked thoughtful. Gabriel glanced up at Clancy, watched her as she watched Remmy think. She looked up; their eyes met.

"No trigger," Remmy said. "And no priming. No way to get the priming inside. I am a soldier, and a weapon like this makes mockery out of everything I have learned about my work. I have a suspicion"—he took the gun in his hand, pointed it out the window—"if I tried to shoot it, it would not fire." *It would not itself-fire.* Gabriel could see Remmy's knuckles turn white as he squeezed the gun. He looked at Gabriel, gave a thoughtful smile. "I owe you my life, Ghibreel," he said, "and my love as well. I do not grudge that you've misled me, but it is very clear that you folk are not from Nanchan, and I think you had best tell me what it is you are."

Clancy looked from Remmy to Gabriel. She nodded, advised him, **I would tell him what he can comprehend, Aristos.**

Gabriel looked at Remmy, jerked his chin yes, then held out his hand. Remmy put the gun in it, and Gabriel hid it away.

"Much of what we've told you is true," Gabriel said. "I am a prince in my country. Clansai is a doctor. Quil Lhur is my secretary, and the others are my servants."

Remmy jerked his chin thoughtfully. His pupils were wide in the darkness as he looked intently at Gabriel's face.

"We are in Beukhomana in search of someone from our country," Gabriel said. "He is a member of our high nobility who has broken our laws and put many lives in jeopardy."

"A prince goes on this errand?" Remmy's tone was not precisely skeptical: he sounded more like someone carefully reserving judgment, waiting for all the facts before he reached a conclusion.

"It is another prince who has committed these crimes," Gabriel said. "Another prince with power, with servants of his own, and with a vast fortune to serve him."

There was the sound of a brass trumpet as Yaritomo, on the box above, blew a signal to the coaching inn ahead.

"A prince, you say?" Remmy asked. Gabriel could see tension in the muscles around his eyes, in the edge that had entered his voice. "They say—forgive me, Ghibreel—that some devils reign as lords in Hell."

Gabriel managed not to smile. "No," he said, "I do not come from Hell."

"Nor Heaven either? Come to find a devil and put him back where he belongs?"

"No. Neither I nor he is supernatural. But our enemy is a very extraordinary and powerful man, and uncommonly dangerous."

Remmy looked more thoughtful than relieved. He had kept sane under torture, Gabriel concluded; he had been driven into an identification with his tormenter, a wholesale acceptance of Peregrino's Manichaean cosmology.

Remmy bowed gravely. "Thank you, Highness, for not condescending to me in that answer."

"You deserve the truth." Gabriel touched Remmy's leg lightly, felt the bandaging under his fingertips. "You have earned it."

Yaritomo sounded the trumpet again. Manfred barked in accompaniment.

"This criminal you seek. Do I know him?"

"Lord Sergius, though we believe his real name is Saigo."

"Sergius?" For the first time Remmy looked skeptical. "Sergius was born in Ter'Madrona, Highness. His lineage is well known, and goes back for centuries."

"We think the man you know as Sergius is, well, an impostor."

Gabriel knew full well how ridiculous that sounded. The skeptical look that crossed Remmy's face seemed more than justified. "Highness," Remmy said, "how is that possible?"

Gabriel gave consideration to his reply. "The answer to that question would not mean anything to you now," he said. "With the proper background, I hope I will be able to make it understandable to you."

There were the sounds of creaking gates, barking dogs,

ostlers running up to guide the horses into the walled inn. The
scent of smoky torches and cedar smoke wafted into the
coach.

"Remmy should be able to walk by now," Clancy reported. "But I wouldn't advise it for at least another day." It
had been almost a full Terrinan day since she'd started inject-
ing him with her medicines, one package to promote healing
and another to remove scar tissue as soon as it formed.

Gabriel swung himself out of the slow-moving coach and
recruited two of the inn's servants to carry Remmy inside.
Remmy stuck his head out the coach window and called to
Gabriel. "Where is it, Highness, that you come from?"

Gabriel looked up at the *Via Lactía*, the glowing veil that
blanketed the southern horizon. He put out a pointing hand.
"There," he said.

To his credit, Remmy did not at all look surprised.

The inn had few rooms available, and those up a narrow stair:
Remmy was bedded down in a small dining alcove off the
common room; Gabriel stayed with him for company's sake.

The innkeeper seemed surprised and a little disappointed
that Gabriel had escaped the bandits who routinely victimized
his lodgers, and Gabriel wondered if he was in league with
them—they might well be his best customers for food and
drink.

Gabriel and Remmy talked into the night, of ships that
sailed between the stars, of medicine, of machines whose
thought was as fast as light. Remmy was more skeptical than
Gabriel could have hoped, but on the whole he seemed open
to Gabriel's ideas. At least he wasn't screaming for the Argosy
Vassals to rescue him from demons.

Eventually Remmy said his prayers and drifted off to
sleep with Manfred lying in the crook of his arm. Gabriel left
the room, climbed the stairs, sprayed himself with repellent
good against lice, ticks, and other vermin, and then joined
Clancy in her soft bed under the thatched roof.

He woke before dawn, looked in on Remmy to make

certain he was sleeping peacefully, then went out into the courtyard to exercise and do wushu. He wanted to center himself, sink his mass deep into the swadhishatana chakra in his abdomen. There he could feel the power of the earth beneath him, power that rose through his heels like a breath. His body glowed with power. He was a warrior, he felt, on a warrior's mission.

Eastward, glowing over a low chain of rounded, green mountains, the pale dawn began to rise.

Within an hour the coach was back on the road. Although their road to this point had been a winding one that went up and down hills, the trend had been generally upward as they climbed out of Vila Real's river valley. Now they found themselves on a long, switchback rise that took them over a pass into the eastern mountains, hours of upward toiling for the lathered Friesians. Everyone but Remmy and White Bear had to leave the coach. Gabriel mounted one of his Arabs, while Yaritomo took the second.

Gabriel and Yaritomo walked their horses ahead of the coach. Fruit trees overhung the primitive road, bright with springtime flowers, their scent perfuming the rutted way. Gabriel entertained the engaging picture of travelers throwing apple cores and plum and cherry pits out of the window of their coaches, of the seeds taking root near the highway and nourishing the travelers' grandchildren.

Eventually the air grew cooler, was laced with the scent of the tall pines that clustered thick on the mountain slopes. Occasional stone shelters had been built for travelers. The horses' hooves were muffled by pine needles. The sigh of wind through the pine forest sounded like the breakers of a far-distant ocean, and Gabriel promised himself to use the sound in an orchestral work.

A few hours past noon the summit of the pass was reached, and the Surveyors could look fore and aft at the blue river valleys laid out before them, the silver, drifting clouds that cast deep shadows on the forests and fields below, the distant, half-glimpsed blue of rivers.

Gabriel had to admit that Saigo had built a fine world.

Manfred gazed at the scenery for a moment with his weak eyes, then found a tree and eased his bladder.

Quiller and Clancy took a spell on the Arabs, and Gabriel and Yaritomo returned to the coach. Gabriel unwrapped Remmy's knees and put them through a series of therapeutic exercises that Clancy had prescribed, working knee and hip flexion from a seated position in the coach. Remmy was astonished at the amount of healing that he'd undergone, though ugly purple bruising still streaked his legs.

Though there was a limited amount that he could do in the coach, Gabriel gave Remmy some basic lessons in breathing and posture, in centering the mind. It was all the sort of thing that children in the Logarchy learned by the age of six. Remmy seemed willing to learn, but still retained the skepticism that Gabriel had observed earlier—willing, on the whole to give the benefit of his doubt that Gabriel possessed some knowledge worth learning, but still prepared to make his own judgments.

Afterward Remmy settled into his usual slouch and gave a look out the window. "I keep wondering if we're going to be pursued," he said.

"Any pursuit will be directed toward the borders," Gabriel said. "The ports may be closed, and border fortresses. But we're going inland to Ocarnío—it's an odd place for fugitives to run to. My guess is that we'll easily outrun any messages."

"But we may have been seen on this road," Remmy said. "Crippled as I am—as I was—I'm not inconspicuous. There may be armed parties galloping on our trail."

"Armed parties won't trouble us. You saw that last night."

"Nevertheless." Remmy's eyes turned to Gabriel. He reached out a big hand and took Gabriel's wrist. "I confessed to a capital crime when I was in the Old Temple, Ghibreel. I don't want to go back there."

"No."

Remmy's grip tightened on Gabriel's wrist. "I want you to use that magic gun of yours, Ghibreel. Promise you'll kill me before you let me fall into their hands again."

Admiration for Remmy's bravery soared through Gabriel's heart. It was unnecessary—the Argosy Vassals, Gabriel suspected, were going to be the least of their problems—but for all that the gesture was completely genuine.

"Yes," Gabriel said. "I'll do that."

"Thank you." Grim humor tugged at the corners of Remmy's mouth. "I don't suppose you've got a dose of the Memory Plague among your bag of tricks, do you? If we could just dose the Argosy Vassals, they might well forget us."

Something hummed in Gabriel's mind, daimones sitting up and paying attention. "Tell me about the Memory Plague," he said. His reno combed its limited files for the phrase, and failed to find it—not surprising, since most of the linguistic data had been aboard *Cressida* or in hard storage in Gabriel's private system memory and accessible only through *Cressida*'s massive renos.

Remmy lifted his eyebrows. "Really?" he said. "Something you don't know?"

"Apparently."

"That's the name my tutor used—he was from Khorar Province, which is pretty remote. It's usually called the Great Devastation or the Wandering Sickness."

Gabriel's reno found referents for both those terms, a major desolation in the planet's history. "Yes," he said. "I've heard those terms."

Listen to this, he broadcast to the others, and opened a channel for Remmy's words.

"Three or four hundred years ago," Remmy said, "a sickness came in from the north and swept through the country. Most people were just made sick and weak, but many forgot things—who they were, who they were married to, how to do their work. Forgot their families, their children, everything. Some just wandered off and never returned. There was great chaos. That was when the Ketshanese and the other barbarians united to conquer us."

The less complex cultures recovered first, Yaritomo said. **They had less to remember.**

That's when the planet woke, Gabriel said. **Now we know the date of this people's birth.**

Not all the implanted memories would take, Clancy said. **Saigo's team couldn't implant every single memory for a whole planetary population—a lot of skills and abilities would have had to be implanted using a kind of fractal algorithm to generate memories and skills. And when it didn't work, or when something important was left out . . .**

The Memory Plague was invented to cover the loss, Gabriel concluded. **So people would be able to blame the illness for what was missing.**

"You look entranced, Gabriel," Remmy said. "Is there something in what I said that strikes you?"

"Yes," Gabriel said. "The Memory Plague explains a great deal."

"A great deal of what?"

"Perhaps we can go into that later. There is so much else to explain first."

Remmy considered this. "Very well."

"Can you tell me everything you know about the Memory Plague?"

"If you'll tell me why it's important."

Gabriel jerked his chin. "I will. But it will take a long time."

Remmy looked about himself, sighed. "I seem to have little else to do but listen, Highness."

"This Saigo, then, is God," Remmy said. "The God that created my world. And you are the God that has come to fight him."

The coach lurched again; Manfred's toenails scrabbled for footing as he propped himself on his hind legs and gazed out the window. The route down from the pass was more rugged than the ascent, and the party would not reach the valley before night.

Gabriel smiled. "We aren't gods."

"What is the difference? This Saigo created the world and everything in it . . ."

"He had help."

Remmy flipped his hands. "He had angels, then. He created the world, and the people, and their works. And now you—" He looked up at Gabriel. "You want to come and change everything. Defeat Saigo and bring about the end of all things. The apocalypse." Remmy gave a hollow, death's-head grin. "You're the Devil, Ghibreel."

Gabriel looked at him. "That's not what's happening."

"For someone like me, what's the difference?" He flipped his hands again. "This Saigo created me for a purpose, even though you don't know what it is. Yet you want to come in and change everything, end my nation, my religion, my civilization. Thwart the unknowable purpose of my God."

"We want to liberate you," Gabriel said. "Give you education. End the sickness that causes such a waste of life, put a stop to the wars that destroy so much life and substance. Saigo has enacted an immense crime by denying your entire world the education that would enable you to live well, and in freedom."

"You tempt me, Ghibreel." Remmy's voice had a hysterical edge to it. "You tempt me with the fruit of the Tree of Knowledge."

"Without knowledge," Gabriel said, "you cannot choose wisely. And without wise choice, there is no freedom."

"That's what the Devil would say, wouldn't he?" Remmy laughed. "You want to give me the knowledge to deny my God."

Gabriel straightened, adopted a commanding posture. Not yet, he thought, an Inflection of Command.

"This is foolishness, Remmy," he said. "This is Peregrino's reasoning, not yours."

Remmy looked at him for a stricken moment, and then tears welled in his eyes. "I'm sorry, Ghibreel," he said. "I didn't realize . . ."

Gabriel took Remmy in his arms. "You're confused, yes," he said. "But we'll take care of you."

"You're going into danger," Remmy said.

"We won't expose you to it. You can't fight Saigo, and we won't expect you to try. Once you're healed, you're free to go, with a purse full of money and all the world before you."

Remmy clutched at him. "You won't abandon me?" he demanded.

"You will have freedom," Gabriel said. "You may do what you wish."

"I don't want freedom!" Remmy said. "I want my God back!"

Gabriel didn't have an answer for that.

Night fell before they came out of the mountains, and the road was too steep and dangerous to drive in the dark. The party spent the night in one of the stone shelters that the locals had built, a warm enough place with dry firewood stacked by the hearth. Remmy took his first careful steps, amazed to be walking without pain.

Moving again at dawn, the coach left the mountains before noon and struck a supposedly ancient military road that ran, straight as a die, cross-country into Ocarnío. Gabriel was amused that Saigo hadn't been able to resist giving himself a first-class road to the capital in case Sergius needed one.

The country was rolling and rich, crossed by rivers and canals. The fords and bridges were well maintained. The inns were crowded, and once Gabriel and the party had to sleep in the coach. Everyone was heading to a public festival in Roméon, the capital of Ocarnío Province, in which the saints' blessing was asked upon the newly planted crops.

"Will Lord Sergius attend?" Gabriel asked.

"Most likely," said one hopeful pilgrim. "He always

blesses the people of the city with vast quantities of beer, wine, and food."

Ah, Gabriel thought. Saigo couldn't resist playing the grand seigneur to his creations.

With luck, he broadcast, **we won't have to face him in his own place.**

Quietly they made preparation.

A handful of gold rented them a room in Roméon that had been pledged to someone else; a handful of silver got them all fast horses for their getaway. The walled town stood atop a hill, and was surrounded by red stone battlements that packed the pilgrims in tight along its narrow cobbled streets.

There was a wooden, garland-wreathed platform on one end of the square, in front of the city hall, with a canopied chair of honor on it. It was the sort of thing that dignitaries occupied. Gabriel hoped Lord Sergius would be one of them.

They had passed the road to Lord Sergius's country house as they came into town. He lived only twelve or fourteen kilometers away, insofar as Gabriel could translate local reckoning.

Their renos' receivers picked up stray, unshielded tachline transmissions when they were in Sergius's neighborhood. Nothing substantial—the sort of leakage their renos were normally programmed to ignore—but it was enough to let them know they were in the right place, and that their enemies had no notion of being overheard.

Lord Sergius had not put in an appearance in person, but his handiwork was plain to see. As well as the long lines of tables, barrels, and tubs that held food and drink, there was the Santo Marco Weavers' College (patron Lord Sergius), the Santa Antonia Infirmary and Hospital (endowed by Lord Sergius), Lord Sergius's Grammar School for Poor Children, and the Santo Sergius Home for the Elderly and Disabled (endowed in honor of his patron saint).

"It's obscene," Clancy said. She didn't dare broadcast for fear it would be picked up by some henchman's reno.

"He's endowing hospitals to cure the population of diseases that he himself has inflicted on them. Not that you'd call it *curing*. Not what they do."

Remmy flipped his hands. "He giveth and he taketh away."

Gabriel looked at him and hoped that what he heard was irony.

They stood in their crowded, low-ceilinged room in a two-hundred-year-old inn built on the central square. Church bells rang out to announce a service. The air smelled of spilled beer, holy incense, and the flower garlands that most of the people in the streets were wearing.

Yaritomo and Quiller, flower-wreathed, were out trying to discover when Sergius was expected.

"I'd like to go to mass," Remmy said. "I've got a lot to say thanks for. Will you be needing me?"

"I shouldn't think so," Gabriel said. "Do pray for all of us, won't you?"

Remmy nodded. He and Gabriel kissed good-bye and Remmy left the room. Clancy looked at the door and frowned.

"He's troubled."

"Who wouldn't be?" Gabriel said. He put his arms around her waist, let her nestle close to him. "But still . . . yes, he disturbs me. He was always pious, as I understand it, but this sudden religiosity has an unhealthy edge to it."

"It was the religious party that tortured him, for heaven's sake. You'd think it would have made him irreligious, if anything."

Some drunken apprentices began a bawdy song. Half the crowd joined in. Gabriel looked out the window and saw Remmy, in the new plumed hat that Gabriel had bought for him, moving through the crowd in the direction of the town's small cathedral.

There was a knock on the door, and then Yaritomo stepped in. He was not tall, but still he had to duck so as not to ram his head into the lintel.

"I had it from one of Sergius's people," he said. "The boss is coming this afternoon to receive an award from the mayor."

Gabriel slid his hands around Clancy's waist, felt the pistol there, under her sash.

"We'll be ready for him," he said.

Oh, Gabriel thought, as Sergius stepped from the coach, *it's not Saigo after all*.

He knew Saigo, and after Cressida's death had studied oneirochronic recordings of him with care—and this Sergius wasn't the man. Saigo was shorter and more powerful, like a badger: this man was eaglelike and slim. They didn't look alike, didn't move alike . . . and the bright look from the sharp Tatar eyes was not Saigo's melancholy glance, but something more elemental, a spark struck by flint and steel.

It could be a puppet body, Gabriel knew, an android or clone controlled through the oneirochronon. But if it were Saigo behind the mask, there was no reason why the puppet shouldn't *look* like him—there was no one here who needed to be fooled. And if it were Saigo, some part of his personality should still be projected through Sergius.

But it wasn't.

Sergius was an Aristos, clear enough, or at least from the Logarchy. He moved elegantly, with gliding feet, held his carriage erect in a Posture of Esteem, had one hand, perhaps unconsciously, set in a Mudra of Receptivity. He wore velvet of a deep violet shade, trimmed with gold; his hair was grey and his beard was pointed. The personality Sergius projected seemed tantalizingly familiar. In a moment, Gabriel thought, he would realize who Sergius was.

The two young men who joined him on the festive program were from the Logarchy as well—they shared Sergius's quiet assurance, his gliding walk and alert carriage. Their watchful eyes glanced over the crowd, drinking in the scene.

Gabriel waited for a moment, listening for inner voices. Perhaps the Voice had something to say.

The Voice didn't.

Gabriel remembered to slouch as he worked his way to the front of the crowd. He'd crowned his wide-brimmed hat with garlands, and flower necklaces draped his neck so profusely they hid his chin. His face was covered with cosmetic, applied artfully so as to reconfigure his face, to make him look as unlike Gabriel as possible. His long dark hair was braided and tucked up under his hat.

The crowd was drunk and cheerful. The mayor, fat and hatless and wearing a medallion, was drunk as well, and walked with exaggerated care on gout-swollen feet. He tottered across the flower-decked platform, kissed Sergius on both cheeks, led him to the chair of honor under a canopy. His two aides hung near the back of the platform—one of them wore a chain of office that probably denoted his status as Sergius's secretary or seneschal or something.

The mayor caressed his white beard and began to make a speech. *"Ridentum dicere verum quid vetat?"* he asked, showing his education, and then loosely translated his Horace for the vulgar: Why should truth not be joyful?

The mayor got two sets of cheers, one from the educated, one from the commoners.

The mayor went into Latin again. Gabriel concluded that this might take a while.

Gabriel reached the front of the crowd, lurked behind the burly shoulders of a flower-draped rustic while he checked his sight lines and looked for the others. Quiller was already in position, on Gabriel's left, with Yaritomo standing just near his shoulder. White Bear's big form was moving into place on the right, near where the two aides stood, and Gabriel could see Clancy's hat following in his wake. She was in male dress again, as skirts would hamper the getaway.

Gabriel continued to lurk behind the big onlooker. Sergius in his violet velvet watched the mayor with an expression of total attention. Daimones were good for such things.

Something crawled across the surface of Gabriel's mind. He could almost put his finger on Sergius's identity.

Gury, he thought, at the precise instant that his team was ready. He had last seen Sergius with a bald head and wide mustachios, opening the door of Zhenling's coach.

There was no time to think about what that meant.

Kill, he commanded, and drew his weapon. His reno flashed targeting displays in the oneirochronon, overlaid them on present reality. He thrust his weapon out of the crowd, out near the big man's hip—no need to raise it to aiming position when the software would do the work.

Sergius was already moving when the first weapons fired. His receptors had picked up the coded tachline pulse—at this close range Gabriel couldn't have helped it—and alerted him to the presence of Logarchic strangers. White Bear's round took out part of his shoulder, Yaritomo's creased his back and exploded with a sharp crack in the hardwood back of the chair, and Gabriel's blew off the right side of his forehead.

Sergius kept moving. He had seen Gabriel and was leaping right for him. Gabriel thought he saw recognition in the man's glittering eyes.

A puppet. Gabriel's daimones shrieked with dismay. It didn't matter how much brain tissue Sergius lost, the real mind was elsewhere. They were going to have to shoot it to pieces.

Gabriel had very likely lost his war, lost it totally at this very instant. Despair sang through him, fired his resolve.

One of the two aides—the one with the chain—went down screaming under White Bear's gun; the other lost part of his face and stayed on his feet.

Gabriel's gun spat out another round before the rustic in front of him swung around in alarm, knocking the pistol out of line. "What's that, stranger?" the man asked, looking at the gun.

"*Gabriel!*" Sergius shrieked, the word deformed by a shattered jaw as Yaritomo and White Bear kept pumping rounds into him. Spraying red, Sergius leaped over the flower-decked railing, his velvet cloak floating out behind him. The mayor, halfway through a Latin tag, had only just

realized something was amiss. The stunned crowd staggered
back, ran into onlookers who were rushing forward to get a
better view. People staggered, fell. There were screams. Gabriel jerked his arm free, fired more rounds before the rustic's
suspicious hand clamped on his wrist. "What is that, stranger?
A weapon?" Sergius was very close. Gabriel jabbed a thumb
into the big man's eye, jerked his arm free, fired again. Sergius's blood-streaked fingers stabbed for his eyes. Gabriel
jerked his head back, slammed the pistol into Sergius's throat,
fired. Fierce clawed hands clutched his shoulders before one
of Gabriel's bullets blew Sergius's spine in half and severed
the enhanced link between mind and body.

The other puppet, one of Sergius's aides, had been blown
to bits by a concentrated volley from White Bear and Clancy.
The man with the chain—a real human—had died long since.

As Gabriel staggered back from the wrecked, blood-
decked corpse, he could see the fiery, accusing intelligence
still gleaming in Sergius's fierce hawk eyes.

Escape was easy: five people knew what they were doing, and
the rest of the crowd didn't. Remmy had been holding the
horses in a side street, and the second everyone mounted—
Manfred jumped up onto Gabriel's saddle—White Bear
formed the Friesians in line abreast and marched them toward
the city gate at an awesome, ground-pounding synchronized
trot. The rest followed in their wake. They were leaving the
carriage behind, but the Friesians were carrying most of their
gear, including their money-generating chest.

To Sergius's estate, Gabriel said. **We've got to find the
real man, kill him, take command somehow.**

Very likely impossible, Clancy concluded.

Very likely.

Very well. There was something mad and delightful in
her acceptance of fate. Love and despair sang in Gabriel's
heart.

Only one of the party, Gabriel was sure, would not die
in the next few minutes.

People scattered out of the Friesians' way. The city gate hovered over them for a moment, then fell behind. Gabriel spurred up to Remmy, kissed him, pressed a sack of gold into his hand.

"We've failed, and we're going to die now," he said. "Run for the border, and go with my love."

He took Manfred in his arms and passed the terrier to Remmy. Remmy looked at him, tears filling his eyes, and then he kicked his horse's flanks and was gone, racing cross-country for the east. His remount followed on a lead. White Bear moved the Friesians out of the way and the rest galloped west on their faster horses, back toward Sergius's estate, with the Friesians following at their own slower ground-shivering pace.

They would have to shoot their way in, Gabriel supposed. But if Sergius—Gury—whoever—was smart, he would already have abandoned the place.

Still, there was nowhere left to go, nothing left to do.

The rich countryside sped past. A dirge sang in Gabriel's heart, horns and bass viols, here and there a rattling snare. He wished he'd have time to transcribe it. The horse moved easily between Gabriel's knees, soaring down the primitive road, shoes striking sparks from the stones.

They almost made it to the house before the end came. Gabriel was in the lead as they spurred up a grass-covered hill. As he topped the rise a vista opened out before him, a white house above a sparkling artificial lake. The house was all glass and gingerbread, an airy fantasy unlike anything else on this planet, all beneath a tower with an onion dome.

Gabriel had only a moment to take this in, to realize the depth of conspiracy and betrayal, before a shadow fell across him. A shuttlecraft hovered above, a private flyer on silent twelve-meter wings. No one was visible as a target, and Gabriel's weapons wouldn't affect the airship.

Scatter, Gabriel ordered, and lifted his pistol to fire off the rest of his magazine—a gesture only, but all he could do. The shuttle was already firing. Gas canisters burst around the startled horses. Gabriel ordered himself not to breathe, but it didn't matter; he could feel parts of himself shutting down as the gas touched him. His horse staggered. The orchestra swelled in his mind, a symphonic Armageddon.

He rode on his stumbling horse to Clancy's side and kissed her before his Arab faltered and the world faded.

Chapter 16

PABST: How will I rate an experimental data point?
A response to stimulus!

The first sensation Gabriel encountered was one of loss. There was a void in his mind, an empty place where there had once been . . . voices? . . . but was now a hollow place filled only with aching sorrow.

Lost, he thought. And perhaps the war with it.

The thought sent a burst of fire through his mind. He snapped awake, leaped to his feet, assumed a Posture of Readiness.

Lord Sergius stood before him, dressed simply in baggy cotton trousers, white shirt, quilted jacket, black slippers on bare feet. He looked like Gury the driver again, with bald head and spreading white mustachios. He stood in the somewhat informal Second Posture of Esteem.

"Greetings, Gabriel Vissarionovich."

"Are you the real one this time?" Gabriel asked. His voice sounded hollow in the room.

He sounded lonely.

The room was a ten-meter cube, hung with dark red

velvet. A massive crystal chandelier hung overhead, its dangling gems waving faintly in a distant breeze, creating a rhythmic movement to the diffused light.

The thick carpet beneath Gabriel's feet was one of the Illyrian Workshop's "Hanging Garden" series, a fact that Gabriel did not appreciate.

"Yes," said Gury. "I'm the real thing."

Gabriel looked around him. There was no obvious door, no guards, no weapons deployed. He was dressed in the same simple clothing as Gury. His hair had been cut short, a centimeter or less, and there was a prickle on his forehead where his eyebrows were growing back.

"You wonder if we're alone?" Gury said. "We are. I have no weapons other than those of my body and mind." His long eyelids lifted, revealing deep, penetrating eyes. "You may kill me, if you want. If you think you can. It seems to be what you desire."

Gabriel called on his daimones, heard only silence.

They were gone.

He stood frozen while his heart thrashed in panic. He pulsed commands to his reno, received no answer.

His reno had been turned off, he realized. And with it the automatic commands that roused his daimones, the parts of the daimones that had been stored in his reno's holographic memory, the communication channels through which they most efficiently spoke to him.

He was alone. The voices that had been with him for eighty years had been silenced, or reduced to the faintest of whispers.

Terror poured through his veins. He could feel drops of sweat breaking out on his scalp.

"Who are you?" Gabriel asked.

The faintest smile touched the corners of Gury's mouth. "I wonder if you can guess."

Gabriel tried to keep a tremor out of his voice. He realized his hands were shivering from adrenaline pouring through his veins. He pressed his hands against his thighs to

ontrol them. "Shall I call you Gury, then? Or would you
prefer Sergius?"

"Whichever fiction is most convenient for you, Gabriel.
It doesn't matter to me."

Gabriel considered the distance between them. They
were seven or eight meters apart, not a distance that could be
rossed without Gury being able to prepare for Gabriel's
attack.

He wondered if Gury's offer to let Gabriel kill him was
genuine.

It occurred to Gabriel, on reflection, that he had little to
ose by trying.

Not yet, though. His mind and body were too shaken,
too unfocused.

In the end he simply walked forward, not charging, not
making any threatening gesture, and ended in a Posture of
Readiness two meters from Gury. Gury's only reaction was to
change his focus, his eyes moving from Gabriel's face to his
midsection, so that he could encompass Gabriel's entire body
within his sphere of perception, not just the upper part.

"What happened to the Lord Sergius in Roméon?" Gabriel asked. He set himself up a careful breathing rhythm,
trying to combat his body's panicked reaction. "Excellent
work, by the way. You seem to have improved puppet technology significantly to create such a machine, indistinguish-
ble from a real human."

"Thank you." A nod of acknowledgment. "Duke Sergius
died, of course. As he was shot to bits, along with his nephew
and designated heir, there was hardly any choice but to termi-
nate his existence." Gury did not trouble himself to look
annoyed. "There will be a splendid funeral. His Orthodox
Majesty will have to find a new adviser."

"Perhaps Saigo can be the next one. Or Zhenling. Though
rom what I understand of the king, he won't be able to keep
his hands off her long enough to listen to any advice she might
offer."

There was the slightest flicker in Gury's eyes at the men tion of Zhenling's name.

"Perhaps," he said merely. His focus on Gabriel's mid section remained unwavering.

Gabriel tried to relax his face, his stance, even the focu of his eyes. He didn't want to give any warning when h moved, and a tense body, every muscle on a hair-trigger, gav plenty of warning.

"And the display of advanced technology in Roméon? he asked. "Do you anticipate any untoward results?"

"Perhaps a few witch-hunters from the cap—"

Gabriel moved. Strode forward with the left, closed th distance, unleashed a right wheel kick aimed at Gury's insid right knee. A feint, because he fully expected Gury to avoi it, most likely simply by raising his leg and letting the kic pass underneath it. Which was all right, because Gabrie planned to plant the right foot forward, then duck down ou of any counterattack and whip the dragon's tail, bring his le leg spinning around to take out Gury's remaining support.

If that didn't work, Gabriel had other techniques in re serve, other feints, other strikes. All attacks, looked at th right way, were feints, except the one that finally struck hom

The wheel kick snapped toward Gury's knee, and Gur reacted as expected, simply lifting his right knee up out of th way. Gabriel planted his right foot, ducked down, swept hi left leg out . . .

Pain staggered him as Gury bounded forward an dropped his raised right foot, with all his body's weight be hind it, onto Gabriel's left kidney. Gabriel's whipping le went nowhere. Gury now stood above him. Gabriel slamme an elbow upward, hoping to catch Gury's groin, but Gur parried the strike and kicked again, catching Gabriel' strained right thigh exactly where it was bearing all his weigh The pain made Gabriel gasp. He rolled away, trying to pu distance between them. Gury did not pursue.

Gabriel rose to his feet, staggered as a bolt of agony sho up his thigh, recovered.

Gury watched him intently from a Posture of Readiness. His expression was neither hostile nor aggressive.

Gabriel's heart was hammering. He took careful sips of air, tried to calm himself.

"A few witch-hunters from the capital, as I was saying," Gury continued. His voice was mild. "Use of witchcraft would be one explanation of the weapons you used. And one of your company was an escaped prisoner from the Old Temple, and he might be recognized by witnesses."

Gabriel hoped he didn't react to Gury's knowledge of Remmy, but he felt the shock roll through him like the touch of ice on his nape.

He shifted to the Fourth Posture of Readiness, with his right side to Gury. His injured thigh muscle spasmed. His left hand, behind him and out of Gury's sight, began tracing the glyph for "beware" on his thigh.

Tzai, he thought.

"I don't think he'll be recognized," Gabriel said. "The man who escaped from the Temple was crippled. When Remmy fled from Roméon he could ride and walk."

He was having difficulty focusing on doing two things at once. Normally his daimones or his reno could do the invocation and leave Gabriel free to engage in this conversation.

Just do it, he thought. The reno was just an aid; he could do it by himself if he needed to.

Tzai. Tzai. Dai.

"They'd say the healing is probably more witchcraft," Gury said levelly. "But perhaps the accusation won't arise. Perhaps people will start remembering gunshots, big pistols, shotguns, assassins with black masks or devils with pitchforks . . . It's the sort of rationalization that's happened before."

Dai, Gabriel thought.

"Why are you letting me attack you?" he asked.

The other man gave a brief nod. "To show you that you can't succeed," he said. "To demonstrate that you can't fight me."

Die, Gabriel thought. *Die, die, die.*

A metallic taste flooded his mouth as he waited for the Voice. Far off, it came.

Submit.

"You'll lose," Gury warned.

Die, Gabriel repeated. *Die, die, die.*

He attacked, lunging forward with the right foot, then planting forward to try a spinning heel hook with the left. He'd chosen a kicking attack and a spin on the injured right leg precisely because that was what Gury would not expect. His teeth clenched as the injured muscle torqued in its spin; he managed to override the pain and keep his attack on target.

Gury avoided the first attack, then stepped inside the second, slammed his knee into Gabriel's right thigh just at the instant of maximum torque. Gabriel's knee almost folded, but he managed to remain upright and fling a back-knuckle punch at Gury's face. Gury blocked with a palm-heel strike aimed at Gabriel's elbow, and Gabriel managed to pull his punch and fold his elbow in time to avoid a stunning slam to the humerus.

Then they were at close quarters, launching one attack after another. Gury fired a short-range punch, Gabriel parried with a palm-up block that shot fingers at Gury's eyes (*die!*), Gury stopped it with an elbow-in block that turned into a vertical punch aimed at Gabriel's face, Gabriel parried with an elbow-up block, launched a low claw to the groin (*die!*) with the other hand, was parried downward, stepped in with an elbow lifting to the chin (*die!*), which Gury evaded . . .

Gabriel lost track of the attacks. Hands, feet, knees, elbows, forearms, body-blocks, sweeps—all followed one another in furious sequence, each of Gabriel's strikes marked by his cry of death.

There was a snapping sound, pain, a break in rhythm. Gabriel tried to keep his mind on what was happening. His feet were swept out from under him and he slammed to the ground on his back, the wind going out of him in a rush. He felt as if he'd fallen twenty feet.

For a moment he lay stunned.

Gury took a calm step back, away from the fight. "I broke your collarbone, Gabriel," he said. "I hope you will be able to master the discomfort."

Submit. The Voice was more insistent.

"You are transparent to me, Gabriel Vissarionovich," Gury said.

It occurred to Gabriel that he knew, and had long known, Gury's name.

Gabriel sat up, crossed his legs. Pain stuttered across his nerves. He focused, tried to make it go away.

Gury's daimones were helping him, he knew, giving the man every advantage.

"I will kill you after you heal my collarbone," Gabriel said.

Gury nodded. "If you wish."

Gabriel bowed politely. "Thank you, Captain Yuan Aristos."

"Ah," said Captain Yuan. "You guessed my name."

"Guessed?" said Gabriel. "Hardly."

Gabriel hoped this would discomfit Yuan. But if so there was no sign.

Saigo and Zhenling entered the room through a door concealed by the shifting, wine-dark tapestries. They were the real people, Gabriel believed, not puppets. Saigo moved with his accustomed deliberation, leaving a faint, sad trail of melancholy behind. Zhenling walked with brittle detachment.

Gabriel wished he had a bomb in his chest. He could behead the conspiracy in a single glorious act of self-annihilation.

As it was he sat cross-legged while Saigo and Zhenling attended to his injury. Little formulas floated through his mind, attempts to contact his daimones. He received a dose of nano to knit his broken bone, a sling to prevent the arm from doing itself further injury . . . no anesthetic, he noticed. Still, the pain was not great. The injury to his thigh muscle hurt far more.

"I am sorry for your injury, Gabriel," Zhenling said. Her tone was soft, not quite businesslike.

"Do your job," Gabriel said, "and leave."

She didn't leave, but instead took a place in the room, forming with Saigo and Yuan a large circle. Gabriel felt heat blossom in his clavicle, the nanos doing their job.

"I believe, Gabriel," said Yuan, "that you should stand and walk in a circle." He set one hand in a Mudra of Command.

"Shan't."

"Are you ready to fight me again?" Yuan asked. "If so, I will send these people from the room and we may begin."

"I'm not ready as yet."

"Fight or walk," Yuan said. "Perhaps a stretch would benefit your thigh in any case."

Gabriel felt a vague mental pressure from his component personalities as they tried to contact him, but they were overwhelmed by a sudden, stinging metallic taste in his mouth, so intense it was almost painful, and the command of the Voice: **Submit.**

Maybe the Voice had a good idea.

Gabriel stood, began to walk the circle defined by Saigo, Zhenling, and Captain Yuan. His bad leg was stiff and he stretched it deliberately. He thought of Eight Trigram Boxing, the style based on walking a circle so as to be able to launch or defend against an attack from any direction. Fantasies of attack and annihilation flitted through his mind.

Not yet.

He walked in silence. Saigo's look, behind his sad cast of features, was hostile, and Zhenling seemed sympathetic. Yuan merely looked intense. Gabriel knew they were trying to wear him down, let pain and weariness seize his mind. *Die*, he thought.

Yuan broke the long silence. "Do you wonder at our purpose, Gabriel Vissarionovich?"

"I don't care, Yuan," Gabriel said.

"We are building an alternate humanity, Gabriel," Yuan

said. His hands formed teaching mudras. "And with it, an alternate future."

Gabriel's hand went to a Mudra of Denial. "I see people starved, tortured by disease and ignorance," he said. "I see them turned into monsters. All this so a few conspirators can flatter themselves by playing at godhood."

"Respect!" Saigo shouted suddenly. "If you wish to live, offer respect to the First Aristos!"

"I offer him death at my hand," Gabriel said.

Saigo turned toward Captain Yuan. Anger glittered in his dark, sad eyes. "He's too dangerous. Kill him."

"We'll see," Yuan said.

Saigo straightened into a Posture of Formal Regard. Gabriel considered slamming a kick into his undefended stomach, but thought better of it.

He walked round the circle.

"Playing at godhood," Yuan repeated. "Perhaps. Yet why does that not bother me? I've been doing it for thousands of years."

Gabriel walked the circle. The pain eased in his thigh. Heat still radiated from his shoulder.

"Your civilization, Gabriel, is largely my creation," Yuan said. "I took a series of scattered, demoralized outposts, and out of them I built the Logarchy. I built *you*, Gabriel."

"You have my gratitude, I'm sure."

Saigo looked as if he wanted to snap Gabriel's neck.

"It was a grand adventure, Gabriel," Yuan said. "Every day a new challenge, a new improvisation. We who had survived the fall of Earth were all terrified of our own technology, afraid to use it even if it meant our salvation. Those who succeeded, those whom I led, we became the first Aristoi."

"I believe I'm acquainted with the histories," Gabriel said. "Though perhaps you overrate your own contribution. The essentials were all there—early tachyon research, the basics of gravity technology, artificial intelligence of sufficient potential to have preserved most of Earth's raw data."

"But who would use them?" Yuan said. "Pan Wengong?

A fine man, but a born follower. Ortega and Shankaracharya had the finest minds, but they died in accidents with nano. That first generation had a terrible mortality rate, Gabriel, far worse than you saw even in barbaric Vila Real. Whose pattern did people have to follow but that of the most successful?"

"Yours, in short."

"Mine."

Gabriel loaded scorn in his voice. "Don't be so proud about what you're trying to destroy, Aristos. You've provoked a civil war, haven't you? How are your battleships faring, by the way? How many innocents have they slaughtered so far?"

Saigo looked up at Gabriel with his shadowed eyes. "None," he said. "We broke your cipher, Gabriel Vissarionovich. We've been sending your little code word back to Illyricum well in advance of the seventy-two-hour deadline." He smiled. "The only casualties have been those on your ship. The ones you brought here to die."

Surprise poured up Gabriel's spine. He didn't know whether to be terrified that he was lost, or happy that the Logarchy hadn't been plunged into fratricidal war.

He forced a sneer onto his face. "The only casualties? What of Ariste Cressida?"

"We regret the necessity," said Zhenling. Her voice was perhaps a little forced, a little loud in the cubelike room. Gabriel gave her a sharp look.

"I'm sure your justifications are very well thought-out, Ariste," he said. "Please spare me them."

"Much rides on our experiment," Saigo said. "The casualties were regretted, but necessary."

"How many more?" Gabriel said. "How many more will you justify? You have all sworn to protect humanity, to elevate and care for them. Yet you inflict entire planetary populations with syphilis, smallpox, typhus, malaria, and you hold back the cures. You've revived the genes that cause cancers, sickle cell, Tay-Sachs, and a thousand others. You've witheld life-extension treatments. You stand by while tens of housands die of starvation."

"Your perspective," said Saigo, "is far too limited."

"What have we done that other Aristoi have not?" Yuan aid. "The human genetic tree has been pruned for generations—the Aristoi promote genes that are useful, allow those eemed harmful to fall into disuse or suppress them entirely. We—my colleagues and I—have recategorized a whole series f abandoned genetics as 'useful.' "

"Schizophrenia, useful?" Gabriel demanded. "Cancer, useful? Huntington's?"

"Yes," Yuan said. He permitted himself a smile. "You've one it yourself. Your little generation of opera singers—you efined an extra voice box as 'desirable,' and you brought it bout."

"I want to bring song into being. But you bring war, lague, starvation. These are useful?"

"Yes."

"Religious bigotry and persecution? Ignorance? Early and enighted death?"

"Regrettable, but necessary. Indeed."

"You make it seem so sordid, Gabriel!" Zhenling called. "You're wrong. This is the greatest adventure in all history!"

"For you. Not for the billions you've created."

"Those billions are more alive than most of us ever vere," Zhenling said. "Humanity is stagnating, Gabriel." Her ands were in teaching mudras, the same Yuan had used. "The Demos are pleasant and polite and unaggressive and tterly without fiber. The Aristoi debate Platonic theory, create stylish unrealities in the oneirochronon, busy themselves vith abstruse matters of physics . . . Where is the glory of hat?"

"What is the glory in misery and death?"

Saigo growled. "Until a few months ago," he said, "your reatest challenge was completing an opera."

Gabriel smiled in answer. "Try it sometime, Aristos. Before you decide it's easy."

"Life must be more than a choice of which affectation to indulge in today," Yuan said. "Every choice should matter. Once, after Earth was destroyed, every decision I made was one of life or death."

"Let's try to bring those heady days of youth back, shall we?" Gabriel said. His shoulder had cooled; the nano had done their work. He felt his daimones singing in the back of his mind—no distinct voices, but presences, things he hoped would help him. He halted in front of Yuan, removed the sling, dropped into fighting stance. "If you others will excuse us," he said, "I'd like to kill Yuan Aristos now."

Saigo gave a grunt of annoyance. Yuan bowed to him and to Zhenling and asked them to leave.

Gabriel used the sound of the closing door as his signal to strike, hoping it would either distract Yuan or cover up the sound of Gabriel's gliding attack.

Yuan broke his nose and shin and left him lying stunned on the ground, spattered with blood.

Zhenling and Saigo returned, gave him more nano. "Walk," Yuan said.

"You broke my leg."

"It's a greenstick fracture. You can walk on it if you want to."

"I decline."

"Then I'll break the other one and give you a better excuse to stay on the ground."

Gabriel rose to his feet and walked. He clenched his teeth at the spasm of agony that seared along his nerves. His blood dribbled out onto the Workshop carpet. Shock drained warmth from his face and hands.

"One of my companions," he said, "was of the opinion that this was all motivated by sheer, monumental sadism." He looked at Yuan, at the intent, glittering eyes, the concentrated expression. "I am coming to share that opinion," he said.

"I don't care enough about your pain to enjoy it," Yuan said, a Mudra of Denial on one hand. "Like everything else I have done, it's a means to an end."

"Consider the scope of what has been accomplished, Gabriel," said Zhenling. "An entire stellar sphere terraformed. Seeded with humanity, complete with culture and memories. False histories buried beneath the ground. The greatest experiment of all time! All of it done in secret, but with scrupulous care."

"It's the future of humanity," Saigo said. "You're only seeing the beginning of it—these civilizations will *grow*, Gabriel. They'll make mistakes, but not *our* mistakes. In time, they'll achieve their own genius. Their own brilliance. Their own glory."

"Then why the secrecy?" Gabriel asked. The conversation helped distract him from his pain. He licked blood from his lips. "Such magnificence—why not display it?"

"The other Aristoi might interfere," Yuan said.

Gabriel gasped as he set his foot wrong. Sudden bolts of sweat spattered off his forehead.

He steeled himself against the sympathy he saw in Zhenling's eyes.

"Could it be that the Aristoi might see through your god act?" Gabriel asked. "Could it be that they would conclude your grand scheme was nothing but an excuse for sadism and vainglory?"

"The Aristoi were irrelevant to my plans," Yuan said. "They are no less my creation than the inhabitants of Terrina."

"What a disappointment we must be."

"Not at all," Yuan chided. "But the Aristoi have concluded that they are an end in themselves. I see them as a part of a process, one more evolutionary step on humanity's ladder—not the end, not the ultimate perfection, but only one more step, like all the steps before.

"When I set out for the heart of the galaxy I hoped others would follow my example—perhaps not to the center of the Milky Way, but *somewhere*. And instead of going on to grander and grander adventures, the Aristoi stayed in their nests and surrounded themselves with things that made them *comfortable*. I realized I had nothing left to say to them. So I cut myself off, and I listened and I planned. And in the end I set myself to this task, to bring about something new, an entire new humanity."

Gabriel, as he paced, began to applaud, banging his hands together deliberately. Yuan looked at him carefully.

"You disappoint less than most, Gabriel. You've shown far more enterprise than I gave you credit for. And you're fearless, I'll hand you that—though I suspect it's more foolish arrogance than genuine bravery."

"Perhaps you underestimate us all."

"If so, I'll be delighted to acknowledge it." Yuan gave a polite bow. "Still, my alternative exists and I wish to protect it. Your civilization has been hopelessly tainted by the destruction of Earth[1]. Every decision you have made errs on the side of caution, of safety. Without that great trauma in history, who knows what might be accomplished?"

"We could be slaughtering each other by the billions. Your dream fulfilled."

"Throughout history," Yuan prosed on, his teaching mudras displayed again, "the greatest drive has been the instinct to reproduce. Yet humanity is so traumatized that the Aristoi took even that instinct away from them, almost without protest."

Gabriel gasped, wiped sweat from his face. "Civilized people control their reproduction," he said. "And everyone in the Logarchy may reproduce eventually. Do you argue otherwise?" There was a blazing heat source in the center of his face where his broken nose was being healed. He blinked furiously as scalding tears jetted across his eyes, trying to carry away the heat.

His leg, at least, felt stronger. Perhaps in a while he'd try to kill Yuan again.

"We're bringing whole civilizations into being," Yuan went on. "Civilizations that will be able to form new patterns, make new choices. Each is on the verge of a technological age, and each planet has sufficient resources to support it."

"Brave new worlds," Saigo added.

"And when they get into interstellar space," Yuan said, "they'll find other civilizations there, to create new patterns. No one source, like Earth[1]. No one great trauma to threaten everything."

"Just a lot of little ones. Plagues, wars, deprivation . . . and an aggressive, barbarized population ready to take up arms at any excuse."

"Nothing humanity hasn't endured before." Equably. "Nothing it hasn't managed to survive."

"I repeat, Aristos," Gabriel said, "why not do it openly? Each Ariste is supreme within her own domaine—" He stopped before Zhenling. "Ariste Zhenling could have turned her terraformed planets into little Terrinas if she desired. It would have been controversial, and there would have been much disapproval, but there is nothing any of us could have done to prevent her. The autocracy of all is guaranteed by the autocracy of each—that is the basis of the power of the Aristoi." He tried to walk again, but he was blind; he took a misstep and pain lanced up his leg. He gasped, and staggered: Zhenling reached out and steadied him. Gabriel took a breath, wiped his eyes.

"Be one of us, Aristos," Zhenling whispered.

It was the first time, Gabriel realized, that any of them had called him by his title.

Gabriel turned away from her. "Be one of *us*, Ariste."

He began to walk again.

"Your argument is naive," Yuan said. "Of *course* the Aristoi could have interfered. They could have declined to loan or sell her the terraforming ships that she would have needed to create her new worlds. They could have used their disapproval as an excuse, or simply pointed out that since her worlds would not be populated by modern humans, she would never generate the capital to repay the loans."

"She could have built her own ships," Gabriel said. "The designs are on file and Aristoi may use nano when they wish.

And of course there are the other members of your conspiracy to give her all needed assistance." He looked at Saigo.

"There are other ways of interference, some more imaginative than others," Yuan said. "Look at how even passive resistance among the Aristoi, imaginatively applied, has hampered Virtue's Icon. But most importantly, Zhenling's domaine would never have expanded naturally. It would have been absorbed by the Logarchy as soon as it began to move out of its home systems."

"She could have made the entire Gaal Sphere her domaine," Gabriel said.

"Only to have other Aristoi putting their domaines on her borders. Secrecy was the only way to assure an uncontaminated experiment."

Gabriel circled until he stood before Yuan, looked straight into the dark eyes of the First Aristos. "Are you saying," he said, "that if Captain Yuan Aristos had reappeared at Persepolis, the Aristoi would have denied him what he wished?"

For the first time Yuan hesitated. "I preferred not to take the chance," he said.

"You lack confidence in your own powers, perhaps."

Yuan smiled. "I lacked confidence in the Aristoi."

"This glory. This adventure. All this greatness you expect from your little sphere of barbarians. What exactly are you looking for?"

"I can't predict that. What I can predict is that they will generate an alternative to the slow-motion decadence of the Logarchy."

"And if Terrina evolves its own Logarchy? Its own Aristoi?"

"Then the Aristoi will have been an inevitable development, and I would have been foolish to think otherwise. Should that occur, I am prepared to accept it."

"Made secure, no doubt, by the fact that only a handful of people will be witness to your embarrassment."

Yuan's face darkened. Gabriel had finally got through.

"What I see," he went on, "is an old man trying to relive the days of his youth. You want to bring back the excitement of a time long past, long dead. You were great once, but your time has passed, and you want it back. And you'll debase and destroy billions before you're finally stopped."

"Wrong," Yuan said.

He seized Gabriel's wrist, kicked his bad leg out from under him, and purposefully dislocated his shoulder. Gabriel's cry of pain was echoed by one of shock from Zhenling.

"You're out of control," Gabriel said calmly.

"Walk."

Gabriel slowly got to his feet and limped onward. Sweat poured down his forehead, spattered the floor. He allowed himself a small, gloating smile as he staggered on—he had shown that Yuan was vulnerable.

He stopped on the opposite side of the circle from Yuan. He bent, took his upper arm in his hand, snapped the shoulder joint back into place. He tasted blood in his mouth—he'd bitten his tongue trying to conquer the pain.

Submit, the Voice said.

I'll kill him yet. Will you help me or no?

I will when you have a chance to succeed.

Gabriel tried to work out what Yuan would have required in order to accomplish his work. The huge terraforming ships—their design was available. Advances in puppet technology, in mind-interface technology—he'd had to program billions of minds at once, and that would have required enormous commitments of communications and computer support.

He'd probably just built them—moons and asteroids were easily converted. Or, he thought, used the Hyperlogos of the Logarchy—Yuan had partly *built* the Hyperlogos, Gabriel realized; he had probably seeded it with trapdoors right from the beginning, so that he could enter the programming and manipulate it when he had to.

No wonder communication was compromised. Yuan's password would take him anywhere.

And there had to be a major advance in life extension
also. Gabriel didn't quite believe that Yuan had survived
Dorian Gray's Disease this long, not when all his contempo-
raries but Pan Wengong were dead.

"I will destroy you, Gabriel," Yuan said. His fingers were
set in a mudra Gabriel didn't recognize. "And then I will build
you again in my image. Your talents are too valuable to
waste."

Very probably, Gabriel thought, Yuan was right. The
Argosy Vassals had it wrong—physical torture was by far the
worst way to make a conversion. Physical pain was beside the
point, except insofar as it worked on the mind. The easiest
way to break someone was just to keep him awake long
enough. Usually two or three days would do, though Gabriel
hoped he could hold out longer. The pain, the fatigue, and the
lack of support from his daimones were going to make him
very vulnerable. Yaritomo had done this to himself deliberately during his rite of Kavandi, his attempt to drive himself
out of his right mind, to open himself to the influences within.

But Yuan was an influence from without. He was strong
and dominant and self-assured, and Gabriel's shattered psyche would look for strength to support it, even the strength
of his worst enemy. In time he'd be agreeing with everything
Yuan said.

Gabriel decided he'd better kill Yuan fast.

The next time he tried, the First Aristos broke both
elbows and his jaw. Not his legs this time, because Yuan still
wanted Gabriel to walk.

This time, as Gabriel slowly healed and walked the circle,
he tried to go deep into himself, to focus his attention inward,
on healing, on summoning reserves of strength. Yuan and the
others prosed on, a continual litany of boast and self-justifica-
tion that Gabriel ignored. He waited till he was healed, then
warmed and stretched his muscles as he walked.

"Now, Yuan Aristos," he said, "I will kill you."

"You cannot stop a single blow," said Yuan.

Gabriel said nothing, just wiped dried blood from his

ace and settled into a fighting stance. He felt his strength
urning inside him, deep inside the swadhishatana chakra in
he pit of his abdomen. He was immovable, he thought, invin-
ible. Yuan was a foolish boaster. He would take his internal
re and project it through his fists and feet. Burn Yuan to a
risp.

"I'll make a bargain with you," Yuan said. "Are you
istening, Gabriel Vissarionovich?"

"Send the others from the room."

"I will strike first, Gabriel. A single blow. If you parry it,
hen I will stand and not resist anything you wish to do to me.
Do you understand?"

Gabriel let Yuan's words penetrate his mind, considered
hem. There was almost certainly a trick involved, but he
couldn't think what it was.

He had parried many of Yuan's blows in the earlier fights.
f he concentrated entirely on defense, he couldn't see how
Yuan could get a single strike through.

"I understand your bargain, and I accept," he said.

Zhenling and Saigo left the room. Gabriel and Yuan prepared themselves.

Then Yuan's two arms flashed into movement. Gabriel
somehow sensed what was coming, knew he should avoid it
somehow, at least close his eyes so that he didn't have to look
at it . . .

His mind emptied. He staggered. His knees were watery,
and there seemed no breath in his chest.

Yuan's kick, his single strike, exploded in Gabriel's solar
plexus. Gabriel collapsed, breath torn from his lungs.

His mind whirled. His heart throbbed in panic. Yuan had
done something to destroy him, something terrible, and he'd
done it before he even launched his blow.

Gabriel couldn't even begin to grasp what had happened.

"Walk," said Yuan.

Gabriel found himself moving to obey before his mind
even comprehended the order.

"Very good," said Yuan.

* * *

"I never loved you," said Zhenling.

Gabriel had been walking the circle for hours. He had trodden a slick path into the plush weave of the Workshop carpet. Panic throbbed in the back of his mind. He couldn't remember what it was that Yuan had used to destroy him, to bypass his defenses and attack his mind.

Yuan had used it twice. Gabriel had managed to reassemble his shattered nerves, fragments of his splintered readiness, then challenged Yuan again. And the same thing happened. Gabriel knocked down by a single blow that he hadn't been able to see because Yuan had somehow unstrung him before the strike had even been launched.

Now he merely walked the circle. He couldn't seem to assemble the concentration for anything else. Yuan had gone away for a rest and left Zhenling and Saigo to continue his work. They would trade off like that, Gabriel knew, making certain that they remained fresh while he grew ever more weary, ever more susceptible to their program.

"It was necessary that we discover how much you knew," Zhenling said. "We knew that Cressida had downloaded the raw Gaal Sphere data, that it was in portable hard storage where we couldn't get in to alter it. We hoped she wouldn't use it. And we had a number of contingencies for what we would do if she did. But no one predicted that she would contact *you.*"

Gabriel walked the circle. This boastfulness was part of their program, he knew, part of their attempt to establish their superiority. They would demonstrate their cleverness ad nauseam until he was compelled to admit their mastery.

"You and she were not friends," Zhenling said, "nor colleagues. You didn't share her scientific interests. But your domaine was closest to the Gaal Sphere, and against all expectation it was you she approached. So it was you that *we* had to make contact with."

Gabriel walked the circle.

"Yuan Aristos felt he didn't know enough about you to

judge how you would act," she went on. "We had built an oneirochronic model of your mind that suggested you would do nothing, but Captain Yuan thought it was based on inadequate data. So I was assigned to keep you . . . intrigued. Every one of our meetings was scrutinized by Aristos Yuan and the others. Even in the oneirochronon, bodies and faces can give away kinesic clues. Your choice of words, the display of your interests . . . it was all valuable. And you voluntarily gave us a chemical analysis of your brain. Aristos Yuan is a master of psychology. The model was considerably improved. Once the model predicted you would come to the Gaal Sphere, I took my ship and came here myself. The Zhenling who climbed Mount Trasker was a puppet that I controlled through the oneirochronon. And every time you and I communicated, we were able to capture some of our transmissions and work on decoding them.

"But you were cautious with what you gave me—either you were suspicious of me or wanted to protect me, but the result was the same. So we faked an emergency—the cutoff in communications when we were on the oneirochronic Mount Trasker was *my* doing. It forced you to give me one of your ciphers. And once we had that to work with—we had every reno in the Logarchy, in their downtime, working on the problem—we broke several of your codes. That allowed us to destroy *Cressida* in safety."

"You thought I was aboard."

There was a moment of silence. "We didn't believe you would surrender to us, Gabriel. And no one on the ship felt any alarm or pain."

Gabriel walked the circle. He realized that all Zhenling's words were intended to wound, were intended to degrade him and demonstrate the superiority of his captors, but none of their meaning seemed to penetrate. His mind was too disorganized to comprehend their meaning.

"I never loved you," she repeated. There was an objective tone to her voice that made it all somehow unreal. "I never *made* love to you, not really. Gregory was there, always—the body he sent to Han Fu was a puppet. He was with me in the Realized World as you were in the oneirochronon. It was Gregory to whom I made love, not you. You were just an electronic phantom."

Gabriel found himself laughing. Even in his disorganized state he found this amusing. "This virtue is somewhat belated," he said. "You prostituted yourself at Yuan's orders!"

Two could play at wounding, he thought.

"Yuan Aristos gave me no orders," she said. "We are equals here."

Gabriel laughed again. "A volunteer! Very well. But I think Aristos Yuan has a way of making his wishes clear, no?"

"We are peers, Gabriel. Our votes each count equally."

"Try opposing Yuan sometime," Gabriel said, "and see what happens."

He was recovering from the shock, he realized. He was scoring points. But still, the debate was meaningless. Fighting Yuan might be meaningless as well, but it was likely to bring bigger dividends.

He had to work out a way to kill Yuan. But first he had to comprehend what it was that the First Aristos had done to him.

His mind refused to encompass it, even to think about it.

He walked the circle.

Yuan eventually returned and Zhenling left to refresh herself. Gabriel was allowed to drink a cup of water.

"If you give us access to your private communications network," Saigo said, "you may eat."

Gabriel flashed him the one-fingered Mudra of Contempt.

A trickle of hope penetrated his mind.

They had broken one cipher only, the one that set the password that prevented word of the Gaal experiment from being revealed. They hadn't broken into his reserves of data— they didn't have the passwords.

He tried, quite consciously, to forget them. Bury them. Pretend they never existed.

He found they faded from his mind quite easily.

It was Saigo's turn to boast. "We have access to *everything*," he said. "We can use the downtime of every processor in the Logachy, and then hide the evidence!"

"Enough of this drivel," Gabriel said. "Yuan Aristos, are you ready to die?"

Saigo looked at Captain Yuan. "Converting an Aristos is too dangerous. Captain Yuan, you must kill him."

Yuan's expression was neutral. "We'll see," he said. "It would be a shame to waste someone of Gabriel's caliber. I disliked the necessity of killing Cressida—she was one of the few Aristoi of whom I approved. I would much prefer to turn Gabriel to our purpose."

He sent the others from the room and dropped into stance.

Gabriel watched carefully this time, but still his mind couldn't quite bear it. Some hours later, after he'd recovered from being knocked down, after his terrified mind had reassembled some semblance of coherence, he realized that the experience had felt, somehow, familiar . . .

He reached back into his mind, brought out a fragment of memory, his first graduation.

The Mudra of Domination.

He remembered when it had been flashed at him during his training, the way his mind and body had staggered.

He'd been deconditioned to that mudra in his first few days as an Aristos, but Captain Yuan had clearly invented another mudra that served the same purpose. Yuan had designed the training program by which everyone in the Logarchy was conditioned to respond to certain signs and symbols, and had understood the psychic programming better than anyone.

He had seen the need for a new Mudra of Domination, one that would enable him to control even other Aristoi, and he had designed it. It was different from the other—it took both hands—but its effect seemed all the greater.

Gabriel realized he would have to decondition himself. He would have to challenge Yuan more often, expose himself to the psychic pressure until he became accustomed to it.

Yuan didn't cooperate. He declined to play the one-strike game again, instead insisted on a bare-handed fight, as he had at first. He broke several of Gabriel's ribs and ordered they not be healed. They weren't life-threatening, he said, and Gabriel could walk without them.

Gabriel staggered on. The pain in his ribs ate at him slowly, along with weariness, hunger, the knowledge of his own failure. He was too injured and weary to challenge Yuan again, and all he could do was hold out as long as he could.

Clancy might not have been captured, he thought. Or even if captured she might be working to free them all. She had developed tremendously, she would be an Ariste, but the others didn't know that. If they were careless around her she might turn things around.

Gabriel walked the circle while the others talked of their glory, their achievement, their successful plotting. Visions began to float before Gabriel's eyes, Clancy storming the room at the head of Gabriel's party, Yaritomo, White Bear, Rubens, Marcus, all armed, energies flying from their weapons to destroy Yuan and the others . . .

He remembered, vaguely, that Rubens and Marcus were dead.

He tried to remember music, concentrate on melody and lyrics so as to drown out the endless droning of his captors. When he realized he was singing aloud, he stopped.

Marcus appeared again, floating into the room through the walls. Marcus kissed him, gave him something to drink. "You should be reasonable, Gabriel," he said.

Submit, said the Voice.

Daimones floated in and out of Gabriel's mind. At times they were in control of his body because his consciousness had abandoned it. They muttered and scolded, cried out in rage, in panic.

At one point he came to himself and realized that he was crawling on hands and knees. He managed to stand and continue to walk the circle. But he staggered and fell and, in the end, had to crawl anyway.

Submit, said the Voice.

Good idea, Gabriel thought. Maybe the Voice knew what it was doing.

Someone gave Gabriel water, and in return he gave a few passwords.

That seemed to make things easier. After a while he realized that he was among friends. He gave more passwords and promised to behave. Someone gave him something that helped with the pain. Someone, Yuan, he thought, kissed him and assured him he was loved.

Gabriel told them everything they wanted to know.

At last he was allowed to sleep in Yuan's comforting, loving arms.

"You will be assigned to assist with terraforming efforts on a planet we have named Dürer," Yuan said. "Terrain needs to be surveyed, divided into climatological zones, and specific recommendations made as to seeding with plant forms and animals. You will work alone, in this room. We will provide you with the necessities of life. We will give specific assignments."

"What about my reno?" Gabriel said. "Without access to my reno I can't do good work."

He wanted to please Yuan very much.

Gabriel remained in the wine-curtained room. It was furnished now, with a bed, chairs, a sofa, a small kitchen.

"We will give you access to an external reno," Yuan said. "But understand that misbehavior will not be tolerated. You will not be permitted outside your account. Your account will be strictly limited, and will be subjected to constant inspection. No transmission or communications will be tolerated."

"Of course," Gabriel said.

"Your first assignments will be very simple," Yuan said. "They will become more complex as you progress."

When Yuan left the room Gabriel began to feel a growing tide of panic. He didn't want to be alone. He didn't want to be without clear direction. But then a message flickered across his optical centers, a signal that the external reno was ready and trying to contact him.

Thankfully he answered the message and received his assignment.

Work was good, he thought. It kept him from thinking about things he shouldn't.

His tasks were fairly easy. He hadn't worked in terraforming since he'd finished creating Brightkinde, but memories and analogies came easily to his thoughts, the software and equipment were familiar, and he finished his surveys and posted his recommendations quickly.

More work appeared. He worked, felt hungry, ate, worked some more, tired, slept.

Every so often Yuan would appear and lead him through exercises designed to firm him in his new character, his new purpose. That and to disperse any anger, any resentment, any inappropriate emotion. Gabriel participated willingly.

Time, days probably, passed. His hair, copper-colored again, grew longer. It seemed to him that he was sleeping much more than he used to, but he had no way to keep track of time.

Daimones occasionally appeared to him in his dreams. Sometimes they cried in fear and loneliness, sometimes they murmured things Gabriel didn't understand, sometimes they came on thundering chords of music, music that filled Gabriel's heart with emotions that left him weeping in sudden terror and wonder.

He asked Yuan if he might spend some of his time composing. Yuan granted permission. He worked on little pieces in the baroque style—no passion, all elaborate ornamentation and technique. When a movement began to say something to

him, to suggest emotion, he changed it. The exercise, paltry as
it was, seemed to ease Gabriel's nights.

Sometimes the music seemed to have the flavor of Spring
Plum to it, sometimes Cyrus. He was accessing the parts of his
mind that contained them, but they couldn't speak directly.

He asked Yuan about his daimones. "I can do better
work with them," he said.

"Perhaps in time," Yuan said. "After you have demonstrated your zealous cooperation in other matters."

"Of course, Aristos," Gabriel said. He threw himself
into work.

Zealously.

Time passed. Gabriel worked, slept, exercised. His
dreams took on strange dimensions. He saw tiny robots at
work, atoms as big as planets moving, sliding into place in an
elaborate dance. For some reason this was all frightening, and
when he woke from such a dream he would exercise until his
unease went away.

His hair grew longer, began to cover the tops of his ears.

A space of time later, lying on his couch, he was surprised to look up from his work and see Remmy entering
through a door behind the curtains.

Remmy was dressed in modern clothing. He pushed
before him a serving cart with food supplies to refresh Gabriel's stores.

Usually a robot did the deliveries.

Remmy answered Gabriel's look of surprise with a shy
smile and a quick nod. "I'm pleased to see you, Ghibreel," he
said. He still spoke Beukhomanan.

"You have been captured as well, then?" Gabriel's
tongue, without his reno's vocabulary and guide to pronunci-
ation, hesitated on unfamiliar words, and again on the word
"captured."

It should have been "yourself-captured," he realized. His
grammar was gone along with everything else.

"Yes, Lord Yuan took me," Remmy answered. He
pushed the cart toward Gabriel's kitchen. "A lone horseman

racing away from catastrophe? My lord's aerial chariot discovered me easily. And I gather there was something in your dog's head that made him easy to locate."

"Yes," Gabriel said. "I suppose there would be." Manfred wouldn't have known not to answer a call on his reno.

Remmy began to restock Gabriel's larder. Gabriel was struck by the remembered grace of his movement, the supple motions of the big shoulders and strong arms.

"I'm very happy that you're not fighting God any longer," Remmy said. "He said that you are beginning to help him."

Gabriel sorted through various contradictory responses, settled for quiet inquiry. "Has Yuan Aristos told you that he is God?" he asked.

"No," Remmy said. "Not in so many words. But I saw him die, and now see him stand before me in his resurrected form. I'm confident that he is divine, and I'm content that he smiles upon me and gives me work." He smiled.

"I'm surprised he brought you here."

Remmy looked at Gabriel with calm green eyes. "Apparently I was thought to be among the rebel angels, such as yourself. And once I was brought here, it was too late to return me to my world."

"Are we off the world, then? I haven't been out of this room."

"I understand that we are under the surface of the world, on the other side from my home. There is a whole network of . . . tunnels beneath the world, and ways to travel that I don't understand."

A secret subterranean base, in short. That was certainly consistent with Yuan's melodramatic style.

"Are you being cared for?" Gabriel asked.

"Oh yes. I'm receiving lessons from some of the automata and minor angels. And soon I'll be given something that will enable me to communicate through the angelic medium."

Implant a reno in him, educate him.

The only appropriate response, Gabriel concluded, was to be happy for him.

He was happy. It required hardly any effort at all.

"I'm glad you're doing well," Gabriel said. "Have you seen any of the others? Clansai, Quil Lhur?"

Remmy finished his task and flowed upright. "No," he said. "I'm not permitted it."

"Do you know if they're alive?"

"I believe so." He paused for a moment.

Gabriel nodded, then remembered to jerk his chin instead. "Good," he said. "I'm glad none of them died on my account."

"I, also. I hope they will all find grace and an understanding of the Lord." Remmy approached Gabriel. "Lord Saigo corrected my error," he said. "He told me that carnal relations between men are not sinful so long as they are not done for the wrong reasons. He said that I might spend time with you, if you wished."

A skein of anger twisted through Gabriel's thoughts. Saigo had sent Remmy here, not Yuan. Saigo had turned pimp, and—given that Gabriel was almost certainly monitored—perhaps voyeur as well.

He suppressed the anger. He knew it was not the thing to do.

"Under the circumstances," Gabriel said, "I think this would be inappropriate."

Remmy gave a little smile. "As you think best, Ghibreel." And then he added, "I'm taking care of your dog, Ghibreel. Perhaps I'll bring him sometime."

Gabriel rose from his couch and held the curtain back as Remmy took his cart out the door. He knew better than to try walking through the door. Outside he caught a glimpse of dark-paneled corridor, fine carpet of the same wine shade as the room hangings.

Gabriel paced for a moment in anger, until he realized he was walking the same circle he'd trodden into the carpet. He made a deliberate effort to break free of the conditioning and sat, facing the wall, until he calmed himself.

He was being monitored, of that he was certain. Every heartbeat, every indicator of stress. If turbulent thoughts came, the watchers would know.

Best to keep everything calm. In time, he managed it.

Time passed. Gabriel worked, slept, ate, and in between tried to think of nothing at all.

Remmy didn't come again.

In solitary confinement, Gabriel knew, people were forced deep inside themselves, deep into their memories, their psyches. But Gabriel didn't want to go there—inside was everything he was trying to forget.

He concentrated on work. Sometimes, when his attention wavered from his assigned task, he found that his left hand was doing something odd, drawing patterns on his thigh or the desktop. He jerked his eyes away from the sight.

He didn't want to look at it. He didn't want to know. His left side was not a part of him, not really.

It was someone else's hand, he decided. Not his. Nothing to do with him.

Visions of dancing atoms haunted his dreams.

After a long space of time Yuan came to him. Gabriel assumed a Posture of Submission.

"You have done very well on your assigned tasks," Yuan said.

"Thank you, Aristos."

"Do you still wish assistance?"

Hope brightened in Gabriel. Perhaps he would have his daimones back. "That would make the job easier, yes."

"I will give you assistants from those captured with you," Yuan said.

Gabriel's heart leaped. "Thank you, Aristos."

"You will meet only in the oneirochronon. Your team will be very carefully monitored at all times. You must be very prudent in what you say and do."

"I will be careful, Aristos."

Yuan formed a Mudra of Approval. "Very well."

"Thank you, Aristos. I am very grateful." Gabriel dropped to a lower Posture of Submission, his forehead to the carpet. Yuan gave an approving smile and turned to leave.

"You are making progress, Gabriel," he said. "Remember your new purpose, and you will do well."

Gabriel returned to his sofa and entered the oneirochronon. Electronic walls patterned around him, red-draped ones. Evidently the environment had been carefully chosen. Gabriel pulsed out messages, heard answers. Clancy, White Bear, Quiller, and Yaritomo appeared.

They adopted Postures of Formal Regard. A bolt of energy shot up Gabriel's spine at the acknowledgment of his authority.

He returned their greeting.

"We have been asked to assist with the terraforming of Dürer," Gabriel said. "I would like to gather data and make assignments."

Their oneirochronic forms shimmered before him. He wasn't receiving their true expressions, he realized; there was some interference, an oneirochronic sensor, that muted their appearance, softened the focus somehow.

"Is it your wish that we do this?" Clancy asked. The sensor did not entirely conceal the directness of her gaze.

Gabriel blinked tears from his realworld eyes. "Yes."

"Then we shall do as you ask."

The team began to function. There were no social aspects to the meetings, only assignments and labor. The work was slow—there were no daimones to supervise the detail work—but in the end excellent. Meetings were scheduled, problems raised, solutions found. The others never called Gabriel "Aristos," apparently having been warned not to. None of them seemed quite themselves: they had to have been subjected to various degrees of personality modifications as well as having their renos and daimones switched off.

Occasionally Gabriel would find his left hand doing something odd, as if it were conducting invisible music. There

was a strong metallic taste on his tongue. He chose not
think about what that meant. It wasn't his hand. It didn
belong to him.

One day Zhenling came to Gabriel in his room. Sh
looked magnificent, her bladelike form clothed in a long blac
cassock covered in cloth-of-silver embroidery. Gabriel ha
seen some of the young fashionable men in Vila Real wearin
something similar.

Gabriel adopted a Posture of Submission.

"Your Dr. Clancy has been caught attempting to subve
our renos," Zhenling said. "While ostensibly trying to do h
work, she was trying in subtle ways to alter the prograr
ming."

Admiration flooded Gabriel's heart. Yes, he though
That's what an Ariste would do.

He pressed his forehead to the floor. "I apologize for he
behavior and accept full responsibility," he said.

"Was this done with your knowledge?"

He straightened and looked up at her so that she coul
see his sincerity. "I knew nothing of it," he said. "I *cou*
know nothing of it."

Her tilted dark eyes seemed to search his thought
"Clancy will be subjected to readjustment," Zhenling sai
"She will not be present at your next work session."

Gabriel bowed. "The decision is fair, Ariste."

"Come sit with me, Gabriel."

Gabriel joined Zhenling on the sofa. "I wanted to se
you," she said, "to let you know that I will be leaving Terrir
in a few days to return to my domaine. A puppet is an inco
venient thing to have to work through, and I wish to be ther
in person. Captain Yuan Aristos will be leaving as well, t
supervise work elsewhere."

A hint of panic throbbed in Gabriel's throat. "Who wi
give me instruction?" he asked.

"Saigo Aristos will supervise you and your team."

Saigo was the most hostile of the three. He would use an
excuse to kill Gabriel.

Gabriel was going to have to be very careful.

"I understand," he said. "I will submit to Aristos Saigo's instruction."

"Good." Zhenling looked at him for a moment, as if on the verge of speech. In the end she said nothing.

"I hope my work has been satisfactory," Gabriel said.

"Yes," she said. "Very."

"Captain Yuan Aristos suggested that if my work was good, I might be granted access to my daimones again. They would make the work go faster, and make things less lonely."

Zhenling turned away, color coming to her cheeks, then mastered herself and looked back. "I wish Yuan Aristos would not make these promises," she said. "He should not raise false hopes."

Gabriel looked at her in rising desperation. She shook her head.

"We can't give you your daimones, Gabriel," she said. "Not ever. It would be too dangerous."

Tears sprang to Gabriel's eyes. He had no daimones to stand between him and his emotions: the agony of life in this forsaken room, confined to its bleak terrain and that of his own mind, was to a brand that consumed his hope with blazing fire.

He collapsed, weeping, facedown on the couch. Zhenling reached out a hand, hesitated, then touched his shoulder.

"I'm sorry, Gabriel," she said.

"I was promised!"

"You will"—she hesitated—"you will have to cope."

Gabriel sobbed on. Zhenling stayed for a moment, hand on his shoulder, then quietly rose from the couch and made her way out.

"I never intended this," she said quietly, and left.

Gabriel tried to master his emotions and failed. He spent the next few days in blackest despair, refused food, ignored his work.

It was the thought of Saigo gloating that sent him back to his tasks.

The team, without Clancy, without a hopeful Gabriel t[o]
motivate it, was less effective. The work dragged on. Gabrie[l]
found that it barely interested him any longer.

Saigo appeared daily in order to make assignments an[d]
walk Gabriel through his exercises. "Any further attempts t[o]
subvert our renos will be met with reprisals," he said.

"I understand."

He looked at Gabriel from out of his melancholy eye[s.]
"This was once an Aristos," he said. "We are surely in de[-]
cline."

Gabriel said nothing.

"Why don't you kill yourself?" Saigo suggested.

Gabriel had considered it. The means were available.

He chose, however, to work on. Sometimes Gabrie[l]
would realize that his left hand was moving in the air, as i[f]
casting a spell. He chose to deny it. *Not mine*, he thought.

His long hair brushed his shoulders.

Much later, weeks probably, Gabriel was eating a meal h[e]
arbitrarily chose to call "dinner," in that it followed mea[ls]
called "breakfast" and "luncheon." There was a bad taste i[n]
his mouth and his appreciation of the food was soured.

Then he was interrupted.

There was a crash, a sizzling sound. The deep red curtain[s]
on one wall blew inward, as if from a violent wind through [a]
suddenly open window. Overhead, the crystal chandelie[r]
pealed like a carillon.

A machine entered, a slick, seamless, night-black thin[g]
on eight disk-shaped wheels. It had a prow like a dreadnough[t]
battleship and a crudely formed seat behind.

Time to go, Gabriel, said the Voice.

Chapter 17

LULU: A knife! Let it sing me to sleep.

Gabriel looked at the machine and concluded that he was in deep trouble.

Hurry, said the Voice.

Gabriel rose slowly, wondering what to do, and then a blazing hope kindled in his heart and he ran for the machine and jumped aboard just as it started to move. He ducked to avoid the low clearance as the machine scrambled through the hole that it had melted in the wall—applied nano at work here—and swung with a hum into the corridor. The seat was slick and difficult to maintain. Numbered doors began to speed by. The machine's wheels were muffled by the thick red carpeting.

I have subverted the base's renos, the Voice said, **but I don't know when some hardwired alarm might go off. That's why I went through the wall instead of the door. It would have set off any number of alarms, and I couldn't suppress them all.**

Where are we going?

The medical unit. I'm going to give you your reno and daimones back.

Gabriel's heart leaped.

Doors sped by. The outpost had been built to a massive scale, but the architecture was merely functional and the place seemed largely uninhabited.

If Gabriel had ever wanted a secret subterranean base, it would have looked far more interesting.

Here. Gabriel almost lost his seat as the machine jerked to a halt. This thing had not been built with his comfort in mind. Gabriel's left hand lifted by itself and pointed toward a door.

Quickly. It's local night here, and most of Saigo's people are sleeping, but you never know when someone might want to check your room or the nano lab—and I've left a mess in both.

Gabriel could imagine. The machine was obviously nano-built, and would have had to get its mass from somewhere. The floor, most likely, the walls, the furniture.

The machine was crude, obviously an improvisation. It had taken the Voice months to build. Gabriel could have designed a much better mechanism in a matter of days.

Can we release the others? Gabriel queried. He entered the medical lab through its sterilizing door, saw gleaming black-and-yellow floors, immaculate countertops, equipment standing ready.

Not without triggering alarms, the Voice said. **Over there.** Gabriel's left hand pointed to a tall wing-backed chair upholstered in soft dark leather.

Gabriel sat. He knew that the back and wings of the chair contained tachline projectors and receivers, sensors, a dedicated reno. From here he could reprogram his own implant reno.

This may take some time, the Voice said. **The toad Yuan has disabled all your reno's functions except the biomonitors, which are feeding data right into his own renos. We have to turn off the biomonitors, switch to a false data feed, and then enable everything else. Yuan's filled every-**

thing with traps and alarms, so I'll have to proceed carefully.

Can I help?

No. Just shut up and stay that way.

Gabriel shut up. Spasms of anxiety tweaked at his nerves—if he was caught now he would be killed. He could feel things happening in his head, little flashes of awareness as if subsystems were being tested. A voice began to sing in his head, Psyche's, then Spring Plum's, then a chorus, and his mind filled with beauty like an endless unfolding origami flower, opening to a realm of possibility.

At your service, Aristos!

He sprang from the chair and laughed aloud. His daimones snarled for vengeance.

Gabriel is himself again, he thought.

Not quite, the Voice reminded. **You've spent months adjusting to a status of submission and dependence. You can't throw off that conditioning in a moment.**

Gabriel considered this. What's the next step, then?

Procure a weapon and kill everyone in your path, starting with Saigo. Before he can use the new Mudra of Domination.

Sounds good. His daimones rejoiced. **Where can I get a gun?**

Saigo's personal ship is docked here, and there is an armory on board. Saigo sleeps in his stateroom, however, and you may have to get by him. I'll have to use the machine to burn our way past the locks.

Gabriel ran for the door, mounted the machine again. It started up with a whine. **How many other people are here?** he asked.

Four Therápontes, not counting the one you killed in Roméon. Our people actually outnumber theirs.

Can't we free our people first, then arm them and overwhelm the opposition?

I can't be absolutely certain I didn't set off an alarm

just now. We should move quickly while we have the opportunity.

The machine made a violent turn. Gabriel's nails scrabbled for purchase on the slick surface. The corridor in which it moved was much wider, the ceiling higher, its floor surfaced in black, soft, rubberlike nonskid surfacing material. Lighting strips provided a cold white glow. At the corridor's end, a half-kilometer farther on, were a pair of wide cargo doors, padded with soft, cushionlike tiles in black and white stripes.

The machine jerked to a stop. Gabriel dismounted, found a control switch, hit the green "open" button. The doors slid open with a hiss.

Frigid air flooded over Gabriel's skin. Breath frosted from his nostrils. He called on Horus to dilate his capillaries and bring more warm blood to his skin, and while he did so he contemplated Saigo's ship.

The giant drydock had been scooped out of the native rock. The *Cold Voyager*—typically gloomy Saigo ship-name, that—lay in a scalloped cradle of sleek black composite, beneath a tented sky of girders, crossbeams, webbed white ceiling material. Illumined by dangling yellow lights, the ship was a quarter-kilometer long, a polished silver spindle with a light golden sheen. *Cold Voyager* was nearly featureless except where maintenance robots clung like limpets to its skin, tuning invisible sensors or polishing its gleaming surface.

There was an unused cradle next to *Cold Voyager*. Another ship—a much larger one, judging from the size of the cradle—had once been here.

Yuan's ship, Gabriel thought. *Discovery*, presumed vanished on its mission to the galaxy's core.

The roadway cantilevered upward from where Gabriel stood shivering in the doorway, ended at one of *Cold Voyager*'s doors, invisible at this distance. Gabriel jumped back on the machine. Warmth flushed his skin as the machine sped the length of the bridge.

I'll have to burn the door, the Voice said.

Isn't there another way to get in?

We could call Saigo and ask him to unlock it.

Gabriel thought about it. **Burn away,** he said.

The machine reached the end of the bridge. Its black ramming prow lightly touched *Cold Voyager*'s silver surface, adjusted itself in a peculiarly repulsive organic way, twitching and flattening like the questing snout of an anteater, and then the prow adhered. Gabriel looked at himself in the mirrored flank of the ship, saw tousled hair grown in long and red again, eyes still dark, skin pale and blotchy. His nose had been broken and healed badly, giving an unbalanced, ferocious aspect to his appearance. There was a hint of unspeakable age in the set of his mouth and jaw—his treatments wouldn't let him grow old, not exactly, but he felt as if he'd aged centuries in the last months and his face reflected it.

You seem to have gained considerable control of Saigo's renos, Gabriel said. **How did you manage it?**

Yuan put trapdoors in *everything*. He wanted unlimited access *everywhere*. He even subverted his own systems so that he could keep tabs on his confederates. The Voice seemed a little smug. **Trapdoors can take only so many forms. Once I knew what to look for, gaining access was relatively easy.**

Easy? Then why did you take so long?

A sizzling sound began to come from the machine's snout. Gabriel felt a wisp of heat rising from the active nano.

I had to move without anyone observing me, the Voice went on. **I am not very . . . efficient . . . and they were *very* alert. I had to use you as a Trojan horse—while they were looking at you, I was able to use your right brain to conduct my own business. I had to move with great deliberation, the task was extraordinarily difficult, and once I was detected.**

< ??? >

Yes. But I managed to set a trail that led to Clancy, and they thought it was she who was attempting the subversion.

Sorrow bit at Gabriel's throat. **What have they done to her?**

Isolation. Deprivation. Demands that she confess.

Has she confessed?

Yes.

Sadness filled Gabriel's heart. Clancy had been degraded for something she hadn't done, something that he—one of his daimones, anyway—had done instead. He imagined her walking the circle, broken, the others shouting at her, perhaps injuring her, demanding that she confess to something she hadn't done.

She would have admitted it, eventually, once she realized that the real sabotage must have been conducted by one of her companions, and that her confession would have helped to conceal the other's—Gabriel's—actions. And then she would have had to make the confession seem sincere enough—summon the strength to make them believe she'd actually done it.

And in that she'd succeeded. Admiration kindled in Gabriel at the thought.

He would reward her, once he got out of this. A thousand orbiting clinics, ten thousand palaces, a hundred thousand temples in her honor. A hegemony . . .

If he got out of this.

Heat sizzled from around the machine's snout. It had inserted itself into the hole it had made, widened it, applied more nano. Large drops of silver metal fell to the distant stone floor.

I don't have full control of the system, the Voice said. **If an alarm goes out, I'll have to crash all communications in order to keep the word from getting out.**

Very well.

I'm going to try to keep it local, only crash the local renos. With luck Yuan won't find out.

Where is he?

At Dürer. Eight days away.

And Zhenling?

Two weeks out, on her way back to Tienjin.

Any other Aristoi in the neighborhood?

No.

Horus was pumping Gabriel's body full of blood and

energy. He shivered, not with the cold but with the adrenaline flood racing through his veins.

He thought of Saigo at the end of a pistol. His blood warmed at the thought.

The machine drew back, leaving a perfect circle in the ship's flank, one wide enough for Gabriel's shoulders.

I could make the hole larger, the Voice reported, **but time is of the essence.**

The Voice seemed a master of cliché.

Gabriel sprang off the machine, stooped, worked his way through the hole. Warm air caressed him. The ship's skin had already dissipated any excess heat caused by the dissolving airlock door, and the nanos had been inactivated.

He ordered Horus to shut down his epidermal capillaries, reserve blood for the major muscles.

His inner ear swam as gravity faded away—the ship had its own local gravity—or lack of it. He had come through a cargo hatch into a wide corridor, spotless gleaming metal with padded edges. Cargo hatches were frequently without gravity: it made moving bulky stuff easier. **Lift around the corner to your left.** Gabriel pushed off with his feet, gently struck the opposite wall, kicked off again, ended in the lift.

Deck four.

Gabriel repeated the Voice's instructions and oriented himself in the direction gravity would come on—his head was now pointed toward the ship's prow and his feet toward its tail. The lift was utilitarian, designed for moving stores from one part of the ship to another, all surfaces coated with soft grey nonskid covering. The door closed and gravity began slowly to increase as the lift began to move. Gabriel's joints cracked as the weight came on.

The armory is in Saigo's personal apartments, the Voice said. **This is his sleep time, and there's no traffic in and out of his reno, but he may be awake. In the event that he sees you, he'll use the new Mudra of Domination. When that happens, you will have to give your body to me. I have conditioned myself to it.**

Gabriel shuddered at the thought of the new mudra. **Yes,** he agreed. He didn't even want to have to think about it.

He was panting, he realized, feeding oxygen to the adrenaline in his system. He gulped and tried to get his respiration under control.

Gravity came on fully. The soft rubberlike floor cushioned slightly under Gabriel's slippers. The door slid open in silence, and Gabriel heard music.

Somber music, a thudding hypnotic pattern at its base, a shimmering, the fall of raindrops. Not music one was meant to pay attention to, just background stuff, accompaniment to the vaguer sort of abstract thoughts. The kind Gabriel hated: he liked music that demanded attention.

It was the sort of thing Saigo would play, though, while he brooded and contemplated the melancholy course of species evolution.

Saigo's personal suite was paneled in dark wood, carpeted in plush deep purple velvet. Lights were provided by brass lamps with phony oil reservoirs and holographic flames. The dark-paneled walls seemed close and suffocating, like a Victorian mansion—a brooding place, built to match its brooding master.

Gabriel stepped silently onto the carpet. Adrenaline howled through his veins. **Take me to the armory without passing the source of the music,** he said.

The music's everywhere in the suite. It's meant to be atmospheric. Go straight ahead, then left at the end of the corridor.

Gabriel padded on, past closed doors bound in brass, each with a brass porthole. There were paintings on the wall, small cramped oils of people in historical garb. Gabriel had no idea who any of them were. Perhaps they were no one at all, just figments of Saigo's paintbrush.

A door opened, and Saigo stepped out, not five meters away.

For a second Gabriel quailed, his nerves turning to water

as the new conditioning gripped him, and then the adrenaline already unleashed in his system picked him up and flung him screaming at his enemy.

Saigo stared in surprise, but Gabriel's hesitation allowed him to recover himself. He stepped fully into the corridor, leaned away from Gabriel's rush, his hands drawn to his hip and out of sight.

Saigo's hands shot toward Gabriel as Gabriel rushed at him. Gabriel's mind dimmed as the Voice's strong personality filled it, as the impact of the mudra struck his psyche.

VOICE: Crashing commo system now! < Commands follow. >

AUGENBLICK: Pupils narrowing, breath controlled, hands cowled to side . . . he's focusing. The mudra!

VOICE: Give me the body! Now!

GABRIEL: < affirmative >

SPRING PLUM: The phoenix rises from a position of supreme disadvantage . . .

The Voice's deconditioning must have been imperfect. The mudra staggered Gabriel as his nerves suddenly unstrung, and Saigo gave a savage cry and lunged forward with a ferocious left kick to Gabriel's solar plexus. But the Voice managed to twist Gabriel's body to one side, the right arm clamping Saigo's foot to Gabriel's side, the left smashing a forearm down on Saigo's knee.

The phoenix had risen.

But it was a young phoenix, not fully fledged. Gabriel's nerves had not entirely recovered from the effects of the new Mudra of Domination, and the Voice's control of his right side was imperfect. Saigo managed to break his leg free of the trap before the Voice's savage attack could cripple him. The Voice drove forward, slammed Gabriel's body into Saigo's before he could recover his balance, an elbow smashing into the ribs and a hand clawing for the eyes. Saigo tried to turn and use the force of Gabriel's attack against him, turn it into a throw, but the move was too forced and hasty, and Gabriel too solidly planted—the grappling attempt failed. The elbow smash stung Saigo, Gabriel could see, possibly broke or bent some ribs, and Gabriel's clawed fingers scored gouges in the sockets of Saigo's eyes.

Saigo counterattacked furiously, suddenly all flashing elbows, clawed hands, driving knees . . . The Voice parried and struck back, but began to give way—he was one imperfect daimōn fighting an Aristos who had a host of daimones at his command.

GABRIEL: Give me the body back.

VOICE: You're too frightened of him!

CYRUS: The tiger cannot fight the wolf pack . . .

GABRIEL: *Let me overcome this daimōn and let him become a part of me!*

Gabriel's invocation of the Sutra of Captain Yuan brought him back to the forefront of his own mind, but the eyeblink's time in which he regained control was an opportunity for Saigo, who drove a palm-heel up under Gabriel's philtrum. There was an audible crack as Gabriel's head snapped back. Pain snarled through his sinuses. His nose was broken again—he knew the feeling by now. He staggered back, blinking tears of pain from his eyes and parrying as he went, all in hopes of luring Saigo into a trap. But Saigo must have sensed Gabriel's intention—he cut his assault short, wiped blood from his eyes, dropped into a guard position, and waited.

Gabriel assured himself of control over his body, lined up his daimones, plotted an attack. He'd wait until Saigo's bloody eyes started giving him trouble, he decided.

"Surrender, Gabriel," Saigo said. Blood was running down his face. "You can't fight the conditioning."

He's trying to revive his commo net, the Voice said. **I'm blocking him.**

"In the name of the Logarchy I demand your surrender," Gabriel said. "I will give you safe conduct to your trial at Persepolis."

It was a lie, of course. He's snap Saigo's neck the first chance he got.

**Can you make it seem as if the Hyperlogos's coming
back on line?** Gabriel asked.

Possibly.

Take command of the reno. Use it.

"You're in no position to make demands," Saigo said.
Blood dripped down his big chest, trailed down his beard.
"You're unstrung, man . . . your fight was totally uncoor-
dinated."

"Then why aren't you finishing me off?" Gabriel
mocked. "I'm an Aristos. You've underestimated me all
along, and now I'm in control."

I'm projecting a start-up sequence, the Voice said.

"You're not an Aristos anymore," Saigo said. He smiled
with pink-tinged teeth. "I've seen you crawl and beg, Gabriel.
I've seen you weep and cry for mercy. Is that the picture of an
Aristos?"

Gabriel's mind filled with Mataglap's howls of rage keening over a loud chorus of daimonic denial. He projected a
contemptuous laugh at Saigo's words, but he felt his insides
twist at the remembrance. At the knowledge that he had fallen
so totally.

He knew he was going to lose.

He wondered why Saigo wasn't attacking now, while
doubts were besetting him. Then he realized that Saigo was
seeing a start-up sequence over his tachlink, that he thought
he was regaining command of his renos. Saigo believed he
could broadcast an alert and wait until his Therápontes
showed up to overwhelm Gabriel and finish him off.

"We'll have to condition you all over again," Saigo said
deliberately. "And this time there will have to be much more
pain."

Panic wailed in Gabriel's nerves. **Give your body back,**
the Voice demanded. **Let me finish him.**

Gabriel thought desperately. **No,** he said. **Reno, give me
a graphic. The four Therápontes here—I want a picture of
them all dead, bloody, and mutilated. I want the glyph for**

"fool" projected along with the image. Nothing but loud laughter for audio—my voice. And I want the new mudra projected as well. For all the effect it would have.

"Pain, Gabriel," Saigo continued. "Enough to keep you in agony for days."

"You have a great future awaiting you, Saigo," Gabriel said. "A stage villain in a melodrama."

Done, Aristos. Reno's voice.

Let his house reno appear to come on line. Flash the image three seconds after he broadcasts the alert. Give me a countdown.

At your service, Aristos. Three.

Gabriel's daimones began keening.

Two.

Gabriel made himself absolutely still, pictured his strike in his mind.

One.

Gabriel sprang forward, claw-hand dropping like a hawk on the bridge of his enemy's nose just as he saw Saigo's eyes widen in shock at the projected image of the bloody bodies of his assistants. There was a crunch as cartilage gave way, and Gabriel's fingers gouged eye sockets again—Saigo staggered back while Gabriel followed up, one lunging strike after another at an enemy falling back too quickly for the attacks to have full effect.

BEAR: Kiai.

GABRIEL: *Die!*

SPRING PLUM: The lion will ever pursue his advantage.

VOICE: Die! Die, you bastard!

BEAR: Breathe. Focus. Strike.

WELCOME RAIN: You're pursuing a ball rolling downhill.

SPRING PLUM: The quarry may turn on his pursuers.

MATAGLAP: Kill him!

AUGENBLICK: Focused now. He's recovered from surprise.

RENO: He's ceased at-

> tempts to use the Hyper-
> logos.

Saigo's presence of mind returned: he tried to grab Gabriel's arm, hammer his elbow joint and pull him forward to convert the attack into a fall, but Gabriel twisted his arm free and slashed with the edge of one foot against Saigo's knee. Saigo's elbow slammed into Gabriel's armpit, spilling wind from his lungs; Gabriel lifted a knee into Saigo's groin, was blocked by Saigo's hip.

Gabriel fired strike after strike, each attack deflected by a parry that became, through furious metamorphosis, a strike. Each of Saigo's strikes was parried by one of Gabriel's counterblows. Gabriel struck high-low, hoping to confuse the defense; he shifted to broken time and back again; he cast feints within feints within other feints.

Nothing worked. Pain crackled through his arms from the force of diverting Saigo's strikes. He could feel his breath rasping in his throat.

As if unwittingly Gabriel let his guard slip high, hoping to lure Saigo into a groin strike that Gabriel could turn into a smash at his supporting leg. Saigo made the strike but anticipated the riposte, and Gabriel saw the counterstrike coming and blocked it.

BEAR: *Breathe!*

AUGENBLICK: He is fully focused. He will kill you if he can.

WELCOME RAIN: There's got to be a way into him.

SPRING PLUM: "A visible spear is easy to dodge, but it is difficult to defend against an arrow from the dark . . ."

GABRIEL: I *am* feinting!

VOICE: We'll cut each other to bits at this rate.

WELCOME RAIN: Give him something. Let him see it and want it.

CYRUS: Groin.

BEAR: A reserve of qi is rising through your heels . . .

CYRUS: < visualizing unprotected groin >

SPRING PLUM: "Knowing oneself and knowing the enemy, in a hundred battles there will be a hundred victories . . ."

GABRIEL: I *do* know him! I do!

Gabriel could think of nothing but to try again. Broken time. Feints. Exposing himself to attack. Everything failed.

He looked into Saigo's mild, melancholy eyes, eyes focused perfectly on his task, and Gabriel saw his own cause failing. The taunting sadist who promised pain had been a mask, and Saigo had no energy for that now—he was centered entirely on Gabriel's death.

Gabriel knew he couldn't stop him.

He had to let Saigo kill him.

He had to accept his own death.

He twisted his body, lowered his center of gravity, struck again and again— feints and preparation. He saw his death in Saigo's eyes.

VOICE: You're *failing!* Let me have your body.

SPRING PLUM: The gods will not accept the sacrifice unless it is heartfelt.

WELCOME RAIN: I concur. We'll have to let him really hurt us.

VOICE: Eyes. Ears. Throat. Let him have something, then turn his death over to me.

SPRING PLUM: < visualizing technique >

GABRIEL: Yes. Bear, summon qi. Horus, try to block the pain.

BEAR: A lake of qi boils in your body.

GABRIEL: Voice, take my body . . .

BEAR: Deep breath. No exhalation at moment of attack.

VOICE: *Now!*

Then he sprang, leaping high, both hands reaching for Saigo. He allowed his chin to lift as the Voice's savagery filled his heart. He was exposing everything, chin, throat, eyes, kidneys . . . Saigo responded with a straight-line strike for the throat, a stiff-armed Y-hand onto which Gabriel fell. The strike and Gabriel's plunging momentum combined to crush Gabriel's trachea.

Pain and panic paralyzed Gabriel's thoughts. But the body was already programmed, the arm that clotheslined Saigo and wrapped his head as Gabriel's body fell past him, the feet that sought purchase on the carpet, the shoulders that twisted, pulling Saigo over Gabriel's back by his neck, a neck that snapped with Saigo's own weight. Saigo fell to the floor with Gabriel on top of him. Gabriel snapped the neck again, more decisively this time.

For a moment he and Saigo were gazing into each other's eyes, and then Gabriel realized it was because Saigo's head was facing backwards over his shoulders.

He didn't have time to take note of exactly when Saigo died. **Voice,** he demanded, **where's the kitchen? I need a knife.**

Up. Back the way you came.

Gabriel's body rose to his feet, swayed, began to lumber down the corridor. **Try to exhale,** Bear suggested. **See if it's possible.**

Let me have my body. Horus, narrow . . .

The pain struck him full-force. He staggered, slammed into the wall, sent one of Saigo's portraits spinning. He would have gasped but it was impossible.

His stomach queased. He hoped it wouldn't try to vomit.

A lake of qi boils in your body, Bear chanted. **It fills your heart and spirit.** Gabriel got his feet moving again, skimmed the wall with one hand to aid in his balance.

Left. Second door on the right.

Aristos? Horus's voice. **You wanted me to do something?**

Narrow the capillaries in my throat. This is going to be bloody. He thought again. **Narrow *everything*. Everything but the blood supply to the brain. Reduce oxygen consumption. The muscles don't need it anymore.**

Horus began to chant body-control sutras. Fire burned deep in Gabriel's chest as he stepped into the kitchen. Stainless steel glowed softly in his whirling vision. Cooking robots stood inactive in corners, most of their tools already built into their design. Gabriel could only hope the place had been designed for human chefs as well.

He started pulling out drawers. Tools clattered on the floor. He staggered through them, found a heavy knife, missed it on the first grab as he almost toppled headfirst into the counter, then braced himself and picked it up again.

Gabriel sat down heavily, tipped his head back. He tried to hum in order to locate the voice box but couldn't get anything more than a breathy gurgle. He felt his throat with his left hand, tried to cry out from the sudden wave of pain. He thought he found the thyroid cartilage, the cricothyroid membrane just below it.

His vision narrowed, faded. He needed to get this over with one way or another. He put the point of the knife against what he thought was the cricothyroid membrane, steadied it with the right hand, then slammed the butt with his left palm.

Pain shrieked through him as the knife went in. Blood spurted over his hands. He hoped he hadn't hit the carotid artery—local variation in the throat was considerable, and blood vessels were tricky.

He still couldn't breathe. Panic flailed in him and he slapped the butt of the knife again, as hard as he could.

He felt the point strike the back of his throat, gagged, felt more pain. He took a grip on the grainy plastic handle of the knife and twisted, felt cartilage grind as he forced it apart—

—and he breathed.

Blood spattered as the long, full breath whistled out. He gurgled as he breathed in.

Never had air seemed as sweet.

He sat still for a long while and felt awareness return. His limbs tingled at the return of oxygen, his daimones sang as the strength-giving blood sped to his brain, light slowly infused to his vision.

When he felt ready he got to his feet. He found a fork and jabbed the tines into his incision, then twisted to keep it open. His lungs kept going into spasm in an attempt to cough the obstruction out. He held the fork there while he stuck the knife in his belt, then went to the armory. He found his own pistol there, fed it his codes, felt it come alive in his mind. He loaded it and went hunting.

Blood streamed from his broken nose, spattered down his chest at every exhalation.

As he opened the airlock door from the inside and stepped out onto the bridge he found the first Therápōn heading for the ship. No doubt she wanted to alert Saigo to the fact the renos were down.

The Therápōn stared for a moment at the sight, the pale bloody man with the bruised face and gaping wound in his throat, then turned to run. The homing bullets caught her before she'd gone two steps.

Gabriel stepped over her body and returned to the underground facility. The Voice's machine followed, its motors whining. Gabriel kept having to reach into his throat with his little finger and pull out half-formed blood clots.

Gabriel located the three other Therápontes and killed them in their beds.

The last was Remmy. Gabriel opened his door, stepped inside, commanded the lights to go on.

Remmy was awake, kneeling by his bed to say his prayers. Manfred was curled up on the mattress. The dog saw Gabriel and his tail began to beat at the blanket in welcome. Remmy looked up at the bloody apparition and turned pale.

"You're fighting God again," he said.

Gabriel shot him in the carotid artery with an anesthetic dart.

Remmy clawed for the dart. "Please don't, Gabriel," he whispered. "You can't fight God."

Just watch me, Gabriel thought, unable to speak.

Remmy fell.

Gabriel checked his vital signs and called Manfred to heel. The dog following cheerfully, Gabriel went to the prison compound. Clancy and the others had been in adjacent rooms, but he'd never known it.

His little finger kept dragging clots out of his throat.

The machine opened Clancy's door. He entered, brushed aside the deep red hangings—the room was identical to his own, he saw—and stepped inside.

Clancy, deep in dream, gave a cry and came up screaming.

She was pale and thin, her rich hair shorn. There were tears on her face from whatever she had dreamed. Her deep-shadowed eyes were slow to recognize him as he stepped into the light.

"You look like hell," she said.

You look like an angel.

He wanted to say it, but couldn't.

Chapter 18

LOUISE: What new hell is this?
    A bottle will make it heaven.

Gabriel rose from his couch in the nanosurgery room of the ruined medical unit. The Voice's machine had been built here, grown out of a Kam Wing container, and it had eaten half the room before it was finished. Much of the yellow-and-black tiled flooring was stripped away, revealing smooth parallel gouges in iron-grey bedrock. Manfred was asleep in one of them, lying lengthwise with his nose on his forepaws.

Remmy, hooked up to a life-maintenance reno, slept quietly on the floor. There was only one couch remaining, and that was needed for Gabriel.

Enough equipment had survived to treat Gabriel's injuries. Nanos had healed Gabriel's broken nose, were in the process of mending the crushed throat. The bleeding had been stanched, the hole in his trachea had been tidied, and he was still breathing through it, cleanly by now. He got to his feet and kissed Clancy gravely.

You are a glory, he broadcast to her. He'd revived her reno and daimones first thing, so they could talk.

"I'm a mess," she said, and ran a self-conscious hand over her cropped head. She was no longer a blushing rose, he thought sadly, but a pale and translucent lily. He kissed her again and put his arms around her. He sensed resistance in her frame.

Is there any medical treatment you require? Gabriel asked. **Have they injured you physically?**

"Yes, but it healed." She looked up at the crooked hump of his twice-broken nose. "I healed better than you, I think." She let out a breath, and her arms jerked up around him, hesitated, touched him. "I was afraid this was some game of theirs. It's not, is it?"

No. He looked at her. **You saved us by convincing them the sabotage was yours,** he said. **I want you to know how important that was.**

"It was . . . difficult." There were dark shadows in her eyes.

We can destroy them now.

Deep conviction hardened her features. "Yes, Aristos. Destroy them utterly."

Across the hall White Bear was restoring the renos of Yaritomo and Quiller. The machine had burned them out of their rooms, collected them, brought them to where Clancy was working on Gabriel in the medical unit.

With Manfred following, Gabriel and Clancy went to the yellow-and-black tiled room where the others worked. Once the renos were up and working, they went to a lounge, reclined on padded chairs and plush sofas, and went to work.

The subterranean installation's powerful renos were brought up and on line. One file after another fell to Yuan's trapdoors. Once they fell, Gabriel's Surveyors rewrote the password file to replace Yuan's passwords with Gabriel's.

First a list of the conspirators. Han Fu, Ctesias, Saigo, Zhenling—only four among the hundreds of Aristoi. About sixty Therápontes involved at one level or another, with hundreds of unwitting accomplices, people like Marcus who had been assigned work valuable to the conspirators without knowing what it was. Gabriel was mildly surprised that Astoreth hadn't been a member of Yuan's team—she shared his ideological agenda—but perhaps Yuan had deemed her too unstable.

He was probably right. She could never have kept the secret this long, would have boasted about it to someone.

But only four Aristoi. Gabriel's nightmare of a Logarchy torn by endless civil war began to fade. Those four wouldn't dare fight the others. They couldn't be that mad.

And Gabriel could do a lot of damage to them right from here.

Gabriel developed a checklist and moved through it methodically. He found where Yuan's battleships, the four whose power had combined to destroy the *Cressida*, were orbiting unmanned in Terrina's system, built phony Trojan-horse battleships in the oneirochronon that would respond to Yuan's orders as if they were the real thing, and then constructed mataglap on the real battleships in order to destroy them, turn them into asteroid-sized chunks of boiling slag. He took the plans for the ships from the Logarchy's files and hid them in a file that would respond only to his, not Yuan's, passwords. Then he substituted a file for the original that would build not warships but lumbering in-system freighters without even gravity generators to propel them.

If anyone was going to have warships, Gabriel thought, it would be his own side. If Yuan wanted any more of them, he'd have to build them from scratch.

Yuan's terraforming ships—there were dozens scattered through the Gaal Sphere—he treated in the same way. This task was easier, as each ship had active nano already on board. Now Yuan wouldn't be able to move his operation to another star system, at least not without starting the whole thing from the very beginning.

Quiller discovered, to Gabriel's amazement, that the *Pyrrho* had been rebuilt by Yuan and his conspirators. There were puppets on board, a puppet Gabriel and a puppet Marcus and thirty-three others, all en route to Illyricum. None of the puppets were currently active: they were held at minimum body function in life-suspension tanks until their arrival. In Yuan's files there was a logged debate among the conspirators concerning what to do with the puppets once they'd returned to Gabriel's domaine. Try to run Gabriel's domaine through the puppets? That would take a lot of effort on the part of the few conspirators involved. Arrange some sort of accident? Too suspicious after Cressida's death. Have Gabriel resign his domaine to one of the new Aristoi and head off on some sort of Yuan-like quest? No decision had been reached, but this last seemed safer.

The puppet *Pyrrho* had nano labs on board. Gabriel unleashed them, and that was the end of the puppets.

It was all very easy. This, Gabriel knew, was how Ariste Cressida had died. Yuan hadn't had to send a rocket filled with mataglap to *Sanjay*'s orbit; all he'd had to do was get into *Sanjay*'s reno and order it to build sabotage nano in Cressida's own labs.

Then Gabriel turned, grimly, to the rebel Aristoi. Han Fu and Ctesias were in their capitals, surrounded by vast populations: he didn't dare unleash mataglap on them. But Captain Yuan was on board *Discovery*, heading toward Dürer to survey terraforming operations, and Zhenling and her consort Gregory Bonham were on her yacht, with four of her Therápontes, en route to Tienjin.

Both, almost certainly, would have nano equipment aboard.

Yuan first, he decided.

He couldn't manage it. Yuan's trapdoors wouldn't work on Yuan's own on-board renos—he'd rewritten the software to make himself impervious to his own brand of meddling. Gabriel worked at it until sweat poured down his forehead from the effort, till he shouted with rage and pounded the arm of his chair. Neither his companions nor his daimones could break through Yuan's electronic wall.

As he fell back exhausted, Gabriel realized he hadn't heard from the Voice in hours. Methodically he traced the glyph for "beware" with his left hand, intoned the mantra *Tzai, dai, die.*

The Voice, when it came, sounded far away. **You wish me, Aristos?**

I am unable to penetrate Yuan's software. You are the expert on subverting his mechanisms.

I don't have anything more to teach you.

I thought you might have a strategy the rest of us overlooked.

I do not.

I want him dead.

He will not die today. Flatly.

There was a pause. **You left,** Gabriel said, **after the fight with Saigo.**

You didn't need me any longer.

I desire your aid.

I cannot help you in this task. The Voice sounded mournful.

I wish you to become a part of my daimonic array. I wish to name you and use you in the tasks ahead.

There was a lengthy pause. **You will not name me. I will not join you.**

The emergency is over, the conspiracy unmasked. There is no longer any reason for you to hide. It took you months to build that nano machine—with the right support you could have done it in only a few days.

There is always reason to hide. Sadly. **There are always new enemies.**

Alarm tingled through Gabriel's nerves. **When we spoke in Vila Real, you said that you came into existence in response to a perceived wrongness. Does that wrongness still exist? Or is there now another threat altogether?**

I cannot tell.

If you can't tell, there's no reason for you not to join me.

You only became aware of me through a mistake of my own. This will not reoccur. I will come if you require me, otherwise never.

I name you. Insistently. **I name you Infiltrator.**

That is not my name. The Voice faded, as if withdrawing down a long, unmeasurable distance.

Gabriel could not invoke him again.

It occurred to him to wonder if the Voice had learned from Yuan's universal access to the Logarchy's systems, if he had gained access to Gabriel's own personality and decision centers. If he, Gabriel, was now a puppet of his own subtle daimōn.

He didn't think so, he concluded, but he would never know for certain.

He thought again of Yuan and how the older Aristos had made himself invulnerable to tachyonic tampering. He wished suddenly that he hadn't taken steps to destroy Yuan's fleet, that he'd ordered the battleships to Dürer to destroy the *Discovery.*

Too risky. Better to destroy the warships than to discover, at the last and worst moment, that Yuan had some way of seizing them again.

Which brought him to Zhenling. He began to give the orders to break into Zhenling's nano labs and ordering the automated equipment to create a fast-growing mataglap nano. He began, then hesitated.

She thought I died aboard Cressida, he thought. *She conspired with the others to ambush and kill me.*

Yes, he thought. He had to behead the conspiracy if he could.

He gave the commands, and decided to despise the part of him that mourned.

To prevent her calling for help, he ordered any emergency transmission routed through Yuan's communication network to be blocked.

After that last order he felt uneasy. **This place is not our**

own, he told the others. **Let's repair the *Cold Voyager* and get off-planet.**

After disabling the nano equipment, Clancy reminded. **So they don't do any of this to us.**

Yes, he thought. Absolutely.

He rose from the oneirochronon into the Realized World, saw the others rising from their couches, heard the breath that whistled from his cricothyroidostomy. His nape hair rose. A sudden moment of doubt and terror possessed him.

He was in the Realized World without guidance. He'd just killed five people without even thinking about it, and given orders that would destroy half a dozen more.

He felt his insides twist. Sweat beaded on his forehead. Suddenly he couldn't understand how he'd dared to do any of this. Kill an Aristos face-to-face, arrange for the death of another, defy the First Aristos.

No, he thought. It was Yuan's conditioning that was causing this uncertainty, this sickening dependence.

Aristoi did not doubt, he reminded himself. The Aristoi simply *became*, while they lived they *were*, and the rest of the universe conformed.

Doubt was a thing he could not afford. Now or ever.

He rose and gave orders to his followers.

"I will follow my God."

Remmy was still drowsy from his enforced sleep; he pushed his long hair out of his face and looked at Gabriel with sadness in his eyes. "How could you betray him again?"

"It was he who betrayed all of us," Gabriel said.

Remmy shook his head. "You cannot beat the Lord Yuan," he said. "Not he who created all of us. He will live forever and revenge himself on those who defied him."

"All humanity will hate him."

"Then all humanity will be deceived." Remmy's voice was eerily calm. "But I misspeak—not *all* humanity. I am part of humanity, and I will remain loyal to my Creator."

Gabriel hesitated, moved by the power of Remmy's faith. Misplaced, built on erroneous information, but utterly sincere. For a moment Remmy's quiet insistence had caused him to doubt.

But that was only because Yuan had conditioned him to doubt, to dependence.

Gabriel firmed his stance of authority, found the reflex of command return.

"I ask you to repent," Remmy said. "You must cease your rebellion and beg the Lord Yuan for mercy."

"I think not," Gabriel said.

"May I then simply leave? I do not desire to be in your company."

FLASH. The alert sounded in Gabriel's skull, and his nerves leaped. But no—it was Zhenling, who had just discovered that her ship was being eaten from the inside out.

Zhenling was using Terrina as a relay station, not firing her tachline beams straight to *Discovery* or Persepolis. The transmission, therefore, would be blocked. Gabriel ordered his reno to record the transmissions but not bother him with the details.

He was killing her, he thought.

Good.

"May I leave, Ghibreel?" Remmy repeated his question.

"No," Gabriel said. He was more brusque than he wanted to be. "I will take you to my home, and care for you there. Once you have more information you may change your mind about Yuan and all the rest."

"Do you have the Argosy Vassals where you live, Gabriel?" Remmy asked. "Because even they could not change my heart." He stepped closer, and his voice turned imploring. "I won't do you any harm, Ghibreel. I couldn't even if I wanted to. I simply want to wander the world and preach the gospel to those who will listen. Won't you let me do that, Ghibreel?"

A death sentence, Gabriel thought. The Argosy Vassals, or someone like them, would kill him quickly enough.

He thought of Zhenling dying in her boiling, bubbling ship.

"No," Gabriel said. "You'll come with me."

He'd save one casualty of his love, if he could.

Remmy didn't resist when Gabriel asked him to come with him to *Cold Voyager*. When they came aboard, Gabriel found that the damage to the cargo hatch had been repaired and that Saigo's body, and that of the Therápōn he had killed on the gangway, had been moved out of the way to a spare room in the Terrina base.

Gabriel's blood still spattered the carpet.

Gabriel assigned Remmy a room and ordered the others, and the ship's reno, to keep a watch on him. He didn't think Remmy could sabotage anything, but it was barely possible that he'd try to do something violent, possibly to himself.

Cold Voyager's nano labs had been effectively sabotaged, the equipment wrecked. All Yuan's trapdoors had been sealed, though it was possible there were more that couldn't be found.

It was time to lift off and let the Logarchy know what had come to pass.

> *"With ravished ears*
> *The Monàrch hears*
> *Assumes the god,*
> *Affects to nod,*
> *And seems to shake the spheres."*

Suspense hummed in Gabriel's nerves as he incanted Dryden's words. He didn't know whether this would work or not.

Yuan wasn't the only one who could use trapdoors. Gabriel had built this one into the personal communications system he'd ordered Fleta to build.

He didn't think he'd told the password—pass*poem*—to Yuan, but he couldn't recall precisely what had happened when he'd come apart.

He didn't want to think about it, didn't want to remember. Either this would work or it wouldn't.

At your service, Aristos.

Gabriel exulted as the Illyricum reno came on line. His private system was still operational, Gabriel was in control of it, and furthermore the Dryden recitation had just locked everyone else out, whether they had the correct passwords or not.

He'd managed to keep at least one secret. Or perhaps, if he'd given it away, they'd thought he was just babbling verse.

Quickly he moved through the system. It was largely intact, though of course most of his codes had been broken, and the passwords he'd given Yuan had allowed the conspiracy to delete all his transmissions and reports about the Gaal Sphere. This was repairable—he could change the code keys and there were copies of the Gaal reports in Yuan's own data banks. He moved them back, put them under his Seal.

The repaired *Cold Voyager* was a half hour out of Terrina. In a majestic rumble of mighty hydraulics, the ceiling of the ship bay had opened like a trapdoor, spilling tons of springtime snow in a minor avalanche, and Saigo's ship rose into the daylight sky, sunlight glowing on its silver skin. Yuan's hidden base had been at the height of over four thousand meters in a huge upthrust mountain range vast as the Himalayas, sparsely populated with no villages in the immediate vicinity. If care were taken, and ships moved in and out at night and without lights, the place could easily enough have kept its secret.

The *Cold Voyager*'s departure in daylight was probably observed by more than a few people. For a moment Gabriel even toyed with the idea of leaving the huge doorway open and allowing the neighbors to get an eyeful.

No, he decided. They might find things that would only get them into trouble. He ordered the door closed behind him.

The inhabitants of Terrina would soon enough get used to the sight of huge ships in the sky.

Just after lift-off Gabriel reviewed the transmissions from Zhenling. She and her crew had discovered the mataglap soon after it was released, but had been unable to contain it. They'd abandoned ship for a small gravity-powered shuttlecraft, and were returning to Terrina while continuing their attempts to contact their fellow conspirators.

Gabriel presumed that they might soon change their minds about their destination.

He moved down his checklist and got to business.

He left his own private communications network and entered the Hyperlogos. First he shut down Yuan's entry, freezing data, altering Yuan's trapdoors into the Hyperlogos so that they would respond only to his signal. The conspirators could still communicate with one another via direct tach-line, provided they had a substantial enough lock on one another's locations, but there was nothing he could do to prevent that.

< Priority One > FLASH to Shikibu, al-Fawzi, Zoë, Reneri, Webster. Order "Stand by."

Done, Aristos.

The Prohedroi of Gabriel's five planets—Shikibu of Illyr-icum, al-Fawzi of Vissarion, Zoë of Lascarios, Reneri of Cos, and the newly elected Webster of Brightkinde—all appeared in the oneirochronon, their skiagénoi showing various stages of respect, alarm, and puzzlement.

"This is Gabriel Aristos Vissarionovich." Gabriel flashed them an oneirochronic image of his seal. In the oneiro-chronon he wore a suit of glowing, rippling armor, orna-mented German High Gothic blackened and chased with silver. It was an image he'd found in his files—he'd worn it long ago for an oneirochronic costume ball with a medieval theme. An iron mace was in his hand, behind him a banner with his seal blazoned on it.

Microwatt lasers scanned his face in Saigo's suite aboard *Cold Voyager.* Let them see the broken nose, he thought, the disheveled hair. He'd earned them both.

He took a Posture of Esteem. "I order you to convert

your economies to a ninety-percent total war footing at once," he said. "Mobilization of civilians will begin immediately, and construction of warships and weapons within hours. Within a short interval I will tell you the names of our enemies. I command obedience and discipline. That is all."

The premieres all stared at Gabriel and one another, their discomfiture visible even in the oneirochronon, but conditioning took hold and they all gave Gabriel Postures of Respect.

"As you wish, Archegétes," they chorused.

"Fini," Gabriel said. He smiled and waited. That had put the fox among the chickens, sure enough.

FLASH queries from Aristoi began arriving within minutes, soon became a high-priority landslide. No one could give a command like that without triggering every alarm in the Logarchy. Gabriel replied to each inquiry that they should stand by for a tachline signal at Channel 6000. Then he loaded the oneirochronic background program for his suite at Persepolis and appeared there, still in his shining, weightless armor.

Chamber music rose from the anthropomorphic quintet. The phantom carpet caressed his feet. An otter in livery offered him a tray of sensual party treats.

Briefly at a loss, he gazed at his suite for a long moment. Unease filled him.

He didn't feel comfortable here.

He canceled the program and hastily assembled another, a bowl-shaped green-grassed amphitheater surrounded by distant rolling plains, a blue sky overhead with high billowing clouds. He didn't have time for a greater level of detail.

In what spring tide will I see again my old village? he recited. *I envy the geese, returning whence they came.*

Perhaps Yuan, with his total corruption of the Hyperlogos, had succeeded in overthrowing the Logarchy.

Lucky thing Gabriel built another one.

At the invocation of *Genji's* flying geese, signals were fired from Fleta's transmitters. Nanos began assembling tachline relays on the skins of almost every ship in the Logarchy.

The Seals of Aristoi began to appear, asking entry to the new communications link. Gabriel let every Aristos into the system except Han Fu and Ctesias. Zhenling, floating in her lifeboat, didn't even try.

Sitting in his stateroom on *Cold Voyager*, he took a careful breath. The time had come.

His armored skiagénos appeared on the lip of the oneirochronic amphitheater. He hefted his mace and allowed the others to appear, Pan Wengong nearest. Aristoi surged forward, demanding explanations of his behavior. Gabriel bowed deeply to the impassive image of Pan Wengong. "May I address the assembly, Eldest?" he asked.

Pen Wengong's slitted eyes moved only slightly. "You may, Aristos."

Gabriel faced the assembly in a Posture of Confidence. Doubts flickered in his belly and he banished them.

Gradually the turmoil, within and without, subsided.

"I come before the Aristoi with accusations of murder, treason, and unacceptable and covert usage of technology," he said. "I bring also a charge of corruption of the universal Hyperlogos, which is the foundation of political stability in the Logarchy."

The Aristoi, silent before him, swayed like a forest in a great wind.

Gabriel spoke again, and the universe changed.

The war was very short. Ctesias surrendered as soon as the word reached him, and placed himself and the Therápontes who conspired with him under house arrest pending the arrival of Logarchy forces. Han Fu fled in his private yacht with the handful of Therápontes who still supported him, then tried to build a battleship out of asteroid material in a system fifteen light-years from his capital. His use of the Hyperlogos betrayed his location, he created (with the phony nano design Gabriel planted) only an in-system freighter, and Gabriel by this point had warships of his own, operating under the Lo-

garchy's flag: a squadron surrounded Han Fu's location and
compelled his surrender.

It was not clear precisely what Han Fu intended to accomplish with the enormous power of this fantasy warship. Perhaps it was only intended to make him feel better about his
chances.

Saigo's surviving Therápontes, those he'd left behind in
his own domaine, alone and without direction, surrendered
quietly.

Of Captain Yuan there was no sign. He had removed
himself from the Hyperlogos entirely, at least as far as could
be detected.

Only Zhenling acted in such a way as to compel Gabriel's
admiration. When word of the situation reached her, she
altered the course of her escape ship to Illyricum.

She would surrender in Gabriel's domaine, she announced, and at her trial before the assembled Aristoi she
would defend her actions.

Even in her small shuttle, she could have got away. She
was closer to the Gaal Sphere than the Logarchy, and Gabriel,
in his unarmed vessel, couldn't stop her. Instead, in her tiny
ship, she was experiencing a foretaste of the imprisonment
that was her inevitable fate.

Sadness wafted through Gabriel at the news of her decision. Her behavior in the dock, he knew, would be exemplary,
proud, and brave.

And hopeless. He almost wished she had run.

That was the end of the conspiracy, barring the remote
chance that Captain Yuan would turn up and challenge the
Aristoi to a debate. The economies of Gabriel's domaine were
returned to a peacetime footing.

Gabriel still had a four-month-long voyage ahead of him,
the long claustrophobic journey back to the Logarchy, in
Saigo's cramped rooms, with only his four companions and
their memories.

They were all wounded, he knew. And the long healing
would not end with the journey.

Chapter 19

ANIMAL TAMER: Walk in, walk into my menagerie
Life and death for all to see.

Gabriel's mind returned from the oneirochronon and reclaimed his body from Horus. He felt the weight of the sleeping Manfred on his lap, saw Clancy patiently waiting on Saigo's boxlike bunk next to him.

"I came to tell you," Clancy said, "that Remmy's implant went well."

"He didn't resist?"

"No," Clancy said. "I don't think he quite understood what it meant. He knew it would help him to understand Demotic, and that was important to his . . . missionary work."

"If we *show* him the oneirochronon," Gabriel said. "If we give him access to the Hyperlogos, perhaps . . ."

Clancy shook her head. "We must be very careful. Step by step. He will choose to believe it, or he will not."

Sorrow floated through Gabriel. "I wish to heal him. Heal all of us."

Clancy scratched Manfred's head. "Horus told me you were just in Persepolis?"

"Yes."

"And . . . ?"

"The news? Ctesias had to be rescued from a mob that was storming his Residence. He's been removed to a more secure confinement in orbit. The Demos were outraged when the oneirochronic recordings of Terrina were released. It seems they identified more with the wretched starvelings of Terrina than with the Aristoi who put them there. Those sights terrified them."

"So should it terrify us all."

"This incident might serve as a caution for those who consider the Demos to be too passive and too polite."

"A pity it came too late."

Gabriel sighed, wiped the sweat that prickled his brow. "We're meeting every day now. An almost permanent session. The logistics of the rescue mission to the Gaal Sphere are incredible. Thousands of ships. Hundreds of thousands of teachers, technicians, medical personnel. Decisions on what to attempt first, who to teach. We'll have to concentrate on the children, I fear—most of the adults are so damaged that many may be beyond help. But what will they say when we take their children, or worse, their childrens' minds? Access to the conspirators' own data will make some things easier, but . . ." He threw up his hands. "And I'm so tired. Sick of it all."

"At least these meetings are a routine you can fall into." She took his hand. "I'm trying to establish a routine here, Gabriel. Routines help. At times I feel quite myself, and at others almost helpless with doubt and terror."

Gabriel took a breath, let it out. "Yes. I feel much the same. When there were things to do, when I had straightforward, obvious tasks . . . when I had Saigo to kill and you to liberate, when I had conspirators to denounce or neutralize or pursue with a fleet, I operated well enough. And there were elements of the Voice's personality still dominant, and the Voice is very self-assured."

"The Voice?"

"A paranoid and psychotic daimōn, but an able one. A kind of hidden genius I didn't know I had. I'll tell you about him later." He shook his head. "But now, when there is little to do but make speeches at Persepolis, I find myself beset with blindness and fear."

Her eyes gazed into his. "They broke us," she said simply.

"They did. And people like us—we're complex machinery, Blushing Rose, and when broken we don't fix easily." He took a long, ragged breath. "I'm finding it very difficult to face my peers," he said. "Those ranks of supremely confident people, all so self-assured, so certain . . . What am I doing among them, I wonder? I've never experienced such doubt. I've never experienced doubt at all. And I'm supposed to be their . . . savior."

She put her arms around him, rested her head on his shoulder.

"What's Yuan done to us? We're his creatures, and he destroyed us."

"Not entirely," Gabriel said. "It was we who destroyed his schemes, remember. The two of us. You most of all, pretending the sabotage was yours, suffering my punishment for me. Thanks to us, he's in desperate flight with an enraged humanity crying for his blood."

"Wherever he is," Clancy said, "he's not as lost as we are."

Gabriel took a long breath, let it out. "No," he said. "He will never face doubt until the moment of his death."

"Hail, Athánatos kaí Sotéhr."

Akwasibo Ariste was in a deep bow with her hands low, the most respectful of the Postures of Formal Regard. Gabriel returned the more informal Second Posture and left his Persepolis apartment, closing the unreal jade doors behind him.

Akwasibo straightened and smiled. Her skiagénos was wearing a burnt-orange robe tied over one shoulder, heavy silver jewelry, hair braided and piled atop her head. She took

Gabriel's arm and began the walk to the Apadana. Her arm was pleasantly warm.

Athánatos kaí Sotéhr—Immortal and Savior—that was now Gabriel's title. The Aristoi had conferred it on him a few days before.

In another few minutes the Aristoi would meet in yet another emergency session. There was one every day.

"Have you heard the news?" Akwasibo said.

"It depends." He tried to be lighthearted, projected a vigor he didn't feel.

"On what?"

"On which news."

"Ah." She smiled again. "We've been tracing Yuan's movements through the Hyperlogos. They were all on record, just hidden from us."

"You've found more trapdoors?"

"Yes. Minor ones, though—it's easy enough to find them if one knows to look. But what I just discovered is that he'd been tampering with exam results."

Gabriel stiffened in surprise.

"Yuan's arrogance is beyond comprehension!" Akwasibo said. "He's been meddling with the linchpins of our civilization. The accuracy of the Hyperlogos and the fairness of the exams are the touchstones of our peace."

"Peace wasn't precisely what he was after," Gabriel said. "And that arrogance was lucky at least for me—if he wasn't so colossally arrogant he would have killed me, not tried to convert me."

"Han Fu should never have been an Aristos," Akwasibo continued. "He missed by more than forty points. But Yuan approved of his ideas, and knew he could manipulate the man—so he added points to his score and then covered up the tampering."

"Anyone else?"

"There are two people that he disrated. Mari Toth and Joel Berlitz, who passed eleven and twenty-six years ago respectively. They were both ultraorthodox, and Mari Toth was an evolutionist whose work was pointing in different directions from Saigo's, so Yuan decided to cut off the threat by devaluing the source."

"Have they been told?"

"They will be shortly." Akwasibo's head rose on its long neck, a kind of hydraulic preening gesture. "Gregory Bonham should have passed the exams twice. And Zhenling should not have passed even once, though her score was very close."

Anger flashed through Gabriel at this manipulation, anger followed by a wave of profound sadness for Zhenling. "She was easier to manipulate than he," he said.

"That's how Yuan must have seen it."

"And her anger over Bonham's failing was Yuan's key to her personality. She must have known that Bonham was better. That any system that passed her and not him must be badly in error."

"It will make their trial difficult," Akwasibo said. "If we accuse Zhenling and Han Fu of misusing the imperium of the Aristoi, they can claim they shouldn't have been Aristoi in the first place."

Gabriel shook his head. "I'm glad I'm not in charge of the trial proceedings."

"You'll be the chief witness for the prosecution."

"If I must. But I pity them more than anything."

Akwasibo looked at him levelly. "Even the most foolish of the Demos knows that murder is wrong, Gabriel. They are guilty of killing over forty people, counting both *Sanjay* and *Cressida*. They thought you were aboard *Cressida* when they destroyed it."

"Yes." He felt weak and dizzy at these revelations, but Horus kept his skiagenetic face impassive.

They rose into the big square before the Apadana. Gabriel found himself looking for the gold gleam of Captain Yuan's statue atop the Mount of Mercy, found it gone. Above, a pale moon, the great reserve data store of the Hyperlogos, floated in the pale blue sky.

Gabriel paused for a moment while memories floated through him.

"Do you remember when we were last here?" Akwasibo asked. "All this was just beginning."

"Yes," Gabriel said. "I remember."

Plumed Aristoi thronged the vast hall of the Apadana. As Gabriel entered the Aristoi turned, offered Postures of Regard, and burst into applause. Gabriel acknowledged their ovation with a Posture of Respect.

He had dressed his skiagénos in a simple white chiton and sandals. He didn't wear elaborate clothing any longer, not once the war was over and he'd put aside his scalloped suit of armor. As an advertisement for himself, the finery had seemed more than pointless.

All considered, he thought, he had little left to prove to anyone.

Pan Wengong called the meeting to order. Tallchief gave a report of his construction of a habitat for the Great Criminals, as Yuan's conspirators were now called. Following their trial and conviction, they would live together on an artificial asteroid that Tallchief had already built. It had no gravity generators, and would be towed from place to place in Tallchief's floating deep-space domaine. The criminals would have a very strictly limited, largely passive interaction with the Hyperlogos. Killer mataglap would be stored in Blushing Rose[1] containers in the habitat, would be let loose at any escape attempt.

It was hoped, after a passage of time, the conspirators would see the error of their ways, repent, and be restored to citizenship among the Demos.

Never would they be allowed access to anything but the most benign technology. That would be an eternal condition of their parole.

After the report had been received by the Aristoi, Virtue's Icon asked permission to speak.

"I wish to address the issue of the safety of the Logarchy," she said. "It was the criminal Yuan's intention to raise a civilization of barbarians on our borders. He took plans for warships that were unwisely left under a corrupted Seal in the Hyperlogos and used these to attack the ship *Cressida*. He *may* still have plans for these ships aboard his own vessel, and in any case he is capable of re-creating this unsound and dangerous work, given time."

Plain in her dull grey uniform, she stood out among the gaudy skiagenoi of the Aristoi. Nothing detracted from the fanatic, assured gleam in her eyes.

"The Logarchy is not out of danger. The only warships we have constructed are few in number. In any case, once our rescue mission arrives in the Gaal Sphere, the barbarized and aggressive genetics of Yuan's creations will soon be in contact with our own populations."

Satisfaction glowed from her face. "I intend to defend the integrity and hegemony of the Logarchy by reintroducing these genetics among my own populations and raising the children in an ideologically sound environment that will guarantee their loyalty. I will also inaugurate a program of constructing a fleet of warships to defend the Logarchy and my own domaine against treason and aggression."

The hall rang with the cries of Aristoi wishing to speak. Gabriel had the opposite reaction, was struck dumb by the horrifying specter of Virtue's Icon barbarizing her population and creating warships of unspeakable power.

She is as fanatic as the Criminals. St.-John's Sealed voice in Gabriel's ear.

Gabriel sent a silent electric signal to Pan Wengong that he wished to speak.

"Gabriel Aristos," the Eldest said, and nodded. The others fell into respectful silence.

Back in *Cold Voyager*, sweat broke out over Gabriel's forehead. He could feel his limbs tremble. Sometimes addressing other Aristoi terrified him, sometimes not. The unpredictability of his stage fright was one of the more terrifying aspects of the problem.

Horus held Gabriel's skiagénos impassive, his tone level. None of his hesitation was visible to the others.

"I respect and applaud the Icon's resolution in the face of danger," Gabriel said. "The defense of the Logarchy must be provided for. But may I suggest that, rather than unilateral action, a resolution be undertaken here in Persepolis to provide for a communal defense, based on a common and reasonable consensus? That each domaine be requested to provide a certain number of ships and other forces held ready at all times?"

Communal, consensus. Some of the Icon's favorite slogans, despite her disinclination to abide by them. Still, the words might reach her.

"Aristos Gabriel's suggestion is a reasonable one," Virtue's Icon replied. "But a common defense may be subverted through common means—we have seen how this may be done through the Great Criminal Yuan's subversion of the Hyperlogos. Any forces under my command will have their security guaranteed by *me*. And I assure my comrades of the Logarchy that I will attend to this matter with the utmost diligence. None of the Great Criminals, their undiscovered collaborators, or future imitators will be able to penetrate *my* security."

Sebastian's silver sphere floated on a graceful arcing curve over the heads of the assembly. "Permit me to observe," he remarked, "that our beloved Icon has obviously given this matter much thought. Perhaps the ideal Form for our mutual security is not Form but non-Form—for each to raise forces as she thinks best, and thus prevent the Great Criminals from subverting the whole."

What, Gabriel wondered, were the two fanatics up to? The one who spoke of community was now acting alone, defiantly building warships, while the one who idealized Form was now speaking of non-Form. Something had clearly been arranged between them.

There had been a profusion of private tachline links set up in the Logarchy since Yuan's schemes had been revealed. Any number of deals could have been struck in private, off the

record, outside the Hyperlogos . . . deals that, lost from
history, might never be known, might never function in the
record to provide examples to future leaders.

You're withdrawing from the civic life of the republic. That
was what Zhenling had said when she'd discovered Gabriel
was setting up his own tachline rig.

Now half the Aristoi had them. Private communications
at the beginning, now private warships and, within the next
generation, private barbarian hordes.

Perhaps the war that had terrified Gabriel would happen
after all. Perhaps he had only delayed it by a generation.

He had nothing more to add to the debate. In his mind's
eye he saw Virtue's barbaric legions swarming across the Logarchy, fanatic warriors raised only to obedience and destruction.

"There has been a great increase of interest in the Faith,
Athánatos Kouros," said Gabriel's mother. "I am moving
very carefully, so as to make the correct doctrinal interpretation of recent events."

"I trust it is a happy occupation," Gabriel said.

Vashti Geneteira smiled. "It is my life's work."

Gabriel suppressed unease.

A vast oneirochronic cathedral space expanded behind
her sculpted face. The sacred symbols she wore in her piled-
up hair glittered with gold and gems. Song hung in the air like
hovering angels, all to the glory of Gabriel.

"If the Logarchy in general could be said to have a God,"
Vashti said, "Yuan was he. Now you have engaged him in
divine battle and overthrown him after great personal sacrifice. The Demos are terrified of the images broadcast from the
Gaal Sphere, all the wretchedness and misery of ordinary
people betrayed by the Aristoi who created them." Her long
eyes glittered. "Yuan has provided the Church of the New
Thoth with something it lacked, Kouros. A divinity of evil to
oppose yours of goodness. Now we have a god of darkness to
battle our god of light, and furthermore our god can be objec-

tively proven to have fought and beaten this new Ahriman."
She smiled. "There is something in people that longs for the
reassurance of fact. In this case we have fact on our side. The
Demos are reassured—you *do* intervene on their behalf. Even
the other Aristoi have anointed you as Savior. We're converting by the thousands."

She sighed happily. "You've done so *well* for us, child!
Poor Marcus and the others will be saints, of course, as well
as your unborn." Her brows narrowed. "And we'll have anti-
saints as well. The Ariste Temptress and the Warrior of Hell
who killed our Kouros only to discover that you were, in fact,
immortal."

Marcus had joined the *Cressida* in order to avoid Vashti
and keep her from the unborn girl: now, Gabriel realized,
she'd have them both forever, prisoners of her doctrine.

Contempt simmered in Gabriel's thoughts. "Is there anything else I can do to assist you?" he asked.

Vashti looked tolerant. "I know you meant that face-
tiously, child, but there are a few things you can do. That fork
you used to hold your windpipe open—did you keep it?"

"No. It's back in Yuan's base."

"A pity. It would make a nice relic." She frowned,
thought for a moment. "Try not to catch up with Yuan anytime soon, will you? It helps enormously to have our wicked
god out there somewhere, conspiring against the peace . . .
The more unease among the Demos, the better they will desire
the comforts of faith."

And if the Demos knew the kind of thinking going on at
Persepolis, Gabriel thought, they'd be even more terrified.

"I don't believe Yuan's apprehension is imminent," he
said.

Vashti smiled. "Oh, good. An eternal struggle is so much
more interesting than a limited one, don't you think?"

The Hyperlogos buzzed with rumors. Virtue's Icon was building warships, training troops. Her nervous neighbors were
looking to their own defenses. Sebastian had done nothing so

far, but was known to be working on plans to assemble warships of various types if he found it needful.

An elite and very secret commission appointed by Pan
Wengong reported on two more Mudras of Domination that
could be used against Aristoi. The Aristoi were urged to
condition themselves against them.

Others may have developed mudras of their own. In
secret. It was impossible to tell.

"It's an interesting tool," Remmy said. He sat in his tiny
bed-sitting room and spoke Demotic with a slight Beukhomanan accent. The fine golden hair on the backs of his hands
glittered in the light of Saigo's phony oil lamps.

"But of course it's a trap," he went on. "Truth has been
so cunningly interwoven with deception that I must make
very careful judgments concerning what I've seen."

Gabriel shook his head. "The implant is not a trap. There
is nothing false in the Hyperlogos."

"How can it *not* be false?" Remmy countered. He bent
forward out of his chair to scratch Manfred behind the ears.
"This 'oneirochronon'—" Gabriel could hear the quotes in
his voice. "—it's false. There are *pictures*. They're like dreams,
they appear in my head when I call them."

"I have shown you nothing false," Gabriel said. Remmy
and everyone else from the Gaal Sphere had been declared
wards of the Logarchy, a legal status like that of children,
which meant their use of the Hyperlogos could be controlled.
Gabriel had given him access only to historical records, scenes
of distant places, to music, poetry, clearly labeled drama.
None of the oneirochronic fantasies that might confuse him.

Remmy straightened in his chair, flipped his hands.
"How can a vision be true?"

"How can you learn to speak a foreign language just by
having Clancy put a tiny machine in your head? It's real.
We're really speaking Demotic, a language you didn't know
only a few days ago. These other images aren't visions—
they're images of things that exist."

Remmy looked at Gabriel with eyes of utter simplicity. "They're a deception, Gabriel. You wish to lead me from the path of virtue."

"Experience will show you otherwise. You can *visit* these places I show you."

"No doubt some of them are real enough." Remmy looked at Gabriel with something akin to pity. "I've seen in the Hyperlogos that there is a church devoted to worshipping you, but you admit to me that it's a false church and you are a false god. You could put a stop to it but you won't. You also admit that there are demons in your head."

"They're not demons. They're not from *outside*—"

"No doubt that's what they tell you. But I have no doubt that they are from the deepest pit of Hell, and that they're prompting you to turn against God and establish your own false religion to lead even more people astray. Why should I follow you when my heart and my intelligence tell me otherwise?"

Gabriel entertained for a moment the fantasy of turning Remmy over to his mother for the furtherance of his education. Let them debate each other endlessly—the new St. Paul versus the new Olympias.

"Continue to use the oneirochronon," Gabriel said. "It will not show you anything false."

Remmy started to jerk his chin before his reno reminded him to nod. "In truth," he said, "I learn much."

"Don't be afraid of it."

"I have my faith to guide me. And I will pray for guidance from Iuso and his saints."

They rose and kissed one another good-bye. There wasn't a trace of passion in Remmy's embrace.

Manfred followed as Gabriel walked to Clancy's stateroom, knocked, entered. Clancy, wearing a simple long Chinese gown of white silk, sat on a stiff little chair holding a flute.

"I've been with Remmy," he said.

Sadness crossed her face. It occurred to Gabriel that he saw it often there. "Ah," she said. "The poor man."

Her hands were in her lap, but her fingers moved along the stops and keys of the flute. "Am I interrupting your playing?" Gabriel asked. "I can leave."

She looked up at him. "Please stay. I was playing only for company."

Manfred trotted up to her and received caresses. Gabriel sat on the carpet at her feet and looked at her. Her color was returning with liberty and exercise. Her skin tone was much better, and she was putting on weight.

"You seem improved," he said.

She sighed. "I suppose I am. I can feel things knitting in my mind. But it's slow, Gabriel, terribly slow . . ."

They met daily, all the Surveyors, for talk and exercise. Discussion of their problems, how best to reassemble themselves after the isolation, deprivation, and shattering of personality that had been their lot. Gabriel and Clancy had access to all the available psychological data about prisoners, about conditioning, about archaic brainwashing attempts from the bad old days of humanity . . . all of it was available to draw on.

They would all heal. They knew what steps to take, what to avoid, what to hope for. The process was slow but inevitable, and its sureness gave them hope.

But still doubts plagued Gabriel. No Aristos had ever been in this situation. The psychological makeup of each Aristos was unique and complex, certifiably unquantifiable, and his had been shattered or altered. Only a cunning, psychotic daimōn had seen him through it. When his mind healed, would it still be that of an Aristos?

He worried as well about Clancy. She had been so clearly on her way to becoming an Ariste, to achieving fusion and synthesis. It was his desperate hope that the process had only been sidetracked, not halted in its tracks.

"Remmy's calm is so unearthly," Gabriel said. "So unlike him. When I met him"—he'd almost said, *when I knew him*—"he was so full of doubt, of uncertainty. And now—"

"The deluded are always filled with absolutes," Clancy said. "The rest of us have to live with ambiguity."

Gabriel looked up at her. "Was I deluded, then?" he asked. "Because I was always so full of absolute certainty."

She left the thought unanswered.

"Remmy and I have changed places," Gabriel said. "I'm the one beset by doubt, and he's the assured one."

She reached out to him, stroked his hair. "Poor human," she said.

"That's what Yuan's made of us," Gabriel said. "You asked me a few days ago what it was he'd done, and the answer just occurred to me. What the Logarchy's done in the last centuries was create a superior type of person, one immune from deprivation, doubt, fear . . . all the horrors we saw on Terrina. But Yuan reverted us to that earlier, desperate type— he made us human."

He paused, her hand stroking his hair, and his fingers formed a Mudra of Denial. Sudden passion filled his heart.

"I hate it!" he said. "I don't want to be human anymore."

"Neither do I," she said. "It's not a good place to be."

"There is a new affectation among the young people in the Logarchy," said Dorothy St.-John. Today she was a scarlet maple leaf floating on the oneirochronic breezes beneath the magnificent roof of the Apadana. "You might be interested in it, Flame. People are having their noses broken, or altered to appear to be broken. Some of them are giving themselves other disfigurements. As jewelry they wear, around their necks, either a fork or something suggestive of a fork." The maple leaf did a little airy somersault, bright against the gold and vermilion of the pillared ceiling. "Fashion à la Gabriel. Don't you find that interesting?"

"Most of us have been imitated one way or another," Gabriel said.

"In general they don't identify with our *pain*," St.-John said; and then her voice turned reflective. "Of course, in general, we don't have any."

Gabriel watched her turn graceful circles in the air. Aristoi continued to file into the Apadana, giving and receiving formal greeting. Back in *Cold Voyager*, Gabriel broke out in a spasm of trembling. Sweat soaked his clothing.

Horus kept his skiagénos in a contemplative stance, his voice steady and thoughtful.

"Let us hope pain remains an affectation for them," he said. "And not a reality."

The leaf nodded sagely. "Apropos pain, Tunku Iskander has written a dramatic work about you. Sort of a Noh drama—it's called *Passion Play*, and you're understood to be a sort of Christ figure. The language is full of incredible power and vigor, even if the action is a little monotonous—endless torture followed by your violent revenge."

"How un-Christ-like of me. I hope my mother doesn't hear about it, or we'll see it, badly performed, in churches."

There was a moment of silence.

"How bad was it, Flame?" The maple leaf fluttered to hover in front of Gabriel's broken face. "As bad as the play would have us believe?"

"I haven't seen the play. But Yuan recorded everything. Look at it yourself."

"It doesn't show what happened inside you."

I became human, he thought.

"Perhaps I'll tell you sometime," he said.

In *Cold Voyager*, Gabriel called on Spring Plum to chant calming sutras.

The maple leaf whirled in the wind, passed on to other, brighter topics.

Pan Wengong called the session to order and reports were made. Mari Toth, the Ariste whose promotion had been scuttled by Captain Yuan, had agreed to make the Gaal Sphere her personal domain and direct the Logarchy's relief efforts. Her work on evolution, she concluded, would be aided by the data generated. She was warmly congratulated.

The other new Aristos, Joel Berlitz, who had decided to take the Mandarin reign name Huan Jiang or Delayed Reward,

would be taking over Zhenling's domain. The domaines of
Han Fu and Ctesias would be dismembered by their neighbors, each absorbing one or two star systems.

Sebastian, globe hovering, announced that he would encourage the reintroduction of barbarian genes into the population of his domaine. "The Ideal for a peaceful Logarchy is
not the Ideal for a Logarchy menaced from without," he
commented.

Gabriel wished he knew what accords Sebastian and Virtue's Icon had reached along their private tachlines. He wished
he could admonish the two for using private tachlines in the
first place.

But the private tachlines, he knew, would be necessary
until the Hyperlogos could be absolutely guaranteed free of
contamination. Until then, Aristoi would have every excuse
to stay aloof from the civic life of the Logarchy.

This business had to be contained. Gabriel signaled that
he wanted to speak.

"How long has it been since a trapdoor was discovered
into the Hyperlogos?" he asked.

The question was rhetorical: everyone or her reno knew
it had been almost a week.

"The autocracy of one is guaranteed by the autocracy of
all," Gabriel said. "I applaud the resolution of Virtue's Icon
and Sebastian Aristos in taking steps to guard against the
Great Criminals. But I remind everyone that the Great Criminals only achieved their success because of a corruption of the
Hyperlogos that goes back millennia. Our first line of defense
against any threat remains not our military forces but our
accumulated *wisdom*—a free, unconditional access to all the
information necessary to conduct a rational and beneficial
commonwealth, as well as best provide for universal defense.
I urge therefore that our best efforts be directed to purge the
Hyperlogos of all outside influences."

"This is being done, Aristos." Pan Wengong, approving.

"How can we know?" queried Virtue's Icon. "How can

we be certain there is not some other means by which the Criminals can break the Seal?"

"When we had no reason to suspect intrusion, we failed to search for intruders," Pan Wengong said. "Now there will be a constant scrutiny of all Hyperlogos software to make certain it isn't being penetrated or manipulated."

Gabriel signed to speak again. Back in *Cold Voyager*, Cyrus had taken command of Gabriel's respiration in order to keep him from hyperventilating.

"When the Hyperlogos is restored," he said, "I will load all files from my private comm link into the Hyperlogos, and then either destroy my private communications system or place it at the disposal of the Logarchy, as this assembly decides. I would find it strangely ironic if those who trusted their Sealed data to a corrupt Hyperlogos should refuse to trust it to a Hyperlogos purified and secured from intruders!"

There was a moment's silence—the comment was unusually pointed—then applause. After it died, Sebastian's smooth voice wafted over the assembly. "Your warships, Aristos? What will you do with them?"

"Once the current emergency is over, I will dispose of my warships as the Logarchy decides," Gabriel said.

"You will keep them in the meantime?"

Denunciations rang loud, Dorothy St.-John's loudest. "Are you suggesting that, after all that Gabriel Aristos has done for us, he would do something improper with his squadron?"

"I suggest nothing," Sebastian said. "I ask for purposes of information only."

The sudden energy that had filled Gabriel faded and cold fear began to pace along his nerves. His temper had become erratic, he knew, timidity mixed with sudden anger.

He could have played it better, he thought.

All at once a new use for the warships swarmed into his mind. Daimones sang in unison.

Yes. Even the Voice, silent for weeks, had an opinion.

For the first time in a long while he felt an Aristos again, all his selves united in one transcendent whole. His body, hundreds of light-years from Persepolis, was flushed with sudden energy, with power.

He asked to speak, held up his hand in a teaching mudra. "I beg to disagree with our esteemed Icon and the honorable Sebastian that reintroducing barbarian genes in the population is the best way of providing a defense against the attack of barbarians from outside our sphere. I believe that our system is better than the Great Criminals', that our assuming control over evolution and reproduction was an excellent step, that a rational humanity, in control of its fate and desires, is a better humanity than that which responds only with brutality and instinct.

"If we are truly the best—the *aristos*—then these barbarians are no threat to us."

He paused, gazed about the room, the chromatic panoply of Aristoi beneath the gold and vermilion pillars. "It is my belief that the Great Criminal Yuan, thwarted this once, will not cease his efforts to provide an alternative to the Logarchy," he said. "No doubt he will flee to what he considers a safe distance, and then will commence his great experiment again in some distant equivalent to the Gaal Sphere."

"Precisely," said the Icon, "why I wish to arm the Logarchy and provide for our defense."

Gabriel spread his arms. "Why arm only passively?" he said. "Why concede the initiative to the greatest criminal in human history?" He raised a hand. "I propose to find the Great Criminal Yuan in whatever starry backwater he may be lurking, to disrupt his schemes, and either to destroy him or to bring him to Persepolis for trial!"

There was a cry from the others: acclaim, shock, sensation.

Flame, that could take centuries! Dorothy St.-John, on a private channel.

Gabriel flipped his hands, the Terrinan gesture. **Let it take centuries, then, he said. Let it take as long as is needful.**

You may not live long enough.

Yuan found a way of surviving for thousands of years. Do you think I can do less than he?

Her voice was skeptical, yet withal admiring. **I daresay you'll find out,** she said, **one way or another.**

The Brightkinde Residence had been built during the early days of settlement and not much used since then. Gabriel had intended to live there during the election and following certification that ended his direct rule over the planet, but events had intruded.

It was small as Gabriel's palaces went, a pillared Georgian portico with white wings extending to either side, above the center part a graceful dome of glass and wrought iron that brought sunlight to a peripteral arboretum filled with miniature fruit trees and statues of an amber-colored marble. The lawns were long and fine, and a kilometer away, in a tree-hedged amphitheater that looked natural but wasn't, was an open-air concert shell where music could be played under the stars.

It was the nearest of Gabriel's houses to the Gaal Sphere. It had taken him over three months to reach it, three months in Gabriel's dark, cramped ship quarters.

By the time he arrived many of his plans were well under way. Plans for a fleet were taking shape, battleships and scoutships and self-replicating probes that would fan out in all directions, that would eventually chart every star in the Milky Way, every star and every planet and every floating rock, everything in the galaxy and neighboring clusters besides. All searching for Yuan, or trace of his work.

Most of the warships would be built well outside the Logarchy, to calm fears that they would be used against Persepolis.

The Hyperlogos was being extended, entire moons devoted to the work of sorting and classifying the titanic mass of data that would flood in from the survey. Huge tachline generators, receivers, and relays were being planned, strung out along the embracing arms of the galaxy. And another moonlet was being dedicated to the task of absorbing everything known about Yuan, to modeling his mind in hopes of predicting his actions.

Where he would flee. Where he would hide. Where he would try again.

But first things first. Tonight was the premiere of Gabriel's new opera. Tonight Lulu would sing and destroy and die, and Louise would dance and play havoc with hearts and drown in gin.

Gabriel had shipped his Illyrian orchestra to Brightkinde for the performance. Rehearsals had taken place in the oneirochronon, then, after Gabriel's arrival, in the amphitheater. The ultrasopranos weren't ready—Gabriel had considered boosting their growth and frog-marching them past adolescence to maturity; but there wasn't enough time to coach their voices into the shapes required for the complex roles, and he'd had to settle for more ordinary vocalists singing into filters. Other than that, all was as he planned.

Gabriel conducted while the music rose around him. He could hear it humming in his bones. Folly marched arm in arm with humanity. Schön died, and the Countess died, and Lulu died embracing a gleaming knife as if it were her lover; Pepi Lederer died, and Pabst shriveled away under the Third Reich and died, and Louise lived a shadow life, trading on her onetime fame, unscrupulous and manipulative to the last, and died—all the mere humans died, voices keening away into the ultrasonic, and as the last chord throbbed away into the stillness, the mourning song of lost humanity, Gabriel thought: *and so with Yuan.*

He would make Yuan human by killing him.

The audience was staggered, overwhelmed; scattered applause broke out, gathered and multiplied, echoed through the Hyperlogos as an audience of billions, watching and listening live, filled the ether with their ovation. Gabriel bowed, the orchestra bowed, and the cast made their curtain calls, and after all the encores Gabriel stepped on stage with the Survey-

ors, all the survivors of *Cressida* and the Gaal Sphere, fellow
saviors all . . . He wanted them there with him, sharing the
success of his *Lulu*, because they had, he thought, undergone
it with him, shared the essential reality of it, that hideous
experience of being human; and they'd survived it and now
they didn't have to be human anymore.

If Gabriel succeeded in his tasks, no one in the Logarchy
would have to be human ever again.

Even Remmy was in the audience, Gabriel saw. Standing
and applauding, understanding the essence of the work even
through his righteous mizzle of illusion. Remmy, who lived in
the Residence and who journeyed into the city every day to
preach and make converts. He had made none so far, Gabriel
thought, nor ever would.

There was a reception afterwards, a giant party that filled
the public areas of the Residence and spilled out onto the
lawns. Gabriel, filled with the blazing energy the music had
poured into him, outlasted them all. In the end, as the pearly
dawn floated over the wooded hills of the Residence park and
the building's solar cells rose to greet it, there were only a
handful left, clear-eyed, pantherlike Rosamund, Clancy, and
a few others, drunken musicians gathered around an antique
ivory keyboard.

Rosamund had stalked magnificently through the part of
Lulu, but she was at heart a shallow little thing, an empty husk
to be filled with the spirit of Gabriel's music—she had little of
interest to say once she'd delivered her performance, so Gabriel kissed her and petted her and sent her to the bed the two
of them, for this brief space of time, shared. He took Clancy
by the hand and left the building, strolling along the gravel
path toward the dawn.

Gabriel gazed up at the fading night, at the invisible ships
and stations that orbited Brightkinde. "Illyricum next," he
said. "And the floating nano lab that waits for your command." He had built it for her, remotely, during the long
months' crawl from Terrina.

.   "I'll have little enough time to use it," Clancy said, "if

you're still planning to have me run everything else as well."
Her long silk gown drew its train down the walk in a little
rattle of pebbles. All about them birds voiced their dawn
songs.

"Protarchōn Hegemón," Gabriel said, saluting her.
"Ruler of my domaine in my absence."

"I don't feel comfortable with the notion, Disturber,"
she said. "It's *your* domaine, not mine . . ."

"You may not be comfortable with the *notion*, Blushing
Rose, but you'll be comfortable enough with the *job* when the
time comes. Consider it practice for when you have your own
show to run . . ." He smiled. "Ariste," he said.

She grimaced. "Not me," she said.

"You mean, not *yet*.'" He raised his hands, as if conferring on her the halo-benediction he'd once given her in the
oneirochronon. "You'll do it, you know. You fooled Yuan,
and that's not something any ordinary person could do.
You're superb, and the sooner you realize it, the better."

"The better for *you*."

"The better for all of us."

He paused in a dappled beam of dawn light, bathed for a
moment in the warmth and golden glow. She leaned gently
against him and he regarded, happily, the roseate luminance of
sunlight on her red-gold skin.

"You've become so ruthless," she said. "The way you
use me, use the others, treat Rosamund like a pet . . . I wonder
how you behave toward your fellow Aristoi in Persepolis?"

"They may regret that title of Sotéhr yet."

"It was always a part of you, that ruthlessness. But you
used to be more charming about it."

"I've less time for charm."

"You're focused entirely, yes. On that battle with Yuan,
wherever he is."

"I'm learning his mind, modeling it as he did mine. I have
a good idea where to look for him. And then . . ."

"You'll decide the fate of civilization between you."

"Something like that."

The purple disk of the sun relinquished its last tenuous connection with the horizon, seemed to bound upward. Gabriel closed his eyes and absorbed the warmth, the moment, the stillness. The peace was perfect.

Perfect except for the distant mocking presence of Yuan. Exorcise that ghost, Gabriel thought, or better yet incarnate it as a human and destroy it forever.

Illyricum, the Residence. Gabriel played his father's thigh-bone in Psyche's room of the Autumn Pavilion, the notes crying out into another dawn.

Gabriel finished the last notes, put the bone trumpet in its velvet-padded case. He would carry it on his flagship, the new *Cressida*, as he searched for Yuan. There would be a shrine there, Vissarion's remains in an honored place along with memories of the crew of the first *Cressida*.

Gabriel rose from his soft-crystal ceramic bench, placed the instrument case on the table, then walked down the opal steps into the still dawn air. He remembered palati pollen floating, Sappho's words drifting through his mind, flower perfume enhancing the air.

Security, human and machine, floated inconspicuously across the lawns, through the park. Machines, Gabriel knew, would not be influenced by any unknown Mudras of Domination.

Zhenling waited on the path, amid a respectful, distant, but larger-than-usual knot of security. Gabriel approached her, gave her greetings.

"You're a savior now, I'm given to understand," she said.

"Not yet I'm not."

"Not till you kill Yuan Aristos."

"Or bring him back, in the unlikely event of his surrender."

Her dark eyes gazed at him levelly. She wore cord trousers, boots, a white shirt, a jacket of hunting green with black braid and silver buttons. There was a tautness in her skin he hadn't ever perceived in the oneirochronon, a parchment brittleness and fragility to her look. Perhaps her skiagénos had been a gilded lily. Or perhaps the drawn look hadn't existed then.

"Shall we walk?" he asked.

"I'd like to see your zoo," she said. "I'm not likely to see many animals where I'm going."

"As you wish."

They walked down the path, security orbiting them like distant moonlets. Zhenling walked with spine erect, shoulders back, looking neither left nor right. Like a soldier, Gabriel thought. Or the proudest prisoner in the world.

"I suppose I should feel flattered," she said, "that I'm granted all these guards. Do you believe I'm such a threat?"

"Were I in your position, *I* would be a threat," Gabriel said. "I'm paying you the compliment of taking you seriously. But the guards, I admit, are intended more to reassure Persepolis than myself. They didn't want you down here at all. But since you agreed to surrender voluntarily, I was able to convince them to take you into custody . . . in my own manner."

"Thank you for the courtesy."

It was rather more courtesy than the conspirators had ever shown Gabriel, he thought. Nor would she have her limbs broken, or be made to walk the circle without sleep or food for days, or deprived of the company of her daimones.

She would be given a scrupulously fair trial and imprisoned on a towed asteroid, probably forever. Perhaps she would have preferred the first alternative.

"My access to news has been rather . . . limited," she said. "I gather I'm the last to be taken?"

"Other than Yuan, yes. The others didn't stay free for long."

"May I ask how they're faring?"

"Ctesias has taken up poetry, sculpture, and resignation. Han Fu made an offer to cooperate and to inform on you all, to tell us all your secrets—he's really most desperate to please.

But the offer wasn't accepted, since you all recorded everything anyway and we have access to your every deed."

"Poor man," she murmured. She shook her head, took a breath. "I'm happy that I chose to surrender, then. I want our intentions to be clearly presented, to go on the record. I want the Logarchy to understand that we intended it no harm, that we only wished to provide an evolutionary alternative. That we did what we did with pride and skill and care, and for the betterment of all."

"Astoreth is claiming that she never agreed with you about anything, that she never knew any of you very well, that she never saw anything wrong with the Logarchy in the first place. We are all very polite and pretend we don't remember it was ever otherwise."

Zhenling said nothing. Her boots moved soundlessly over the gravel.

"I'm proud of what I did," she said.

"All of it?"

She looked at him. "All of it was necessary," she said.

"Given your premises, perhaps."

A group of mountain gorillas strolled out of a grove of bamboo and crossed the path. The adults ignored him, but babies on their mothers' backs stared at Gabriel curiously. The white buildings of the zoo began to appear beyond the trees.

Gabriel watched the gorillas until they disappeared, then turned to his companion. "You know of course that Bonham passed his exams, but that Yuan suppressed the results and promoted you instead."

"I've been told that. I don't know that it's true."

"Why wouldn't it be?"

"Persepolis might be trying to discredit my ideas by degrading me."

"But then why upgrade your companion Bonham?"

She only shrugged. The white buildings were closer. Gabriel heard the cry of howling monkeys.

"I wonder, though," Gabriel said. "If Gregory Bonham

had been made an Aristos, would he have followed Yuan's program?"

She eyed him. "Will this have any bearing on the legal outcome of the trial?"

"I doubt it. And your opinion of him isn't evidence, anyway."

"Then I don't see why my answer matters." Gabriel said nothing, just walked along. Zhenling reluctantly filled the silence. "I'd like to think that Gregory would have joined our group—he joined readily enough when *I* asked him—but I can't say for certain."

More little data points, Gabriel thought, for his model of Yuan's mind.

The monkeys howled on. Gabriel and Zhenling walked under an arch—sculpted birds and beasts, flowing together like a river—and into the zoo proper. Sadness tugged at Gabriel's heart as he remembered walking with Rubens here, with Marcus.

"I like the big cats," Zhenling said. "Let's start there."

The animals were kept in large enclosures, open to the sky, as reminiscent of the home environment as possible. The cheetahs had plenty of room to run, and the leopards were provided with trees to climb and rest in. Were it not for the arched walks over the enclosures, they would have been difficult to locate.

Gabriel knew the names of all the animals. He pointed to each one and told its history. Still, Zhenling's look saddened as she watched her fellow prisoners.

" 'It seems to him there are a thousand bars, and behind the bars, no world.' " Rilke, he knew. "Let's leave," she said. "This was a mistake."

"If you like."

She looked over her shoulder as they left the skyway, at one she-leopard lying asleep in the crook of a tree. "Poor evolutionary dead end," she said.

"She's better off than in the wild. She'll live longer, eat better."

"She won't bear as many young."

"But a higher percentage of the young will live. That's the advantages of civilization for you."

"In the wild she would be herself. Now she's the pet of an Aristos."

"There are still worse things to be."

She looked at him. There remained a silent tilt of sadness in her eyes. She stopped, took a deep breath, let it out. "Freedom," she said, "while it lasts." Then she forced a smile.

"Have you considered," she said, "that you may be fulfilling Yuan's plan? He wanted to shake up the Logarchy, get it to examine itself, provide an alternate point of view . . . get things moving again."

"Things always were moving. It was the fact that he wasn't at the center of them that bothered him more than anything."

"*You're* moving. And you're moving toward Yuan. With fleets, a communications array, a universal blanket of probes, with *everything* . . . It's a quest, Gabriel! A battle of wit and skill with all the future of humanity at stake! And even if you don't find him, your probes will find other things . . . and the Aristoi will want to study them, come out of their tidy little Logarchy and have a look." She paused on the walk, laughed. "It's just what Yuan would have wanted! A chance for real splendor at last!" She looked at him, eyes blazing. "And at the end . . ."

" 'Is it not passing brave to be a King, and ride in triumph through Persepolis?' "

A smile tautened her parchment flesh. "Yuan's plan fulfilled. And you're doing it in the name of opposing him."

Gabriel looked at her. "We'll see, when I find him, whose plan is fulfilled."

"He's the most formidable mind in history. It won't be easy defeating him." She looked at him intently. "In order to defeat him you'll have to *become* him. You'll have to know him that intimately. And once you've become him, it doesn't matter which of you actually wins."

Gabriel looked at her, shook his head. "If I thought it didn't matter, I wouldn't bother going."

"In another ten thousand years, we'll know if you're right."

He nodded. "Ten thousand years. In Persepolis."

"Ten thousand years! Ten thousand worlds! Persepolis!" A wayward gaiety had claimed her. She spun about, headed back toward the zoo. "The hell with it, Gabriel," she said. "Let's have a look at my fellow prisoners."

Her long-legged strides took her toward the cages.

His own, he considered, had somewhat further to go.